The Girl She Was Before

By Jess Kitching

KINGSLEY
PUBLISHERS

First published in South Africa by Kingsley Publishers, 2021
Copyright © Jess Kitching, 2021

The right of Jess Kitching to be identified as author of
this work has been asserted.

Kingsley Publishers
Pretoria, South Africa
www.kingsleypublishers.com

A catalogue copy of this book will be available from the
National Library of South Africa
Paperback ISBN: 978-0-620-94127-3
eBook ISBN: 978-0-620-94128-0

To Jack - none of this would be possible without you.

And to Mum and Dad, for believing in me from day one.

"Bullying is a horrible thing. It sticks with you forever. It poisons you… but only if you let it."

Heather Brewer

"Can you believe they didn't show? I wore my good bra for nothing," the passenger grumbles, flicking her hairspray-crunchy curls forward and tying them in a messy bun on top of her head. "Honestly, Hallie, why do we bother with dating?"

With her eyes still fixed on the dark road ahead, Hallie takes a break from gnawing her lower lip to reply. "It's fun, apparently."

"Yeah, well, clearly anyone who says that doesn't have friends getting hitched left, right and centre and the onset of wrinkles to keep at bay." The passenger snorts at her own joke, but she's the only one laughing. She turns to her friend, only now noticing how pale she is. "Are you okay?"

"What? Sorry, you know I hate driving at night. The idiot behind me won't back off, either," Hallie replies, flexing her clammy hands before tightening her grip on the steering wheel. As if on cue, the vehicle behind lurches forward, so close the two cars almost kiss.

"Fucking hell, what a dick! Just go faster," the passenger instructs.

"I don't know, Bree. I'm already over the limit as it is…"

"So what? No one comes down here. Not at this time, anyway."

Hallie bites her lip but does as she's told. She's usually the one who calls the shots in this friendship, but tiredness and agitation from being stood up seems to have given Bree a new sense of decisiveness. After a long day of teaching and a tedious staff meeting afterwards, never mind the dating no-shows, Hallie's only too happy to have someone else do her thinking for her. She presses her foot on the accelerator and the humming engine leaps into life.

The car behind mimics the movement, their engine snarling back in response.

"What the fuck is their problem?" Bree snaps, winding down her window and waving her arms at the encroaching vehicle.

That only seems to antagonise them more. Their engine roars into life, their glaring headlights blinding in the rear-view mirror.

"They're speeding up!" Bree shouts, but Hallie doesn't need Bree to tell her that. She can see the outline of the bigger vehicle homing in and dwarfing her car as if this is a game of cat and mouse that's got out of hand. Her speedometer climbs faster than she's comfortable driving, especially on somewhere like Carlton Road at night, but what can she do? They won't back off. They won't slow down. It's almost like they want her to drive faster.

With adrenaline coursing through her veins, Hallie glances in the rear-view mirror once more. Headlights shine so close they're dazzling. White spots dance in her eyes. She winces and turns the steering wheel ever so slightly, but at that speed the slightest movement is all it takes.

The wheels spin out of control as the car hurtles off the road towards the unknown.

There's a scream, the last thing either woman hears before the sickening crunch of metal rings out into the night. Then... nothing.

<u>Then.</u>

A painful growl escapes from underneath the girl's shirt. She raises her hand to muffle the sound, cupping the concave curve of her stomach protectively.

"You'll get there soon," she tells herself, thinking of the row of artificially lit vending machines that will greet her on arrival. Two bars of chocolate and a can of Coca-Cola, her breakfast for the last two weeks, paid for by stealthily siphoning money from her mum's savings jar.

The thought of the jar makes her already aching stomach spasm with anxiety. She reckons she has another four or five days' worth of funds in there, tops, and then it's back to life with no breakfast. Back to feeling lightheaded and nauseous from the moment her sleep crusted eyes open in the morning to the moment her weary head hits the pillow at night.

Worse than that, though, in four or five days her mum's pitiful life savings will be completely gone. She will have stolen it all.

An icicle of dread traces its way down her spine at the thought.

She is glad He doesn't know about the jar. If He knew she had been stealing money He could have used for beer, He would kill her. She wishes that were a dramatic statement, but it's not. Not with His temper.

Sometimes she is surprised she has made it this far in life.

Sometimes she wishes she hadn't made it this far at all.

Two minutes later than scheduled, the bus pulls to a stop in front of her. As the double doors hiss open, she silently repeats the mantra she has recited every morning for the past three years – 'another day closer to leaving'.

She's jostled aggressively as students push past her from all directions, desperate to sit with their friends, desperate to not be at the front with the losers, desperate to not be stuck next to her.

She lets them force her to the side without a fight. What's the point in trying to battle her way onto the bus first, anyway? There's nothing waiting for her on there. Nothing good, at least.

When the eager clamouring is finally over, she climbs aboard and flashes the driver a nervous smile. His nostrils flare as she approaches. His eyes bulge. He doesn't say anything, but he doesn't need to. She knows exactly what he is thinking. He's willing her to take a seat and be quick about it - he can't hide his disgust for much longer.

Head down, cheeks burning, the girl walks on.

She tried to wash her clothes last night, but there was no detergent left. There hadn't been for over two weeks. Her mum was too sick from her latest round of treatment to go out and get some, and since when did He do anything to help around the house?

She had put her ratty underwear and pungent uniform in the chipped bathroom sink and soaked them the best she could, but with no soap either it was hard to get them clean. Still, she had hoped the water would have an effect.

It had an effect alright, but one that made the smell ten times worse than before. Not only had the build-up of sweat clung to the fibres of her clothes mercilessly but washing them added a dampness that caught in the back of the throat.

Personally, she can't smell it anymore, but it's clear from the way people clamp their mouths shut and shuffle away as she walks past that everyone else can.

A part of her feels like apologising to them - I'm sorry for the smell. I'm sorry you have to sit near me. I'm sorry I exist – but would they even hear her if she did?

A dramatic cry comes from the back of the bus. "Oh my god! What is that smell?!"

The pit of the girl's stomach falls heavy as she takes a seat, far from them but not far enough to be out of their firing line.

"Seriously, I'm going to barf! What is it?!"

Chrissy Summers's voice rises loud and clear above the chorus of over-the-top gags. "What do you think it is? It's Fish Sticks!"

The beautiful girls at the back of the bus fall about laughing at their own cruel joke. The rest of the bus sniggers along. Their laughter hits the girl's chest like poisoned arrows.

"Fish Sticks! Fish Sticks, over here!"

She doesn't turn around. She made a vow to herself years ago – she will never respond to that name, even though it's the only one anyone ever calls her. She looks out of the window and does her best to ignore their taunts, the cruel name stinging like antiseptic in a papercut every time it's screeched in her direction.

"Fish Sticks, are you deaf as well as dumb? We're talking to you!" Amira Johal barks.

The girl forces herself to count the number of letterboxes the bus passes. Through the blur of her tears, she makes out letterbox five... then six... then -

Suddenly, something hits her hard on the back of the head.

A cold liquid runs down her neck, soaking into her shirt. For a moment, she panics it might be blood, but as a bottle of chocolate milk clatters to the floor and brown liquid pools at her feet, the girl realises what they have done. It's an injustice far more painful than cutting her could have ever been.

She will wear that chocolate-stained shirt until next Thursday when she finally comes home to washing powder. The smell of sour milk will mingle with her already toxic odour, growing increasingly stronger and more putrid with every day spent in the summer sun.

They will conveniently forget they had thrown the milkshake and will use the dark stain against her, not that they need more ammunition in the first place. They will call her shit stain and ask why she can't wipe her arse properly at fifteen. They will gag theatrically when she walks past, and every time they do, a part of her will die. Every time they do, she will feel smaller and more insignificant than she ever thought a person could possibly feel.

<u>Now.</u>

1

"The sky looks amazing," I comment, marvelling at the sun kissed world on the other side of my windscreen.

Sunaina glances up from replying to messages on my behalf and whistles. "Not a cloud in sight! It would be a great backdrop for content."

"I don't know. We've got to drop the goodie bags off with Joelle…"

"We'll still have time."

Sunaina's words hang between us while I weigh up my options. "Jay will be okay for a few more minutes, won't she?"

"She always is," Sunaina shrugs, putting my phone away and getting the camera ready.

I take the next right, pulling my four-wheel drive into the almost deserted carpark of Coral Bay Beach. At 2:50pm on a Wednesday, most people are either still at work or out on the school run. The timing of this spontaneous photoshoot couldn't be better if I tried.

We hop out of the car and I open the boot. A sports bag stuffed with a variety of outfits for all occasions greets me. My husband thinks I'm crazy for having a second wardrobe in the back of my car, but I like to be prepared for all eventualities. He doesn't understand that sometimes the lighting is just right and I can get four posts worth of content in one location… but only if I have clothes to change into.

"Should I wear something else?" I ask, plucking at my black, fitted trousers.

Sunaina eyes me analytically. "Roll your hems up and grab one of the hats. We can write a 'taking a moment for myself after my big meeting with the gallery' style of post."

I nod and reach for a wide brimmed hat, thanking the stars for the millionth time today alone that Sunaina came into my life just under a year ago.

At just twenty-one, Sunaina strikes me as someone who has the skills to take on the world, but for my own sake I hope she stays with me forever instead. She has expertly managed my life after things unexpectedly took off and I could no longer keep up with running a popular social media page, painting full time, and looking after a newborn by myself. Most days I trust her opinion more than I trust my own. After all, she got me from thirty thousand followers to well over eighty thousand – clearly, she knows how to style an impromptu photo shoot.

"Not that hat," Sunaina instructs with a shake of her head. "Go for a 'Dress to Impress' one. They've been nagging for another ad for a while now."

I rummage around in the back of the car and pull out a straw trilby.

Sunaina nods approvingly. "We should use the stats from this post to negotiate a raise. I know 'Dress to Impress' have been supporters from day one, but you can charge triple what they pay you now."

After making a mental note to call Suzanna at 'Dress to Impress', we step onto the beach. Warm sand spreads between my toes and instantly I am at peace.

"Stand there and look out to sea," Sunaina instructs. "And look cute!"

As I scan the shimmering horizon, the green-blue waves crashing onto the shore with a satisfying fizz, I realise how, even if someone offered me all the money in the world, I would never want to move away from here.

Coral Bay, with its picture-perfect ocean views and sunsets that need no filter, has always and will always be my home. Well over an hour away from the nearest city and so laid back the suits stay away, it's the perfect slice of chilled, coastal life. That's what my followers tell me, anyway.

My Instagram account, 'Finding the Good Life', started just over three years ago when I moved back to Coral Bay after falling out of love with city life. Storming around bars in short skirts with a patchy fake tan was fun when I was a student, but astronomically rising rent and the only romantic prospects being fleeting encounters with emotionally unavailable bankers lost their appeal soon after graduating. I stuck it out for a few years, but one day I decided I just couldn't do it anymore. City-girl life wasn't me, no matter how hard I tried to make the identity fit. I wanted the ocean on my doorstep, space to create and a life not bound by the ties of a 9 to 5.

So, Coral Bay beckoned me home.

To say I was nervous about coming back is an understatement. I once swore to myself I'd have to be dragged back to Coral Bay kicking and screaming, but I still pulled up in my battered Nissan with a pounding heart and a chest full of hope.

I rented a small house on the edge of town and set up a painting studio in the spare bedroom. I started posting photos of my artwork and the coastal life that inspired me online. To my surprise, the orders and followers were soon rolling in. Within my first year of dedicating myself to my passion, my canvases were stocked by Arlene Davies in one of the biggest contemporary galleries in the country, with pieces selling almost as soon as they were unveiled.

When musician Michelle Obanye shared a photo of one of my seascapes in her living room, everything kicked into overdrive. My prices quadrupled, my follower count skyrocketed, and my life changed forever.

Suddenly I didn't have to hide away. Doors opened to me that were once firmly shut. After years of being invisible, through self-preservation not choice, all of a sudden I was the one people wanted to talk to. I was the one they invited. I was popular, a sentence I never thought I'd say other than in my daydreams.

Pretty soon, I was real life friends with Hallie Patterson, Brianna 'Bree' Jackson, Bex (or Becca, as she likes to be known now) Harper, Amira Johal, and Melissa Curtis. Fifteen-year-old Nat would have never believed it to be possible, but it's true. They called upon me to join them, and I've never looked back.

These days, instead of hiding in the background and wanting to disappear, you'll find me at the head of the table for every cocktail fuelled girls' night. A place I've worked hard for and one I never want to lose.

The biggest surprise of my homecoming, though, was Lucas Redding. Voted most fanciable male at formal, captain of the football *and* cricket team and now my husband. Sometimes I find myself studying my wedding ring or counting the stretch marks left on my stomach from carrying our nine-month-old daughter Esme to remind myself that it's really true - *I* am married to *the* Lucas Redding.

Coral Bay called me home, alright. It called me home and made up for all its past mistakes, and for that I'll forever be grateful.

"Whatever you're thinking about – stop. You look kind of smug in these photos," Sunaina says, cutting into my disbelieving trip down memory lane.

"You mean smug isn't the vibe we're going for?" I joke, but there's nothing to laugh about. There isn't a day that goes by where I'm not beyond thankful for how my life U-Turned, or a moment I'm not terrified the tide will turn and drag me back to how things were before.

As I hold onto my hat to stop it from blowing away in a sudden gust of wind, Sunaina snaps away.

"That's the shot," she says, turning the camera to face me.

She's right – she's got it. She caught me mid laugh, free, easy, and light, the epitome of 'Finding the Good Life'.

With our spontaneous photo shoot now over, we drive towards Joelle Nichols's house. In the passenger seat, Sunaina edits the picture. I'm not one for blurring out wrinkles or redefining my waist, but a little upping of the contrast and fiddling with the brightness never hurt anyone, right?

I pull to a stop, smiling at Joelle's multicoloured windows and rainbow door. Joelle, my Coral Bay Arts Council co-chair, is the only other creative in town earning a full time living from her work. She makes beautiful ceramics and holds workshops in schools all around the country. Every three weeks we host classes for the local community to help them get in touch with their creative side. They're rewarding sessions, and the least I can do to thank the people of this town for never reminding me of the girl I used to be.

Hauling a mound of carrier bags from the backseat of my car, I make my way up Joelle's path, her overgrown, wildflower garden like something from a fairy tale.

"Nat! So good to see you," Joelle enthuses from the front porch. She pulls me into a bosomy hug, her bright red corkscrew curls tickling my cheek.

"I can't stay long – I've got to get back for Esme – but I thought I'd drop off the goodie bags you asked for while I was in the area."

Joelle takes the bags from me, her eyes dancing with delight. "The kids are going to love these – thank you so much! You really are a treasure."

"Oh, it's nothing," I blush, my chest swelling with pride. "I'd best be off, but I'll see you at the next meeting, okay?" Joelle nods and I wave goodbye as I hurry back to my car.

"Was she happy with the bags?" Sunaina asks, not once looking up from her laptop.

"She loved them."

"So she should – it took you weeks to source those materials."

"I know, but it's nice to do something for someone else," I shrug, but Sunaina's right. Joelle's little favour had turned into hours of painstaking research and reaching out to different suppliers. The effort is a small price to pay for belonging though and I'm happy to go the extra mile if it keeps me in Coral Bay's good books.

We set off towards the four-bedroom house with panoramic sea views I'm lucky enough to call home, all the while Sunaina works on perfecting our impromptu post.

"For the caption, how about 'after a busy day of meetings with gallery owners, the beach was calling. Never forget to make time for yourself, even if that time is spent trying to keep hold of your hat'?" Sunaina suggests.

"That's great. I've noticed my shorter captions get the most engagement."

"As do posts about Esme," Sunaina reminds me, her tone cool but her words hard.

I smile tightly. Lucas isn't keen on the idea of Esme being 'all over the internet like a meme', as he so eloquently puts it. I see his point, but I can't help wondering what my following would be if he let me share photos of her rather than just referencing her existence.

As we reach Maple Drive, I shelve the thought. "A conversation for another day," I tell myself.

We roll into the driveway just as Sunaina hits post. Unclipping my seatbelt, I slide out of the car. I can already feel the likes rolling in, but I ignore them and smile at the building in front of me instead.

I know in my bones I will never tire of this house. Whitewashed and hidden from the street by a luscious garden, it is my paradise within paradise.

"We're home!" I shout, dropping my handbag and walking into our recently renovated kitchen-diner where I find Jay prepping dinner. "Sorry we're a little late."

"Oh, it's no problem. I know how these gallery visits run over."

I beam at Jay, our exceptional and exceptionally understanding nanny. Jay joined us a little over six months ago and became part of the family overnight. She moved to Coral Bay after a bad breakup, one I don't ask about after she explained that the scar by her left eyebrow was a parting gift from her ex and not the result of a childhood accident. Jay's arrival in town was a well-timed kiss from fate, and life has been pretty perfect ever since.

On days like today when everything seems to align just right, I find myself thinking 'pinch me'. After 'pinch me' always comes 'please don't let this all be taken from me'.

The urge to grab everything and hold tight could consume me if I let it. Lucas says when your childhood was as rough as mine, life owes you a favour or two. That sentiment, however sweet, always sets off a spark of fear in me. I know better than most that life owes us nothing.

Blessings counted, I walk to Esme. "Hello, angel," I coo, scooping her up and showering her with sloppy kisses. She erupts into a fit of giggles so pure my heart soars. She is the spitting image of Lucas, apart from the springy curls she has inherited from me. They're going to be a nightmare to comb in a few years' time. I can already hear the tantrums.

I turn to Jay. "How has she been?"

"Good, as always."

Jay's report makes me glow and I plant another kiss on Esme's forehead. "Aren't you an angel?"

Just then, the front door clicks shut.

I glance at the clock above the fridge and frown. "You're home early," I call to Lucas, but my blood freezes when I see him – ashy faced, pale, traumatised. Questions pour out of me in a breathless stream. "What is it? What's wrong? What's happened?"

"There's been an accident," Lucas says, swallowing so hard I hear his gulp from the other side of the room. "Bree's in a coma and Hallie... Hallie's dead."

2

The room tilts off kilter for a moment. The white tiles seem too bright, too harsh. My vision clouds. "That's not funny Lucas," I say softly.

Lucas blinks. "Why would I joke about that?"

"Why would that be true?!"

In my arms, Esme starts to whimper. I open my mouth to tell her mummy didn't mean to shout, but I can't find the words.

Like an angel, Jay appears at my side. "Come here, cutie. Mummy's just had a nasty shock, okay?" Jay says, her tone children's entertainer high and grating, but it does the trick because Esme stops fussing.

I turn to Lucas and his features slip back into focus. The sadness covering them hits me like a barbed wire whip. "That can't be true," I whisper, but his crestfallen expression tells me it is. I go over the news in my mind – Hallie is dead, Bree is in a coma.

Hallie is dead, Bree is in a coma.

Then I break.

In seconds, I'm in Lucas's arms. He strokes my hair and tells me everything will be alright but, as I cry for my friends, his words couldn't seem further from the truth.

"Here, sit down," Sunaina instructs, pulling out a chair. Gratefully, I collapse into it. Lucas sits beside me, my hand small inside his.

"What happened?" I manage to ask.

"No one knows exactly. When Hallie didn't show up for work and no one could get hold of her, Tim called the police." Tim is the head of Coral Bay High where Lucas teaches PE and where Hallie works - worked - as an English teacher. "There was no one at home, so the police did a drive about. They found Hallie's car in a ditch off Carlton Road."

"Carlton Road?! That's miles away!"

"And in the middle of nowhere too, which is why they weren't found until the police went looking for them. It turns out they went on a double date to some sketchy bar in Whitehaven. Apparently, the guys didn't show – Hallie text Chloe and told her they'd been stood up. That's the last anyone heard from her. The theory is that Bree and Hallie stayed out. Hallie was drink driving. The police think she took a wrong turn and…"

"And?" I ask, even though I already know the answer.

"And they crashed, Nat. By the time the police got there, Hallie was already dead. Bree's alive, but it's not looking good." Lucas rubs his temples, exhaustion radiating from his every pore. "We had to break it to the kids this afternoon. No one can believe it. Everyone's devastated."

I stare at my hands and allow my tears to fall freely.

"I'm so sorry, Nat. I know they were good friends of yours," Jay says softly. Nodding, I flash her a wobbly smile.

"You never know, Bree might be okay," Sunaina offers, but she catches Lucas's eye and instantly regrets the glimmer of hope her words give me. Lucas doesn't need to say anything for me to know that even if Bree is alive, she is most definitely not going to be okay. I choke on a sob.

Lucas cradles me. "I'm sorry, babe. I know how close you three got."

I know he means well, but his words strike me as reductionist. How close we got? Those women were my *best* friends.

Hallie and Bree were the first people to really welcome me back to Coral Bay, even though they were probably last on the list of people I thought would be glad to see me again. When I bumped into them outside Coffee by The Sea, my heart was in my throat. Instantly, I recognised Hallie's upturned nose and Bree's electric blue eyes. Even with a few years, a few kilos and a few too many late nights between us, I could never forget what they looked like, but they did a double take when they saw me.

"Natalie Evans?!" they shrieked.

The first thing that shocked me about their response was that they knew my name. I'd only ever heard them refer to me as a derogatory slur. The second thing was how happy they were to see me.

"I can't believe it's you!" they cried, pulling me into warm, welcoming hugs.

Things only got better from there. We caught up briefly over a coffee, then two nights later we went out for cocktails. We spoke about the past, glossing over the parts of our shared history that weren't so pretty until eventually Hallie faced it head on.

"Can we take a moment to address the HUGE elephant in the room?" she interjected. "I was a bitch in school, Nat, and I'm so, so sorry. I teach at Coral Bay High now and I can't believe some of the shit I used to do, especially to you. If any of my pupils did that, I'd lock them in detention for the rest of the year. I am so embarrassed about who I once was. I was such a bitch."

Following her lead as always, Bree nodded in agreement. "We both were. We were kids, you know? We never really thought it through. We just followed Chrissy -"

Hallie had shaken her head adamantly at this. "Chrissy was the leader, but we made our own choices. We knew what we were doing was wrong and we did it anyway, and for that I'm so sorry."

"Me too," Bree added.

I remember sitting back in my chair and thinking, 'if only teenage Nat could see me now!'. Two of the most popular girls at Coral Bay High saying sorry to *me*. I used to apologise to them for walking past, for breathing, for simply existing, but there they were, wanting *me* to be nice to *them*... me!

A part of me wanted to laugh in their faces as they had done in mine so many times before, but at the sight of their earnest expressions and guilt-tinged cheeks, something inside me tugged. They wanted *my* approval. They cared what *I* thought. A world I'd only seen from the periphery suddenly opened up to me, a rainbow footpath leading the way to belonging in a way I could only ever dream of.

"Water under the bridge," I shrugged, raising my cocktail.

The three of us toasted each other and, just like that, the ugly past was laid to rest. We never mentioned it again, not even when I was introduced to the rest of the gang and Amira dug her old yearbook out one wine fuelled night. No one commented on my absence from their grinning, pouting group photos, but it hung heavily between us until Hallie squeezed me close and told me the past was the past, we were friends, and this was where I belonged.

She was a wonderful person like that. Her friendship quite literally changed my life. No call was ever too late, no favour too big, no conversation off limits. Hallie was so important to me that Lucas and I made her Esme's godmother, a move that reduced her to tears and a role she fulfilled with such love and care. She was the best friend I ever had, and now she is gone.

My pain sticks in my throat, choking and oppressive.

How can Hallie be *dead?* She was only twenty-nine. You don't die at twenty-nine. It's not the way things are supposed to go. You're supposed to be travelling the world, falling in love and building a life for yourself, not leaving it all behind.

And Bree in a coma? What will become of her?

My body shudders involuntarily.

As I spiral downward, my phone buzzes into life, the vibration loud against the dining table.

Sunaina glances at the screen. "It's Amira."

I flush and shake my head. "I can't talk to her, not yet."

Sunaina nods and lets the call ring out. When the phone finally stops ringing, her eyes widen. "Nat, you've got twenty-six missed calls and over fifty texts already."

A hand wraps itself around my throat. Of course I have that many notifications - Coral Bay is reaching out to soak in the misery of the moment with me. In a small town like this, sadness is communal, only I'm not ready to share my grief with anyone. How can I be expected to speak about what has happened when I can barely wrap my head around it myself?

"Can you take care of it for me? Please?"

Sunaina nods, slipping my phone into her pocket. A weight lifts from my shoulders, but my chest is still crushed from the blow of the news. I struggle for air in this grief filled atmosphere.

As if sensing my sadness, Jay reaches for my hand. "Why don't I put Esme in her playpen? Then I'll get you a glass of wine and we can talk for a bit?"

I smile a watery smile. "That would be nice."

"I'll stay too," Sunaina adds supportively.

"If it's a late one, you can sleep in a guest room if you want," Lucas offers.

"I will do – we don't all have the luxury of onsite accommodation!" Sunaina jokes, grinning at Jay.

Lucas and I built a guesthouse next to my painting studio in the garden a year ago. Little did we know how perfect this would be when Jay came into the picture. The onsite accommodation saved her from having to hunt for a place in Coral Bay's notoriously tricky rental market and gave us the benefit of having Jay on hand for Esme at short notice.

After a much-needed cuddle, Jay carries Esme away and Lucas brings me a large glass of wine. He sets two more bottles on the table. Teetotal Sunaina raises her eyebrows but doesn't comment.

The alcohol burns my throat as it makes its way down to my hollow stomach. "I just can't believe it. It feels like a bad dream."

"Me either. It really makes you think, doesn't it?" Sunaina says, taking a delicate sip of water, a sharp contrast to my desperate gulps of Shiraz.

"Life's so short. You never know what's going to happen next."

"It's just like when Blaine Rankin jumped off that building, do you remember?" Lucas asks.

A shiver runs down my spine as the memory of the first time I found out someone my own age had died floods back into my consciousness.

Blaine, the loudest mouth in school with the ultimate playboy reputation, jumped from the roof of his fifteen-storey apartment block in the city at the start of the year. It was a huge shock to everyone. With no suicide note left and no apparent motive, no one knew why Blaine had done it. He had a good job, a beautiful apartment, and a different girl on his arm every weekend – the life he always wanted. He became the poster boy for the idea that you never really know what's going on inside people's heads.

Even though they hadn't seen each other since they were eighteen, Lucas was shaken to the core by the death of someone who had once been so prominent in his life. For the first few weeks after Blaine's suicide, he held me tighter and told me he loved me more. He wore his hurt like it was a suit.

I guess it's my turn to wear the grief suit now.

I wipe my tears and finish my wine. Seconds later, Jay re-enters the kitchen with a baby monitor in her hand. "She's playing with pretty much every toy she owns, but she's okay."

"Thanks Jay. What would we do without you?"

"Struggle," Sunaina winks, and I laugh, an act that feels wrong given the circumstances.

"Someone could do with a top up," Jay says, nodding at me.

Lucas obliges, pouring wine until my glass nearly overflows. I don't stop him.

We sit and we drink. We talk about Hallie and Bree until the words become too painful to say out loud, the stories too raw to recite. It is then that Jay swoops in and tells us about Esme's day. Her stories are a welcome distraction, but the news of what happened to Hallie and Bree has soured the night. Every colour is now sepia. Hallie and Bree lit up a room; I guess it's only right the world would seem duller without them in it.

3

My hungover brain screams as soon as I open my eyes the following morning. I groan, the sound rattling around my head like a pinball machine. Heavy limbed, I fumble for my phone, but it's not on the bedside table. My heart lurches, visions of losing followers and missing deadlines bursting into my mind, until I remember I offloaded it to Sunaina last night.

Panic subsiding, I brave sitting up. My head swims. Blinking my pristine, white bedroom into focus, I look to the clock on the chest of drawers opposite the end of the bed.

"Shit!"

I shuffle to the bathroom and guzzle water from my scooped hands. My mouth is so fuzzed from alcohol I barely taste it. Catching sight of my reflection in the vanity unit, I grimace. Swollen, puffy eyes, skin streaked with mascara and patches of crusted foundation dotted around my face.

"Hot," I mutter, then a stab of guilt winds me. How can I be worried about what I look like when Hallie died yesterday?

Squirming eels of shame writhe around my stomach. I pinch the flesh of my thigh hard so it will bruise, a habit I haven't been able to break since my teenage years. When my guilt is less all-consuming, I let my skin go.

After quickly cleansing, I pad into the kitchen where I find Esme in her playpen and Lucas packing his lunch into his backpack. "You're up," he smiles. "I was going to leave you sleeping this morning."

"I've too much to do today to sleep."

Lucas pours me a cup of coffee then puts his backpack on. Seeing him ready to leave sends a jolt of panic through my body.

"Can you stay home today? Please?"

Lucas brushes a stray strand of hair from my face and cups my chin. "I wish, but I need to be in for the kids. They were just as cut up about Hallie as the staff."

My wobbling chin betrays me. "I don't want you to leave me," I confess.

"I know, babe, neither do I, but you won't be alone. You've got Jay and Sunaina with you, and I'll be back before you know it." Lucas gives me a coffee-tinged kiss then waves goodbye.

I watch him leave, a fizzing mixture of conflicting emotions brewing in my stomach. I know normality needs to restart, but I don't want it to. Without Hallie, life will never be the same again anyway.

Hallie. Just thinking of her name tears me apart.

Sighing, I kneel beside Esme's playpen, waving her favourite teddy in her face. She squawks and takes him from me, grasping the matted toy in her chubby arms.

Tears fill my eyes as my daughter stares at me expectantly, wanting more from me than I can give her today.

"What a bitch you are, Nat," I think scornfully. "Hallie would have given anything for a family, yet you're shying away from your daughter while she lies in a mortuary."

It's just not right.

I'm just not right.

Hallie never got to experience motherhood. It was all she ever wanted, but she never found the right person. The men she met were either already married, commitment-phobes or only with her for sex. Her useless picking ability became a running joke in our group, albeit a sad one.

"Laugh it up ladies, but one day my prince will come!" she would cry. "We will have lots of wild sex and make ridiculously cute babies – then who'll be laughing?!"

I smile at the memory, then deflate. If only that was how things had worked out for her.

Jay enters the kitchen and studies me. "Why don't you go for a run? I'll let Sunaina in when she gets here."

Temptation snaps at my heels, but I hesitate. "I don't know if I should…"

"Nat, take some time for yourself. You deserve it. Hell, you need it."

Deliberation over, I flash Jay a grateful smile and jog upstairs to change into my running gear. A few minutes later, I'm out the door.

There are many great running spots around Coral Bay, but my favourite is Hillman's Trek. Not only is it the quietest track, but it's also the most beautiful. In the right season, the path is framed by the most stunning array of brightly coloured wildflowers. The terrain is uphill and challenging halfway through, but once you get past that part you end up at the most stunning lookout that shows all Coral Bay beneath you like a miniature village. It's my favourite spot in the entire world.

My running philosophy is usually slow and steady, enjoy myself and take in the sights, but not today. Today I run to escape what I know. I turn up the volume of my workout playlist and plough down Maple Drive.

The buzz of activity throughout Coral Bay jars with my sombre mood. Everything is open, business as usual. The sky shines bright blue and birds flutter from tree to tree. Last night, the world felt like it was ending, but today life continues. People are still taking card payments and serving customers. People die, but the world keeps turning.

My heart hurts at the sight of it all.

Racing towards Hillman's Trek, I wave to the familiar faces who spot me. Everyone's features twist in sympathy as I dash past, but only Fiona, deli-owner and relentless gossip, tries to stop me for a chat.

"Can't stop – I've got to get back for Esme soon," I lie.

Finally, I reach the start of Hillman's Trek. My feet slap against the ground, dust clouds forming with every punching step. I'm sweating profusely before I reach the incline, but I don't slow down, not even with my heart pumping so hard I can't hear my music over the pounding in my ears.

The path bends before me, rising like a snake about to attack its prey. I push onwards, ignoring the screaming in my calves and straining in my lungs. I don't dare stop. If I stop, I'll fall apart.

Suddenly, I spot a lone figure doubled over in the distance. For a moment I wonder if it's a mirage, the sight of another person on Hillman's Trek so rare, but when I blink, they're still there.

It's a woman. Her clothes are last season's H&M, well-worn and covered in dust from the dry path. Her sports bra is shocking pink and too tight, as are her leggings. As I draw nearer, I discretely eye the bulk of flesh hanging over her waistband and the terrible box dye job on her straw-like, blonde hair.

I debate running past without interacting, but the woman hears my footsteps and straightens up. She turns to face me, and I stop dead in my tracks.

The only sound is that of my racing heart.

"Chrissy? Chrissy Summers?" Her name tumbles from my lips before my brain has time to register who I am addressing. When it does, it shrivels in fear.

The woman blinks, trying to locate me in her memories, but I know she will struggle. I don't look anything close to the person she would remember.

But then again, neither does she.

Chrissy Summers, head of the school, all-star, beautiful, popular, ringleader, bitch, nightmare inducing bully… none of those words seem right to describe her anymore. She looks old before her time, like she has been washed, wrung out and left on the side to airdry. Her wrinkles are deeply etched and savage. A poorly designed flower tattoo takes up most of her left arm and one of a badly executed butterfly spreads across her ribcage like an exploded fountain pen.

There is something incredibly sad about seeing her like this. I almost want to run back home at the sight of what has become of my biggest tormentor, the girl I used to loathe with every breath I took and envy with all my heart.

Most of all I want to run back home at the sight of her back in Coral Bay.

"It's me," I find myself stammering. "Natalie Evans."

Chrissy takes a moment to place me, my real name never the one she called me. When she does, her eyes bulge in shock, then embarrassment sweeps over her. She's thinking what I'm thinking – if people saw us now, they would imagine she was the loser and I was the popular one.

How wrong they would be.

"Natalie," she says, her voice still carrying with it the same harsh edge it always did. She straightens up to her full height, a good few inches taller than I am, perfect for leering over me. Something she had plenty of practise at. "Don't you look different."

"So do you," I add, then cringe. "Older. More grown up I mean, not older, sorry!"

"I guess we all change a little when we leave school," she shrugs, scrutinising me up and down.

Suddenly, I'm fifteen again, cowering in the girls' changing room and trying to get dressed without Chrissy teasing me, without being forced to notice her body, already so curvaceous and adult compared to my own.

In my head, I know I'm not fifteen anymore. I know my outfit costs at least four times as much as hers. I know my skin looks younger, my hair healthier… but still, I am cowering. Still, I am fifteen.

"You look well," she says in a way that makes it sound anything but a compliment.

"So do you."

Chrissy tilts her head. "You always were a terrible liar."

I open my mouth to protest, but I don't waste my time. Chrissy sees right through me. She always did. Those dark, cold eyes see through everything.

"Did you hear about Hallie and Bree?" I find myself asking.

Chrissy cocks her eyebrow. "No?"

"They were in a car accident the other day," I explain. "Hallie's dead."

Her eyes widen. "And Bree?"

"In a coma."

Chrissy blows air out of her mouth, thinking for a moment. I wait for her reaction but the one she gives is not one I expect. Her laughter hits first, cruel and menacing. "Fuck! Those two always were terrible drivers."

I take a step back like I've been slapped.

Chrissy eyes me with amusement. "What? It's not like you were friends."

"We were," I say defiantly, trying to ignore the fact that I'm shaking. "We have been for the last few years."

"You and them?" Chrissy asks, then laughs once more. "Fuck, things really did go downhill when I left!"

I fold in on myself, which only entertains Chrissy more. She looks up at the rest of the track before turning back to me. "Good luck with the run. There's a beautiful view at the top. I think you'll like it," she says before brushing past me and heading back towards Coral Bay.

I watch her go, amazed it's really her, amazed that, even after all this time and when so much about us both has changed, she can still cut me down to nothing without batting an eyelid.

Suddenly, Chrissy stops and turns around, a devilish smile dancing on her thin lips. My heart freezes, knowing all too well that whatever comes next is not going to be pleasant.

"You know, I lost my virginity up there," she says.

"Oh?" I reply, the only thing I can think to respond.

"To Lucas Redding. He's your husband now, right?"

My jaw drops.

Chrissy laughs and walks away before I have time to think of a comeback. I watch her disappear, the acidic pink of her neon sports bra burning my eyes. I think of all the things I should have hissed after her, choking on the snarling, bitter words stuck in my throat and blocking my airway. Words I'd never dare say, not to Chrissy Summers.

What I don't think of until much later, though, is how the hell Chrissy knew I was married to Lucas in the first place.

4

The shock of seeing Chrissy again takes the thrill out of Hillman's Trek, but only when I'm sure she's gone do I dare make my way back home. My legs tremble with each step, my mind swimming with memories I have tried so hard to forget.

Sunaina and Jay are nursing cups of tea at the dining table when I get in. It's such a normal, everyday scene it seems at odds with the fact that Chrissy Summers crashed back into my reality mere minutes ago.

"Feeling better?" Jay asks, her eyebrows knitting together. "You look a little pale."

I slide onto a chair, hoping that being in my own home and anchored to a seat will calm my nerves. It doesn't.

"I've just had the biggest blast from the past," I say. My voice comes out reedy and thin. One interaction and I'm already losing myself to Chrissy. I shudder at the thought.

"With who?"

"Chrissy Summers."

Jay and Sunaina look blank. I sigh, remembering how Jay didn't grow up in Coral Bay and Sunaina wasn't even in high school when I graduated.

Even though everyone in Coral Bay knows everyone else, Chrissy hasn't been back since she left for university. Over the years her name has lived on in legends told by those who survived her torment, but not in the everyday gossip that filters through the streets we call home.

But now she is back.

God help us all.

"Who's Chrissy Summers?" Jay asks, a question I don't know where to begin answering. How do you explain poison to people lucky enough to never know of its existence?

"She was the queen of school when I was younger. A real bitch," I explain.

Sunaina wrinkles her nose. "Was everyone in your year a bitch? Your friends always tell me how they're 'ex-bitches' like it's something to be proud of."

"Well, they were bitches back then. To be honest, from my point of view it seemed like everyone was a bit of a bitch."

"Were you not popular?" Jay asks, evidently shocked by this idea.

"Me? No, not at all. People used to tease me all the time."

"You? What did they have to tease you about?"

"What didn't they have to tease me about? I was poor and shy and geeky and…" I trail off, remembering my fifteen-year-old self with her sketchbook and fearful expression. She was worlds apart from who I am today, but she wasn't a bad person. She didn't deserve what she was forced to put up with.

I shake my head. "Do you know what? There was nothing wrong with me, but they made me feel like being myself was the worst thing I could possibly be."

Jay reaches out and squeezes my arm. "Girls can be so cruel."

I blink back tears, doing my best to not remember just how cruel that is, but with Hallie's death, Bree's coma and now the return of Chrissy Summers, a good cry seems inevitable.

Sunaina types something on her phone then turns the screen to me. "Is this her?"

A photo of a grinning Chrissy fills the screen.

"Yes!" I cry, taking the phone and studying the image. "I didn't know Chrissy had Facebook. I thought she'd disappeared off the face of the earth. Surely my friends would have found her account and told me all about it?"

29

"It's a fairly new profile, plus she calls herself 'Cee-Cee Summers'. They wouldn't have found her unless they knew to search for that name," Sunaina explains.

"How did you find her?" I marvel, flicking through Chrissy's photos. They all show a much more glamorous version of the woman I just bumped into but still a person I would have struggled to accept as *the* Chrissy Summers.

"There's always a way," Sunaina grins ominously.

Jay takes the phone from me, her eyes widening at a photograph of a pouting Chrissy holding an elaborate cocktail. In the picture, Chrissy's heavy black eyeliner is smudged into her well lined eyebags, making her glassy, intoxicated eyes appear even more tired. "She was the most popular girl in school?" Jay asks disbelievingly.

"Honestly, she was stunning," I say because it's the truth. Chrissy was beautiful, probably the most beautiful person I've ever seen in real life, but she was also evil. My God was she evil.

I crack my knuckles to stop myself pinching my thigh again. One bruise I can shrug off to Lucas as an accident, but a collection might make him suspicious. My penchant for small acts of self-harm is something I've managed to hide from him so far, and I'm not about to break that record, even if Chrissy Summers is back.

"When she left Coral Bay, she fell out with everyone, even her parents. As far as I know, no one has heard from her since. I wonder what happened to her."

Sunaina examines Chrissy's profile. "Drugs," she says a few seconds later. "It looks like she got into partying in a big way. She got out of rehab at the end of last year. By the sound of things, she'd been a few times before, only they didn't work out. She posted a status about it. It's the first post on the 'Cee-Cee Summers' profile."

Sunaina shows me her screen.

Well, I did it!!!! For good this time I promise. I have made it this far and I will NOT be going back to where I was ever, ever again. Wild Chrissy is gone. She is dead and buried.

The new and improved Chrissy is here and she's here to stay!

So, here's to the future. New life, new start, new me. I'm not going to mess it up this time. #chrissysbackbitches

I nod, not really knowing what to respond. I know I should pity Chrissy for her life going down a dark route, but her struggles don't excuse her for everything she did to me. She wasn't on drugs when she was pushing me into lockers or throwing food at me in the canteen. Her merciless, endless, and brutal treatment was a fully sober decision.

My stomach twists as I recall my teenage years. I haven't thought about how bad school was in such a long time but seeing Chrissy again has brought it flooding back like a tsunami of trauma. The taunts, the violence, the isolation… it's all I can see.

I force down a shudder. I hate being reminded of who I once was.

While I stew on memories I would rather bury forever than remember for even a split second, Sunaina and Jay scroll through the 'Cee-Cee Summers' profile.

"Wait, isn't that the name of the guy you mentioned last night?" Sunaina says suddenly. "Blaine Rankin?"

Sunaina shows me a photo of Chrissy and Blaine cuddled together in a busy bar. They're both smiling at the camera like it should be grateful to get a photo of them, the way only people born with confidence can.

"Yep, that's him." I look at the date of the post. The photo was taken two weeks before Blaine's suicide. My spine frosts over.

Jay peers at the screen. "He's so good looking! He killed himself?"

I nod. "A few weeks after this photo was taken."

"Maybe this Chrissy is a bigger bitch than you first thought and drove him to it," Sunaina comments, taking a sip of tea.

"Maybe," I respond, flashing a polite smile, but Sunaina's words lay heavy in my stomach. I know it was a throwaway comment but, when you've experienced Chrissy Summers like I have, anything seems possible. It wouldn't be the first time she had driven someone to the edge.

I know that better than anyone.

5

I do my best to push Hallie, Bree and Chrissy from my mind to focus on work. While Jay takes Esme for a walk, Sunaina and I map out 'Finding the Good Life' content for the next few weeks. A healthy mix of in the studio shots, my latest canvases, beach walks and body image chat, 'Finding the Good Life' is going from strength to strength. Every idea Sunaina has pushes it that little further and I couldn't be more grateful for her input.

"Honestly, it's looking amazing! Thank you so much."

"No problem," Sunaina shrugs, but the smile on her face says it all. I make a move to stand, but Sunaina clears her throat. "There is one more thing, though."

I slump back down. "If this is about featuring Esme…"

"No, it's about Hallie and Bree."

My throat closes at the mention of their names. "What about them?"

"I think you should address what's happened online. People love the idea of the life you sell, but sometimes it can be a little… unauthentic," Sunaina choses her words carefully, but I read the subtext well. "That's not to say your life isn't relatable, just that –"

"Just that not every day is rainbows and sunshine and living by the beach."

"Exactly. I think you need to post about Hallie's death and Bree's current situation. Show your followers you're human. Bad things need to happen to 'Finding the Good Life' too, you know? We can move today's post to next week so your posting schedule is consistent. I've even found the perfect photo of the three of you to use." Sunaina flicks through her laptop before showing me the screen.

The image confronts me like a slap. It's of the three of us stood in a sisterly huddle on Bree's balcony last summer, laughing so hard we've broken free of our breathe-in-breasts-out poses. That's the beauty of the image, though. It's natural and unposed. It's the way I want to remember us – free, happy, loving… friends.

When I can no longer cope with being face to face with the people I have lost, I push the laptop back to Sunaina. "What should we write?"

"I didn't know if you'd want to write the caption yourself with them being your friends."

"I… I don't know if I have the words," I admit.

"I get it," Sunaina says with the flippancy of someone who doesn't get it at all. I suddenly realise how young she is, how untouched by loss, and I'm envious of her.

"Why don't we write something like, 'it is with the deepest sadness that I post this photo, a photo of a night I will never forget, now a treasured memory. My beautiful, witty, one-of-a-kind friend Hallie sadly passed away in a car accident. Bree survived, but is in a coma. My heart breaks for myself, my friends, and their futures. Please send as much love and positivity as you can, especially for Bree. Strong, wonderful Bree - you can get through this' and then a heart emoji?"

I nod, unable to speak.

Sunaina types away then hits post. The photo is now online for the world to see. Words that aren't mine but echo my every sentiment stare back at me without flinching.

It seems so real now it's written down in black and white. It hurts. It hurts more than I can bear.

"You should write sympathy cards," I manage to say.

"I should do a lot of things, but I like working with you too much," Sunaina grins, glancing at the incoming notifications. "You're on fifty likes already."

I smile tightly and stand. I couldn't care less about the likes. Unlike Sunaina, I am unable to look at the numbers. When I look at that photo, all I see is my loss.

"I'm going to paint," I say, my signal to Sunaina that we are done.

"Wait," Sunaina shouts after me, her chair scraping across the tiles as she stands. "There's so much more to go through. You've had three new collaboration offers this morning alone and Jenny Drysdale is wanting to confirm your attendance at her 'Women of the Internet' luncheon. Plus, Arlene Davies has called twice. She wants an update on the progress on your latest pieces."

My airway blocks. There's so much going on, so many people reaching out for a comment or something from me. Life's hectic at the best of times, but the last few days have kicked it up to inhumane levels of stress, and that's without remembering that Chrissy is back too.

"What do you want me to tell Arlene?"

I grimace. With only one of the three pieces I promised Arlene started, I know I'm going to be a disappointment to not only the woman whose gallery brings me in the most sales, but also my assistant who will have to have the awkward conversation where we admit I can't meet the deadline. Sitting and painting seascapes isn't on my mind right now, though. Holding onto everything because it all feels like it's slipping away is.

"Tell her I'm working on them," I respond vaguely. "And I trust you to make a decision on the rest." I make a move to leave once more, but Sunaina grabs my arm.

"Nat, stop. We need to talk. What should I do about your messages? Amira, Becca and Melissa are going out of their mind trying to contact you."

Guilt freezes my blood. I haven't taken my phone back from Sunaina since finding out about the accident. I haven't wanted to face the world, but I know I can't avoid it for much longer.

"I don't know what to say to them," I confess.

"They're your friends, Nat. They need you right now. You can't hide from them forever."

Sadness swallows me whole. I know what Sunaina is saying is true, but it's not what I want to hear. Lucas leaves me to soak in my misery, but my friends won't. They will want to dissect every flickering emotion like we are pulling apart a text from a suitor. They will share anecdotes that will only remind me Hallie is really gone. I'm not ready to be around that yet.

Hallie was the person I was closest to out of everyone. We got each other on another level, clicked in a way that was almost cinematic it was so perfect. How can I share my grief over losing her? She's the only person who would understand how I feel, but she's the one who's gone.

"Amira wants everyone to go to hers tomorrow," Sunaina informs me.

I swallow with difficulty. The idea of walking into Amira's memory filled home and there only being four placemats at her table instead of six makes my skin crawl.

"Nat, you should go. It looks really weird if you don't."

Biting back a sigh, I nod. "Tell her I'll be there."

I leave Sunaina to respond to my messages and head to the sanctuary of my studio to spend the rest of the day painting. Pulling down the blinds, I shut out the world as if not seeing it will remove the chokehold of anxiety surrounding me.

I layer the canvas with thick, dark colours and create something much harsher than my usual by the sea, happy go lucky pieces. What I produce goes completely against Arlene's brief, but it's the purest expression of my emotions. My brush strokes are angry and confused. My brush strokes are me.

I paint until there's nothing left in me to give to the canvas.

It's dark by the time I stumble back to the house. My stained, filthy hands push on the back door, my eyes burning from exhaustion. Once inside, I find Lucas at the dining table, a beer in his hand and the weight of the world on his shoulders.

"Where's Esme?" I ask.

"Asleep. It's after nine."

I blink, bruised. "But I didn't get to say goodnight to her!"

"I didn't want to disturb you when you were working. I thought you might need the time alone."

"I'd have liked to say goodnight to my daughter," I reply frostily.

Lucas sighs. "Please, Nat, not tonight."

I look at Lucas properly, noting his drained features and how dead behind the eyes he is. Concern wraps around my throat like a noose. "What's wrong?"

"I have something to tell you, but I'm not sure where to begin."

Immediately, alarm bells sound in my mind. "What is it?"

"The police…" Lucas trails off, then shakes his head, pulling himself together. "The police came into work to talk to everyone today. They found tyre marks on the road. It's as if… it's as if Hallie's car was swerving when she crashed." Lucas reaches for my hand and grips it tight. "Nat, the police don't think what happened was an accident. They think someone purposely forced Hallie to drive off the road."

6

I fall into a seat beside Lucas, his hand in mine the only thing making sense right now. "Why would anyone do that?" I whisper.

"Why would people do a lot of things?"

A heavy silence cloaks us as I try to absorb Lucas's news. Someone... someone *did* this on purpose?

I imagine Hallie and Bree in the car, the terror they must have felt as an unknown vehicle stalked them, headlights blinding, speed intimidating. I hear their screams, tingle from the rush of terrified adrenaline coursing through their veins as Hallie desperately pushes her foot on the accelerator to drive, just drive. I feel the air catch in the back of their throats as they lose control of the car and plummet into a ditch, the rattle of their rasping breath as they struggle to cling onto life.

Bree, the one who always had a story to make me smile, and Hallie, the best friend I ever had... how could this happen to them?

I tremble with repulsion. My movement stirs Lucas from his thoughts. "I'm sorry I had to be the one to tell you," he whispers, rubbing soothing circles on the back of my hand with his thumb.

"It's okay. I'm glad I know," I reply, but the lie sticks in my mouth like treacle. Knowing my friends were in an accident is one thing, but it being a deliberate attack is another entirely.

My airway tightens. I want to sleep, to close my eyes and for this nightmare to be over, but I won't be sleeping tonight. Not after this news.

"What did the police want to know?" I ask.

"What you'd expect, I guess. They wanted to know if everything was okay with Hallie and Bree, if threats had been made against them, if they had any enemies."

"What did you say to that?"

"I said no, of course. Hallie and Bree were good people. Everyone loved them."

"That's true, but..." I trail off, biting my lip.

Lucas frowns. "But what?"

"I mean, they weren't always good people, were they?" Even though what I'm saying is something Hallie and Bree admitted themselves many times over the course of our friendship, I still burn with shame for saying it out loud. Friends aren't meant to admit their friends' flaws, but not everyone is friends with the people who pushed them so close to the limit there was a time they thought they would topple over the edge.

"What's that supposed to mean?" Lucas asks sharply.

Instantly, I regret speaking. My face burns red, but the fire in my husband's eyes demands I explain myself. "Come on, Lucas," I say as lightly as I can. "You might have spent your time in school on the sports field, but you weren't blind. Hallie and Bree hurt a lot of people when we were younger."

"But that was years ago. Who carries a grudge for all this time?"

I struggle with the naivety of his logic. "I know it was a long time ago, but people's words don't disappear from memory just because we're no longer kids. When you bully someone, you bully them for life."

I want Lucas to understand where I'm coming from, but he drains his beer in one long gulp and stands, his body stiff and unapproachable.

"If you're telling me someone would purposely force two people off the road because they called them a few names in school, then this world is madder than I thought." Tossing his empty bottle into the recycling bin, Lucas walks away.

His footsteps thud heavy on the staircase, but I don't follow. Instead, I stare at my hands, lost in thought.

I'm angry. Angry at whoever hurt my friends, of course, but I'm also angry at my husband for not even attempting to understand what it was like to be on the other side of the popularity divide. Seeing Chrissy today brought it all flooding back, and it's not pretty.

It's easy for Lucas to shrug off what Hallie and Bree did as a few names and nothing more. He was one of them - how could he know what it was like to not be eternally adored? He had the glow, the popularity, the appeal. He didn't know how bad they could be. He was never on the receiving end of it. He could turn a blind eye. He could forget.

But I can't, ever.

While I forgave Hallie and Bree and loved them like sisters, I could never forget what they did. Sometimes I wondered how I could smile at the people who caused me so much pain. Countless times over the years I have wanted to ask them if they realise that to this day the doubting, negative voice in my head telling me I'm hideous or useless or unloved is actually theirs.

Whenever Hallie made a joke at my expense, no matter how friendly she meant it, I fell back into my old self-hating ways. Whenever Bree laughed along, I wanted to curl up, burst into flames and be swept away as a pile of nothing in the breeze.

Hallie always threw her arm around my shoulders to show she was only joking, but even as our friendship deepened over the years there was still a part of me on edge in her presence. I was always waiting for the day she laughed and said, 'the joke's on you! Did you *really* think we wanted to be your friend?!'.

Because of them, I live my life waiting for the flip. For everything to fall apart and for me to be left the empty, hollow shell they told me I was.

Sadness envelopes me as I realise no matter how much Lucas loves me, he will never be able to love all of me because he does not understand all of me.

I sigh so forcefully my bones rattle, then trail upstairs after him.

He's reading in bed by the time I make it to the bedroom. He glances in my direction when I enter, his face an indecipherable mask.

"Lucas, I only said they weren't always nice because the police asked if they had enemies. I thought it might help the investigation. I don't want the person who did this to walk free. You know I loved Hallie and Bree more than anything," I say, my voice wobbling at the honesty in my last statement.

Lucas puts down his book and I walk to him, slotting under his arm like a key in a lock.

"I'm sorry I overreacted. I just don't like the idea of who they were as teenagers casting a shadow over who they were as adults, you know? They did a lot of good to make up for who they used to be, Hallie especially. She was the biggest advocate for anti-bullying in the school."

"I know."

"She changed - they both did."

"I *know,* Lucas. Do you think I would be friends with them if they hadn't? Out of the two of us, I'm the one who wouldn't put up with them being how they used to be."

Lucas strokes my hair away from my face. "I always forget you were a little different in high school."

"A little different? I was a social pariah."

"And now you're a social butterfly," he says, pressing his lips on mine. I melt into the kiss. My stomach still churns with an undercurrent of anxiety, but right now my husband not hating me is all can ask for.

I break away from Lucas and head into the bathroom to remove my makeup.

"To be honest, I think the only reason I brought up school is because it's been on my mind a lot today. I had an unfortunate blast from the past this morning," I call out as I splash my face with cold water.

"Oh yeah?" Lucas replies, his casual tone telling of the fact he has started reading again and isn't fully listening.

"Chrissy Summers. She's back," I say, leaning against the doorframe

41

to watch his reaction.

Lucas drops his book and faces me. "Chrissy Summers? You're kidding? She's back in Coral Bay?"

"Out of rehab and back with a vengeance."

Lucas's eyebrows dart upwards. "Rehab?"

"It seems her partying days were as wild in her twenties as they were when she was a teenager. She had a lot to say about you too," I respond, wrinkling my nose.

"Me?"

"Oh yes. She got a lot of pleasure from telling me how you took her virginity."

Lucas laughs heartily. "Nat, if you think Chrissy Summers waited for me to lose her virginity to then you are very much mistaken. She'd been with half the boys in the year above before she got around to me."

"Lovely," I grimace.

Lucas sees my face and pulls me towards him. "We had one night together when we were sixteen and it wasn't even good. Why is this bothering you?"

Realising how irrational I must look to my carefree, go with the flow husband, I sigh. "She was just rude and smug and mean and… she was just Chrissy Summers, that's all. It got to me. It made me feel like nothing from school has changed."

Lucas bites my lip playfully. "Look at yourself, Nat. Everything from school has changed."

Smiling, I lean in and kiss him. Lucas - the love of my life. The man who was oblivious as his friends brutally destroyed me when we were younger. The man who didn't care who I used to be, only what we could be together.

As I mount him, I think of how far I have come. Things have changed. I have grown. Chrissy will have to accept it – no one can make me go back to the girl I used to be.

No one.

<u>Then.</u>

She stares in horror at the red stain in her underwear. If only Mr Isaac had let her out of class when she asked to go to the toilet, the blood would never have made it this far. But he had to stick to the school rules. No students in the bathroom during lesson time, even though he let Chrissy go in the middle of class. On top of that, he didn't say a word when she came back over twenty minutes later.

But with Chrissy it was different, right? With Chrissy it was always different.

"Is it an emergency?" Mr Isaac had asked in front of everyone.

She could hardly tell him it was, could she? So, crimson, she shook her head in response.

"Then you're just going to have to learn to control your bladder," he scolded.

"Like she can do that. Has he smelled her?" Chrissy muttered, a spiked comment that created a ripple of laughter across the classroom.

*She was sure Mr Isaac heard her – Chrissy hadn't spoken **that** quietly – but he didn't call her out on it. None of the teachers ever did.*

As soon as the lesson ended, the girl ran to the toilet, but it was too late. The blood had done its damage.

Her eyes sting with humiliation as she bunches up toilet paper and stuffs it into her greyed underwear. She knows the other girls use neat, discrete tampons or pads that absorb all evidence of their hormonal bodily functions, but she can't exactly ask Him to buy her any, or her mum. He doesn't trust her mum with money, and there's no chance she would ask Him to get her a box of tampons.

Just as the girl is about to flush the toilet, the door to the bathroom swings open.

"Chrissy, you're so bad!" Giggles a voice. Bree Jackson's voice.

"That's what they tell me... I'm bad to the bone!" Chrissy sings.

The girl's blood runs cold. The walls of the bathroom cave in. Spit dries in her mouth with every ragged breath she takes.

No, no, no! How could she find herself alone with them?! She's always so careful to avoid situations like this, following huddles of other girls and trying her best to blend into the crowd. Not that other people being around stops them from attacking her, but sometimes their punishments are just a little less cruel in front of an audience.

The girl stands with her back to the wall, hoping that if she makes herself small, that if she quietens her breathing, they won't sense she's here.

"Hallie, can I borrow your lip gloss?" Chrissy asks.

"Sure."

Their voices are so close now, just outside the cubicle door. One wrong move and she's theirs.

She's the most scared she's ever been, even more afraid than the time He held her by her throat when she accidentally knocked over His beer. She would take that beating over this torment any day.

"You know, this colour suits me more than you. I think I should have it."

"Oh, well it's actually my mum's so -"

"Thanks, Hallie. You're the best."

Footsteps echo throughout the room. Footsteps travelling in the opposite direction to her.

The girl doesn't allow herself to exhale just yet, but her fingertips tingle with relief. A quick cosmetic touch-up, that's all they're here for. She could cry with happiness.

"Wait! Do you... do you smell something?"

In that moment, something inside the girl dies.

"I smell something, don't you?" She hears a chorus of sharp sniffs, then a loud wretch.

"Oh my god!" Amira Johal screeches. "It's disgusting! What is it?"

"Not what... who!" Hallie Patterson cries.

"Fish Sticks!" they scream, then fall about laughing.

She shrinks, almost crouching now. She prays to a god she doesn't believe in, to anyone who will listen, anyone who will save her. "Please don't let them find me."

"Fish Sticks, where are you?" they call out, sniggering.

She says nothing.

"Come on, Fish Sticks – come out and say hello!"

Again, she says nothing.

Suddenly, she hears a loud bang, then another.

"They're opening toilet doors!" she screams internally. She covers her mouth with quaking hands, desperate to muffle her fear. The door of her cubicle is locked, a barrier between them and her, but since when did that stop them? If they want her, they get her. That's the way it always goes.

"Fish Sticks, oh Fish Sticks!" she hears Chrissy sing.

"Please, please, please," she whispers, closing her eyes and willing them to stop, just stop.

Another bang. More laughter.

Their excitement builds. They know she is near. They know she is alone.

BANG.

They're closer now, the bangs louder, their anticipation stronger. It fills the air like a choking cloud of perfume.

BANG!

The walls of her cubicle tremble. She squeezes her eyes tight. Make it stop, make it stop!

BANG!!

Her cubicle ricochets violently, but the lock on the door holds strong. Slowly, she opens her eyes.

They can't get in. They can't get her.

She will stay in the toilet all day if she must, she realises, just as long as they can't get her.

Silence.

The girl counts four pairs of shoes underneath the door of her cubicle, but they're not moving. They're not trying to break down the door. They're not coming for her.

They've given up.

She lets out an unsteady breath and rises to a stand on trembling legs. No one calls for her, no one laughs, no one speaks. It's quiet, peaceful almost.

Almost.

"Boo!"

The girl looks up to find Bex Harper and Amira Johal leaning over the top of her cubicle, their smiles leering, their joy so strong she tastes it. She screams and tries to duck, but a fistful of her hair is grabbed by Bex. The searing pain makes her gasp out loud.

"She's in here!" Amira cries gleefully.

The girl struggles, trying to break free, but Bex has her in such a tight grip. Her hair follicles roar in agony. Instinct begs her to wriggle away, but if she manages to do so then the clump of hair in Bex's hand won't be going with her.

Amira shimmies over the top of the cubicle, dropping to the floor in front of her. "You smell even worse close up," she spits, then she does the worst thing she possibly could do – she unlatches the lock.

The cubicle door swings open to reveal Chrissy, Melissa, Hallie, and Bree stood in a smiling, triumphant cluster.

"Hi, Fish Sticks," Chrissy says sweetly before lunging at the girl.

Chrissy's nails dig into her flesh, the sound of her victorious laughter amplified by the echoey bathroom. The girl's head is smashed into the wall. Her vision doubles. She wants to cower and cover herself from the attack, but she knows whenever she tries to protect herself, they only come for her harder. She's learnt over time that trying to break her becomes yet another game for them, so she holds herself loose, an easy, unmoving target.

"We just want to say hello!" Chrissy coos, throwing the girl into the wall of cubicle once more. Her body slams into it, knocking the air out of her lungs.

As Chrissy reaches for her again, someone shouts the last word the girl ever thought she would hear.

"Stop!"

The girl thinks she's misheard but, when the grip on her shoulders relaxes, she realises she hasn't.

Head throbbing, she blinks. She looks for Bex, her unlikely hero, only when her vision comes back into focus, she sees Bex is not the ally she had hoped for, but the person she knew her as all along.

Bex smiles like it's Christmas Day.

Bex points at the toilet. The toilet filled with blood and urine.

"You don't flush?!" Hallie cries. "That's disgusting!"

"What do you expect? She is disgusting," snarls Bree.

"I-" the girl tries to explain, but Chrissy's hand whips her across the face, a hard, brisk slap that silences her immediately.

"She needs a lesson in cleanliness," Chrissy sniffs.

The girl knows what's going to happen before they grab her. This time she tries to fight back, but it's no use. She is outnumbered. Amira has her arms. Her legs are crushed by Hallie and Melissa. She's hauled to the toilet, Chrissy taking the lead as always.

Her screams drown out as she is dunked into the toilet bowl. Bloody tissue invades her open mouth. Red stained, piss filled water gargles in the back of her throat.

Shame, humiliation, disgust... she's filled with them all.

They dunk her twice for good measure, then let her go as if she is poison to touch.

She slumps against the cubicle, soggy paper stuck in her hair, toilet water drenching her uniform. She doesn't look at them. She can't bring herself to. Instead, she sits and stews in her degradation.

"Shame... I hoped washing her in piss would have made the smell better," Chrissy sniffs before walking away. The others follow, never once looking back to witness the harrowing reality of what they have just done.

The girl curls into a ball, her self-hatred so strong she chokes on it. Only when she is sure they are gone does she allow herself to cry.

Now.

7

I'm late. I spy the others clustered together through the window, clutching glasses of wine like a lifeline. The house beckons me to join them, the welcoming glow of Amira's living room emitting the perfect 'come in and get comfortable' vibe, yet my legs won't obey orders. They scream every time I try force them into action, begging me to stay put.

It's not that I don't want to see my friends; it's that I want to see *all* my friends.

Only that won't ever happen again. When I go into that house, two will be missing. The thought breaks my heart.

I love these women, I really do, but to me Hallie and Bree were the heart of the group. They were the ones who first welcomed in. Without them, where is my place?

I swallow down the lump in my throat and glance back through the window.

Fuck. Amira has spotted me. She waves me to come inside and join the gang.

I force a smile and wave back. There's no chance I can drive away and feign a sudden illness now.

I haul myself out of the car, remembering just in time the bottle of wine I bought for the occasion. Grabbing it, I head inside without ringing the doorbell.

I see them before they see me. Huddled together like they're conspiring against the rest of the world, these women are as tight-knit as ever. An impenetrable clique saved exclusively for those they deem worthy.

High school might have been years ago, but they all still have the same glow they did back then. Individually they are so different – from dark hair to blonde hair, curvy to thin, activewear to corporate wear – but together they make a coherent ensemble that makes perfect sense, like a well-groomed girl band. Hair perfectly styled, makeup emphasising and concealing where appropriate, clothes both chic and effortless at the same time… one look and you'd know they were the popular kids. The only sign their life isn't completely charmed is the red-rimmed, puffy from crying eyes they all sport.

"Nat!" Amira cries when she spies me, her well-known flair for dramatics coming out in full force. "Oh Nat, can you believe it?"

I shake my head and hug her. The queen of the fad diet, Amira is tiny and breakable in my arms, exactly how I feel inside.

"How can we live without them?" she whispers thickly. "It's killing me. Is it killing you?"

I don't get chance to answer the question because I'm peeled out of her hug and pulled into another.

"I'm so glad you're here," Becca croaks as she holds me. Her perfume invades my nostrils, overpowering and choking. I cough, a noise Becca mistakes for a sob. She squeezes me harder, patting my back as though she is winding a baby.

Melissa is the last one to greet me, her false eyelashes damp with tears. She clutches me like she never wants to let go.

When we are done with our tearful greetings, we stand back, the air thick with emotion and our circle notably smaller. No one moves, no one speaks, but the empty spaces in our line up scream louder than any conversation could. We study each other, unsure what to do without two of the gang here to complete us.

"This is weird," I comment, a sentiment I'm not sure I'm supposed to say out loud.

"Tell me about it," Amira echoes, taking the bottle of wine from my hand and setting it on the coffee table, not before scanning the label to gauge how much I spent on it. "We're going to need lots of this to get through tonight!"

Once we each have a full glass, we take our usual places on Amira's giant sofas, doing all we can to ignore the glaring gaps in our seating arrangement. Talk focuses on the only thing it was going to be about – Hallie and Bree.

"I keep waiting for them to walk in and laugh at us for believing this could be real," Melissa admits.

"The ultimate practical joke, except nobody's laughing," Becca sniffs.

"No laughter, just comfort eating and lots of tears. Does anyone have an update on Bree?" Amira asks, popping a stuffed olive into her mouth.

"Her mum said she's stable but unresponsive. There's no change there. I called the hospital earlier today too, but it's still family only for visits," Melissa informs us.

"Maybe we'll hear more at Hallie's funeral next week."

My heart lurches. "The funeral's next week?"

My friends frown.

"We spoke about it in the group chat earlier? Surely Hallie's mum messaged you too?"

I flush but nod along. "Sorry, my mind's all over the place. Of course we did." My friends accept my words on face value. They have no reason to suspect they've been texting my assistant all week and not me. I make a mental note to drive to Sunaina's on the way home and get my phone back.

"It's going to be such an awful day! Seriously, I don't know how I'll get through it," Amira wails.

"I know," I agree. "It's going to be so tough. Especially now the police think it wasn't an accident."

As soon as the words leave my mouth, I know they shouldn't have. Gasps ring out. Amira drops the olive she was about to eat. It rolls to the floor, but no one bothers to pick it up.

"What... what do you mean, not an accident?" Becca stutters.

Panic grips me as I realise what Lucas told me was probably confidential. It was about an active police investigation, after all. I curse myself for speaking, but I can't back out of this now. The truth is out there, the seed of murder already planted.

I pray Lucas won't be in trouble for divulging the information to me because I know once I tell these women the police suspect foul play, the whole of Coral Bay will know by morning.

"The police went to Coral Bay High and asked if Hallie and Bree had any enemies. They think they were purposely scared off the road by someone," I explain.

The room shivers.

"Why would someone do something like that?!" Melissa cries.

"That's horrific! And how ridiculous of the police to ask if Hallie and Bree had enemies," Becca scoffs. "What a dumb question."

"Exactly! There isn't a single person in Coral Bay who'd have a bad word to say about either of them!" Melissa adds.

For a moment I think I've misheard her, but as my friends echo Melissa's sentiments, it dawns on me that I'm the only one who remembers my friends for all the colours of their personality, not just the pretty ones.

I listen to emotionally recalled stories of Hallie and Bree's angelic behaviour in stunned disbelief. Tales of spontaneous acts of kindness and thoughtful gifts are devoured like leftover Christmas chocolates. Hallie and Bree's souls are buffed and shined; their positive attributes exaggerated to saintly status.

It's almost bizarre to watch.

A part of me wants to burst out laughing at the absurdity of it all. Hallie and Bree never hurt anyone, ever? Can anyone say that about anyone on the planet, especially people who used to be bullies?

I want to stop the conversation and ask everyone to think of Hallie and Bree without rose tinted glasses, but what would be the point? My friends are adamant Hallie and Bree were angels in human form.

"They were good people. Solidly good people through and through," Becca proclaims.

Her statement is met with emphatic nods, but it's those words that wake me to the truth – Hallie and Bree were never solidly good people in my eyes. How could they be after what they did to me?

There's a reason why I'm the only one who remembers their flaws – I'm the one they bullied. They never could be perfect in my eyes, none of these women can. I love them and I would be lost without them, but can I blindly defend them?

No, never.

It's only now I realise that, while I love my friends and know they love me, I will never be one of them. Not really. There will always be a part of me that doesn't quite fit here. I'm not an original. I wasn't always a chosen one. They can sit here and edit the past in their favour. They can think of Hallie and Bree and only remember the good. They can do so because their teenage years aren't full of scars, but mine are disfigured by them. Because of these women, I have wounds that will never fully heal, no matter how much I wish they would or how many times I share a bottle of wine with them.

My biggest fear is confirmed – I don't fit here, and I never did.

The realisation tastes sour in my mouth.

"Are you okay, Nat? You're kind of quiet," Amira asks.

I stir from my thoughts and fake a smile. "I'm just thinking of Hallie and Bree," I respond, an answer that isn't a complete lie.

My friends shoot me a sympathetic grimace. Melissa reaches out and squeezes my hand, uniting me with her grief. "We'll get through this. We're strong women and strong women lift each other up," she says, no doubt reciting a quote from her Pinterest affirmations board.

"To Hallie and Bree," I say, raising my glass in the air.

"To Hallie and Bree!" The girls chorus, then we drink to their memory, to whatever version of our friends we each choose to remember.

8

Lucas must have taken one of his painkillers before he went to bed because he is dead to the world when I get in, so I have to wait until morning to tell him about my foul play faux pas.

I'm halfway through feeding Esme when he enters the kitchen dressed unusually smart in a shirt and tie. "Please tell me how you're going to teach athletics in tailored trousers?" I joke.

"I could do it if I had to," Lucas grins. "There's actually an assembly this morning for Hallie. I didn't think wearing a tracksuit would be appropriate."

"Maybe not," I agree. "Are you feeling okay about it?"

Lucas shrugs. "I've got to be, right? It's important the children get the chance to grieve. The school is closing for the funeral so staff can attend, but Hallie's mum asked for no students at the church. It's not big enough to fit everyone she was friends with *and* the kids too."

I arch my eyebrow. "She's expecting that many people?"

Lucas pours a coffee for the both of us. "Why wouldn't she be? Hallie was very popular."

I nod, my heart fluttering in my chest as I build up the courage to verbalise my confession. "Lucas, I have to tell you something. Last night I kind of told everyone the police don't think it was an accident anymore."

Lucas says nothing, his silence my cue to panic.

"I'm so sorry - I didn't think it was a secret. You never said not to tell anyone! I thought because I knew then it must be common knowledge, but I don't think it was. It just slipped into conversation then everyone reacted. I couldn't take it back once I'd said it and -"

Lucas rests his hands on my shoulders. "Babe, don't worry about it. It was bound to get out somehow – this is Coral Bay we're talking about, after all. Technically you weren't meant to say anything, but the girls were going to find out when the police spoke to them anyway."

I recoil from his touch. "The police want to speak to us? Why?"

"Because you're Hallie and Bree's closest friends. You're more likely to know of people who might have a grudge against them than their colleagues." Lucas drains his coffee and glances at his watch. "I have to go. Have a good day, okay?" He kisses me goodbye then heads for the door. I stare after him, my lips still parted from our hasty kiss.

The police want to speak to me? I shudder at the thought.

Maybe it's from being bullied for years with no one taking a stand for me, but authority figures make me uneasy at the best of times, never mind when they're digging into the past I so firmly like to keep behind me.

Besides, what can I say to them? It's clear I remember things differently to everyone else. I can easily reel off a list of at least ten people who might not have the best things to say about Hallie and Bree, but it hardly screams 'Nat is a good friend' if I do. The last thing I need is to tell the police the truth and have everyone hate me for it.

From her highchair, Esme gurgles. I pick her up and she nuzzles into me like I am home. "What's mummy supposed to do? Is she meant to tell the police her friends were little bitches, hmm?" I ask in a squeaky voice.

The sound of someone clearing their throat behind me makes me jump. I spin around to find two formal looking strangers stood in the kitchen doorway.

"Good morning, Mrs Redding. Apologies for the intrusion, but we're here to ask you a few questions. We passed Mr Redding as he was leaving and he told us to come straight in," says the female. She smiles politely, trying to pretend she hadn't overheard me, but from the dancing intrigue in the eyes of the man beside her, I know they both heard exactly what I just said.

9

I ask the strangers if they would like a cup of tea, an offer they both accept. My hands shake as I fill the kettle. I pray they don't notice, but the way the man's dark eyes scour every inch of the room tells me he is someone who doesn't miss a trick.

"Thank you," beams the woman when I hand her a steaming mug.

"Is there somewhere we can sit?" the man asks without smiling or thanking me for the tea. Then again, smiling doesn't look like it comes naturally to him. His face is well lined and craggy, his misery twisted features almost painful to look at.

With my fluster still burning bright on my face, I gesture towards the dining table, and we take a seat. Esme, mouth crusted with the remnants of her breakfast, warbles.

The woman smiles, deep dimples piercing her cheeks. "She's beautiful."

"Thank you. Her name's Esme."

"Hello Esme!" the woman coos, clucking my daughter's chin and pulling a silly face. The man barely looks in Esme's direction, his disinterest in her so strong it's almost insulting.

Jay enters the kitchen from the garden, her hair still damp from her morning shower. Her eyes widen at the sight of two formally dressed, sombre strangers sitting at the dining table.

"Jay, this is…" I trail off.

"Didn't we tell you our names? How rude of us, I'm sorry. This is Detective Andrew Baldie, and I'm Detective Julia Stone."

"Good morning," Jay says politely.

"This is an informal visit, Mrs Redding, so there's no need to worry. We're just after some background information on Miss Patterson and Miss Jackson. We believe they were friends of yours?" Detective Stone asks, her eyes crinkling as she smiles.

I nod.

Starved of attention, Esme shrieks. Instinctively, I turn to Jay. "Do you mind taking her?"

"Of course." Jay swoops in and picks Esme up. "Let's go to the garden!"

We watch Jay as she carries Esme outside and sits her on the grass. Once the door is closed behind them, the detectives and I turn back to each other.

"And that is?" Detective Baldie asks.

"Jay Scott. My nanny."

Detective Baldie raises his eyebrows and I blush the same way I always do whenever the fact that I have a nanny is met with judgement. "I work from home as a painter. I need someone to look after Esme while I work. Jay was new to the area, experienced in childcare -"

Detective Stone waves her hand in the air. "Oh, you don't have to explain yourself to us, Natalie – is it okay if I call you Natalie?" I nod. "I have a young one myself. It's hard going back to work and finding appropriate childcare. You're lucky - trying to find a decent day care that doesn't charge over the odds or have an enormous waiting list is a nightmare."

Her words of exoneration allow me to exhale. "Exactly, and painting is such an irregular job. Sometimes I can be in the studio solidly for a week, other times it's only for a few hours every couple of days. We needed childcare that reflected that, and along came Jay. We have free accommodation for her onsite too, so everyone benefits."

"You have accommodation for your nanny? Painting must pay well," Detective Baldie comments. Something about the way he addresses me makes me squirm.

I force myself to sit straighter and feign a confidence that doesn't come naturally to me. "I do alright. Anyway, what can I help you with? You said you had questions about Hallie and Bree?"

"That's right. We have a few questions that should hopefully help build a better profile of your friends and figure out what happened on the night of the crash," Detective Baldie says. "Are we okay to start?"

I nod, plastering my best 'eager to impress' smile on my face.

Out of the corner of my eye, I spy Detective Stone pull a notebook from her pocket and ready herself to take down everything I say. Realising this chat isn't quite as informal as it had been made out to be, I'm suddenly terrified.

"What do you need to know?" I ask, my throat tight.

"First of all, can you describe your relationship with Miss Patterson and Miss Jackson?"

"Sure, we were friends."

The look on Detective Baldie's face tells me I need to give them more than that.

"We were part of a group of friends. There are six of us in total - me, Amira Johal, Becca Harper, Melissa Curtis then Hallie and Bree."

"And have the six of you always been friends?"

I scrape my thumbnail across my finger. "No, not exactly."

Detective Baldie's eyes flash. "What do you mean by that?"

"It's all water under the bridge now, but when we were in school, I was bullied by them," I admit.

"By Miss Patterson and Miss Jackson?"

"All of them, and Chrissy Summers."

Detective Stone writes down Chrissy's name. Her pen scratches deep into the paper like the needle of a record player destroying a vinyl.

"Tell me, how did you become friends with these women if they used to bully you? It's not every day you hear stories of people forgiving their former tormentors, never mind befriending them."

I shrug. "Well, I did. It wasn't a big deal. I changed and they did too. The things that matter as a teenager aren't really important when you're an adult. Cliques don't exist. So, when I moved back to Coral Bay we made up."

"That's nice," Detective Stone smiles. I catch Detective Baldie pulling a face and indignation sweeps over me.

"It is. We grew to really love each other. It's good to be friends with everyone here, to be honest. Coral Bay is a small town, you know?"

"We wouldn't know – we're not from here," Detective Stone explains.

I swallow. The seriousness of what has happened sinks into my consciousness another level. You don't send city detectives to rural coastland for nothing - someone really did want to kill my friends. Every hair on my body bristles at the thought.

"Look, when you walked in... when I called them bitches." Admitting what I said makes me burn with shame. "I didn't mean they were like that now, but I didn't know whether to tell you that they used to be. When Lucas told me someone might have forced them off the road..." I study my hands to stop myself from crying.

"It's okay, Natalie. It's not a crime to call the people who used to bully you bitches," Detective Stone replies. I flash her a small, grateful smile.

"They really did change, though. We were great friends in the end."

"Well, that's good. I do love a happy ending," Detective Baldie says dryly.

Detective Stone rolls her eyes. "Aren't you Mr Grumpy today!" she jokes before turning back to me. "I'm glad you told us. It helps build a better picture of these women. We can only solve cases when we know all the facts. When someone dies, especially in circumstances like this, people often edit out the bad bits. It's hard to know where to start when we're only told people are saints."

I sit forward in my seat. "Exactly. I don't want you thinking I didn't like them – they were my best friends – but they were human too. Their bad bits were as much a part of them as the good bits. I just want to help."

"If you want to help, can you think of the names of anyone they might have bullied in school, anyone who might not think that Miss Patterson and Miss Jackson were so great?"

"Where do I start?" I admit with a grimace. "Everyone got a little bit of shit from them, some worse than others. There was Mohammed Abad, they were nothing but toxic to him. Or Hannah Mead, she had a speech impediment, or maybe their harassment gave her one, I can't remember, but they were never kind to her. Then there was Josephine Riley, she got a really raw deal. So did Bethan Wright and Sonny Peters. Look, I don't mean to be awful but point to anyone in the yearbook and I could tell you a story about how they had been bullied at one point in time by those girls."

Detective Stone scribbles the names I said down while Detective Baldie studies me closely. I burn under the intensity of his gaze.

"They were great people, in the end. They were just…"

"Bitches," Detective Baldie finishes my sentence for me. The bluntness of his tone hits like a slap.

Detective Stone glosses over the rising unease in the room. "You mentioned Chrissy Summers as someone Hallie and Bree used to be friends with, but I noticed she isn't in your group now. Can you tell me why that is?"

The words 'because she's evil' are on the tip of my tongue, but I hold them in. "The other girls haven't spoken to Chrissy in years. They fell out when we were younger. I wasn't in the group back then so I'm not sure of the details. All I know is Chrissy moved away, but she's back in Coral Bay now." Detective Baldie tilts his head at this, and I sit up straighter. "I saw her the other day, actually."

"Where?"

"Hillman's Trek. It's a really lovely running track along the coast."

"I'll have to check it out after my detox tea and morning yoga," Detective Baldie mutters.

Again, Detective Stone rolls her eyes and writes down what I said. "That's great, thank you. Now, on the night of the accident, Miss Patterson and Miss Jackson were on their way to meet two men they had been speaking to online, only the men never showed. Do you know anything about this?"

My forehead scrunches as I try to remember some of the last conversations I had with my friends. "I mean, Hallie and Bree went on a lot of dates. They wanted to get married and have children. They kept saying they had to play the field because they weren't getting any younger, you know?"

Detective Stone nods like she understands exactly. "Did they tell you about their dates or who they were talking to?"

"Oh, all the time. They used to show me photos of people on dating apps or have me read over conversations and give my opinion. The usual things women talk about with their friends, I guess."

Detective Stone roots through her bag and pulls out a folder. "These are photos of the men Hallie and Bree were supposed to meet on the night of the crash. Do you recognise either of them?"

As she lays two photos on the table, I gasp, my entire body turning to ice. "Recognise them? I... I know them!"

10

The detectives sit forward, their eyes illuminated like festive lights.

"That's Aaron Chambers and that's Rory O'Connell," I say, pointing to each picture with an unsteady hand.

The natural frown on Detective Baldie's face deepens. "Aaron Chambers and Rory O'Connell? Are you sure?"

"Yes, definitely. We were friends at university. I haven't seen them for a few years, but I'd recognise them anywhere. Aaron studied graphic design and I think Rory studied accounting – it was something to do with maths, anyway. I have them both on Facebook, see?" I pull my phone from my pocket and type Aaron's name into the search bar.

When his profile loads, Detective Baldie takes my phone. "Aaron Chambers," he confirms. "Do you mind if I search for Rory O'Connell?"

"Not at all."

Detective Baldie types in Rory's name then turns the phone to Detective Stone. "Rory O'Connell."

Confusion bubbles in my mind. "Hallie and Bree were meeting Aaron and Rory? But that can't be right - Rory O'Connell is married."

"Plenty of married men use dating websites," Detective Baldie shrugs.

"But Rory seems so happy."

"Where did you deduce that from – social media?"

"Detective Baldie isn't a big fan of social media, can you tell?" Detective Stone asks with a shake of her head.

I smile weakly. "Just a little."

"Although I hear that's where you've made your fortune," Detective Baldie says, taking in his surroundings in a way that's half appreciative, half disgusted.

"It's helped, yes," I reply, suddenly embarrassed by the gifted appliances surrounding us. "But most of our money comes from my painting and Lucas's teaching salary. We work hard."

Whatever attempts I made to exonerate myself from Detective Baldie's disdain, they don't work. He's just as disinterested in me as ever when he hands me back my phone. He turns to Detective Stone. "I think we've got everything we need here, don't you?"

Detective Baldie rises to his feet and I follow his lead. I reach out to shake his hand, but he doesn't reciprocate the gesture. Rather than leaving me hanging, Detective Stone accepts the handshake, a move that only just saves me from crippling embarrassment.

"If we have any more questions," she begins.

"Feel free to come over anytime."

I walk the detectives to the front door in a surreal silence. When we reach it, Detective Baldie stops. He picks up the ornate vintage candlestick sitting on the side table by the front door and turns it over in his hands. "This is a little different to your usual décor."

I take the candlestick from him, excruciatingly aware of the over-the-top decorative moulding and poorly executed mock vintage paintwork. "It's the first thing I bought when I left Coral Bay. It made me feel grown up somehow, like the start of a new me." I sit the candlestick back down, noticing how out of place it looks against its minimalistic backdrop. "Silly really."

"We all hold onto mementos from our past," Detective Stone smiles. "I have all my sports trophies from when I was a kid, would you believe it?"

"I guess it's nice to look back and see how far you've come," I conclude.

"As long as you can look back with fondness, not fury. Enjoy the rest of your day, Mrs Redding. I'm sure we'll be seeing each other again soon," Detective Baldie says coolly as he exits, his words leaving me rooted to the spot.

11

Lucas comes home from work to find me sat at the dining table staring at my phone while a grizzly Esme plays by my feet. "Haven't you started her dinner yet?" he asks, unable to hide his irritation.

"Huh?" I glance up from my phone and realise the time. I leap to my feet, but Lucas presses on my shoulders.

"Sit. I'll make it. You look exhausted."

"Thank you," I mumble, crimson faced. I reach for Esme, only now noticing how cranky she is, and press my lips onto the top of her head. Her cheeks are red and furious, but she softens. She will forgive me. My accidental sway from her schedule won't scar her for life. My tension lessens, but the guilt over my maternal failing goes nowhere.

"We're nearly out of food," Lucas calls.

"I know. Jay's gone to the supermarket," I reply, flushing again as I am forced to admit I have let yet another thing slip from my control this week. "I was going to go myself, but Jay thought the gossip at the checkout might be too much for me right now."

"That's brave of her. She hates going into Coral Bay."

"I know. She's been great, especially after my chat with the police this morning."

Lucas stops rooting around the cupboards and gives me his undivided attention. "How did it go?"

"They grilled me, Lucas," I say, suddenly on the verge of tears. "They made me feel like I'd done something wrong by having this house and this life."

"Babe, I'm sure they were more interested in finding out about Hallie and Bree than seeing what your house looks like."

I bristle at his dismissive tone. "I'm telling you Lucas, it was awful. The male one, Detective Baldie, he hated me. You should have seen the way he looked at me, like I was a speck of dust or something. He made me feel like shit for having a nanny."

"A lot of people don't understand that we have a nanny, but so what? It's not their life, it's ours. It's no big deal."

I open my mouth to protest that criticism from other people *is* a big deal to me, but Esme chooses that moment to nuzzle into my chest and I am silenced. I squeeze her close and drop it. Esme is happy, healthy, and content – that's all that matters. That's what I'll tell Detective Baldie the next time he makes me feel bad for how I live, anyway.

"What did they say about the investigation?" Lucas asks.

I stroke Esme's fluffy hair. "They think it's foul play, that's for sure. They're looking for suspects and motives at the minute, but this is the weird bit - Hallie and Bree were going to meet two people I knew from uni the night they died."

Lucas's eyes widen. I set Esme down and go to Lucas, handing him my phone so he can see what I've been staring at for the last few hours - Rory O'Connell's Facebook. "Rory O'Connell and Aaron Chambers, only they were using fake names when they were talking to Hallie and Bree."

"Why were they -" Lucas begins, but he stops when he sees a photo of Rory and his wife. "Oh."

I take my phone back and study the smiling photo of the seemingly blissful couple. "I just can't believe it. Any of it. Why would Rory cheat? Why is Hallie dead?" I can't fight the emotion of the day anymore. I burst into tears.

I'm in Lucas's arms in an instant. "Babe, I'd be worried if you could understand any of this. Some people do bad things. The fact you don't get it just means you're a good person."

"I just wish none of this was happening," I sob.

"Me too, babe, me too."

We stay locked in an embrace until Esme's anguished cries pull us apart.

"Hey, baby girl," Lucas soothes, grabbing her and kissing her cheek. "Daddy's sorting your dinner, okay? I'm sorry it's taken so long."

Even though he is being the good dad his daughter needs, I'm still tortured by the reminder that I didn't feed my child. "I'll take her," I say, reaching for Esme.

"I've got it," Lucas says, walking past with my baby still in his arms.

"Lucas -"

"Seriously, go rest. I've got this."

Unreasonable fury grips me. I want to snatch Esme from him, to scream that I'm her mother, that I just lost track of time, but I don't want to make a scene. I have no right to shout at Lucas, especially when he's smoothing over my failings.

Instead, I slope off to the living room, angry at my husband for breezing in and saving the day, but angrier at myself for needing him to fix it in the first place.

As I flop onto the sofa, I plunge into self-deprecation.

It's rare for Lucas to see me as anything other than composed. I have Jay and Sunaina now to help me maintain an air of total control, but even before they were in my life Lucas never saw me rattled. I never let him. I kept on top of everything, juggling painting and social media and managing the home with a smile on my face and a weight that never fluctuated more than 2lbs either way. Lucas thought I could take on the world because I made him think I could. He saw hiring Jay and Sunaina as a mark of how successful I was, not an admission of defeat. To him, I've always been an in control, I-can-do-it-all-by-myself-thank-you, self-made woman.

Yet he found me glued to Facebook and forgetting to feed my hungry daughter. What must he think of me now?

"You're a mess. A disgrace. You don't deserve to be a mother," my brain snarls.

My phone lights up with an Instagram notification, but I ignore it. I don't feel like participating in anything today, even if the online version of me has a life that's still perfectly in place. No, right now is a time to fester in my failings and fears.

The voices of my old tormentors wash over me, reminding me who I really am, telling me I deserve nothing in my life. I rake my nails over my thighs again and again until the skin is red raw.

I only break from my stewing thoughts when the front door closes to mark Jay's return. Rising to my feet, I go to help carry the groceries into the kitchen.

"Nat," Jay breathes when she sees me, her usually pale cheeks tinged pink with excitement. "You'll never guess what I heard when I was paying!"

"Please don't say it's about Curtis's infected foot…"

"No, not this time. It's Bree – she's awake."

12

The group chat is alive with suggestions of what to bring with us to the hospital when we visit Bree. After an intense debate where Becca at one point even suggests we hire a musician to play Bree's favourite songs, I manage to convince my friends that the simple act of showing up is all we need to do. However, Amira's suggestion of spraying Bree's pillow with her favourite perfume was an idea we all agreed on. Seeing as it's the same perfume I wear, I'm in charge of that.

The bottle weighs heavy in my bag as I set off, but the weight is a welcome reminder that I am still here. With everything sliding from my usually tight grasp, I need that right now.

I pay for parking and follow a maze of artificially lit corridors, hunting for Intensive Care. My shoes squeak against the overly polished lino, the noise abrasive against the silent backdrop. I'm disturbing the peace just by being here. I think of Lucas and Esme having dinner at home and wrestle the urge to turn around and run into their arms.

The eerie silence makes me almost wish I hadn't been so adamant about coming alone. Amira suggested carpooling, but I made Esme related excuses and drove myself. I needed time with my thoughts before I could come here. Time to prepare myself for these corridors, for the harsh, chemical smells that remind me so clearly of the last time I went to visit someone seriously ill.

I haven't thought about that day in years. The memory drains all life from my soul.

I take a right at the end of the corridor and blink in the sombre sight of my friends waiting outside the ward. They smile when they see me and we hug, tight, squeezing embraces of support.

"I can't believe we're actually doing this. I can't believe this is real," Melissa sniffs.

We murmur in agreement, no one quite knowing what to say. I try breathing normally, but the atmosphere is so thick with unease it's suffocating. We look to one another to make the first move while simultaneously comforted by the fact that no one else is in a rush to see what has become of Bree either.

"Come on," Amira says, straightening up to her full height. "Bree needs us, and I for one am not going to let her down."

Buoyed by Amira's uncharacteristic show of leadership, we push open the doors to the ward. Inside, crushing silence is replaced by the faint rhythmical beeping of medical machinery. It makes me almost long for the absence of noise in the corridor.

A curvaceous blonde nurse behind the front desk looks up from her paperwork. "Can I help you?"

"We're here to see Briana Jackson."

The nurse eyes our huddle. "I'm sorry, but there's a three-person limit. I can't let you all in at once."

Her words deflate us like a pin to a balloon.

"But we've driven over an hour to see her," Melissa begs. "We've been friends since high school. It's killing us not knowing how she is!"

"Please," I implore. "We won't stay long. We just need to see she's alright."

The nurse sighs. "Alright, you have ten minutes - Miss Jackson needs her rest. Her room is at the end of the corridor. You can go join your other friend."

"Our other friend?" I frown.

The nurse nods, clicking her pen and returning to her paperwork. I turn to the rest of the group who look as perplexed as I do.

"Her mum is probably with her," Melissa says.

Amira nods. "I've heard she hasn't left Bree's side since she got here."

Appeased, we make our way down the corridor. Melissa links her arm through mine, and I squeeze her hand gratefully. However torturous these steps are, I'm not taking them alone, a stark contrast to the last time I visited this hospital.

Light shines from the room at the end of the corridor, signalling that there is life behind the door. But what is left of that life, we do not know.

As if realising my terror, my senses kick into overdrive. The lights seem too bright, the disinfectant too strong, the silence too loud. I can't be the only one feeling the tension rise because, just as we approach the door, we all instinctively stop.

"This is it," Becca whispers. "Everything changes from here."

"Hey, everything's already changed," I joke, my eyes shiny with tears.

My friends choke on a half laugh, half sob. With one last smile at each other, we step into the room.

As soon as we cross the threshold, we freeze, but it's not the sight of the violent, ugly, purple bruises covering Bree's swollen face or her half shaven head that causes such a violent, jerking reaction.

No, the thing that forces the air to catch at the back of our throat is sitting beside our injured friend and stroking her hand.

13

"Chrissy, is that you?" Melissa asks, her eyes popping out of her skull.

Chrissy rises to her feet at the mention of her name. Her gaze flicks from one ex friend to another, drinking in the sight of them as adults. A faint smile dances on her thin lips, a sight terrifying enough to strike fear into even the bravest of hearts.

She looks better than when I last saw her. Instead of ill-fitting sports gear, she wears a patterned wrap dress that makes her silhouette appear even more curvaceous and womanly. Loose, wavy hair frames her face, her makeup minimal but well applied.

Only no matter how much more polished she looks, there's still no denying her glory days are long gone. There's a tiredness to her that only comes from years of tough living.

"Chrissy *Summers*?" Becca repeats.

Chrissy doesn't flinch at their startled reaction, even though it must hurt. "It's good to see you again," she says, then glances at Bree. "Even if it is under terrible circumstances."

Her casual acknowledgement of Bree reminds everyone why we are here. We scoop our jaws from the floor and rush to Bree's bedside.

There's no other way to say it - Bree looks terrible. Her skin is sunken, her figure small and alien like, almost as if her body has caved in on itself. Angry cuts line every visible inch of flesh, giving the impression that a child has scribbled on Bree's skin with a thick, red crayon. A large, plastic breathing tube is stuffed in her mouth. It's hard to imagine anything that looks so suffocating could help someone breathe. Bree's eyes are closed as if she is sleeping, but she appears far from peaceful.

"Fuck," Melissa chokes, then the tears fall. Instinctively, I wrap my arm around her.

Chrissy notices this, her lips curling, before focusing her attention back on Bree. "Apparently she opened her eyes yesterday. It was a big moment. They think that's about all she'll be able to do from now on."

The pit of my stomach falls to the floor. "What?"

"Didn't you know?" Chrissy asks innocently. "She's badly brain damaged. She can't move, she can't speak. She'll need constant care for the rest of her life."

There's no holding back the tears now. Amira reaches out and grasps Bree's hand, sobbing so hard she looks like she's vibrating. Melissa trembles in my arms and Becca leans in for a hug too. Grief chokes us.

Bree, fun loving, loyal, larger than life Bree. How could this happen to her?

We cry for our friend, for our loss, for our disbelief that any of this is real.

The only person not crying is Chrissy. If anything, smugness lines her features. Couple that with the airy way she delivered the horrific news of Bree's condition and I'm ready to throttle her.

I pull back from my friends and wipe my eyes with the back of my hand. "Why are you here?" I ask, my voice heavy with accusation.

"I could ask you the same thing," Chrissy fires back. The shock of her retort strikes me like a baseball bat to the chest. Chrissy sucks her teeth to hide her snidey smile. "I'm here to visit my friend, of course."

"So am I," I reply hotly.

"Oh, I know you've been a bit friendly recently, but there's something about the friends you've had since you were a kid, isn't there? You know that no matter how long it's been since you last spoke, you will always have a special place in their heart. That's true friendship." Chrissy looks past me and smiles at the rest of my friends. "Remember when Bree snuck a couple of her dad's beers to my house and we all convinced ourselves we were drunk after two sips?"

Despite their all-consuming sadness, the girls laugh.

"None of us even liked beer," Melissa smiles.

"Bree didn't want to bring them, either. She only did it because Hallie told her to," Becca adds.

"Didn't she always do what Hallie told her to?" Chrissy quips.

"Always!" Amira laughs. "Sometimes it was like they morphed into one person. Do you remember when Bree cut her hair like Hallie's even though it did *not* suit her?"

"Of course I do - I gave her the scissors!" Chrissy grins.

"You always were the bad one," Becca smiles.

"Me?" Chrissy pulls an innocent face, and the others laugh.

Their giggles hit me like punches. Like an outsider looking in, no laughter escapes my lips.

Chrissy looks from Bree to us, her false smile faltering. "Those two really show you the value of true, lifelong friendship, don't they?" she simpers. Her words are aimed at my friends, but her gaze is fixed on me.

As everyone else murmurs in agreement, I stay silent. Exactly how Chrissy wants me to be. I can't share fond memories of sleepovers or talk about the good old days because I wasn't there. I was at home, crying over whatever poisonous antic they had inflicted on me that day.

I want to grab my friends and steal them away before Chrissy can say another word. I want to suggest we all go back to mine, an invitation I would not stretch to Chrissy. I want to leave her alone in this clinical, depressing room and take *my* friends back to *our* shared life, but I don't. I don't say a word. I'm too hurt to.

I leave the hospital distraught over what has happened to Bree, yes, but also distraught for myself. For every step I've taken over the last few years, in one night Chrissy has knocked me back three. All my worries about being cast out again not only surround me, but they're now stronger than ever.

Chrissy is back, alright. She's back and determined to pull apart everything I have worked so hard to build.

14

My cloud of anger and fear carries over into the next day, filling me with inspiration. Knowing the Arlene Davies deadline is looming closer and closer, I lock myself in my studio and get to work.

I paint a girl in purple, small, isolated, and alone. I paint angry, red figures closing in and towering above her until eventually the paint drips over the purple girl and she is consumed by it.

When I stand back, the canvas is smeared in various shades of violent, raging red. Droplets of paint even drip onto the floor like blood from an open wound. There is just a small, dark, smudged spot where the girl once stood.

The piece is not at all on brief, but I don't regret spending my day on it. I needed the freedom of attacking the canvas with my unfiltered thoughts. And by the looks of things, my thoughts are pretty dark right now. Taking them out on a canvas is much better than taking them out on the world, or myself.

When I finally emerge from the studio hours after disappearing into it, I find Lucas playing with Esme in the sunset lit garden. He raises his eyebrows when he sees me, paint smeared and rosy cheeked. "Good session?"

"Therapeutic."

I kiss him quickly then head for a shower. Paint stains the water red, turning my whiter than white bathroom into a crime scene re-enactment.

When I am clean, I slip on a loose dress and head into the garden to join my family. As I take a seat on the grass, Esme reaches for me. Her chubby fingers lace around mine.

"You're such a good girl," I coo, snuggling her close. She grips onto me and all the uncertainty and wobbling emotion of the last few days disappears. "She is what matters," I tell myself. "She is the only thing that matters."

I don't realise how much I've needed time with my husband and my daughter until after we've put Esme to bed. I curl under Lucas's arm on the sofa, the warmth of his embrace like healing magic. "I miss this," I say.

"Miss what?"

"You, me, cuddling."

Lucas squeezes me. "I always cuddle you."

"I know, but I just wish you'd never me let go," I whisper, my voice catching in the back of my throat.

Lucas pulls away to study me, his worry lines out in full force. "Are you okay? You've been quiet ever since you went to visit Bree."

I toy with Lucas's hand. "It was tough seeing her like that, but to be honest it was Chrissy who made it worse."

"How so?"

"Well, first of all, she shouldn't even *be* there."

Lucas shrugs. "I guess she just wanted to see her friend."

I pull a face. "A friend she hasn't bothered with in years."

"Still, when something bad happens to someone you were once close to, you feel it. Take me and Blaine – his suicide rocked me, and I hadn't seen the guy since the second summer of university."

"His death was a huge shock, though."

"And Hallie and Bree's accident wasn't?"

I sigh irritably. "That's not what I mean. I just… she shouldn't be there, that's all. She has no right."

"Nat, she was their friend. She has as much of a right to be there as anyone," Lucas says, squeezing my hand.

"But she's toxic," I snarl, my fury bursting from me like a snapping dog.

Lucas raises his eyebrows, a sharp tone and bitter language something he's not used to seeing from me. No one is. This side of my soul is one I work hard to keep under wraps, but there's just something about Chrissy that seems to pull a venom from me I thought I had long buried.

"Don't let it get to you so much, babe. She might have changed."

I can't resist scoffing. "People like Chrissy *never* change."

"You don't know that."

I press my lips together to stop myself from protesting that after only seeing Chrissy twice, I *do* know that. There's no point pushing it. Lucas likes to look at the world and only see the good. To him, I must seem unreasonable and petty, and maybe I am being unreasonable and petty, but I know Chrissy more than he does and I can safely say she has not changed at all.

I also know that she was not at the hospital to be a good friend. Chrissy hasn't bothered with Coral Bay or anyone here for years, but now all of a sudden she's back and wanting to reunite with her old gang?

Bullshit.

No, Chrissy Summers is back for a reason. She's up to something. She's always up to something.

Lucas kisses the top of my head, interrupting my thoughts. "Come on, cheer up. I hate seeing you like this."

I sigh. "I'm fine, it's just... I just... I just wish she didn't make me feel so..." I struggle to find the words.

"So?"

"Left out," I admit.

"Babe, if you think Chrissy Summers showing up again is going to change anything for you then you're mad. The girls love you!"

"I guess," I mutter.

"There's no 'I guess' about it - you're irreplaceable! As soon as you stop feeling so down, you'll see that too. Now, let me grab a bottle of wine and we can spend the rest of the night cuddling." Lucas kisses me and stands. I watch him leave the room.

For a moment, I believe him. For a moment, I think he is right. My friends will always be my friends, even if they decide to befriend Chrissy again. I am not the person I used to be. I have changed. I have built a life to be proud of. No one can take that away from me, not even Chrissy Summers.

While I wait for Lucas to return with the wine, I check my phone. I have two missed calls from Arlene Davies which I ignore. Conversations about my artwork – or lack of artwork – are not what I need right now. Instead, I head to Instagram, bypassing the mountain of comments and bursting inbox waiting for me and flicking through the images on my feed.

My heart stops inside my chest at the third post I see.

Two hours ago, Amira posted a picture from the local pub, The Oaks. It's of a group of women huddled together sharing a bottle of wine. In the photo, there's Amira, Becca, Melissa... and Chrissy Summers.

The plug is yanked from the bottom of my world and with it all sense of peace and contentment swirls away and disappears forever. Bile rises in my throat as I read Amira's sickening sentiments.

There's nothing like a tragedy to bring people together. Catching up with old school friends – it's like nothing has changed!

The four of them are smiling, their arms wrapped around each other's shoulders, all stylish clothes, whitened teeth, and sparkly eyes. They look like a proper group of friends, the kind you walk past on a night out and think, 'I'd love to be part of a group like that'. They look complete. They look like they don't need me.

My heart beats hollow.

I focus on Chrissy until the pixels of her face burn my eyes. Her beaming smile oozes with smugness. It dawns on me that it's no coincidence everyone but me was invited to their cosy night out. Chrissy did this to oust me, to show me my real place in the world, and my friends have happily let her.

"Of course they don't want you anymore," I tell myself. "Did you really think they were your friends? Are you honestly *that* stupid? You need to remember who you are, Nat, who you always have been."

I squirm under the intensity of my self-hatred, but I don't fight back. I let those words and the truth in them sink into my soul, knowing they will stain it forever.

Lucas returns with wine, but I don't feel like drinking anymore. I cuddle up under his arm, waiting to melt into the safety of his embrace, but serenity never comes. I hold onto my husband tighter, praying for him to anchor me, but I still feel like I am bobbing out to sea, lost and alone. Always, always alone.

<u>Then.</u>

Lunchtime.

The worst time.

She used to eat in the library, nestled safely between endless shelves of books. She would devour a new one each day, falling headfirst into fictional dreamworlds where she could be anyone but herself.

Only one day the librarian told the headteacher she was worried for the girl's social development because she was spending every day alone instead of making friends. That's what the headteacher said, anyway.

Really, she knew the librarian had complained about the smell and asked him to remove her from the library.

So here she is, excluded from the one place she felt safe and forced to sit in the canteen. Alone in a sea of people who wish she weren't there as much as she wishes she weren't too.

But one day, completely out of the blue, something magical happens - two girls sit at her table. She blinks in the sight of them. Are they lost? Is this a joke? No one ever sits with her.

Ever.

Ever.

But there they are, and they've not moved yet. In fact, they've even started to eat. They're on the table for the long haul.

She can't believe it.

Each table in the canteen has room for eight people, yet she has always, always sat alone. One time she saw a group of four girls stand to eat rather than sit with her. She tried to pretend it didn't upset her to watch them balance their lunchboxes on their skinny forearms and nibble their neat, white bread sandwiches standing, but she was fooling herself. The fact that people would rather eat like a savage than sit beside her was more cutting than she could express.

But here they are, two girls sat at her table, eating.

They're from two years below. They aren't cool – one has books with her, a girl who makes the cardinal sin of publicly declaring she reads for fun – but that doesn't matter. They're two girls, two people, and they're sitting near her without laughing, pulling a face or calling her names.

She smiles shyly as the red-haired girl makes eye contact. To her amazement, the red-haired girl smiles back.

Heart pounding, the girl looks back at her lunch. She can't believe it. The girl hadn't stuck her tongue out or mouthed 'fuck off' or asked what she was looking at... she had smiled back.

Suddenly, the girl isn't hungry anymore. She knows this food will be the only meal she will have all day and that really, she should finish the lukewarm, greyish Bolognese, but she can't. Her mouth is too dry to swallow, her hands too clammy to grip her fork. She sets down her cutlery and wipes her hands on her skirt.

The girls are talking about maths – 'I swear, Mr Jenkins hates me!' – but, even though she doesn't mind maths, that's okay. It's nice to listen to a conversation that isn't about her and how hideous everyone thinks she is.

The book girl catches her staring and smiles. "Hi."

*She blinks. The book girl said hi. The book girl said hi to **her**.*

Pulling herself together, the girl smiles back, praying that her features align right and her smile doesn't come across as weird. "Hi," she says, her voice soft and cautious.

"I'm Jenny, this is Carmen," the book girl says. "What's your name?"

"Fish Sticks," she thinks, but of course that's not her name, that never was her name. She opens her mouth to reply but her words stay stuck in her throat as someone else joins the table. She doesn't need to look to

know who it is. She would recognise that perfume anywhere. Expensive, fruity, overpowering - the smell of dread.

"Is she bothering you?" Chrissy barks.

Jenny and Carmen blink. They might not have known who they were sat with, but they know Chrissy. Everyone knows Chrissy. And right now, Chrissy is pissed off.

"Is she?" Chrissy demands.

"N-no."

"Good, because if she is – you tell me. Fish Sticks bothers everyone. Well, the smell of her does anyway." Chrissy waves her hand in front of her nose to reiterate her point.

The girl spies a flash of pity in her could-have-been-friends' eyes, but she knows all too well what will happen next. They have shut down, the warm, friendly glow they emitted evaporating in the blink of an eye. They are scared, scared of Chrissy, and scared they will end up another of her victims if they stay on this table any longer.

"Why don't you have lunch with us today?" Chrissy suggests, an offer nowhere near as friendly as it seems.

"Oh!" Carmen exclaims, her shock palpable. "Really?"

"Sure, why not? Our table's in a much better spot. Plus, we can save you from feeling sick every time you take a breath. Come on," Chrissy commands.

*Like little sheep, the two girls collect their things. Carmen follows Chrissy straight away, but Jenny hesitates for a moment. She makes eye contact once again and it's clear there are a hundred things she wants to say, but she doesn't. She can't. She might be young, but she knows how it works. Someone must be at the top of the ladder, and someone must be at the bottom. Everywhere else is okay, it's survivable, but you do **not** want to be at the bottom.*

Red cheeked, Jenny bows her head and scurries after Chrissy.

The girl watches her two almost friends as they join Chrissy's table.

85

They are given a hero's welcome. Amira laughs at their jokes and Hallie reads the blurbs of Jenny's books. Bex even shares her lunch with Carmen. They make them feel like they belong, like they have made it.

The girl knows they will never make the mistake of acknowledging her again. She will remain alone on this table until the day she can finally leave this place.

She wants to be sad they have gone, and a small part of her is, but in all honesty by sitting at her table they gave her more than they will ever know. They gave her the knowledge that she isn't completely invisible after all, and that is something Chrissy can never take away from her, no matter how hard she tries.

Now.

15

The contents of my wardrobe stare at me from the bed. Nothing is right. It's either too colourful, too casual or too light-hearted for a funeral. Besides, I don't want to taint anything I already own by wearing it to say goodbye to Hallie. I want something new, something I can throw away as soon as the funeral is over and never see again.

I glance at the time. Sunaina is scheduled to arrive to shoot content in half an hour, but looking at the scene before me, it's clear that isn't going to happen.

To say Sunaina is less than impressed when I cancel our plans is an understatement. "I know you're going through a tough time at the minute Nat, but you really need to sort your shit out," she snaps. "Arlene Davies will not leave me alone, there are a million and one emails I need your input on before I can reply to them and we're falling behind with content. It's starting to come across as sloppy."

I make whatever promises I must to appease her, but my words are hollow. How can I focus on content creation or painting seascapes when Chrissy is back and I'm about to bury my best friend?

When the call ends, I beg Jay to head into Coral Bay with me so I don't have to face the gossip alone, but she recoils at the suggestion. "Sorry, Nat, you know I hate heading into town. Those women scare me."

I whine in response but concede. I struggle with the Coral Bay rumour mill at the best of times and I grew up here, so I can only imagine what it's like for an out of towner.

Begrudgingly, I head into Coral Bay on my own. I park on Main Street and politely wave back to Hank the florist as he pauses outside his shop to greet me. "Morning, Nat," he calls.

"Morning Hank," I reply, trying to slip past, but I should know better than to think I could get away with that. In Coral Bay, there's no slipping past anyone.

"Terrible news, isn't it? Hallie and Bree… who'd have thought it. You were such good friends too. I'm sure you're just cut up inside! Any news on what happened? I've heard the police think it wasn't an accident," Hank asks innocently, but I'm an expert now – I can recognise subtly fishing for a story a mile off. Sometimes, I play along with it, dropping juicy bits of information into a conversation or starting my response with Coral Bay's favourite line, 'you didn't hear it from me but…', but not today. Not about Hallie and Bree.

"Nothing more than you already know," I reply, pushing on before Hank can respond.

As I make my way towards Dot's Designs, I am stopped every few steps and forced into more well-meaning but intrusive conversations. After walking just five metres away from my car, I'm already exhausted.

While it's true that 'Finding the Good Life' has made me somewhat of a celebrity in some circles, even without it walking down Main Street would be like this. Everyone in Coral Bay is a friend, or at least someone who knows your most intimate secrets. Even though I've barely spoken to anyone recently, I know that Linda caught her son smoking the other day and that Len found a lump on his testicles but won't get it checked out. That's just the way it is here. Shops stay open for generations because people's children take over the business. High school students go on to become high school teachers. Most people, people like Lucas, never leave and never want to. Then there are those like me who do leave but who always return in the end.

Coral Bay ebbs and flows like the tide of the sea it looks upon, moving but somehow always staying the same. Today, I really hate that about it. I almost find myself wishing I could go back to being my old, invisible self, just for five minutes of peace. It's a thought I quickly shake away. Nothing could make me want to go back to that life. Nothing.

The door of Dot's Designs chimes as I push it open. From behind the counter, Dot looks up, her eyes crinkling into a sad smile when she sees me. "Oh Nat, darling, come here!" She holds her arms out for me to fall into.

"Hi Dot," I reply, squeezing her body to my own. I swear, Dot's hugs could heal the world. Barely five-foot tall but with the biggest heart of anyone I've ever met, Dot is a local hero.

"I still can't believe it. Awful, just awful!" Dot sighs, peeling out of the hug. "I suppose you're here for an outfit for the funeral?"

I nod and Dot leads me to a rail of dresses.

"This one will be too big for your lovely figure, but it could look great with a belt. The other is more fitted, but you might think it's a tad too much for a funeral. Try them on and see what you think." Dot hands me the two dresses then studies me sadly. "Do you know, it seems like just yesterday you and Hallie were in here finding an outfit for Poppy's wedding."

My throat tightens at the memory. Me, exhausted and cripplingly insecure about my post-baby body, crying in a fitting room because nothing looked right until Hallie threw open the curtain with an armful of ludicrous ensembles for us to try on. We spent the rest of the day pairing wacky dresses with formal trousers and running shoes until I was laughing so hard I forgot all about my self-consciousness.

The memory pulls inside my chest like a weight on a spring.

"Tell me about it," I reply thickly. "It still doesn't feel real."

"I know, love, but you'll get through this. You have all our love and support behind you," Dot soothes, squeezing my arm. Suddenly Coral

Bay doesn't seem like such a bad place to be in a crisis after all.

Just then, the door of Dot's Designs chimes and in walks the last person I want to see.

"Chrissy." Her name leaves my mouth without being instructed to.

"Oh, hi Nat. Fancy seeing you out shopping and not at work or with your daughter."

My eyes narrow with hatred while Dot's pop with shock. Her mouth hangs open as she registers who has just walked into her shop, but the saleswoman in her recovers quickly. "Chrissy, dear, is that you?"

"Hi Dot," Chrissy says, beaming as if butter wouldn't melt.

Dot rushes to Chrissy and hugs her close. "My goodness – what a blast from the past! It's so good to see you!" she enthuses with all the warmth of a heatwave.

With those words, my heart turns to stone. It seems, just like the rest of Coral Bay, Dot has forgotten who Chrissy Summers is and the damage she caused when she last lived here.

How can I be the only one who remembers Chrissy telling everyone Dot sold old lady clothes and laughing at anyone who shopped in her store? Dot's Designs nearly closed because every teenager in Coral Bay insisted their mother took them to the city for their clothes, but Dot seems to have erased that sour, unprofitable period from memory.

As Dot and Chrissy excitedly catch up, I force myself to watch the scene.

Chrissy's charm offensive is on top form. She acts as if she is genuinely pleased to see Dot and Dot glows from the attention, coming to life with each artificially sweetened compliment. If I didn't know better, I might have really believed they were happy to see each other, but I know Chrissy better than that. Her niceness always comes with a catch.

"How does she do it?" I marvel. "How can she be so vile yet so universally adored?"

A familiar burning sensation swells in the pit of my stomach.

I hate her.

I hate her so much.

"Dot, I'm just going to try these on," I call, but Dot barely registers me. She's too busy showing Chrissy her latest summer dresses to care what I have to say.

I drag myself into the fitting room and strip to my underwear, catching sight of my reflection in the mirror. My stomach sags a little, my skin rippled from accommodating my daughter. I am beyond proud of what my body has achieved, but sometimes it's hard not to panic at the sight of the doughy pouches and softened curves that didn't used to be there. It brings back old insecurities that I have worked so hard to try and move past. I reel them off in a list – hip dips, cellulite, thread veins.

When I was younger, Chrissy made me believe I was nothing short of hideous. I can still hear her cruel taunts and wicked laughter in the changing room before PE.

Even now, years later, her voice still takes over my thoughts whenever I stand exposed and vulnerable in front of a mirror like this. Her jibes buzz around my head like angry wasps. No matter how hard I try, I can never forget the things she said.

As a ripple of laughter erupts from the shop floor, I clench my jaw.

I pull on the bigger dress and add a belt as Dot suggested. It's stylish, but I don't love it, so I try on the more fitted style. It's definitely a lot sexier than the other but paired with the right shoes it could be appropriate. Wearing it, I feel bolder and more confident. I feel like someone who could take on Chrissy Summers and win.

I change back into my own clothes and exit the fitting room to find Chrissy and Dot still catching up like old friends. My stomach turns. "I'll take this one," I say loudly, cutting Chrissy off mid-sentence.

Dot turns to me, wiping tears of laughter from her eyes. "Okay, dear. I knew it would suit you."

"It fits perfectly," I smile, ignoring Chrissy until I feel her hand on my arm.

"Can I see that?" she asks, pointing at the dress I just dismissed.

"Oh… sure," I stumble, handing it over.

Chrissy holds the dress in the air, admiring the fabric closely. "Dot, this is beautiful!" she exclaims, her voice dripping with insincerity, not that Dot picks up on it. I fight the urge to roll my eyes.

"Do you like it, dear? Why don't you try it on?"

"Do you think it will fit me?" Chrissy asks, chewing her lower lip.

I study the dress and Chrissy's curves sceptically but say nothing.

"Only one way to find out!" Dot leads Chrissy to the fitting room, telling her to shout if she needs anything else. I can't help but feel a tug of envy as I watch Dot coo over Chrissy instead of me.

While Chrissy is changing, Dot bags up my new dress. "Can you believe Chrissy Summers is back in Coral Bay?"

"No, I really can't."

I take my purchase and say goodbye to Dot, who responds pleasantly but who clearly has her mind elsewhere. I head for the door, ready to go home and shut myself away for the rest of the day, but I stop when I hear Dot shriek.

"Chrissy, you look amazing!"

I turn on my heel and blink, taking in the sight of Chrissy wearing the dress I had just tried on. The difference is Chrissy is *wearing* the dress. Whereas the fabric bagged and bulged awkwardly on me, it clings to Chrissy, her womanly silhouette bathed in swathes of luscious material. She somehow looks both thinner and more curvaceous at the same time. I hate to admit it, but she looks beautiful. She looks like Chrissy again.

From her beaming smile, she knows it too.

"Should I get it?" she asks Dot, knowing what the response will be but still eager to hear the compliments.

"Are you kidding me? Yes! Yes, you should! You look *amazing!*" Dot fusses around Chrissy, admiring her from every angle.

Chrissy faces me, her eyes sharp. "What about you, Nat? Do you think I look good?"

Everything around me stops.

I swallow hard.

I want to tell Chrissy that I know what she's doing. I want to tell her to stop toying with me and to leave me alone. I want to remind her that we are no longer teenagers, that she has no power over me, but my words would be futile. Chrissy knows as well as I do she will always have power over me.

"Chrissy, you look amazing," I say, then I leave and don't look back to see the sickening smirk of triumph on her face.

16

Unsurprisingly, running into Chrissy at Dot's Designs leaves me in a foul mood. The mountain of work I must do calls out, but I ignore it. Instead, I find myself resorting to aggressively cleaning the bathroom to burn off rage, an act that doesn't have the desired effect.

After snapping at Lucas when he phoned on his lunchbreak to see how I was doing, I decide to call an emergency girls' night to cheer myself up. I've barely pressed send on my invitation text before replies from Amira, Becca, and Melissa roll in.

Such a good idea babe! Just what we need x

Thnx 4 thinking of this, doll. Ill B there! x

You're the best Nat – see you later tonight! xoxo

Girls' night planned, the pace of my day kicks up a notch. Melissa messages to remind me about picking up a bag of donations I promised to supply for a charity auction her work is hosting. With everything that's happened, it completely slipped my mind. I quickly run around the house and collect a few things for her. Then I head back into Coral Bay to stockpile wine and cheese, smiling through gritted teeth as I'm lured into conversations about Hallie's funeral until I finally get back to the safety of home.

House tidied and dressed for a cosy evening with the girls, the front door opens just before five. "You're early!" I call out, but my smile freezes when I see Sunaina breezing into my kitchen and not my friends.

She blinks at the sight of me prepping a cheeseboard. "What's going on?"

"I'm hosting a girls' night."

Sunaina's face screams with irritation. "Don't tell me you forgot we were shooting tonight? You literally said this morning that we could take the photos once you got your dress for the funeral."

The memory of palming Sunaina off with whatever she had wanted to hear sits uncomfortably on my chest. "I'm sorry -"

"Great, I guess I'll just drive all the way back home and -"

"Wait! Why don't we use this as a backdrop for content? A girls' night is surely part of 'Finding the Good Life', right?"

"You're meant to be wearing the red 'Oh So Pretty' dress for a date with Lucas. It's a sponsored post. They've paid a lot of money for this, Nat. We can't fuck it up." Sunaina's tone is that of a disappointed parent and suddenly I'm flooded with dread. I hate it when she's mad at me.

"Why don't I wear the dress for girls' night?"

Sunaina raises her eyebrow. "That dress for a night at home?"

"Why not? Come on, let's go."

Sunaina follows me upstairs and I slip into the dress. In my desperate rush to make peace, I had forgotten how fitted and cleavage enhancing the dress is. Totally inappropriate for a girls' night in, but I stay silent.

Sunaina instructs me on what makeup to apply and how to style my hair. Before I know it, I am overdressed and back downstairs feigning pouring wine as she snaps away.

"We can pretend this is a date night at home," Sunaina compromises halfway through the photoshoot. "The main idea is still the same and I guess as parents of a young baby it adds a little more realistic romance to the image."

"Great idea! We can tell 'Oh So Pretty' that the angle is that every day should be treat like date night, so every day is an occasion to wear a beautiful dress," I enthuse, decanting the glass of wine I just poured back into the bottle so we can take the photos again from another angle.

"Sounds like the kind of bullshit they will love."

Sunaina's words sting like salt in an open wound, and I force a tight smile.

While it's true that the work I do sometimes blurs the line between what's real and what isn't, I like to think it's at least a little authentic. I post photos of my home, the town I live in and the work I paint. I'm no stranger to sharing photos of my cellulite and stretchmarks or admitting my character flaws. I don't want Sunaina to think what we do is bullshit, or worse, that I am insincere.

I catch sight of myself pouring the same glass of wine for the fifth time in a row and wonder if there is anything authentic about what I do after all.

We're fifteen minutes into the shoot when the front door opens.

"That will be them," I say, putting the bottle of wine down. Wordlessly, Sunaina makes a move to grab her bag. "What are you doing?"

"Going home."

"What? No! Stay – you're one of the girls!"

Sunaina shifts on the spot. "That's really kind, Nat, but your friends are -"

I don't get to hear the rest of what she has to say because Amira, Becca and Melissa burst into the kitchen at that moment in an explosion of noise, casual outfits, wine, wine and more wine.

"Thanks so much for having us over, darling!" Amira coos, kissing me on both cheeks. "It's so nice not to be the one who's hostess for once."

I smile, glossing over the double-edged compliment. "It's not a problem. I thought we could all do with being together before the big day tomorrow."

"Too right! Although I've got to say, Nat, you didn't let us know girls' night had such a nice dress code!" Becca grins, pulling at my dress. The others study me with the same frozen smiles.

"Oh, it doesn't," I laugh, burningly conscious of how over the top I look. "Sunaina and I were just shooting my latest promotion."

My friends turn to Sunaina as if they've only just noticed her presence.

She waves awkwardly, a gesture my friends do not return. I can't help but notice how she's shrunk in on herself in their presence and I'm hit with the sudden urge to hug her.

"So good to see you, Suzie!" Melissa says.

Sunaina's expression remains flat. "It's Sunaina."

"Is it? I thought it was Suzie, but I suppose Sunaina is a little bit of an unusual name," Melissa shrugs. I wince as I listen to Melissa almost blame Sunaina for having a name she can't be bothered to remember. "Are you heading home now?"

"No, she's staying for girls' night," I say, flashing Sunaina an encouraging smile that she struggles to return.

"Oh, how lovely," Melissa says, her politeness barely covering her disappointment.

"So is Jay," Sunaina interjects. "I'll just go get her."

Sunaina has barely left the room before my friends turn to me.

"It's really sweet of you to ask Sunaina and Jay, but I kind of hoped tonight would be just the original gang," Becca pouts.

"Me too," Melissa nods.

Awkwardness cloaks me. "I know, but Sunaina and Jay have been great these last few days. It seemed only fair to ask them."

"Here, here, the more the merrier," Amira calls, pouring wine into six glasses. I put my hand over the last one to stop her from filling it.

"Sunaina doesn't drink," I explain.

"And she's coming to girls' night because…" Melissa mutters, but not quietly enough that I don't hear her.

We move to the dining table just in time for Jay and Sunaina to enter the room. Jay's dressed in a faded t-shirt and looking severely confused as to why she is here, but she greets everyone warmly. My friends return the 'hello', but not the warmth.

I pull out two chairs for Jay and Sunaina and raise my glass for a toast. "To tonight! To remembering Hallie and Bree and cementing the strong friendships we already have."

My friends echo my sentiments, we clink glasses, then the gossip begins.

"So, did you hear about Crystal Myers?"

"No! What about her?"

"Well, you'd never guess from her happy marriage bullshit on Facebook but she's having an affair!"

I watch as Sunaina's eyes glaze over and Jay deflates before me. Suddenly, I'm painfully aware of how cruel my friends seem as they discuss this intimate secret as casually as they would talk about what to wear to work. The back of my neck burns.

"Maybe Crystal Myers has her reasons. Maybe we don't need to talk about it," I say loudly across the table.

My friends turn to me, perplexed.

"Who's given you a conscience?" Amira jokes, her smile faltering when she sees I'm serious.

I struggle under my friends' gaze, their bemused, slightly pissed off expressions reminding me of a time in my life when that was the only way they ever looked at me. "What she's doing is terrible, I know, but we don't have all the facts and -"

"We do have all the facts – she's boning her neighbour!" Becca cuts in. I flinch at her crass wording.

"Uh oh, Nat's gone soft!" Melissa laughs. She reaches out and pats my hand. "It's okay, Nat, we will still love you even if you're boring!"

"Although girls' night without gossip is just any other night," Becca adds, pursing her lips.

"It's just not nice, that's all," I mutter, embarrassed at allowing myself to be spoken to like this in my own home, but more embarrassed at myself for even going down this route.

"Oh, come on, Nat – do you honestly think Crystal Myers really cares how you and Lucas are doing when she asks? She's just looking for something to bitch about when she next sees her friends," Amira dismisses.

"Actually, Crystal Myers is really nice," Sunaina interjects.

Her words silence the table. My whole body clenches.

"I'm friends with her daughter Maddy," Sunaina adds as if to explain herself.

"I'm sure she's *nice*," Melissa says. "But she's still a cheat."

"Doesn't Becca only exclusively date married men?" Sunaina asks, her expression indignant.

My friends look at each other then burst out laughing.

"She's got you there, Bec!"

"Wait, wait, wait," Becca grins, taking a glug of wine and holding her hand in the air as if pledging on a bible. "*I'm* not the one who's married. How can I cheat when I have no one to cheat on?"

My friends nod as if her reasoning makes it all okay, but I spot the barely disguised disgust on Sunaina and Jay's faces. I cringe so hard it physically pains me.

Inviting them was a mistake, I see that now. They are as important to me as my friends, but there is a reason these two sides of my life stay separate. They are simply too different. Jay and Sunaina would never understand what it's like to be in this group. They don't know that these women have been talking like this since high school. To them, this is normal. This is just part of surviving at the top of the pile.

I ransack my brain for a way to steer the night back on course, but how? I can't exactly tell my friends they shouldn't talk about Crystal like that or tell Sunaina and Jay to lighten up because maybe gossiping is what my friends need to do to stop themselves from obsessing over the funeral.

So, I sit in silence, cringing as the conversation veers from offensive to embarrassing and back again until eventually there's a knock at the front door.

"I'll get it," Sunaina says, leaping to her feet before I can excuse myself.

"She's well trained," wine-drunk Melissa quips.

Amira and Becca snigger while I avoid Jay's eyes.

"Anyway, now the gossip squasher has gone, you'll never guess what else I found out today," Becca smirks, her eyes glinting with mischief.

"What?"

"Well, it will come as no surprise to you to hear that Chrissy Summers's return has officially rocked Coral Bay."

I can't help myself – at the mention of Chrissy's name, I'm hooked. "What do you mean?"

Becca grins triumphantly now she has my full attention. "Well, Chrissy is estranged from her parents, as in completely and utterly cut off. Apparently, they haven't spoken since she left Coral Bay. No one knows why, but it must be bad because I was chatting to Priya, and she said Chrissy's mum didn't even know Chrissy was back in town. Priya met her for drinks at the golf club and said she had bumped into Chrissy at Pilates. She said Chrissy's mum literally got up and walked out of the bar without another word. How weird is that?"

"Really weird," I confirm. "Do you have any idea why they don't speak?"

"Well, I have a theory," Becca begins, but just as she is about to get into it the kitchen door opens.

"Nat?" Sunaina calls.

"Yes?" I ask, unable to hide my irritation at being disturbed at such a pivotal moment.

"You need to come to the door. Now."

"What?" I turn to Sunaina and suddenly notice how pale she is.

"You're needed at the door. It's the police. They want to speak to you."

17

I excuse myself and quickly head into the hallway where I find Detective Baldie and Detective Stone waiting for me. Their eyes pop when they see me, and I'm reminded once again how inappropriately I am dressed.

"We're not interrupting anything important, are we?" Detective Stone asks.

"Not at all. I'm just having a girls' night," I explain, wishing more than anything I had a jumper or cardigan to throw on over this ludicrous dress.

"I wish my girls' nights were as glamorous as yours," Detective Stone smiles.

"Me too," Detective Baldie says, the sarcasm dripping from his voice practically creating a puddle at his feet. "May we have a moment of your time?"

"Of course," I nod.

"What car do you drive, Mrs Redding?" Detective Baldie asks.

"A Toyota. Four-wheel drive. Why?"

"A car matching that description has been spotted on CCTV near where Miss Patterson and Miss Jackson crashed. The driver's face isn't visible on the recording, but the make and model of the car is. We would trace the licence plates, but they had been removed from the vehicle. We've asked around and a lot of people have said that's the car you drive."

It's as though I've been hit on the head with a hammer. Everything around me slows. "You... you think I did this?"

"No," Detective Stone replies, a little too quickly to be convincing. "But I'm sure you understand that this is a murder investigation, and we need to explore every avenue that opens to us. For us to do that, we will need to see your car. Where is it parked right now?"

"In… in the garage."

"Is that where it's always parked?"

"Sometimes it's on the driveway, sometimes the garage."

"Can you take us to it?"

Dumbly, I nod. On shaky legs, I walk the detectives to the garage. A wide eyed Sunaina follows. I try to find comfort in her presence, but the nervous glances she shoots in my direction do little to help me do so.

"Does Sunaina actually think I did this?" I wonder as I suffocate from breathing in her tension.

I flick the garage lights on and stand back so the detectives can see my car. With clammy hands and a dry mouth, I watch them at work. Detective Stone takes photos and Detective Baldie walks around the vehicle, eying it from all angles.

"It's very clean," he comments.

"Lucas took it to a carwash at the weekend."

"How kind of him," Detective Baldie says, squatting and inspecting the licence plate intently.

In this terrifying context, I'm painfully aware of how gleaming my car is. It practically sparkles like new under the fluorescent lighting of the garage. Lucas is a neat freak who gets our cars cleaned regularly, but the detectives don't know that. Should I tell them? Does a clean car make me look suspicious?

My head pounds from the barrage of questions.

"Surely I'm not the only person in the area to drive a Toyota? I've seen plenty around town before."

"No, of course not. We just need to follow all leads, that's all," Detective Stone reassures.

Detective Baldie rises to his feet. "Just out of curiosity, where were you on the night of the accident?"

I recoil from the shock of being asked such a question. I glance at Detective Stone, waiting for her to tell Detective Baldie to shut up, but she doesn't.

My lips tremble. "I was at home. I was at home in bed where I should be."

"Can anyone vouch for that?"

The question cracks me across the face, but I answer as calmly as I can. "My husband. Jay, I suppose, even though she will have been in the outhouse."

"Did you go out at all?"

I shake my head.

Detective Stone smiles. "That's great, Natalie, thank you. That's all we need for now."

"It is?"

"Unless there's anything else you want to tell us?" Detective Baldie asks.

I shake my head and the detectives make a move to leave. I follow them in a trance, detaching from myself almost as if my mind is walking three steps behind and watching the scene from a distance.

How could they ask me those questions? How could they think I had anything to do with the crash?

"I didn't do it," I blurt out as we reach the front door.

Both detectives turn to face me. I blush, mortified by my sudden outburst. I've seen enough TV shows to know the person protesting their innocence without being asked to is often guilty, but it's too late now. I've already said it.

"I didn't hurt my friends."

"No one's saying you did, Natalie. We're just following leads."

"Surely you want us to catch whoever did this?" Detective Baldie adds.

"Of course, I just -"

"That's settled then. Goodnight, Mrs Redding," Detective Baldie interjects, seeing himself out as if he owns the place. Detective Stone smiles goodbye then closes the door behind her.

There's a beat of silence before Sunaina breaks. "Fuck, that was intense," she exhales. "Are you okay?"

I nod, but the overwhelming urge to cry threatens to betray my cool exterior. "Do you think they think I did it?" I manage to ask.

Sunaina shakes her head adamantly. "No. Like they said, they have to follow every line of inquiry, right? They're just doing their job."

I so desperately want to believe Sunaina, but I can't. I've seen the way Detective Baldie looks at me. He wouldn't have any difficulty believing I hurt my friends. Sometimes, when I look into his eyes, they seem to sparkle as if they *want* me to have hurt them, as if he knows that's the kind of person I am behind the image I present to the world.

"Come on," Sunaina says, nudging me back to reality. "Everyone will be wondering where you are."

Inhaling deeply, I nod and we head towards the kitchen. Just before we open the door, I grab Sunaina. "I'm really sorry about some of the things they've said tonight. They're not usually like this," I begin, but Sunaina shoots me a 'cut the crap' look and I concede. "Okay, maybe they are, but I'm still sorry. Sometimes they take it too far."

Sunaina shrugs. "Don't worry about it. I'll put up with their shit for one night if it means I can be there for you."

I well up, my heart fit to burst. "Thank you," I whisper before pushing open the door and heading back into the lion's den.

"What did the police want?" Amira asks as soon as we enter the room.

"To check my car. Apparently, a white Toyota with no licence plates was seen on CCTV near the where the accident happened." The words still don't seem real even as I say them out loud.

"They can't seriously think you did it, can they?!" Becca exclaims.

"Nat's our queen, why would she hurt us? Besides, she's too soft to do that. Too soft and cute like a... like a baby bunny," Melissa hiccups, leaning her head on Becca's shoulder and laughing.

"Uh oh, someone's drunk," Amira sings.

"Fuck off," Melissa replies, moving her arm to swat Amira but knocking over a bottle of wine instead. Jay leaps to her feet to clean the mess while the rest of the group giggle like naughty schoolgirls.

"She's a good one, isn't she? Joe... Jackie? Jenny? Whatever her name is," Melissa slurs, her head lolling backwards as if it's too heavy for her neck.

"I think it's time for Melissa to go home," Amira laughs.

"We'd all better go. It's a big day tomorrow."

Becca's mention of the funeral sobers everyone but Melissa up.

"Just let me get the..." I begin, but with one look at Melissa I realise she's not in a fit state to carry the clothes and homewares I hastily collected for her. "Never mind."

I help my friends bundle Melissa's ragdoll body into a taxi and we say a quick goodbye. I wave as they drive away, dizzy with relief that they are finally out of the house, then head back inside. Sunaina and Jay have cleared everything away and are wrapping up the leftovers by the time I return.

"What a night, eh?" I joke, running my hands through my tangled hair.

"Tell me about it. Those women really are something," Sunaina says, shooting Jay a knowing look.

"They're not that bad," I protest feebly.

Sunaina shakes her head. "I love you Nat, but I can never believe you're actually their friend."

"They're nice! Sometimes they say the wrong thing, but they aren't terrible people. I wouldn't be friends with them if they were."

"You don't have to justify anything to us, Nat," Jay smiles.

"I just can't imagine what you talk to them about. All they do is bitch!" Sunaina cries.

"I guess we all bitch sometimes. We all do things we aren't proud of."

"Go on then," Jay says cheekily. "What's the worst thing you've ever done?"

Somewhere buried in the pit of my soul, the memory of the worst thing I have ever done stabs me, but I push the thought down. I don't need to torture myself by reliving that moment, not tonight.

"I'm not sure. Probably said something to Lucas in a fight I shouldn't have," I lie.

Sunaina rolls her eyes affectionately. "You two are sickening," she laughs. "Anyway, I'd best get home. Are you okay if I leave? The police haven't upset you too much, have they?"

I sigh. "I'm okay. Tired, but okay. Just watch your back, though. If the police are questioning me about this then they're clearly clutching at straws. The next thing you know, you two will be suspects. The killer nanny and the killer social media manager," I joke.

"Please, Hallie and Bree were the only friends of yours I liked," Sunaina says, giving me a hug goodbye. "Good luck tomorrow."

With the kitchen tidied and Sunaina gone, I say goodnight to Jay and ascend the stairs to my bedroom.

Exhaustion overwhelms me, but I briefly fill Lucas in on the night. He doesn't seem phased by the detectives checking my car – 'plenty of people have that car, don't worry,' he decides – but I am worried. After those questions, how could I not be?

My stomach knots, but I don't have the energy to deal with it right now. Hallie's funeral has drained me and it hasn't even happened yet. I want to close my eyes and forget the events of the day.

But most of all, I want to be rid of the panic creeping up on me, telling me that things are only about to get much, much worse.

18

As soon as my alarm blares into life, I'm aware what day it is. My subconscious doesn't allow me even a split second of peace before reality crushes my chest.

Today is the day I bury my best friend.

I roll onto my side to find Lucas's face inches from mine. "Hey," he whispers. "How are you doing?"

I open my mouth to reply, but no sound comes out.

Lucas pulls me close. "It's going to be okay," he says into my hair, words we both know aren't true but words we both know I need to hear. We lie together in silence, locked in an embrace I never want to end.

My head pounds with the events of the last few days. I think of Bree's bloodied, swollen body and how her future has been so cruelly torn from her. I think of Hallie in her coffin, how she will never hold Esme again or be there with her witty jokes whenever a mood gets too serious. I think of how life is fleeting and how after this day mine will never be the same again. The sudden onslaught of fresh grief catches in the back of my throat.

Through the baby monitor on my bedside table, Esme's cries pull me into reality. I stir, sitting upright.

"I'll go," Lucas offers.

"No, let me."

Sliding out of bed, I kiss Lucas and head to Esme's room. She reaches for me as soon as I open the door. I scoop her up, her warm body leaning into mine, needing me, loving me. My whole world, my reason for waking up every morning. Motherhood, the best thing I have ever done.

If I could exist forever in this cuddle, I would.

I rock my baby backwards and forwards, humming a gentle tune, until the creak of a floorboard startles me out of the softness of the moment. I turn to find a blushing Jay in the doorway.

"I'm so sorry for intruding. I heard Esme crying and thought you might want to be alone this morning."

"Thank you, but I think I'm okay," I say, kissing Esme's forehead.

"Are you sure? Not even to go for a run?" I pause for a moment, giving Jay the ammunition she needs to take Esme. "Go. Taking some time for yourself won't hurt. If anything, it's needed today more than ever."

Esme appears to be more than happy in Jay's arms, so I cave.

A few minutes later and I'm off, headphones in, music blaring, feet pounding. I run and I run until my lungs are ready to burst. At the top of Hillman's Trek, I wretch, stumbling to the ground, panting, spent.

As I struggle to catch my breath, a crippling tightness overcomes my muscles and I'm forced to admit I've pushed myself too hard. Only it doesn't seem hard enough. When I look around, I still see the problems surrounding me. Every thudding beat of my heart reminds me of the life in me but no longer in Hallie.

I want to outrun the day, but that's impossible. It's here - I'm already living it.

And if I don't leave Hillman's Trek soon, I'm going to be living the nightmare of being the girl late for her best friend's funeral.

With a sigh, I haul myself to my feet and limp back home, each step more tortuous than the one before.

The low hum of conversation filters through the house when I enter, but I ignore it and head straight for the bathroom. I peel off my damp clothes, dropping them to the floor and climbing into a too hot shower. Scalding water singes my skin, but I don't turn the temperature down. Let it burn. My sweat and the grime of Hillman's Trek swirls down the drain, but not my sadness. That's too engrained in me to disappear.

When my red raw skin finally screams at me to stop, I turn off the shower and reach for a towel. The fibres rub against me like tiny shards of glass, but I'm numb to the pain.

Once dry, I apply a discreet layer of makeup and slip into my new dress, then inspect my reflection in the mirror. Smart, sophisticated, stylish. Powerful and in control, the exact opposite of how I feel.

It's perfect.

I skip downstairs, following the sound of Jay and Lucas's laughter, and find them both playing with Esme in the kitchen. They look up when I enter, Lucas's eyes widening at the sight of me. "That's what you're wearing to the funeral?"

"What's wrong with it?" I ask, but I catch sight of my reflection in the window and don't need Lucas to answer the question. I notice for the first time just how fitted the dress is, how it clings to my exercise honed curves in a manner that's more cocktail night than funeral.

"Isn't it a little... much?" Lucas chooses his words carefully, but they still slice me open like a pathologist's knife.

"The people in this town expect me to look a certain way, Lucas. Besides, I wanted to feel good about myself today, not that I do now thanks to you," I snap.

Lucas's cheeks tinge pink. "Nat -"

"Save it, Lucas."

Jay rises to her feet. "Well, I think you look great. Hallie knew you as a glamour queen, so why shouldn't you dress like that for her funeral?"

Lucas hauls Esme into his arms and approaches me. "Jay's right. I'm being silly. You look great." He kisses my forehead and smiles, but I'm still stung. Not because he's wrong but because he's right - I *am* dressed inappropriately for Hallie's funeral. I'm a woman saying goodbye to her best friend. How could I think wearing something so extravagant would be okay? What's wrong with me? It's like I'm regressing back into teenage Nat. Outcast Nat. Nat who can never, ever get it right.

"Maybe I should change…"

"No way!" The unexpected sound of Sunaina's voice makes me jump. "You're taking funeral styling to a whole new level. They'll start a funeral fashion hashtag in your honour when people see you in that!"

"Sunaina, really?" Lucas asks, his tone clipped. I put my hand on his chest. Sunaina's ability to spot the Instagrammable in life makes her a valuable asset to me, but a pain in the arse to my down to earth husband.

Sunaina shrugs. "I'm just saying."

"Well don't, not today," Lucas mutters.

Before anyone can say anything else, I steer Sunaina towards my laptop. "There's an email from Arlene Davies that needs replying to and Athletica are calling at eleven. You'll have to explain my absence."

"I know my job, Nat."

I flinch at Sunaina's sharp tone, a knot twisting in my stomach. Lucas and Sunaina's temperamental relationship is usually something I can manage with ease, but today it feels out of my control.

I squeeze Sunaina's hand. "I know you do. You're the best at it!"

Sunaina offers me a small smile, her way of saying she still loves me, even if she is annoyed at my husband.

Suddenly, Lucas clears his throat. "Nat? We best get going."

And just like that, it's time to leave. Just like that, it's time to say goodbye to Hallie.

19

It seems like everyone in Coral Bay is at the funeral and they all want to consume part of my grief. As I stand outside the church, person after person comes over, their questions attempting to drag words from me that hurt to say.

"Oh Nat! What will we do without them? What will you do without them?"

"I'm so sorry for your loss, sweetheart. You must be feeling dreadful! You look like you've not stopped crying for days."

"Tragic. It's just tragic. I'm crushed about it, so I can't imagine your pain!"

I echo their sentiments and return their hugs, but deep down I want to push their clawing hands away and run in the opposite direction.

These people knew Hallie, but they didn't *know* her. They served her at the butchers, cut her hair or exchanged small talk while buying milk, but they didn't know of her burning desire to be a mother. She never called them crying at 1am when her latest boyfriend turned out to be a cheat. They hadn't accompanied her to the doctors when she found a small, hard lump in her breast. They hadn't held her hand through some of the most painful moments of her life and cheered her on through some of the best. They didn't know Hallie like I did, but they all want a piece of her.

However unreasonable it is for me to feel this way, I hate them for it.

Lucas senses my anxiety and squeezes my hand. "I love you," he mouths. I mouth it back.

An arm snakes around my waist and instinctively I stiffen, only to relax a second later when I realise it's Amira.

"I thought you could use a friendly hug. You know, a *real* friendly hug," she whispers, her dark eyes scanning the crowd. "I'm getting a bit sick of everyone coming to me and crying like today is so hard for them. I want to snap and say, 'you sat next to Hallie in Biology for half a term in year nine... get over it'. I swear, if one more member of the 'Coral Bay Walking Club' invites me to their memorial hike next weekend, I'm going to scream. I don't need an excuse to burn off my excess back fat and pretend it's out of respect for Hallie, thank you very much."

I nudge Amira in the ribs. "You're terrible."

"You know I'm right. Some people here are such drips. It should be them in the coffin, not Hallie. Us girls need to stick together today," Amira says, slipping her arm through mine. "You too, Lucas."

Lucas, who had been politely ignoring Amira's catty comments, turns to us. "I'm flattered to be thought of as one of the girls. I didn't think I had the fashion sense to make the cut."

I smile at his joke, but my smile falters when I spot Becca trying to weave her way through the crowd towards us. I note her drawn features and trembling hands. "Hey, Bec. How are you holding up?" I ask when she finally reaches our huddle.

"I don't think I can do this, and not just because I'm a little hungover from last night," she wobbles.

"Yes, you can. We all can. We're going to get through this together."

"Yes, just us... no walking group members allowed," Amira adds.

Becca offers us a watery smile then scans the congregation. "There are so many people here."

She's right, there are. Every available patch of grass outside the church has sombre groups clustered on it. Coral Bay centre must be a ghost town. No businesses can be open because everyone who owns them is here to pay their respects.

"Hallie would like to see all these people here and know how loved she was," I think, smiling sadly to myself.

Suddenly, Amira frowns. "Can you see Melissa anywhere?"

Becca shakes her head. I check the crowd myself, searching for my missing friend, but failing to find her.

"You don't think she'd miss the funeral, do you?" Becca asks, chewing her lip.

"I guess we'd all skip it if we could. It's not exactly going to be a nice day," I remark.

"I know, but still… maybe I should go check on her and see if she's okay?" Becca wonders out loud.

"I wouldn't," Amira replies. "If she's bailed, she's bailed. What can you do about it?"

"I know, but…"

I squeeze Becca's arm. "Look, you're already here. You don't want to miss anything. Besides, everyone is watching you. If you leave now, you know there'll be a big Coral Bay style drama about it."

"Exactly. You don't want to give these vultures any more to talk about than Nat's fabulous dress already has," Amira adds, flashing the nearest huddle of people a dazzlingly false smile.

Becca nods but her teeth still gnaw away at her lower lip.

Just then, a taxi pulls up.

"This could be her," I say.

We watch as the passenger door opens, but Melissa doesn't emerge from it. Chrissy Summers does.

Inwardly, I curse.

Wearing the dress from Dot's Designs, she somehow looks even better in it than I remember. A pair of dramatic, fake designer sunglasses perch on the end of her nose. She holds a well-worn clutch bag to her chest like a shield, but nothing can protect her from the disbelieving reactions of Coral Bay's residents.

A rustle of shocked whispers ripple through the crowd. Every eye is glued to Chrissy, taking in every minute detail of her new appearance. She shrinks under the scrutiny and, for the first time since she came back into my life, I'm happy.

"Is that…" Lucas is unable to finish his sentence, so I do it for him.

"Chrissy Summers," I confirm.

The clipped sound of her heels against the path rings out over everyone's hushed tones. People are trying their best not to drop their jaws, but they're not doing a very good job of it. She looks incredible, yes, but different too. It's like people don't know whether to applaud or laugh.

Suddenly, Lucas breaks from my side. "Chrissy! It's so great to see you again," he calls, hugging Chrissy close and instantly evaporating the tension in the air. She squeezes him back, grateful for her hero.

Me? I feel like I've been slapped.

Lucas places his hand on Chrissy's back and steers her towards us. Time seems to move in slow motion, their every step like a bolt of lightning to my heart. I blink twice to check I am really seeing *my* husband with *his* hand on *her* back.

"I believe you've already been reacquainted with these ladies," Lucas says as Amira and Becca reach out to hug Chrissy.

The moment my husband's gaze meets mine, I shoot him daggers. He mouths 'what' at me, but I don't have time to respond because before I know it, Chrissy is facing me head on. "Oh Nat, darling, how will we ever get through this?" she cries, forcing me into a rib crushing hug.

Unable to breathe never mind speak in her vice like grip, I say nothing.

Chrissy pulls away from me and reaches for Becca's hand, her calculating eyes shiny with tears. "Do you mind if I sit with you? You're the only people who truly understand how I feel. You've lost one of your oldest and best friends too."

Becca squeezes Chrissy's hand. "Of course!"

"Coral Bay High girls stick together, right?" Chrissy simpers, shooting a purposeful glance in my direction, and just like that, I'm shut out.

I turn to Lucas in disbelief. He frowns, unable to understand why I'm so angry. In his world, everyone has the potential to get on. Lucas-land has no drama, no trauma, no previous pain to hold back because of.

But we don't live in the same world. We never have. He doesn't know what it's like to be on the receiving end of Chrissy Summers, but I do. I've done it before, and I won't let it happen again. I am nobody's victim, especially not hers.

I straighten up to my full height. Smaller than Chrissy, but still a force in my own right. "Actually Amira, Becca and I –" I begin, but Chrissy's gasp cuts me off.

"Look," she exhales, pointing in the distance. "The hearse… Hallie's coming."

I spy the black car slowly making its way towards us and suddenly arguing over seating arrangements seems insignificant.

My best friend is in that car.

My best friend is gone, and she is never coming back.

A strangled sob breaks free from my lips. Amira reaches out to me, but Chrissy takes Amira's hand in her own. Amira smiles at Chrissy, seemingly believing her intrusion on our moment was a genuine mistake, but I know the truth.

Chrissy blocked Amira on purpose. It's clearer now more than ever how badly she wants me out of the picture and how she will stop at nothing to make sure that happens. Shutting me out at my best friend's funeral is only the start.

I've not just lost Hallie and Bree – Chrissy isn't going to settle until I've lost everyone else too.

20

Eight hours, endless tears, too much wine and more time being elbowed out of the way by Chrissy than I would care to admit later, I am done. The funeral, the wake and all the fake niceties are finally over.

Hallie is buried.

She is gone and I am dead inside.

Without waiting for Lucas to get out of the car, I head into the house. Rage and hurt clouds my vision. Stomping into the kitchen, I grab a bottle of wine I don't need from the fridge. I down a glass in one, then pour myself another.

"Nat?" Jay's voice from the dining table makes me jump. "Is everything okay?"

I open my mouth to reply, but at that moment Lucas enters the kitchen, his tear-stained eyes tired, his tie loose. "That's what I'd like to know."

I narrow my eyes. "What's that supposed to mean?"

Lucas sighs. "Don't play dumb, Nat. You've been foul to be around all day."

"Sorry I wasn't the life and soul of the party, Lucas, but I buried my best friend today."

"We *all* buried a friend today."

"Oh sorry, I forgot – Coral Bay High students stick together, right?" I mimic, downing more wine.

"Bingo – we've got it!" Lucas cheers sarcastically. I raise my eyebrow, a move that only serves to further irritate my usually placid husband. "Don't play innocent with me now, Nat. You've been like this ever since Chrissy showed up."

My skin prickles at the mention of her name. "You'd know all about her showing up, wouldn't you, with your little hero act. Going over to her, inviting her to sit with us - 'here Chrissy, come hold my hand, come cry on my shoulder'," I spit.

"She never held my hand, she never cried on my shoulder!"

I roll my eyes. "She might as well have done. Sat there fake crying, simpering, playing the victim... and you lapped it up! You all did! You all fell for it!"

"Nat, the woman was really fucking brave today! She went to that funeral completely alone. She faced a crowd of people all staring at her, all noticing how different she looks, all speculating about what happened to her. It can't have been easy."

"If it can't have been easy then she shouldn't have bothered coming."

Lucas shakes his head. "I don't know why you have such a problem with the fact that she was there. She was Hallie's friend as much as any of us were."

"And you just *had* to make her feel so welcome, didn't you!"

"I was just being nice!"

I turn to Jay who is shooting desperate glances at the back door and clearly wondering if she can slip out of the room unnoticed. "Jay, how would you feel if your husband was being *nice* to a woman he knows made your life miserable?"

"Oh, I... I..."

"Don't bring Jay into this, Nat. You're the only person in the world who sees anything wrong with being nice to someone at a funeral."

That's when I explode.

"Chrissy Summers does not deserve your niceness! Chrissy Summers is a bitch!"

"Not this again," Lucas groans. "Look, I get it - she was horrible to you in school, but that was years ago! We're all adults now. We were at a funeral, for fucks sake! It's no time for petty grudges."

"Petty grudges? Lucas, she made my life hell!"

"You weren't the only one, Nat. What about Sonny Peters? He needed counselling after what she did to him, and don't tell me you think you got as raw a deal as Josephine Riley because you did not."

"If you know she's such a bad person then why be nice to her? Why put your arm around her?" Tears stream down my cheeks, but I can't stop. I'm so hurt by him, by the day, by the pure cheek of Chrissy showing up in Coral Bay and trying to push me out of my own life.

"Because it was a funeral, Nat. Because we weren't there to make a scene. Because people aren't the same person they were at sixteen. Do you need any more reasons?"

Lucas's soft tone grates against the rage I radiate with. I drunkenly teeter on the edge of reasonable, then take a step forward and fall into hysteria. "Chrissy Summers does *not* deserve your niceness - she ruined my life!"

Lucas gestures to his surroundings. "Take a look around you – your life looks pretty good to me! Chrissy hasn't ruined it at all. If anything, the only person doing that here is you."

"Oh, of course, it would have to be *me*, wouldn't it? I'm the problem here, not Chrissy. Not precious Chrissy."

"Precious Chrissy?! Nat, you sound fucking crazy!"

"Don't call me crazy!" I scream, hurling my wine glass through the air towards him.

The sound of glass shattering against the wall silences us.

Lucas holds my gaze, his simmering rage a mirror of my own. His jaw clenches and his hands ball up into tight, fury filled fists, but he won't act on his feelings. He will hold back, not break and allow his anger to explode into the atmosphere like a toxic bomb. He's a better person than I am, than I could ever hope to be.

"You," he says, his tone quiet but as sharp as a knife. "You need help."

With that, he turns and walks away. A few seconds later, the front door slams so hard the walls of the house rattle, then the engine of his car roars into life.

I inhale sharply, then choke on a sob.

"Nat," Jay says, rushing to my side, but I push her away.

"Fuck off, Jay! Leave me alone! You don't have to help me all the fucking time!"

Jay backs away, her hands held up innocently, her eyes brimming with hurt. "Sorry, I'm sorry," she stammers, before running to her outhouse.

I stand alone in my designer kitchen, the silence around me screaming louder than a crowd of thousands. I slump to the floor, my head in my hands, my tears uncontrollable.

I cry until there is nothing left in me to give to my tears. My face is sore, my eyes sticky, my skin swollen. I'm as empty as the bottle of wine I reached for when I arrived home.

Dragging myself to my feet, I survey the scene. Carnage, just like my life right now, and it's all my fault.

Strangled by guilt, I hunt for a dustpan and brush to sweep away the shower of broken glass littering the kitchen floor. On my hands and knees cleaning up the mess, shame overwhelms me.

I have never thrown a glass at Lucas before. I have never been violent towards him. I have never felt this level of rage burning away inside me. Chrissy is turning me into someone I do not recognise. I am becoming the hideous outcast she always told me I was, the person I have fought so tirelessly not to become.

Halfway through sweeping the smashed shards, my phone buzzes inside my handbag. I let it ring out, but then it rings again.

Panic chokes me.

Lucas.

He drove off in such a fit of fury. What if something has happened to him?

I stumble to my feet and frantically tip my bag out onto the counter, a messy concoction of mascara-stained tissues and bank cards spilling across the surface. Finally, I locate my phone. "Hello?" I pant down the line.

"Nat! Oh Nat," Amira sobs. "You need to come quick. It's Melissa. I think… I think she's dead!"

21

I don't think – I just run. In seconds I'm pounding down the street in my bare feet, heart pumping, mind racing.

Melissa, dead? It can't be. We just buried Hallie today... how can Melissa be dead too?

It doesn't make sense. It can't be real.

I take a left, then a right, my feet slapping hard against the pavement. Streetlights line the way, illuminating my route while keeping the rest of the world cloaked in blackness. Everyone else in Coral Bay is asleep, worn out by the funeral and already moving onto the next day. They're not racing to find out if yet another of their friends has been struck off.

I tear down Miller Street and stop at number seven. The house I've been to so often over the years stares back at me. Everything about it appears normal for this time of night – blinds down, door closed, lights off. The only sign anything is amiss is a hysterical Amira rocking herself back and forth on the front step.

I rush to her. "What's happened?!"

Amira's sobs tangle with her ragged breath. "I... I..."

I fight the urge to shake her into making sense. "What's happened?!"

Amira's bloodshot eyes meet mine. "When she didn't show at the funeral, I got worried. I came to check on her and... and..."

"And?"

"And there was no answer. I tried her phone. I could hear it ringing by the door so I looked through the letterbox," Amira shudders and pulls her knees to her chest, shaking her head to tell me she can't go on with her story.

I glance at the door. An icy shiver runs down my spine. It looks like any other front door, but I know that's not the case. I know that beyond that pristine exterior is something I don't want to see.

Another nightmare is coming to life.

Inhaling deeply, I climb the rest of the stairs. Amira's devastated cries are the soundtrack to my ascent. My palms sweat, but I keep moving. Three steps to go, then two, then one.

Even though I know it's futile, I try the door handle. Locked.

My eyes flick to the letterbox. It stares back at me, daring me to peek inside.

"Come on, Nat. Come on," I whisper, urging myself into action.

Slowly, I lower onto my knees. My heart beats in my throat, my breath caught in the back of my mouth like a fluttering bird. I will myself to make the move.

"Melissa?"

Everything in me hopes Melissa will suddenly throw open the door and ask us what the hell we are doing on her doorstep at this time of night, but there is no answer, and the door remains firmly closed.

"Melissa?" I call, my voice louder this time.

Nothing.

There's no avoiding it. I know what I must do.

Hand unsteady, I reach out. The letterbox is cool to touch. I push it open. The hinges squeak softly in the silence of the night, then I lower myself to look inside.

At first, I can't make anything out. With no lights on in the house, everything is dark and indistinguishable. I reach into my pocket, take out my phone and illuminate the torch. Shining it through the gap in the letterbox, I look.

Instantly, I wish I hadn't.

Behind a mass of matted, bloodied hair, Melissa's glassy, lifeless eyes stare back at me.

"Fuck!" I scream, scrambling backwards and dropping my phone in the process.

My horrified reaction confirms Amira's worst fears and she crumples. "She's dead, isn't she? She's fucking dead!"

"We don't know that yet," I lie. "We need an ambulance, and we need the police. Did you call them?"

Amira shakes her head. "I only rang you."

"Me? Why me?"

Amira wipes her nose on her sleeve and stares at me steadily through her tears. "Because you're the only one who knows what's going on here."

Fear twinges in my chest like a plucked violin string. "What's that supposed to mean?"

Amira lets out a strained laugh. "Everyone pretends we were such fucking saints," she hisses so ferociously a bubble of spit appears in the corner of her mouth. "But you and I both know who we were in school, Nat, and you and I both know someone is coming for us. One by one, they're going to get us. They're going to make us pay for what we did."

<u>Then.</u>

She walks down the corridor, books in hand. Everyone files out of one class and rushes to make their way to the next. Loud chatter fills her ears, snippets of conversations standing out more than others.

"Can you believe she said that?"

"I swear, he's so hot it makes me want to cry!"

"Why do they give us so much homework? It's like they don't want us to have a life."

The girl smiles at her classmates' dramatics. She imagines what she would say to people if only they would open themselves up to speaking to her.

"I can't believe she said it, what a bitch! Do you really think he's hot? I think his friend is way hotter! I know right?! Biology and maths homework – do they think we're machines?!"

She continues the imaginary dialogue in her mind. Sometimes she's the funny friend, sometimes the quiet friend, sometimes the loud one. It doesn't matter who she plays, though. She is happy with any role as long as it's a friend.

She weaves in and out of the crowd as discreetly as possible. She's almost reached the English block when two moronic, jostling boys from the football team knock into her, sending her flying into the person beside her.

There's a scream as they stumble and drop everything they were carrying. Their books scatter. Their pencil case rolls across the floor.

Small, hot pink and inscribed with the names of her closest friends.

Melissa Curtis's pencil case.

The girl freezes. Of all the people in school, why did she have to be pushed into Melissa Curtis?!

"What the fuck, Fish Sticks?!"

She's grabbed by the back of her shirt and flung against a locker. She may only be light, but the impact of her body hitting metal makes a sound so loud it silences the entire corridor.

"It was an accident. I was pushed!" she protests, but Chrissy is in her face and having none of it.

"Oh really? Pushed like this?" she snarls, throwing the girl against the locker again.

While some people scurry to class, desperate to not witness something they will never be brave enough to stop, a sizeable crowd gathers to watch what happens next. The girl burns under their gaze.

"Pick it all up," Amira Johal snaps, pointing to Melissa's belongings.

"What?"

"Get on your knees and pick it up!" Hallie Patterson shouts.

The girl stares at the furious huddle of her tormentors for a moment, but a moment is all they need. Amira kicks the back of her legs, making her body crumble in on itself. The next thing the girl knows, she is on all fours scrambling to collect Melissa's belongings.

Someone spits on her.

Tears sting her eyes. She scuttles across the floor like a cockroach, stacking up Melissa's textbooks and planner. She reaches for the pencil case, but just as she is about to grab it, someone puts their foot on top of it. They're wearing expensive trainers, not uniform regulation approved shoes but somehow, they get away with it.

"Say please," Chrissy instructs.

The girl gulps. "Please."

Chrissy glares at her, her piercing eyes boring into the girl's skull, then she kicks the pencil case. It skids across the floor.

"Fetch."

Humiliation sears her skin, but the girl does as she is told. The crowd parts to let her past, watching her scuttle towards the pencil case. Chrissy and her friends laugh. Other people join in, the girl's degradation their sick source of entertainment.

Once she reaches the pencil case, she piles it on top of the rest of Melissa's belongings and hands them back to her.

"I might as well burn everything now she's touched it," Melissa snarls.

Chrissy snorts then takes a step forward. Her hot breath, scented with fruity chewing gum, tickles the girl's cheek. "You need to watch where you're going. If this happens again, we might not be so kind."

With that, Chrissy marches away. Her friends follow and the crowd disbands, but the girl remains rooted to the spot. She knows she will be late for class and will get a red mark against her name because of it, but she can't make her legs move. They don't want to take another wrong step. They want to stop, to stand still, to stay safe.

But how can she ever be safe when Chrissy and her friends patrol every inch of her life?

Now.

22

Screaming sirens and flashing lights wake Melissa's neighbours. Within seconds of the emergency services arriving, the street is lined with curious faces craning their necks to see what on earth is happening on their sleepy, suburban street at this time of night.

I don't meet their eyes. I don't want anyone to see the pain on my face. Instead, I huddle beside Amira, wrapped in a blanket a kind paramedic gave me when she saw I was trembling uncontrollably.

The door of Melissa's house is broken open.

Seconds later, the paramedics confirms what I already knew – Melissa is dead.

They don't use the word murdered, but I saw the blood. I know it was no accident.

We are taken away from the house so it can be cordoned off as a crime scene. As soon as the tape goes up, the crowd on the street is up in arms. Their gasps ring in my ears. They're shocked, but I'm not. I saw the blood.

"What happened?!"

"Is Melissa okay?"

"Oh my god… what is going on?!"

Their disbelieving words pierce my soul. I close my eyes as if to shut them out, but when I do all I see is blood.

An officer whose name I forget as soon as she tells me it takes my statement. The cogs of my mind whir into overdrive, but somehow, I manage to robotically go over my timeline. The officer tries to press me for details, but all I can tell her is what I saw. I saw the blood. I saw the body.

I saw my friend dead.

By the time I'm taken home in a police car, my eyes are fighting to stay open. All I want is to crawl into bed and howl, but as soon as I open the front door, Lucas flies into the hallway in a furious rage.

"What the fuck, Nat? The front door was wide open -" he yells, but he stops when he sees my pale, traumatised face and the officer escorting me inside. He takes a tentative step towards me. "What's happened?"

"Melissa's dead," I state as if I'm telling him what I had for lunch.

Lucas pauses, the words ticking over in his mind. I see the moment they finally register like a punch. He comes to me, our raging fight forgotten, and then I am in his arms.

I burrow into him. I want to cry, but I can't. Everything is stuck inside me, a gluttonous stack of pain clogging my airway more and more with every second that passes. I need to breathe, to let it out, but I know as soon as I do, I won't be able to control it. My grief will take over, my heartbreak will crush.

"What happened?" Lucas directs his question to the officer.

"At this point in time, we aren't exactly sure," the officer responds diplomatically.

"But Melissa's dead?"

I bury my head into Lucas's shoulder, trying to shield myself from the exchange.

"That's right," a different voice answers. I peel away from my husband to find Detective Baldie entering my home. "Murdered, actually, if you want to be more specific."

"Fuck," Lucas exhales, shuddering so hard his entire body trembles.

"Detective Baldie, what are you doing here?" I ask, blinking and taking in the unwelcome sight of him.

"Well, Mrs Redding, I'd have thought it would be obvious, but I'll explain if you need me to. You are a witness. It's my job to ask questions and find out what you know. Do you mind if I come in and we get started?"

I open my mouth to say of course, but I notice Detective Baldie is already inside my home. I then realise that I never really had a choice in the matter – he was going shake me for answers no matter what.

My stomach squirms, my body warning me what's to come might be even worse than what's already happened.

23

A mug of tea steams on the table in front of me, a token of Lucas's support even though he isn't allowed to be in the room while I am being questioned.

"Please, just let me sit beside her. I won't say a word, I promise, but I don't want to leave her alone right now," he pleads.

"Lucas, it's fine. I'm fine," I respond, my words as much for my benefit as his.

"Babe, you've just seen -"

"I know what I've seen," I snap. I exhale unsteadily, then force a smile. "But I'm okay. If these questions help find whoever did this, then I need to answer them."

Even though I'm doing my best to please him, Detective Baldie says nothing. He watches Lucas and me interacting, taking in every detail and unspoken word like a vulture eying its prey.

Lucas nods half-heartedly and takes himself to the living room. He puts the television on then lowers the volume. Knowing he's keeping one ear out for me is a comfort, but not one that makes much difference to my anxiety.

Exhaustion radiates from my every pore. I want nothing more than to crawl into my bed with its fresh white sheets, to close my eyes and not see Melissa's lifeless gaze staring back at me. I don't want Amira's terrifying theory to plague my thoughts. I want to sleep. I want my friends to be alive and well. I want this to be over.

Rubbing my eyes, I force myself to focus on Detective Baldie's stern face across the table. Another officer sits beside him clutching an open notebook and a poised pen. A Dictaphone is laid out, ready to take down every word I say. I ball my hands into fists under the table, pressing my nails into my palms so hard I know I will draw blood.

Detective Baldie takes a gulp of his drink and sighs happily. "Your husband makes a good cup of tea," he praises. "Now, let's get started, shall we? When was the last time you saw Melissa Curtis?"

I wince as Melissa's bloody face flashes before me but force myself to speak. "Last night. She was here when you came to ask me about the car, then left a few minutes after you had gone."

"Melissa wasn't at the funeral today?"

"No."

Detective Baldie raises an eyebrow. "She skipped the funeral? But I thought you were all such good friends?"

"We were. We are."

"One of Melissa Curtis's closest friends dies, and she misses the funeral... didn't you think that was strange?"

Instantly, my defences are up. "Of course I did, but we had all said how we didn't want to go to the funeral. I just thought Melissa had decided she couldn't handle it. By the time we realised she wasn't going to make it, the funeral had already started. We couldn't exactly walk out and get her."

"Maybe not, but it still must have been worrying to think of your friend in such distress they couldn't make the funeral. Why didn't you check up on her afterwards? I would have thought you would have. You know, being the good friends you are."

I tense at his words. "It had been a long day. I was going to message her tomorrow, but to be honest after the funeral I just wanted to get home and go to sleep."

"I see," Detective Baldie says in a way that makes it sound like he really doesn't see at all. "Can you walk me through your night after the funeral and explain how you ended up at Melissa Curtis's house?"

"I already gave a statement about that at the scene," I respond wearily.

"I know, but I wasn't there, so fill me in."

Taking a deep breath, I begin. "Lucas and I came back from the funeral together. We got into a silly fight -"

"About?"

I bristle. "Does it matter?"

"This is a murder investigation, Mrs Redding. I would say yes, it matters."

I sigh. "Chrissy Summers," I admit, my body burning from head to toe. "She was at the funeral. Lucas was nice to her and I… I got jealous."

"What was there to be jealous of?"

"Nothing really, but Lucas was nice to her, and it didn't make me feel very good."

"You don't like your husband being nice to other women?"

I grit my teeth. "I don't like my husband being nice to Chrissy Summers. We don't exactly have the best history."

"Ah, she was one of the bitches from school, right? Like your friends used to be?" I flinch as Detective Baldie uses my careless words against me.

"She wasn't very nice, no, but as Lucas pointed out, that's all in the past."

"But not enough in the past for you to not argue about it."

"Husbands argue with their wives, it's not uncommon, especially after a tough day and a lot of wine," I respond icily.

Detective Baldie shrugs, his sceptical expression making me burn with injustice. "So, what happened after your argument?"

Thinking back to the glass I threw, the pure horror in Lucas's eyes and the ear-splitting slam of the front door, I squirm. "Lucas… Lucas left. Sometimes when we argue he goes for a drive to calm down."

"And you?"

"I stayed here. I went over the day in my head and realised how silly

I was being. Chrissy is a girl from school, someone I haven't seen in years... why was I letting her bother me? Lucas and I are happy."

"Apart from when you argue."

"Again, people argue," I reply, my tone spikier than I intend it to be.

Detective Baldie's eyes scan the room, pausing for a moment on the pile of broken glass I had only half cleared away. I don't follow his gaze. I'm ashamed of my outburst enough as it is without witnessing his judgemental reaction too.

"So, after your big revelation about Chrissy, what did you do?"

"I didn't want to go to sleep on a fight, so I waited for Lucas to come home. Then my phone rang. It was Amira. She was crying. She told me... she told me she thought Melissa was dead." I gulp at the memory and dig my nails further into my flesh. A spike of pain jolts through my palms, one so intense it almost calms me.

"Those were her exact words?"

"She said, 'I think Melissa's dead' and asked me to go to the house."

"What did you do?"

"I did what she asked – I went to Melissa's house. I literally ran there."

"You ran from here to the victim's house?"

"Yes. It's not far. Besides, I'd been drinking at the funeral – I couldn't exactly drive."

"So, you ran from here to the victim's house, leaving your infant daughter asleep alone upstairs?"

His words pin me to the chair. The police officer making notes looks up, unable to hide the shock in her eyes.

Detective Baldie doesn't say anything else, but he doesn't need to. He knows what he has done, what he is forcing me to admit.

"We have a nanny," I try to explain as if alerting people to Jay's presence makes my abandonment any better.

"Was she in the house at the time?" Detective Baldie asks.

Remembering Jay running from me after I shouted at her, I shake my head.

"Did you tell her where you were going?"

I pause, but there's no point lying. Detective Baldie would only find out the truth anyway. "No, I just left," I admit, sweat trickling down my back.

"So, like I said, you left your daughter alone?"

"She wasn't alone! We have a nanny."

"Who didn't know you had gone..." Detective Baldie trails off suggestively.

"I panicked, okay? Amira said she thought Melissa was dead! I didn't know what to do."

"You were rational enough to know not to drive when you'd been drinking, but you were unable to pop your head into your nanny's on-site accommodation and ask her to keep an eye on your sleeping baby..."

Hot tears spring into my eyes. "Stop trying to make me look like a bad mother!"

Detective Baldie holds his hands up. "I'm sorry if you feel that way, Mrs Redding, but I'm just repeating facts. I need to know exactly what happened tonight, and you've told me that you left your daughter alone in this house while you ran to Melissa Curtis's."

"Fine, I left her alone," I admit. A frustrated tear falls from my eyes.

The officer flashes me a polite smile, but her eyes sparkle with judgement. One look at her and I know exactly what she is thinking – 'she left her daughter alone *and* she has a nanny. She probably thinks of her baby as an accessory, something to tick off on a 'life to do list'. Rich influencer... she doesn't *care,* not really.'

The shame of her thoughts pierces my heart.

Detective Baldie clears his throat. "After you ran from your home to the victim's, what happened?"

I turn my attention back to him, his serene, smug face filling me with rage. "Amira was sat on the stairs. She was crying. She told me to look through the letterbox… so I did."

"What did you see?"

I gulp and stare at the grain of the wood on the dining table. What did I see? Blood, so much blood. Melissa's mouth downturned, frozen forever in a terrified scream. Her eyes boring into mine, begging me for help.

But I was too late to save her. She was already dead.

"I saw Melissa's body," I whisper, then I burst into tears.

"That's enough," Lucas's voice cuts across the conversation like a guillotine.

Through the blur of my tears, I watch him stride across the room towards me. When he is by my side, he puts his hand on my shoulder.

"Mr Redding, we need to ask your wife -"

"I've heard the questions you've asked and the things you've implied. Nat is a good mum, a great mum. What would you do on the day of your best friend's funeral if you got a call saying your other friend was dead? Would you think straight? Would you?"

It's the officer's turn to be embarrassed now. She shoots me an apologetic smile, a blush creeping up her neck. I want to be soothed by her change of heart, but I'm not. The only reason she has realised the error of her ways is because Lucas made her think twice. Had he not burst in, she would have told whoever would listen what a terrible mother I was. That gossip would have been all over Coral Bay by sunrise.

"I should have been here, but I wasn't. We argued, I got hot headed, I left. That's on me, not Nat. So, the next time you need to speak to my wife, I would appreciate it if you didn't spend your time trying to crucify her character and instead stick to your job of getting information about the crime that has happened. You're here to catch a killer, not persecute my wife for making a split-second decision after a traumatic day."

I look up at my husband, his body pulsing with tension, his exterior composed and protective. I have never loved him more.

"This was just a friendly conversation, Mr Redding, but I'm sorry if it came across otherwise. Mrs Redding has been very helpful with our inquiries so far. There was no offence intended." Detective Baldie rises to his feet and turns to me. "Thank you for your time, Mrs Redding. I think it's best we leave you to get some rest now, but I will need to speak to you again."

I give him a small nod, then Lucas walks Detective Baldie and the officer to the door.

As soon as I'm alone, I collapse in on myself.

"Am I really a bad mother?" I question. Esme hadn't even crossed my mind when I raced to Amira's aid. The blind panic of the moment had taken over.

But Detective Baldie, however awful he had been, was right. I *had* left my daughter alone. I even left the front door open. On the same night Melissa was murdered in her own home, I left my child alone. A vulnerable, easy target. Anything could have happened, and it would have been completely my fault.

The thought congeals in my stomach.

I love my daughter more than anything. She is the best thing in my life. I look at her and can't believe she is mine. I would give everything up for her in a heartbeat, but sometimes it's a relief to plant her in Jay's arms. Sometimes I spend a little longer painting than I need to. I am proud of the fact that being 'mum' is just one of many labels I have.

But if my child is not the only thing in the centre of my universe, should I even be a mother?

"Stop," Lucas orders as he walks back into the room. "Stop thinking whatever you're thinking right now. You're a good mother, Nat."

"That's not what Detective Baldie thinks."

"Well, fuck him. He was completely out of order tonight. You're the best mum I know. The best wife, the best friend, the best person."

"Lucas, I didn't even think of her," I admit, my voice thick.

"No, you thought of Melissa, which was exactly where your thoughts needed to be."

"But she's my daughter."

"She's your daughter and she was fine. Melissa was your friend, and she wasn't. You did what any of us would do. Do not let Detective Dickhead make you doubt yourself. Esme is lucky to have you as her mother."

"Even if I have a nanny?" I half joke.

"A nanny that allows you have to have a career your daughter will be proud of. That's nothing to be ashamed of." Lucas reaches for me, and I fall into his arms. "Nat, I am so, so sorry I wasn't there."

"No, I'm sorry. I was so out of line. Chrissy just -"

Lucas shakes his head. "Let's not mention her name again, not tonight. Let's just go to bed. This day needs to be done with."

I take my husband's hand and follow him to the bedroom. We curl together, my head on his chest. His heart beats against my cheek. I close my eyes tight and know that even though so many things are falling apart around me, I am lucky to have Lucas as the constant holding me close no matter what. I pray there never comes a day where he lets me go.

24

After a night spent tossing and turning in and out of nightmares imagining Melissa's terrified last moments, exhaustion consumes me. A day watching mind-numbing television calls to me, but those daydreams are interrupted by another email from Arlene Davies. With my deadline looming, avoiding her work isn't an option anymore, so I spend the day painting.

Luckily for me, inspiration flows through my veins. The red washed fury that took over me before is back, only this time it's even stronger. My brushstrokes grow with aggression and confusion. I'm sweating profusely, the shapes on the canvas taking on a life of their own bigger than anything I can control.

By the time I'm finished, I'm drained but proud. I stand back and survey the piece.

It still needs a little work, but so far, it's perfect. It sums up exactly how I feel right now – enraged, lost, and bewildered. Once again, it's not my usual painting style, but to me it is some of my best work yet.

"Arlene might love this new direction," I tell myself as I wash my brushes. "My 'loving life by the sea' images are getting a little predictable."

I take one final look at the canvas. There is nothing predictable about this painting. The abstract nature and frantic technique show a side of me no one has seen before. I just hope the world is ready for rawness instead of perfection.

Buoyed by my burst of unfiltered creativity, I head back to the house where I find Jay feeding Esme. I startle when I see her, the taste of the last thing I said to her sour in my mouth. "Jay, about last night. I'm so sorry -"

I begin but she shakes her head.

"Don't apologise. You had a rough day, I get it."

"I know but -"

"No buts, Nat. Seriously, if I had just buried my best friend, I think I'd have said far worse than that. Just forget it. I know I have."

I well up. "I really don't deserve you!"

"Oh, come here," Jay says, pulling me into an embrace. "I heard about Melissa too. I can't believe it. To think she was at this table just the other night..." Jay shudders. "If you need anything, please just let me know."

"Thank you, but I think all I need is for my friends to stop dying," I joke, then flinch. "Sorry, that wasn't funny."

"Don't worry, I've got used to your strange sense of humour by now! These came for you earlier, by the way." Jay indicates to an impressive bouquet of pink and white flowers on the kitchen side. "I didn't know where you'd want them."

The sickly-sweet scent makes my head swim, but I grab the card and read it:

Dearest Nat,

Sending love at this difficult time.

Love all your friends in Coral Bay

My chest tightens. "That's nice of everyone," I manage to say, hoping my words don't hint at the drowning sensation my brain is flooded with.

"Beautiful, aren't they? I think news must have got around about you being there to find... well, you know."

Melissa's blank, lifeless face flashes before me, so detailed it's like her body is laid out on my kitchen floor. I fight the urge to be sick.

Just then, the front doorbell rings. I freeze, dread filling my soul.

Jay squeezes my arm. "I'll get it." She hands Esme to me and leaves the room.

I hold my baby close, watching her babble away and grin impishly at me. My heart flushes with pure, blissful love, but something niggles in the back of my mind. How could I leave her alone? With the weight of her in my arms, I almost can't believe it of myself. She's so small, so dependent, so fragile. How could I leave this ball of cuteness, this half of my soul? Had I lost my mind?

The sound of Amira's voice cuts through my spiralling thoughts. I look up from Esme to see her entering the room alongside Jay. I note her red raw eyes and steely expression – the look of a broken woman. A mirror image of me. "How are you holding up?" she asks.

"I've been better."

"Tell me about it." Amira glances around the room and nods at the flowers. "Let me guess – your Coral Bay fan club?"

I blush tellingly. "Didn't they send you flowers?"

"I'm not you, Nat. I don't get the flowers."

The uncomfortable truth in Amira's words hangs heavy in the air. Jay shifts on her feet before walking towards me with her arms outstretched for Esme. "We'll give you two some space."

We watch Jay pack Esme into her pushchair. She speaks excitedly about their impromptu walk and Esme beams at Jay like she's the best thing she's ever seen.

Something tugs inside my chest. Does my daughter prefer her nanny to her mother? When I think of how many hours I've spent away from her this week alone, would it really be that surprising if she did?

Amira walking past my line of sight drags me back to reality. I follow her to the living room. As soon as we are alone, she turns to me. "Enough of this bullshit - we need to figure out who is doing this."

"Amira," I sigh, sinking into the sofa, exhausted by the conversation already.

"Don't *Amira* me, you know as well as I do something fucked up is going on here." I've never heard Amira be so decisive before. I raise my eyebrow; a move she takes in with irritation. "What? My life is on the line here, Nat. Can I break character yet or am I expected to be subservient, fun Amira forever?"

"What?"

"Oh, come on, don't give me that wide eyed bullshit! We all have a role to play, right? We all have the same shitty dynamic as ever – Bree was Hallie's puppet, Melissa was the dumb one, I'm the fun one, Becca's the slutty one."

"And who am I?" I ask, stung not to be included in the line-up.

"You? You're our Chrissy."

I sit back, gobsmacked. "I am *nothing* like Chrissy Summers!"

Amira rolls her eyes. "Of course you are. You're our leader. You're the one we all want to be."

I wrinkle my nose, but Amira shakes her head furiously.

"Don't pretend to be so down on yourself, Nat – it's one of the things I hate most about you. Why wouldn't we want to be you? Amazing house, gorgeous husband, adorable kid, cool career... you have everything we've all ever wanted."

"But I earned those things!"

"Yeah, I get it, you had an 'ugly duckling' transformation like in movies," Amira says with another roll of her eyes. "We all got it, okay? The whole, 'I used to be the one you bullied but now you're my friends' shtick, it was cute!"

"It wasn't a shtick - you said you were my friends!"

"Of course we were your friends! We liked you, you idiot, but we were looking for a leader and there you were. You know as well as I do you couldn't believe your luck when you came back and we wanted you to be a part of our group, never mind be in charge of it. You couldn't wait to take Chrissy's place."

My lungs constrict. "Is that the only reason you wanted me to be your friend, to replace Chrissy?"

"Honestly? Yeah," Amira shrugs. Her cool, calculated tone makes me flinch. "Don't look at me like that, Nat. Hallie would have argued otherwise and pretended she *loved* you for you, but the reality is when Chrissy left, we didn't know what to do. We were so used to being the top girls, then high school ended, and we were like… what next? In that group, we knew where we belonged. In the real world, we didn't have a fucking clue. Hallie tried to be in charge for a bit, but it didn't work. Why would you take advice from a girl who over plucked her eyebrows and once asked if you could get pregnant from anal sex? For a long time, we were a mess. Fuck, Bree even worked as an exotic dancer for a few weeks, can you believe it? Then you came along with your Instagram fame and your disdain for everything that was too twee and coastal, and we became a group again, just like in school. We served you. We belonged. We were back on top."

My whole world teeters on a knife edge now the carpet has been pulled from beneath my feet. I almost can't believe I've been so stupid to think my place in their life was genuine, but of course I can believe it. Everything my friends do has to benefit to them.

Besides, Amira's right – I couldn't believe my luck when they wanted me. I would have done anything to be a part of their group. Anything to prove to the girl I used to be that life didn't have to be empty forever.

My heart hangs heavy. "So, it didn't matter who you were friends with. You just needed someone to fill Chrissy's shoes."

"Of course it *mattered*. It couldn't just be just anyone. Fuck, there are plenty of women here desperate to be our friend. I mean, have you ever managed to go to the supermarket without some ex-Coral Bay High loser trying to make small talk?" Amira shudders at the thought. "No, it had to be someone who elevated us, someone who made us look better than the lost kids we were. It had to be you. You're a decent person, Nat. Sometimes a little wet, sure, but you made us better people. We were a good group for a while, but someone remembers us as we were before. Someone wants us gone."

A shiver runs down my spine. With the body count of my friends stacking up, every word Amira says rings true to me, but I don't want to admit it. My head is too warped from her last revelation to take another bombshell.

"Amira, don't."

"Don't what? Don't say what's staring us in the face? Don't admit we're all fucked? First Bree and Hallie are forced off the road, then Melissa is murdered in her own home. Do you really think we can afford to ignore the facts anymore? Someone is coming for us, Nat. Someone is killing us off."

My blood runs cold. "Who do you think it is?"

Amira flops her head back against the sofa, an ugly smirk twisting her features. "Narrow it down to the whole school, why don't you? We were fucking terrible people."

I don't smile. "You were."

"Tell me about it."

"It's not funny, Amira. You can't sit here and tell me someone wants to kill you because of the shit people you were when you were younger and smile about it. You can't laugh about the hideous things you used to do."

Amira eyes me challengingly. "Well, you can't have thought we were that hideous. After all, you forgave us like that." Amira clicks her fingers to reiterate her point, the snap sharp against the silence of the house.

I open my mouth to protest, but what's there to argue against? Those girls ruined my life. They belittled me, humiliated me, made me do and think things I never thought were possible. I had nightmares about them well into my second year of university, yet the lure of being one of them was so strong I jumped at the chance to become part of their group. I didn't think twice about it. I never even confronted them about what they did - I just swallowed my pain down for the promise of popularity.

I laughed at people's bad haircuts and passed on rumours I'd overheard on the bread aisle. If I heard any gossip, I typed it into the group chat without even considering the person I was speaking about.

I did everything a popular girl should do. Everything they did all those years ago that drove me to the point of hating myself so much I thought the world would be better without me in it.

Teenage Nat would be disgusted in me.

"We need to make a list of everyone you wronged," I say, trying to shake off the bitterness of the truth that just exploded in my face.

Amira pulls a face. "It will be a long list."

"Then we'd better get started."

25

I can't remember the last time I braved looking through my yearbook. Over the years I've often thought about throwing it away but at the last minute I always stop myself. Sometimes I need the reminder that however my life looks now, it hasn't always been this way.

Nothing proves that more than my yearbook. It is a compilation of evidence of how hated I once was. The photos I'm not in, the blank pages that should be filled with well wishes but aren't, the gut-wrenching insults scrawled into it whenever it got into the wrong hands... it's the story of who I used to be.

I set it on the coffee table.

"I haven't seen this in ages!" Amira marvels. She flicks through the yearbook, her neatly plucked eyebrows raising as she notices the distinct lack of signatures and kindness. "You really weren't liked, were you?"

"Nope. You all saw to that."

Amira's gaze meets mine. "I guess saying sorry now wouldn't fix it, would it?"

"Would you mean it?"

Amira shoots me a sheepish glance then turns her attention back to the yearbook.

As I watch her flip through the yearbook in delighted fascination, I try to not feel bitterly hurt. No matter how hard I try, though, the agony of the truth cuts deep. I allowed her into my life under the guise of being genuine friends, but it was a pretence all along. I was a way for Amira to cling to her glory days, just like her penchant for unnecessary Botox and excessive dieting. How had I not noticed it before? More worryingly, did everyone else look at being my friend in the same way?

I feel more stupid for believing anyone could like me than I did at fourteen for thinking life wouldn't always be this cruel.

Amira suddenly jabs one of the photos, pointing to a picture of a boy with deep acne scars and an overbite. "Him! Max Potter. I'm pretty sure we got the football team to shave off one of his eyebrows."

"It was both of them, actually."

"Really?" Amira grins. "Savage."

A bubble of anger rises in my stomach. I'll never forget the sight of Max, head down to hide his tears, running from the laughter of the football team into the safety of the school building. The memory makes me tingle with injustice, but Amira brushes it off like it's a speck of dust on her coat.

"Her," Amira says, pointing to a photo of another ex-Coral Bay High student. Faye Dennis, a size fourteen girl who was picked on enough to develop anorexia so severe she was in and out of hospital for four years after high school. Even now I spot her at the supermarket obsessively reading the nutritional information on everything that goes into her trolley. "Fat Faye."

I suck in a breath. "Faye Dennis."

"Is that her married name?"

"No, Amira, that's her *name*," I snap, snatching the yearbook from her manicured hands and rising to my feet.

Amira blinks, bewildered. "What's wrong?"

"I can't do this," I say, turning to walk away.

"But you have to help me!" Amira cries, scrambling to her feet.

Her words light a firework in my soul. "I don't *have* to do anything. I can't sit here while you go through a list of people you hurt with a smile on your face and pretend I think it's okay. You were nasty people, Amira. All of you. If someone is making you feel one ounce of how you made them feel, then I'm…"

Amira sticks her chin out. "Then you're what?"

"Then I'm glad! You spent years of your life torturing others and you still can't find it in yourself to feel bad about what you did!"

"We were just kids!"

I shake my head furiously. "You stopped being kids the moment you took away someone else's right to be a child with your nastiness."

Amira's mouth hangs open. I hold her gaze, standing up for myself, for all of us, like I should have done so many years ago. The silence is static. Amira's chin wobbles, but I stand my ground.

"Nat, I'm scared," she whispers. "Please, I'm begging you. I need your help."

"I spent every day of my teenage years scared. Where were you to help me then?"

Amira looks at her feet. "I know I can't make it okay. I know it makes you sick to sit opposite me while I list what we did – what *I* did – but I don't know what else to do. Everyone around me is dying, Nat. They are *dying*. You have to help me. Please." Amira grasps my hand. "Please, please help me find out who is doing this. I don't want to be next."

I want to push Amira away, to call her all the names she once called me, but witnessing the fear in her eyes reminds me I can never be that person. No matter what those girls did to me, I will never sink to their level.

Maybe that makes me a better person, maybe that makes me weak, I don't know. All I know is I am not going to let Amira be alone with her fear like I was with mine.

"Fine, but no more looking back fondly at the shitty things you did, okay?"

"Deal."

After two hours, we have a list of over twenty names. The list could be much longer, but we decide to only write the names of people who were hurt so badly their lives altered dramatically. In the end, the list is made up of people who had been pushed to things like self-harming, developing eating disorders or moving away to escape the torment.

"Fuck," Amira whispers, her eyes wide as she reads over the list. "That's a lot of people."

I nod. I wonder what it's like to hold in your hand a list of people whose lives were negatively impacted as a direct consequence of your actions. People who had family, friends, feelings... forever changed because of you. The thought makes me shiver.

"I guess when you look at this it makes sense why someone would want us dead," Amira admits.

I scan the list. "The good thing is that ninety-nine percent of these people still live in Coral Bay."

"Why is that good?"

"It means you can interact with them and see how they react to you."

"But most of these people were at Hallie's funeral. I saw some of them crying. Just because they're nice to me, it doesn't mean they don't want to kill me."

I grimace at the truth in Amira's logic. "Can you take the list to the police? Maybe they can investigate the people on there."

Amira gnaws her bottom lip. "Do you think they'll take it seriously?"

"Who knows. But if you're worried for your life, surely it's better to try than to not?"

Amira nods. "I guess I'd better start making friends with the locals rather than laugh at them behind their back!" she jokes.

I don't laugh back.

Amira makes a move to leave, but before she grabs her handbag she pauses. Her eyes lock on mine, her skin paler than I've ever seen it before. "There is one other person who's not on the list but maybe should be," she says softly.

"Who?" I ask, but the glint in Amira's eyes tells me she knows I am thinking of the exact same person she is.

"Chrissy Summers. The biggest bitch of all."

My stomach clenches at the sound of her name. The cruellest, most evil person I have ever met. The only person I can think of who I would bet all my money on being capable of murder. "Do you think she would do something as sick as this?"

"Do you really have to ask that?" Amira challenges, flopping back onto the sofa and flicking through the yearbook once again. "Chrissy, Chrissy, Chrissy…" she murmurs. Amira stops on a photo of her group of friends and the football team. "Wait, Chrissy met Blaine right before he died. I remember seeing a photo of them together on Facebook. So obviously filtered, but still. Chrissy is there when Blaine dies then comes back to Coral Bay and suddenly Hallie and Melissa are dead too?"

"It looks suspicious to me," I admit, trying to act nonchalant about the fact that I am essentially accusing someone of murder.

"Right? She had none of us on social media, but she somehow knew *everything* that had gone on in Coral Bay whilst she was gone. She even knew about Melissa's boob job and Becca's affair with that married guy who stalked her. She brought it up over drinks."

At the mention of their catch up without me, my stomach knots. "I forgot you went for drinks with her," I lie.

Amira flashes me a pitying smile. "We only went to play the game, Nat. You've got to do what you've got to do to survive as a top dog, right?"

I nod, but I don't agree. I will never view friendship in the same way Amira does. I could never be so calculating.

"She kept asking about you, you know. She wanted to know everything about your life. It was like she was obsessed," Amira says.

My heart skips a beat. "Obsessed with me?"

"Is it really that surprising? You took her crown, why wouldn't she want to know about you? Although to be honest, she knew a lot already. It wouldn't surprise me if she's been stalking you on Instagram for years."

I gulp, my mind racing back to bumping into Chrissy on Hillman's Trek. "The first time I saw her, she already knew I was married to Lucas even though I never mentioned it."

"You're actually shocked to hear she's been keeping tabs on this guy?" Amira says, turning the yearbook to me.

The photo on the page confronts me like a home invader. It's a snapshot of a time I'd rather forget, of faces I've tried to push to the back of my mind forever. The football team and the popular girls, their smiles leering back at me. The faces of my tormentors.

But the bit that really sticks is Chrissy and Lucas. If the love heart eyes emoji were a photograph, this would be it. Lucas has thrown his arm over Chrissy's shoulders and Chrissy beams at him adoringly. They look like the epitome of childhood sweethearts.

Envy turns me nauseous. I push the yearbook back towards Amira. "She definitely did love attention," I quip dryly.

"Especially from Lucas."

Amira's words knead my stomach, not that she notices. She's too engrossed in the reminder of her youth for that. She traces over the grinning faces of the people frozen in that moment with her forefinger.

"It makes sense Chrissy would keep up to date with Lucas's life. She thought he would be under her spell forever. It must have killed her to see him with someone else, especially you. We all thought you'd be bottom of the barrel forever."

I try to shake off Amira's last comment, but it's a dagger to my heart. "Chrissy fits the timeline of the murders, but why would she kill her friends?"

Amira looks at me like I am stupid. "Why wouldn't she kill us? We dropped her when things got tough and replaced her with you. You took her friends, her man. You took her life, Nat, and we let you. Chrissy is all about loyalty. What kind of friends would let you do that?"

Once more, I turn my attention to the photo of Chrissy and Lucas. It burns my eyes to see them together. "I guess she'd be jealous."

"Jealousy and Chrissy Summers are two things you do *not* want mixing," Amira says darkly.

I stare at the photograph until the pixels etch into my memory. Chrissy's wicked smile mocks me from the page. "Do you really think she's a suspect?"

"Everyone on this list we hurt because she told us to. I can't imagine the hatred she must feel for us now she's back and seen we've moved on with you instead of her. She'll be angrier about this than she's ever been about anything before. Knowing that, do you really think we can afford for her not to be?"

26

I want the rest of the day to stew on Amira's words and retrace Chrissy's whereabouts over the last few years, but I have little chance to do so. Sunaina comes to the house soon after Amira leaves to shoot my latest paid promotion, a blender that will apparently be the answer to every time-strapped mother's prayers. After weeks of careful negotiation on Sunaina's part, the fee for the ad is hefty and the expectation I can present myself as the perfect mother high. Usually I would relish the challenge, but after the events of the last few days I don't feel like I can portray 'World's Best Mum' on camera without the words 'fraud' somehow appearing on my forehead.

"Nat, no one who sees this will know you left your daughter alone in the middle of the night," Sunaina dismisses when I voice my concern.

I open my mouth to protest I'm not camera ready, but Sunaina's steely expression silences me. She lays out a dazzling white dress for me to wear and, by the time I come downstairs, my kitchen has been transformed into the blissful domestic setting of dreams. Carefully chopped fruit sits proudly on an expensive ceramic plate and my nicest glassware waits patiently to be filled with a smoothie.

"I told you that dress would look amazing," Sunaina comments, glancing up from unpacking the so-called miracle blender. I give a twirl and Sunaina laughs. "See, I knew you'd come around – just fake it 'til you make it, girl!"

So, I do.

I smile and I preen and I pose like I don't have a care in the world, following Sunaina's instructions until we get the perfect shot.

Sunaina looks exceptionally pleased with herself and, when I see the final image, it's clear why. The house looks amazing, the shoot styling is impeccable, and I can already tell the client will be incredibly happy with the results. There isn't a trace of guilt on my face. I look exactly how the brand wants me to pretend to be – composed, in control and the kind of mother every woman fantasises she will be one day. It's completely inconsistent with how I feel right now, and I love it.

After packing away the blender, we sit and snack on the chopped fruit.

"How are you coping with everything?" Sunaina asks through mouthfuls of banana.

I grimace. "How do you cope when two of your friends are dead and another will never be the same again?"

"Fair point. For what it's worth, I think you're handling it all really well. If two of my friends had died and I'd found one of the bodies, I'd still be crying in bed."

"Well, I did try, but you said I had to do the shoot."

"No rest for an influencer," Sunaina jokes.

"Life goes on, right?" I say sadly.

Beside me on the table, my phone leaps into life with a call from an unknown number. I answer tentatively. "Hello?"

"Natalie? It's Detective Stone. I'm just wondering if you're free to answer a few questions about last night?"

"More questions? But I answered them twice yesterday."

"I know, but we need to go over a few things with you and some new evidence has come to light. Could you come here, or would it be easier for us to come to you?"

I'm stuck. There's no way I'm braving a police station today, but I also don't want Detective Baldie in my house again. Add that to the fact that I don't want to recite last night's events again and I'm on the verge of tears. But what choice do I have?

"Come over anytime," I respond. I hang up and run my hands through my hair.

"What's up?" Sunaina asks.

"The police want to talk to me again."

Sunaina pats my hand. "I guess they need your help finding whoever did this."

"I just don't know how many times I have to say I saw my friend dead before they leave me alone," I snap, my tone so sharp Sunaina jumps. "Sorry, I didn't mean to scare you. I just can't keep going over what happened. Every time I close my eyes, I see Melissa staring back at me. I can't keep thinking about it. I just can't."

"I know it must be hard, Nat, but your friends need your help right now. Look, how about I wait with you until the police arrive so you're not alone?"

"That would be great," I smile, blinking back tears.

We carry the plate of fruit into the living room, ready to get lost in mindless reality TV.

As we take our seats, Sunaina turns to me. "Just a thought – do you think you'll finish with the police before your arts meeting tonight?"

I groan. How could I forget my Coral Bay Arts Society meeting? It's central to my monthly calendar. A way to nurture local talent, share ideas and for gossip to spread, so many people look forward to these sessions. With Hallie barely buried and Melissa now gone, there will probably be a queue for tonight's meeting. I don't know whether to thank the police for getting me out of it or hate them for making me miss a night of distraction.

"I'll call Joelle."

The phone only rings twice before she answers, diving straight into conversation. "Nat! Oh Nat, how are you, dear? You must be in terrible shock. No one can believe what's happened! First Hallie, now Melissa too. And for you to find her like that, you poor thing. It's all anyone's talking about."

My stomach knots at Joelle's friendly but intrusive monologue. "I know, it's terrible. I can't talk long, but I just called to say I can't make the meeting tonight. Something... something's come up." I don't dare tell Joelle that what's come up is another chat with the police. Gossip about that will be everywhere by sunrise if I do.

"Oh, no worries at all, sweetheart! I'll handle this meeting for you. It should be a good one. We've a new starter joining us."

"Who?"

"Chrissy Summers."

My heart stops. "Chrissy is joining the Arts Society?"

"Yes, isn't that wonderful?"

I pull a face. "Can she even paint or draw?"

"I don't know, dear, but even if she can't, we welcome beginners, don't we? It will be wonderful to have her with us."

"Wonderful, yeah," I reply, my mouth making the right noises, my soul full of dread. "Anyway, I'd best be going. See you next time."

"Bye, love," Joelle trills, then the line goes dead.

"Everything okay?" Sunaina asks from the other end of the sofa. I nod, but of course it isn't. Chrissy coming back to Coral Bay is one thing, but stealing my friends and now worming her way into my Arts Society? She's weeding me out. Soon there won't be a place left for me.

I pull my knees to my chest and hold them close, lost in my thoughts until the doorbell rings.

"I'll get it," Sunaina offers.

I rise to my feet and smooth down my appearance, trying to prepare myself for what is to come. When Detective Baldie and Detective Stone walk in, I offer them my brightest smile. "Hi," I chirp. My warm greeting is returned by Detective Stone, but not Detective Baldie. "Shall we talk in the kitchen?"

"That would be great," Detective Stone replies.

I lead the detectives into the kitchen, the remnants of the photoshoot still littering the surfaces. Detective Baldie's gaze lingers on the camera.

"Back to work already?"

"We had a deadline for a brand. It had to be shot today or we would be in breach of contract," Sunaina lies, offering me a supportive smile. We had until the end of the week to shoot the ad, but the detectives don't need to know that.

I return Sunaina's smile and transform into the perfect hostess. "Please, take a seat," I say, gesturing to the table. "You said you had new evidence?"

Before answering my question, Detective Baldie sets a Dictaphone on the table and turns it on. My jaw clenches, my teeth on edge by the gesture. He recites the date and time, then fixes his gaze on me. "There are some things that have come to light since we last spoke, yes. First of all, the two men you identified as Rory O'Connell and Aaron Chambers have solid alibis for the night of the accident."

"That's great news. Rory and Aaron really didn't seem like the type of men to cheat, never mind hurt anyone."

"It's great their names are cleared, but that means we now have to look elsewhere for suspects," Detective Stone explains.

"Oh?"

"Someone was fraudulently using photos of the two men and messaging Hallie and Bree under false pretences. So far, the only link we can establish between Mr O'Connell, Mr Chambers and the two women in the car is you."

I blink. "Me?"

"You attended the same university as Mr O'Connell and Mr Chambers. You are the only Facebook friend shared between the two men and the two women." Detective Stone offers me a reassuring smile. "That's not to say there's a huge significance in that – people take strangers photos from social media all the time – but I'm sure you can agree it's a little strange."

I nod slowly, my heart thudding inside my chest. "It is strange. I don't know why there would be a link between what happened and me other than I was friends with Hallie and Bree."

"Another thing," Detective Baldie says, pulling my gaze from the supportive face of Detective Stone to his stern one. "There were no signs of forced entry at Melissa Curtis's house, which means whoever murdered her was someone she invited inside."

My mouth hangs open. "You mean she was killed by a friend?"

Triumph flickers across Detective Baldie's face. "I never said a friend. It could have been someone she recognised from about town."

I flush furiously. "No, no, I never… I didn't mean -" I stumble over my words, heat tickling the back of my neck.

"I need to ask you, Mrs Redding – where were you yesterday morning?"

The air catches in the back of my throat. I look at the two detectives, their eyes fixed on me, the atmosphere in the room suddenly dense and oppressive. Sunaina watches from the kitchen, open mouthed. She seems just as astonished as I am to find me on the receiving end of this line of questioning for a second time, but that doesn't offer me much comfort.

"Are you… are you accusing me of something?"

"No," Detective Stone says. "We just need to establish your whereabouts to eliminate you from any further inquiry, that's all. It's routine."

Her words do little to soothe me. Neither does her smile. I know she is the good cop to Detective Baldie's bad cop. I know she is acting as though she is on my side to encourage me to open up. I know their game, but I'm also a part of that game, whether I like it or not.

"I was at home. Lucas and I slept in a little, then I went for a run before the funeral."

"Where did you go for your run?"

"Hillman's Trek."

"Who with?"

"I ran alone," I reply. Detective Baldie's mouth twitches and panic sets in. "I always run alone though. I wanted to clear my head. It was the day of the funeral, things were overwhelming -"

"It's not a crime to go for a run," Detective Stone smiles, but I don't smile back.

"How about the night of Hallie and Bree's accident? Where were you then?"

I jump at the question, my body cloaked in disbelief. "I've already answered this."

"Would you mind answering it again?" Detective Baldie's question is more an instruction than request.

I sit back, flabbergasted. "I was in bed with my husband, asleep, where I should be."

"And Mr Redding can verify that?"

"Of course!"

Suddenly, from behind the kitchen counter, Sunaina speaks. "Unless he had taken one of his tablets."

Time suspends. I turn to Sunaina who looks as shocked as I do at her interjection.

"What was that?" Detective Stone asks.

Sunaina opens and closes her mouth like a goldfish, the surprise at hearing the words leave her lips still etched onto her face. Her pleading eyes lock with mine and scream 'I'm sorry', but then she speaks and her apology means nothing.

"Lucas... Lucas has a bad back. When it plays up, he takes a tablet. They're really strong. They make him sleep," Sunaina mumbles, her face scarlet from her betrayal. "That's not to say there's any significance in that, though. Plenty of people use them," she adds feebly.

I keep my eyes fixed on my pained assistant, not quite believing what I am hearing. Slowly, I turn back to the detectives to find they have been watching my response the whole time.

"Lucas has a bad back from an old sporting injury," I reply, choosing my words carefully. "Sometimes he takes medication for it. Not every night, but sometimes. If he's had a tablet, he tends to sleep deeply."

"Did he take one that night?"

"I don't know," I reply with a tight smile. I might look serene on the outside, but inside I am on fire. "Am I being accused of something?"

"No," Detective Stone rushes, but I don't quite believe her. "Establishing alibis is a routine part of every investigation. We need all the facts to create a timeline and understand what's happened, that's all."

"I've lost two friends, that's what's happened," I say, a lump forming in my throat.

Detective Stone looks down, but Detective Baldie doesn't. He holds my gaze without flinching. "Miss Johal came to the station earlier today. She backs up your admission that your friends used to be bitches, as you referred to them. She came with a list of people she thinks are worth investigating. A list of names you helped her compile."

I nod, swept away in a wave of gratitude towards Amira. "That's right. Amira thinks someone is coming after her friends because of the things they used to do."

"Did you help her with that theory?"

I see Detective Baldie's trap, but I won't fall victim to it. I hold my head high. "No. She came to me with it. It's what she thinks is going on."

Detective Baldie cocks his head. "And what do you think is going on?"

I hold his gaze. "I think that list is a good place to start looking for suspects."

Detective Stone clears her throat. "There's a name on there, a name you mentioned the first time we met– Chrissy Summers?"

I bite back my irritation at hearing her name for what feels like the millionth time today. "Yes."

"Do you think she killed your friends?"

A loaded question. If I say yes and she didn't, I look like a bitch. But if I say no, the police might not look at her as a suspect and something in the pit of my stomach tells me Chrissy Summers coming back to Coral Bay at this time is no accident.

"Everything started to go wrong when she came back into the picture," I reply diplomatically. "I'd say that makes her about as suspicious as a person can get."

Detective Baldie's eyes stay fixed on mine, but I hold his stare. He wants me to look guilty, but there's nothing for me to feel guilty about. I compiled the list because my friend asked me to. I rang the police as soon as I got to Melissa's house. I told them about Aaron and Rory. I did everything I should. I am a good person. I came back here a brighter, better version of myself. I forgave those women for what they did. I didn't kill them. I wouldn't hurt anyone. Not intentionally, anyway.

"Thank you for your time, Natalie. You've been very helpful," Detective Stone says, reaching out to shake my hand. Limply, I take it, then I show the detectives out.

Only when they are gone do I dare breathe.

With the door firmly shut behind them, I stand immobile in the hallway. The white walls burn my eyes. The minimalistic decor that was once so serene and peaceful now feels clinical and oppressive. There is nowhere to curl up, nowhere to hide from the onslaught of pain and accusations that keep coming my way.

I want a moment to collect my thoughts, but I don't have a second of peace before Sunaina bursts into the room and launches into a grovelling speech.

"Nat, I'm so sorry! I didn't mean to say anything. Their questions the other day about the car threw me off, then to hear them again just felt weird. I was thinking about Lucas's back pills, then suddenly I'd said it out loud! I didn't even realise the words had left my mouth until you were all looking at me."

I turn to my blushing assistant, her eyes wide and pleading for me to understand.

"You made me look like I have something to hide," I say softly.

"No, I didn't -"

"Do you think I have something to hide? Do you think I have something to do with this?"

"No, I'd never -"

"Then why?!" I scream, the words exploding from me and making us both jump. "Why make me look like a bad person? Haven't I always treated you with kindness? Haven't I always looked out for you? How could you throw me under the bus like that?"

Sunaina blinks back tears. "Nat," she begins, but I can't stand the sight of her anymore.

"Get out."

"What?"

"Get OUT! And don't bother coming back - you're fired!"

A stunned Sunaina's mouth hangs open, her chest heaving as she tries to catch her breath. "Nat, you don't mean that -"

"OUT!" I screech, pointing to the front door.

Sunaina scrambles for her handbag, hot tears spilling down her cheeks. She looks so young all of a sudden. Watching her choke on sobs, I know I should feel something for her, but I don't. The only person I feel sorry for here is myself.

Sunaina pauses at the front door, clearly wanting to say something to me before she leaves, but with a hiccup she decides not to and goes without another word.

When the door closes behind her, I stand in the cavernous silence of my own home. Loneliness wraps around my neck like a noose.

As I trail into the kitchen to clear away the last of the photoshoot, I catch sight of my reflection in the hallway mirror. The strained, pale face staring back at me isn't one I recognise. There are lines at the sides of my eyes that didn't used to be there. I look exhausted, but how could I not? Everything I've spent years building is crumbling around me.

27

To stop myself from spiralling over my chat with the police and Sunaina's departure, I spend the rest of the day cooking dinner. I sit Esme on the kitchen counter and give her the job of my assistant. She's enthusiastic, even if her need to grab fistfuls of chopped vegetables and throw them onto the floor makes her a little unhelpful.

"Daddy is going to be so surprised when he sees what we have made him!" I coo, kissing Esme's nose.

I take a photo of the two of us cooking together and post it to 'Finding the Good Life'. It's not a Sunaina approved shot or even a particularly Instagram worthy photo, but the act of regaining control over *my* account makes me feel powerful.

"Who needs Sunaina?" I think as the likes roll in.

With dinner ready to go in the oven, I change into a dress and put Esme in an adorable outfit. The more I focus on creating the perfect evening, the more I forget the turmoil of the morning and I feel myself blooming again.

When Lucas arrives home from work, Esme and I greet him at the front door. "Well, isn't this a sight for sore eyes," he beams.

I light up at his words and lead him through to the kitchen where Jay is laying cutlery on the table.

"This smells amazing," Lucas compliments, kissing me on the cheek. "My wife, the genius chef."

Beaming, I serve the meal and take a seat next to my husband. Lucas's eyes glimmer as they meet mine, lighting up with the same loving glow they did on the night we met.

Picking up my wine glass, I extend my arm to the table. "To happiness like this," I toast.

We clink glasses and tuck into our dinner.

"This is really good, Nat," Jay says.

"Thank you," I smile. Beside me, Esme gurgles and I fluff her hair. "And thank you for all your help in the kitchen today!"

"Our little chef, huh?" Lucas says, pulling a face at Esme. She giggles in response, a sound that makes my heart flutter.

A rush of love overwhelms me. "This right here is everything that matters, the only thing that matters," I tell myself. My soul soars. This is exactly what I wanted tonight to be.

But of course, all good things must end.

"It's a shame Sunaina isn't here. She'd love this!" Jay enthuses.

At the mention of Sunaina's name, I freeze.

"What's wrong?" Lucas asks.

I toy with my wineglass. A drop of condensation trickles down the stem, puddling on the table. A mess. I wipe it away with my thumb, but a tell-tale smear stays behind. "Sunaina won't be working for us anymore."

My words are met with shocked silence.

"What?" Lucas eventually asks. "I thought you loved Sunaina?"

"I do – I did - but she really let me down today."

"What do you mean?"

I sigh. "The police came earlier and asked me where I was when Melissa was murdered and when Hallie and Bree had their accident."

Lucas's frown deepens. "Why did they ask you that?"

"I don't know, Lucas. Because they're clutching at straws? Because they have no leads now they know someone was fraudulently using Rory and Aaron's photos? Because they think I did it?" Saying the words out loud makes me want to cry. "Sunaina basically told the police you couldn't be my alibi for the night of Hallie and Bree's accident because you take medication that makes you sleep."

Lucas sits back in his chair, absorbing what I've just said. "But... but I do take medication that makes me sleep."

"I know, but don't you see how Sunaina saying that makes me look?"

I look around the table, only now noticing an atmosphere that wasn't there before. Jay appears to be inexplicably engrossed in her meal while Lucas stares at me as if I've grown two heads.

"Nat, you've got nothing to hide. What does it matter if Sunaina said I take medication? If anything, she did the right thing. You can't sack the girl because she told the truth to the police."

"But it was a truth that didn't need to be said! She made me look guilty."

"But you aren't guilty. So what if the police know I can't say you were at home for definite? If you didn't cause the accident then you didn't cause the accident, that's all there is to it. There's nothing to worry about."

"You didn't hear their questions, Lucas. They were talking to me as if I've done something wrong."

Anger flashes in Lucas's eyes. "Was it Detective Baldie again?"

I nod. "He's making it sound..." I begin, but my voice catches.

Lucas grips my hand. "Look, they can't accuse you of something you didn't do, okay? So don't worry. Everything will be fine."

I smile at Lucas, but my smile doesn't meet my eyes. I want to believe him so badly, but he wasn't there. He didn't see the way the detectives looked at me or feel the mistrust that radiated from them. He wasn't there to witness the glee on their faces every time I tripped up over my words.

"I'm sure Sunaina didn't mean anything by it, either," Jay adds.

I exhale. "I'm sure she didn't, but I feel like I've been betrayed. I need support right now, not this."

Jay offers me a small smile and nods, but Lucas doesn't look so sure.

"Why don't you take a couple of days to cool off and see how you feel afterwards? You might look at things differently then. Maybe you'll want to speak to Sunaina again when the police have new leads and things are less frantic. Hiring her back might not be such a bad thing."

I tilt my head at my husband. "I thought you disliked Sunaina?"

"Dislike her? I don't agree with some of the things she tries to push but I don't not like the girl. She's been great for business and a good friend to you too."

"Oh," I respond, pushing my dinner around my plate, suddenly not quite so sure about the way I acted earlier.

"She is really good at what she does," Jay chimes in. "She posted such a cute photo of you and Esme earlier. It was the sweetest thing I've ever seen!"

Lucas reacts immediately. "What?"

The world around me stops. My throat closes. I clutch my knife and fork and pray Lucas isn't as angry about this as he seems, but the way he grips his wineglass tells me he is raging.

"What photo?"

Jay blinks, looking from Lucas to me like a rabbit caught in headlights.

"What photo, Jay?" Lucas repeats, but he doesn't wait for her to respond. He opens his phone and goes to 'Finding the Good Life' himself. Sure enough, the photo I had taken of Esme and myself earlier is published for the world to see. And with a large following like mine, so much of the world has already seen it.

An angry snarl bursts from Lucas. "I said no photos of Esme on here!"

"I know, but -"

"There are no buts, Nat. This is non-negotiable, you know that! Now Esme's out there for the world to see like an animal in a zoo! She's a baby, not a celebrity. Do you have any idea the kinds of people who look for photos of children on here?"

"She's fully clothed -" I protest, but Lucas shakes his head.

"It doesn't matter how many layers she's wearing – I don't want her online! Every time you post, you leave a digital footprint. From 10 seconds of looking at your profile, I know the town you live in, where you shop, what beach you go to. Fuck, you've even posted photos of the front of our house! I could find out everything about you in just a few clicks. If you want to put that information about yourself out there then fine, but not Esme. Anything could happen to her!"

The room radiates with Lucas's anger and I'm pinned to the chair by the sinking feeling that once again I have majorly messed up.

"I know I seem really strict about this, but I'm a teacher, Nat. We have training on this stuff. People can find out anything online - people can *do* anything. I thought I made it clear that Esme wasn't to be on the page. I thought we'd agreed on this?"

Lucas's disappointment is so strong it's choking. I shrink under the intensity of his glare, the man I love now full of contempt. It hurts to have him as anything other than an ally.

So, even though it makes my organs shrivel with shame, I do what I must to survive unscathed. I do what I must to keep my husband viewing me as the woman he loves and not the enemy.

"You did, I'm sorry. I should have checked what was scheduled to be posted. I showed Sunaina photos of us in the kitchen a few weeks ago, but I thought I'd passed on the message about not sharing pictures of Esme strongly enough. Clearly not," I lie, struggling to swallow down the truth that begs to burst from me.

"Sunaina posted this?" Lucas asks.

I nod.

Lucas sighs, shaking his head. "Well maybe firing her isn't such a bad thing, after all. If she can't respect this basic rule, then maybe this is for the best."

The lie squirms inside me, twisting and turning, embedding itself in the pit of my stomach alongside the other searingly shameful moments of my life.

"I'll delete the photo after dinner," I promise.

"Good," Lucas says. "Now, let's not let this spoil tonight. How was everyone's day?"

I turn my attention back to my dinner, only the food looks anything but appetising now. Jay chirps up with a story about her latest French lesson failure and Lucas laughs along. I try my best to join in with the conversation, but my mind is on the photo I posted and the lie I told to cover my tracks.

"Is this what good people do, Nat?" I scold myself. "Lie to make themselves seem like a better person? Chrissy was right – you are a waste of oxygen."

While Jay stacks the dishwasher and Lucas runs Esme's bath, I go to delete the photo. It's been liked over twenty thousand times, a fact that makes me glow even though it shouldn't. I scroll through the comments, beaming at every gushing expression of adoration.

Oh WOW! She is soooooo cute!

She looks just like Nat!

Life goals and now family goals... is there anything @findingthegoodlife can't do?!

My sense of self swells. I feel loved. I feel like me again. I want to reach out and shake every stranger's hand. I want to thank them for their kindness while inhaling every word like a greedy child.

I scroll further, lapping up the attention, until I spot a comment that makes my heart stop.

Putting her baby high up on the kitchen side WHILE using a sharp knife AND the hob is on too... is @findingthegoodlife for real?! Mother of the year... NOT!!

I have to read @coralbaygirl747's comment twice for the words to sink in. When they do, any sense of joy I felt is leeched from me.

Worse still, the comment has one hundred and thirty-three likes and seventeen comments. One hundred and thirty-three people agree I'm a bad mum.

With a wobbling chin and clammy hands, I read the seventeen

responses.

My thoughts exactly… wtf was she thinking?!

It's all about likes with these 'influencers'. They don't care about their children! Cute child = more money. It's sickening! Some people shouldn't be mothers!

Wow… Nat is so desperate for likes that she would even put her baby in danger for them #youdisgustme

My fingers itch to respond and defend myself, but what would I say? Maybe it was a bit dangerous to have my daughter on the counter while I cooked but I was present and would never let anything happen to her? Would I tell them my daughter is my world and her safety is my number one priority?

Can I even say that after the other night? Anything could have happened when I raced out of the house. If I told my followers I left Esme home alone, what would they think of me then?

Maybe these comments tell the truth. Maybe I am a bad mum.

I swim in self-hatred until Lucas calling my name hands me a lifejacket. "Bath's ready!"

"Coming!" I shout, hastily deleting the post.

But deleting it doesn't make a difference. I've still read the comments. I still know what people think of me. Their words are burned into my mind, joining the long list of names and insults I have learned to take on as part of my identity ever since high school.

<u>Then.</u>

The sun beats down on her as she sits alone on the grass, her skin fiery from the intensity of its rays. The girl doesn't mind the sunburn, though. Red raw skin is an easy trade for a moment of peace. A small patch of grass at the back of the science block, who'd have thought it? But here she is, enjoying her lunchbreak uninterrupted for the first time in longer than she can remember.

She's had over a week of this bliss. She's never been happier.

She stretches out and closes her eyes, the sun kissing her cheeks.

"Life isn't all bad," she thinks, giving into the serenity of the moment. A blanket of tranquillity cloaks her. Her limbs soften and her mind wanders as she drifts into the calming waters of nothingness.

"Fish Sticks…"

She hears the name like a ghost's whisper. She whips upright and looks around. There's nobody there, but she's sure she heard it.

"Fish Sticks…"

There it is again!

The hairs on the back of her neck stand to attention. She looks from left to right, turning around, scouring her surroundings, but no one's there.

"Have they finally broken me?" she wonders. "Finally taunted me so much I hear them even in my private thoughts?"

The voices come back, louder this time, less ghostly, more monstrous.

"Fish Sticks, why are you so disgusting?"

"Why can't you just disappear?"

"Can't you see how much everyone hates you?"

Her cheeks flush. "Who's there?" she calls out, but no one emerges. She picks up her bag, but she doesn't leave. She doesn't dare. What if she walks into a trap? What if she's already in a trap?

Her bottom lip trembles as her limbs root themselves to the spot, fear coursing through her veins with every beat of her terrified heart.

"Fish Sticks, you're a gross bitch," someone whispers.

Tears sting her eyes. "Leave me alone," she cries out.

"Never. We will always find you, wherever you go," calls a voice. "We will follow your scent."

Hysterical giggles ring out as Chrissy Summers emerges from the side of the building, her friends following her lead. Their smug smirks burn more than the sun.

The girl takes a step backwards, terror biting her throat.

"Aww, Fish Sticks, we've missed you!" Melissa grins.

"Don't look so sad – we just wanted to say hello!" Bex adds.

"We just wanted you to know we were thinking of you. We're always thinking of you, and we can always find you," Chrissy warns, her voice serious, her face smiling.

Then she tosses her thick, glossy hair over her shoulder and walks away. The others follow like obedient sheep.

The girl watches them go, but the ghosts of what they said remain behind. They lodge into her consciousness where they will stay for the rest of time, their clawing fingernails embedding themselves in the core of her soul. You can't forget words like that. They stick, they fester, they poison.

You can't forget fear like that, either. It stays with you, always.

<u>Now.</u>

28

Sleep doesn't come easily for me, not with the weight of the trolling comments crushing me to the bed. On top of that, whenever I close my eyes the moment I lied about Sunaina plays in my mind and reminds me what a terrible person I am.

When I do eventually drift off, all I dream of is Chrissy. She comes for me, her hands still caked in Melissa's blood. She takes the stairs of my home one at a time, evil dancing in her eyes, leaving me immobilised by fear. An easy, unmoving, soon-to-be-destroyed target.

I wake dripping with sweat.

A night spent staring at the ceiling takes its toll the next morning. I need two cups of coffee before I feel remotely human, but even then, my eyes still burn with exhaustion.

"Are you okay?" Lucas asks, eyeing my dubiously as he grabs his lunch.

"I'm just a little tired."

"Why don't you head out today with Esme? Go for a walk or a coffee in town. Some fresh air might perk you up."

Leaving the safety of home is the last thing I want to do, but I take Lucas's advice and force myself to go into Coral Bay with Esme.

Walking down Main Street, I'm stopped every few feet. My clothes are complimented, my daughter adored, my spirit restored. After just a few minutes, my life no longer feels like it's falling apart but is instead in the palm of my hand where it should be.

Floating on air, I push Esme into the supermarket.

"What shall we make daddy for dinner tonight?" I ask as we walk through the fresh produce section. "Carrot and orange soup? Strawberry and potato pie?" Esme roars with laughter and my stomach fizzes with love.

Further down the aisle, Anna Townsend stops stacking groceries and turns to me with puppy dog eyes. "Oh Nat, she's such an angel!" She leaves her work and approaches us, beaming at Esme.

"Thank you," I simper.

"It's so great to see you out and about. We've missed you, you know. I can't imagine what you've been going through, first with Hallie and Bree then finding Melissa like that."

The ground gives way beneath me as Anna's unexpected words remind me of all I have lost. I struggle for composure, Melissa's bloodied face suddenly appearing before me. Her lifeless eyes bore into me, begging to know why I didn't save her from Chrissy.

"Have you any news on Bree?" Anna asks, her question attempting to pull me back to reality, but Melissa holds strong. Her desperate nails cling to me, imploring me to help her even though we both know it's too late.

Somehow, I manage to shake my head in response. Heat tickles my neck. I blink, desperately wishing to wash images of Melissa's blood from my line of vision, but all I see is red.

From inside her pram, Esme squawks. Anna beams at her. "I'll say it again, Nat – she's an angel, she really is! You are such a good mum."

With conversation now on neutral ground, I push myself to flatten thoughts of Melissa and fake a smile. Anna and I chat for a few more minutes before I wish her a good day and walk on. At the end of the aisle I take a left, but terror blocks my airways as soon as I do so.

Chrissy Summers is in the supermarket.

Nausea clamps my stomach. I look from side to side to find an ally, a scream trapped inside my throat, but midday and midweek the store is quiet. On trembling legs, I duck into the next aisle and peep around the corner.

Chrissy studies the promotional section two aisles away. A full basket digs into the flesh of her arm. Her hair is swept back from her face and her skin is dewy and fresh. She looks so normal, so unphased by what she has done. A true psychopath.

I take a tentative step forward to get a better view of her.

She picks up a Mexican meal kit and reads the back of the box before dropping it into her basket. After a quick glance over the rest of the day's deals, she walks away.

I weigh up my options for a split second before deciding to follow her. My legs move on autopilot, creeping discreetly behind Chrissy as she makes her way towards the frozen section. My palms sweat, my knees knock, but I don't fall back. There's too much at stake for me to do that.

Chrissy's phone suddenly rings, and she pulls it from her back pocket. "Amira! So great to hear from you!"

"Amira?" I frown.

Bloods pounds in my ears as Chrissy laughs at something Amira says and adds a pack of chicken to her basket. As she makes a move to go down the next aisle, so do I. She's so close I can smell her perfume and see the glint of evil in her eyes.

My cautious steps mirror hers until an unexpected eruption of sound has me leaping in the air.

"Natalie! Wait!"

Spinning on my heel, I turn to find Detective Stone rushing towards me with Esme's pram. "Did you forget something?" she smiles, parking Esme in front of me.

All life exits my body. "I... I..." I stammer, my heart in my throat as I look from the detective to my daughter and back again.

Detective Stone's face falls into a concerned frown. "Are you okay? You're as white as a sheet."

I glance over my shoulder to find Chrissy watching the scene unfold alongside a few key members of Coral Bay's gossip community. Her lips twist into a gleeful smirk and she holds her phone to her ear. "It's Nat. She just left Esme in the supermarket. She's with a detective now."

Her words scorch my skin. I open my mouth to protest, but the sight of everyone watching silences me. Andrew Wright covers his mouth and whispers something into Ellen Wright's ear. Ellen nods in response, her eyes sharp with accusation.

Suddenly, Detective Stone's hand is on my arm. "Shall we go for a coffee?"

Dumbly, I nod and follow the detective out of the supermarket, never once looking back to see the swirl of rumours about me I know will be forming.

29

Sat by the window of Coffee by The Sea, my body trembles with the shame of what I have just done. I take Esme from her pram and hold her to my chest, rocking her backwards and forwards.

"I'm sorry, I'm sorry, I'm sorry," I whisper into her hair. She looks at me as if I've nothing to be sorry for, but of course I do. I left my baby… again.

"What's wrong with me?" I wonder, my eyes dampening.

My legs had worked on autopilot. The need to find out what Chrissy was up to had just taken over. Self-preservation ruled me, but it also left my baby behind. What kind a person leaves a child alone? What kind of mother?

"Here you go," Detective Stone says, setting down our coffees.

I force a smile and wipe my eyes. Detective Stone pretends not to notice my tears. "Thanks," I reply, taking a sip.

We sit in amicable silence for a moment before Detective Stone speaks. "You're looking much better now. For a moment there I thought you were going to faint."

"For a moment, so did I."

"Do you want to talk about it?"

I pause to study Detective Stone. She's pretty in an 'I don't wear makeup and I'm cool with it' way. She radiates with a confident, kind energy. In another life, I imagine we would have made great friends.

But not this life. In this life, she thinks I might be guilty of the worst crime imaginable. How would admitting I was following Chrissy around the supermarket when she found my abandoned daughter make me look?

"I was just going to get some bread. I left Esme for a minute. It's Coral Bay, I knew she'd be safe -"

Detective Stone shakes her head and silences me. "You don't have to explain yourself – you're not being questioned here. I was just worried about you, that's all. You've gone through a lot recently."

"I'm fine," I say, words we both know are a lie.

Gloria, the owner of Coffee by The Sea, chooses this moment to appear at the side of the table. "I'm so sorry to interrupt, but I just wondered if you have any news about what's happened? Everyone's sick with worry, you see. We don't want a killer loose on the streets. Coral Bay's a safe place. It always has been."

Detective Stone smiles politely. "I'm afraid I'm not at liberty to say more than what's already out there."

Gloria's disappointment is palpable.

"But we have lots of lines of investigation open, some of which look really promising."

"That's good to hear. I'm sure talking to Nat will help, too. She knows Coral Bay like no one else. She's practically Coral Bay royalty," Gloria says, clapping me on the back.

I falter. I know her words are meant as a compliment, but I'm not sure making me out to be someone who knows the innermost workings of an entire town is a good thing.

When Gloria walks away, Detective Stone turns to me. "Don't worry, we don't have to talk about the case."

"I'd rather not," I admit, then panic sets in. "Not that I don't want to help find who did this, of course, just that -"

"Just that you didn't expect to run into me today?" Detective Stone laughs. Right on cue, Esme giggles back. "I know I've said this before, but she really is adorable."

"Thank you," I reply, stroking my daughter's hair. "You have a little one too, am I right?"

Detective Stone's features come alive. "Archie. Four years old and the best thing in my life. A real sportsman already, and such a comedian. He drives me mad, but I love him. I'd love to raise him somewhere like this." Detective Stone stares wistfully out of the window. "I can see why you moved back here. The beach is beautiful, the people are kind, and the coffee is to die for. If I had the money, I'd consider moving here myself."

"Coral Bay's great. There's not a day that goes by where I don't feel lucky to be here."

"If you don't mind me asking, why did you ever leave?"

I chew my lip for a moment before I answer. "High school wasn't easy for me. I was unpopular, bullied and… and my mum was sick." Detective Stone's eyebrows furrow together with sympathy, an expression I've grown used to seeing whenever I touch upon this subject. "When she passed away, there didn't feel like there was much to stick around for."

"That must have been terrible. I'm so sorry for your loss, Natalie."

I toy with the handle of my mug. "Coming back here wasn't easy, but Coral Bay is my home. Some of my happiest memories are here. Some of my saddest too, but I wanted to stop looking back and only seeing the bad. I didn't want to be afraid of the place I think of as home forever, so here I am."

"Well, that was a brave decision. It doesn't sound like you had the easiest of times here."

"No," I say softly. "No, I really didn't."

Memories of humiliation and hurt cloud my vision. Taunts fill my head. I wince at the sudden, unexpected onslaught of trauma.

Detective Stone studies my sadness. "For what it's worth, I think bullying is the most disgusting thing."

The corners of my mouth flick in acknowledgement.

Something between us shifts. A barrier breaks. Detective Stone's warm eyes stare into my own. I notice the smatter of freckles across the bridge of her nose. Her top lip is a little too small in contrast to her bottom one.

Her face melts, kind, friendly, approachable. I want to trust her, and more importantly, I want her to trust me.

"I didn't hurt my friends," I blurt out.

Instantly, Detective Stone shuts down and the moment dies. She pulls back in her seat, but I reach out and grab her hand, an act of desperation that surprises even me.

"I didn't hurt my friends," I repeat, my tone forceful and urgent.

Detective Stone removes her hand from my grip, but she takes in my earnest expression. "Do you really think Chrissy Summers did?"

Without hesitating, I nod. "I know her. I know what she can do. Chrissy Summers is capable of more evil than you can even begin to imagine."

Detective Stone's features soften. "We're looking into every lead we get, Natalie. We're doing all we can, that I promise you. Now I best get back to work. Enjoy the rest of your day and take care of yourself, okay? You had me worried back there."

Detective Stone waves goodbye, a friendly act I mirror, but I am dead inside.

I can't tell if she believes me or not. I can't tell if I'm clutching at straws by trying to get her on side. All I know is I believe in my heart that Chrissy is behind this, and I will stop at nothing until my name is cleared and she is outed as the murderer she is.

30

Much to my surprise, when Lucas gets home from work, he doesn't ask me about leaving Esme in the supermarket. I would have thought he would have heard all about it through the Coral Bay grapevine, but if he has, he doesn't show it.

Instead, he's the same doting husband as always, asking about my day and cooking dinner for the two of us. I try to be the wife he knows me as, but something about my performance is off. My reactions are flat, my responses delayed. I will myself to be present in the conversation, but my mind can only focus on Chrissy and how she crops up at every opportunity like a second shadow.

"Was dinner okay?" Lucas asks, taking my barely touched meal and putting into a plastic container to take for lunch tomorrow.

"It was great. I'm just not that hungry," I reply, reaching for my phone to flick through social media. My fingers itch to search for Chrissy's profile but, just as they are about to do so, a text comes through. "Amira wants me to go to yoga with her tonight."

"You should go. Go on, let your hair down!"

"There was a time when 'let your hair down' meant going for a cocktail, not an exercise class…"

"What can I say, we're getting old," Lucas jokes. "Now go get ready!"

That's how I find myself half an hour later dressed in spandex and parked outside Amira's house. With no one around to distract or stop me, I find Chrissy on social media and dig for dirt.

From only a few minutes of searching, I already know so much more about her.

Chrissy's drug problem was serious. She went to rehab four times, but she's clean now, or at least she says she is. She has bounced around a few different cities for the last few years but is back in Coral Bay for the foreseeable future. She used to have a dog called Ringo, but he passed away just over a year ago.

While all of that is great to know, it's just a list of meaningless facts about past Chrissy. It's present Chrissy, murderous, ruin your life Chrissy I'm interested in.

In a short space of time, Chrissy has added most of Coral Bay as a friend. I'm not on her friend list, but that doesn't surprise me. I'm the one to get rid of, not include, right? And Chrissy is going out of her way to include anyone and everyone but me. Her leeching tentacles are embedding themselves in life all over Coral Bay. She's sharing posts from local businesses, wishing people she previously wouldn't dream of speaking to a happy birthday and throwing herself into conversations that before would have been beneath her.

Worse still, she's been meeting up with everyone who matters to me. There's a photo of her and Joelle having a coffee and one of her and Dot together. She's gone for a hike with Becca and drinks with Amira. Bit by bit, person by person, she's pulling them all on side and away from me.

It's not just how social she is that frustrates me, but the content she's producing too. She posts artful shots of the beach and shares pretty selfies daily. Inwardly, I snarl to myself that the photos must be edited, but I know they're not. Chrissy, however old or tired she looks now, will always be beautiful. There's just something about her. She didn't have to run away and transform herself completely like I did. She was just born this way. Born better than the rest of us and knowing it.

Every photo she shares is met with lavish compliments and endless likes. Chrissy's profile already has over one thousand followers. That's four times as many as when I last checked. What if that number keeps growing?

I take another look at her feed and my stomach spasms. There's no artwork on there, but other than that it has loud echoes of my own social media page. Small town, coastal life in all its sunny glory, that's the image she's projecting, and she projects it well. It's painful to admit that some of her beach photographs are even more impressive than my own.

Not only are her photos eerily like mine, but the location tags inform me she's been going to the same beaches, cafes and shops as me. Coral Bay is a small town, but it's not *that* small. Everywhere I have been, so has she. Every step I take, she is one step behind me. The realisation makes my body bristle.

How can I feel safe when Chrissy is circling my life like a vulture just waiting to swoop in and end me?

The car door opening startles me so much I nearly drop my phone. Amira slides into the passenger seat and flashes me a toothy grin. "Are you ready?"

"As I'll ever be for yoga," I joke.

"Just put on your Kate Middleton smile and we'll have a good time," Amira laughs, then she turns to me with a serious expression. "Although I've got to ask – what's this I hear about you ditching Esme in the supermarket?"

My eye twitches at her comment. "I didn't ditch her. I just went to get something from another aisle."

"And left her?"

"I was going back in a second," I protest. "Is everyone talking about me?"

Amira waves her arm dismissively. "Don't worry about it. They'll soon forget. Plenty of women here have done way worse than that. Do you remember when Carole Saunders left her son in Bed World and didn't realise until she got home? Now *that's* a bad mother."

I force a smile, but Amira's words of exoneration do little to soothe me. Clearly I'm the talk of the town, a title I don't want at all, especially when it's because of something so terrible.

Amira clips her seatbelt in and tells me about an upcoming visit from the head of her company. I half listen, but I can't focus on the details. All I can think about is how black and white things seem to Amira, how someone can either be a good mum or a bad mum, popular or unpopular. I wish I had the same courage in my convictions. Everything in my life right now seems grey and wobbly.

Just as we pull up to the gym, Amira hits me with a confession. "I forgot to say, I invited Chrissy tonight."

My body turns to stone. "What? Why would you do that?"

"Keep your enemies close, right?" Amira shrugs, hopping out of the car without a second thought for how I might feel about this.

I want to speed away right here, right now. I can't believe Amira would put me in this situation. We think this woman has killed our friends... why would I want to be around her? Watching Chrissy from afar on social media is one thing but being in a downward dog beside her is something else entirely. I turn icy at the thought.

Amira bangs on the back window of my car, beckoning me to join her. Begrudgingly, I grab my yoga mat and scurry after her. "You could have warned me she was coming."

"But you wouldn't have come if I did."

With a sigh, I concede. "Is this why you rang Chrissy today? I overheard her on the phone to you at the supermarket."

"Why else would I ring the beast?"

"That's what I was trying to figure out," I admit, and then I see her.

Dressed in another lurid gym kit, Chrissy waits patiently outside the gym. My mouth dries at the sight of her, my fear solidifying when she spots us and waves.

Amira hurries over. "I'm so glad you could make it!" she coos, hugging Chrissy close.

My gut tugs at the falseness of it all. I can't believe how good of an actress Amira is. She fusses over Chrissy like she's a puppy, and I can't help but think of all the times Amira has been that way with me.

"Was it all an act?" I wonder. "Does she even like me?"

I can't obsess over the thought for long though because suddenly Chrissy turns to me, her arms outstretched. "Nat, it's good to see you again! I wasn't sure you'd be coming after the embarrassment today at the supermarket, but I'm so glad you decided to show your face in public. Love the leggings, by the way. Did you get them in last year's H&M sale?"

I narrow my eyes. "No, they're -"

"Strange, I could have sworn I saw them then," Chrissy shrugs. "Shall we go in?"

We head towards the door in a three, but it's not wide enough for us all to fit through together. As Chrissy launches into a story about her day that has Amira in stitches, I realise there is no chance Chrissy will let me walk in with Amira, and I'm right. The pair walk through the door together while I trail alone behind them.

All eyes are on us as we enter the yoga studio. The room seems to hold its breath. Hafsah Khan sucks her stomach in self-consciously and Elise Wyatt, another of Chrissy's victims, shrivels like a wilted plant. I offer everyone a smile, but they seem just as intimidated of me as they do Chrissy.

"I'm a nice person!" I want to scream. "Don't associate me with her because we walked in together! She is *not* my friend!"

Taking matters into my own hands, I turn to the nearest person to me. "Elise!" I gush. "So good to see you!"

Elise blinks, a reaction that sits heavy on my chest. While it's true we haven't spoken since I bumped into her at The Oaks a few months ago, Elise is still someone I like.

"How are the kids? How is Anton?" I chirp, trying my best to show Chrissy she isn't the only one making friends in town.

"Good. They're good," Elise replies. "I like your leggings."

"Oh, thanks," I begin, but Chrissy jumps into the conversation.

"Great, aren't they? H&M sale, last year," she says. I glare at her and she smiles back. "Come on, let's get a good spot."

Chrissy pushes her way to the front of the room. No one stops her. I blush at her brashness but follow. If I had it my way, I would shrink away at the back of the class and wobble my way through the moves unnoticed, but I'm not leaving Chrissy and Amira alone for a second. Chrissy's already pushed me out once, but I won't let her do it again.

With a place now secured at the front of the room, the instructor announces the class is about to start. While Amira fawns over Chrissy, I sigh and set out my yoga mat.

For the next hour, I sweat my way through the session, twisting and turning my body into an array of different positions in a room I would do anything to not be in. Amira is a seasoned pro at yoga so she flies through the class, but Chrissy is better than I thought. She tackles every move head on, holds herself strong and barely breaks a sweat.

"That was amazing," she says at the end of the class, throwing her arm around Amira's shoulders. "Thank you so much for asking me!"

"Oh, it was nothing," Amira says, her beaming smile betraying the fact that she is secretly over the moon that Chrissy had such a good time. I try to not show my disgust. As we walk out together, Amira turns to Chrissy. "Do you need a ride home?"

My eyes nearly pop out of my skull. Chrissy in *my* car? Is Amira crazy?!

"That's so kind, but it's okay. I've got a few errands to run. I'll see you later, though – you too, Nat. Don't be afraid to come to the next class. We'll have you able to keep up with us in no time!" Chrissy says, her subtle dig a dagger in my back. She waves as she walks away, then she disappears into the night.

"Bitch," I mutter under my breath when she's out of earshot.

"Well, I thought she was lovely," Amira replies, then bursts out laughing. "The look on your face, Nat! Of course she was a bitch! That's just who she is, and tonight she was on top form. The H&M sale comment still makes me laugh."

"It's not very funny when it's directed at you," I snap as we walk towards my car. "How could you be so nice to her? You think she's murdered our friends, Amira. I don't get it."

"I did what I had to do," Amira says, tensing at the mention of the friends her simpering actions betray.

"And what's that, pretend to be Miss Popular?" I scoff. I slide into my car, slamming the door to prove my anger. "What was the point in asking her tonight, anyway? I had to put up with her bullshit, and we learned nothing."

"That's where you're wrong. We learned so much. One, she hates you."

"Like I didn't know that already," I grumble.

"Still, it's something to note. Two, we know she's hiding something."

My eyebrows furrow. "What do you mean?"

Amira pulls a face. "Errands at this time? Who does she think she's kidding? Something's up with that. She wouldn't let me pick her up when we went for drinks, either. She doesn't want us to drop her home because she doesn't want us to know where she's staying. I'm telling you, Nat, she's hiding something. The next chance we get to find out what that is, we're going for it. We're going to prove she's the killer. Are you in?"

"I'm in," I say without a second thought.

31

I drink a herbal tea and leave my phone downstairs, but I still can't drift off. The idea of being an unconscious, easy target forces me to stay awake. My thoughts are consumed with visions of Chrissy tiptoeing towards me, a knife in her hand, her eyes glinting with triumph like my death is her ultimate prize. I feel her all around me, watching and waiting to pounce.

After tossing and turning so much I wake Lucas, I give into my restlessness. "I'm going downstairs," I whisper into the darkness. Lucas grunts in response, rolling onto his side and falling back asleep.

I slip out of bed and pad into the living room, taking a seat on the sofa. Even though I tell myself not to, my hands work on autopilot and I find myself on Chrissy's Instagram once again.

She's posted another selfie since I last looked, one in her gym kit this time. She looks pretty, her cheeks flushed, her smile wide and carefree. There are twenty-three comments, all of which tell Chrissy how gorgeous she is. One comment even reads, '*you are beautiful inside and out'*.

I want to scream.

In need of relief from the Chrissy loving, I open 'Finding the Good Life'. Since my dismissal of Sunaina, things have slowed a little, but I tell myself that's to be expected. I haven't committed to my online life as much as I used to. A growth of one hundred followers over the last few days is still growth, I remind myself.

I click the comments on my latest post - a flattering, sweat free photo of me taken just before a run. Even though it was posted today, the photo is a few weeks old, not that my followers need to know that.

Seeing as Chrissy posted her workout selfie ten minutes after I shared mine, this is yet another post she has mirror imaged from me.

But the thing that stands out about these photos is not that they are essentially the same, but that Chrissy's is so much better than mine. Not because she looks prettier or because the lighting is more impressive, but because it looks *real.*

She looks like she has really pushed herself. I look like I've changed into gym clothes, headed into my garden to take a photo then gone back inside to relax. Sure, Chrissy's photo is as posed as mine, but it's the message her post sends that's so different to my own. She doesn't come across as someone pretending to be perfect. She looks like someone who naturally *is* perfect, sweaty, out of breath and all.

My hatred swells like a balloon.

I flick through the comments on my post, waiting for a sense of calm contentment to overcome me like it usually does when I read messages from my devoted followers.

U go beautiful mamma!

How have you had a baby and STILL look this good?!

I definitely don't look like this when I work out... you gorgeous girl!

I read and I read and I read... but the feeling doesn't come. The words blur into one, their sentiments hollow.

Then I see it.

You didn't wear those clothes to yoga... is this 'Finding the Good Life' or 'Finding the Bullshit'? Keep it real Nat – your followers deserve better than your lies!!

My mouth hangs open as I reread the comment. Each word spears me like a dagger, not least because in some part they scream the truth.

The handle - @coralbaygirl747 – vaguely rings a bell, then it hits me. @coralbaygirl747 was who commented on my photo with Esme. They started the abuse last time. That's twice they have sent hateful messages and stirred up trouble with my followers.

I click on their profile. There are no photographs posted, no followers and only one person the page follows – me.

My blood turns to ice. Why would this profile only be following me?

I head back to the original comment and see people have replied to it.

Are you suggesting Nat is fake? I've always thought this but never dared say it!

Finding the Bullshit – good one! Nat's turning into just another carbon copy wannabe like the rest of them. I'm so over her #yawn

My cheeks flush as I read comment after comment from people not only agreeing with @coralbaygirl747 but encouraging her and laughing along. All the thoughts and feelings I squashed down when I left high school flood back at such speed my head spins. Then I spot another comment from @coralbaygirl747.

Nat is not who she seems - the truth will out.

The truth will out... what does that mean?

Even though it's not cold, goosebumps line my arms. I check my last few posts, all of which @coralbaygirl747 has commented on in the same slanderous tone.

Yeah, sure you woke up looking like that... how about some honesty on this page for once? You're boring and we are all SO over you now!!

I saw Nat at the supermarket this morning and she did NOT look like that #filtermuch #maybeshesnotbornwithitmaybesheneedsmaybelline

I wish your followers knew what you were really like... YOU FAKE BITCH!!

My hands tremble. I can't believe I didn't notice these comments sooner. I know I've let the ball slip recently, but not spotting such spiteful messages takes ignoring my social media presence to a whole new level. Since when did I become so detached from the things that matter in my life?

Tears fill my eyes as I read the comments over and over again. It's crippling to realise how many people have liked them, how many people have replied in the same vein, how many people find me disingenuous.

Frustration bubbles in my gut. Every day I try so hard to be a person people want to be around, and all it takes is one person to hide behind a keyboard and post a few nasty comments for the tide to turn against me. How is that fair? What did I do to deserve this?

And, most importantly, who the fuck is @coralbaygirl747?

There's only one person I know who would do something this toxic.

I look back to the comment on my running post and snarl. '*You didn't wear those clothes to the gym*' – of course it's Chrissy. She was the only one who was fixated on my leggings.

Naming the profile @coralbaygirl747 too, how clever. She knows I will figure out it's her but never be able to prove it.

"Why would I create a fake profile to harass you, Nat?" she will say patronisingly. "Do you really think I don't have better things to do with my time?"

But of course she'd make a fake profile to target me - she's out to destroy my life. With two of my friends dead and the foundations of my life trembling, where does this end?

If my life the last time I was in Coral Bay is anything to go by, the answer to that question isn't good for me.

32

I wake up groggy, which is unsurprising after I resorted to sneaking one of Lucas's pills to help me sleep. Lucas would be furious if he knew what I'd done, but when I got back into bed all I could think of was Chrissy waiting for the perfect opportunity to destroy me. A pill was the only way I was going to rest.

Lucas pours me a coffee before he leaves for work. "You look wiped out, babe. I'll tell Jay to spend the day with Esme. Just get some rest, okay?"

I nod, but rest isn't on the cards for me. With yet another missed call from Arlene Davies, I need to crack on with work.

I'm in my studio finishing my latest furious, grief washed canvas when my phone rings. I debate not answering, but after the last unexpected call resulted in finding Melissa's body, I'm hardly in the mood to screen calls.

Amira's name flashes on the screen as I pick up my phone. "Hello?"

"Nat, come quick – I've just spotted Chrissy going into the bakery!"

"So?"

"What do you mean, 'so'? Get here so we can follow her! We'll need to be in your car. Chrissy's seen mine before."

I hesitate, eying my half-complete work. I know I should finish it while I'm in the flow of painting, but can I really in good conscience send Amira after Chrissy alone? If anything happened to her, I would never forgive myself. And with Chrissy, anything *could* happen.

"I'll be five minutes." I hang up and exit the studio. "Jay?" I call as I enter the house.

"Yeah?"

I follow the sound of her voice and find her reading a story to Esme in the living room.

"I'm heading out for a few hours – Amira needs me." I don't bother explaining more or changing out of my paint splattered clothes.

Instead, I set off as fast as I can. My fingers drum against the steering wheel as I do my best to focus on the road ahead and not the thudding of my heart.

I reach Main Street in record time. Pulling into the closest available parking space, my tyres screech to a halt. Seconds later, Amira slides into the car dressed in black and wearing large, dark sunglasses.

"Nice disguise," I comment.

"I know you're being sarcastic, but I really don't want Chrissy spotting me. If she is the killer, then she won't be too pleased about being followed, will she?"

Amira's words wipe the smile off my face. I open the glove compartment of my car, pull out a pair of sunglasses and tie my hair up. It's about as inconspicuous as I can be but with Chrissy on the loose it doesn't seem inconspicuous enough.

"What have you seen so far?" I ask.

"Not much. I was just getting into my car when I saw her, then I called you. I figured she can't do anything to me if I'm with someone else."

My stomach knots as I remember all the times Chrissy came for me even with a crowd around. I try to peer into the bakery, but the blinds are angled so I can't see inside. "Has she come out yet?"

"No. That's her car over there," Amira says, pointing to a battered Volkswagen a few spaces over.

Disappointment sideswipes me. "The car they think scared Hallie and Bree off the road is the same as mine."

"They only said they'd seen that car on CCTV. It had no plates so of course it stood out to the police, but that doesn't mean it was the car involved. Besides, Chrissy could have easily borrowed a car and traded it in for that piece of junk to throw the police off her scent. Never underestimate her," Amira warns.

"You don't have to tell me that," I mutter.

Nerves climbing, we sit in silence and watch the bakery. Amira chews the side of her nail, a habit that's already annoying me. The silence swells until it becomes unbearable and Amira cracks.

"I talked to Becca last night. She said she hasn't heard from you in a while. Apparently, she text you about visiting Bree again and you ignored her."

I shuffle in my seat. "I didn't ignore her. I've just been a little distracted."

"That's what I said, but she said you weren't distracted enough to miss going to the gym with me and Chrissy."

"How does she know I went there? Is she talking to Chrissy?"

"I'm telling you Becca is upset with you and all you can take from that is that she might be talking to Chrissy?"

My cheeks flare. "I just don't want Becca putting herself in danger, that's all."

"Hmm," Amira responds, eying me coolly.

"How is Becca, anyway?" I ask, hoping my interest will make me seem less of a shit friend even though it's what I've been.

"The same as the rest of us, I guess. Upset, hurt... scared."

"Does she think someone is going after you all too?"

Amira sighs. "I tried to talk to her about it, but she wouldn't listen. She kept saying how we weren't bad people and how no one cares about school anymore. It's like she's told herself Hallie and Bree drove themselves off the road and Melissa caved her own head in."

I shudder at the thought of Melissa's skull splintering. "Is that how she died?"

"Yeah, blunt force trauma. She'd been stabbed a few times too, but the police said that a blow to the head was what killed her."

I turn to Amira. "They told you that? When?"

"They came over the other day to ask me a few questions."

I remember Detective Baldie's stern, mocking face and grimace. "What did they ask?"

"The usual stuff, I guess. They wanted to know where I was on the morning of the funeral and when Hallie and Bree had their accident."

Relief washes over me like a tidal wave. "They asked you that too?"

"Of course, why wouldn't they?"

I open my mouth to respond but Amira jumps and points ahead. "There she is!"

My heart leaps into my throat as I watch Chrissy wave goodbye to someone inside the bakery and head towards her car. Freshly dyed hair cascades down her back like a blonde waterfall. She's wearing a short skirt despite the grim weather, showcasing impressively toned legs.

"Isn't she terrifying?" Amira breathes.

I don't reply. I'm too scared to. Being in the same vicinity as Chrissy is always terrifying, but in light of recent events it's scarier than ever.

Chrissy unlocks her car and climbs inside, dropping her bags onto the passenger seat. She turns on the ignition and glances over her shoulder, ready to reverse.

"Right, let's go," Amira says, clipping her seatbelt in place.

I don't move. I watch Chrissy pull out of her parking space and set off down the road.

"Nat! What are you doing?! Go!"

Slowly, I turn on the ignition, keeping an eye on Chrissy all the while.

"Nat, come on - she's getting away!"

"This isn't a movie, Amira. We can't get too close, or she'll realise she's being followed."

"We also can't let her get away!"

"Relax... she's gone down Main Street. She can either go right at the end to go to the beach or left to head to the motorway." In the distance,

Chrissy's car turns left. "Motorway it is," I say as I pull out of my parking space.

"But there are houses on the left too."

"I know, but if Chrissy wants to re-establish herself in Coral Bay, she isn't going to waste her time befriending people on that side of town."

Amira scrunches her face. "Didn't you grow up on that side of town?"

"Exactly."

At the end of Main Street, I turn left, navigating my way past the smaller, less expensive houses in Coral Bay. As we pass the familiar turning for Ridge Street, my heart tugs. I haven't been back to my old house since I first left town and still haven't braved going down that street in the following years. There's nothing there for me. Not anymore. Not since mum died.

A fresh spasm of pain tears through my already aching chest.

"Don't think of mum, not today," I command.

I turn my attention back to what's going on inside the car and immediately wish I hadn't. Amira's anxiety is choking. She looks out of her window, scanning the sideroads for Chrissy's car.

"How do you know she won't be stopping here?" she asks.

"I just do."

"But how?"

"Because when you spend so much of your life trying to avoid someone, you learn pretty quickly how they tick."

Amira shoots me a sidewards glance. "You'd better be right, Nat. If I end up in a body bag because of your stupid hunch, I'm going to come back and haunt you so bad you'll wish you were dead too."

I ignore her. I know I'm right. Unfortunately for me, I know Chrissy almost as well as she knows herself.

We join the motorway and I accelerate a little above the speed limit, passing cars either side of me, none of them the car I want to see. Amira's panic rises to suffocating heights the longer we drive without spotting

Chrissy, but I push on.

"There!" Amira shrieks suddenly, pointing in the distance. "She's there!" Amira faces me, impressed. "Good job."

"I told you I knew her well."

"Poor you."

We follow Chrissy from a distance for over twenty minutes before she indicates to leave the motorway. Amira frowns. "Rosevale? What the hell is she doing in Rosevale?"

"No idea," I reply, taking the exit too.

Rosevale is just outside Coral Bay but couldn't be further from it if it tried. Property is cheap, schools are undesirable, and the people are nowhere near as friendly. All the things that make Coral Bay great are things that do not exist in Rosevale. It's an area greasy estate agents would describe as 'up and coming' before shoving you inside the property so you don't realise 'up and coming' is code for shithole.

"Wow," Amira mutters, unable to hide her disgust as we drive through seemingly endless dilapidated streets. "What the fuck is Chrissy doing here?"

I shrug, but I'm thinking the exact same thing. "Maybe she's meeting someone."

"If she's meeting someone from Rosevale then she's definitely the killer. Nothing good – or legal - comes from here."

"My mum's boyfriend was from Rosevale."

"What was he like?"

"He was a dick."

Amira lets out a snort of laughter. She turns and looks out of the window just as we pass a row of boarded-up houses. "Get me back to Coral Bay," she mutters, but she's only half joking. She toys with the sleeve of her shirt, her theory of Chrissy the killer becoming more real before her eyes and making her sweat.

"Just because she's in crime capital, it doesn't mean she's the killer,"

I say diplomatically, but Amira's shrivelling glare silences me. I don't blame her for looking at me like that. I don't believe myself, either.

"Can we cut the bullshit, Nat? Do you really think either of us would be in this car if we didn't honestly believe she was the killer?"

My mouth is too dry to respond, the truth in Amira's words too fearful to fully confront, but I nod.

At the end of the street, Chrissy takes a right. I follow and watch as her car swings into the carpark of Rosevale Motel, which happens to be the most horrific place I've ever seen with my own eyes. Paint peels from the walls and the sign looks like it's about to fall and crush anyone who walks underneath it.

"Rosevale Motel? I know she's not speaking to her parents, but surely she's not staying here?!" Amira gasps.

I slow to a stop, and we watch Chrissy exit her car, grab her shopping and walk to a door labelled with the number 16. From her pocket, she pulls out a key and unlocks the door.

"No *way!*" Amira shrieks. "Chrissy Summers is staying *here*?!"

I must admit, I'm shocked too. Chrissy is not from a poor family. In fact, her parents own one of the biggest houses in Coral Bay. Her mum is one of those glamorous women who swears she's never had cosmetic surgery but clearly has had the best that money can buy. Her dad made a fortune as a divorce lawyer before retiring early. Her parents spend their time holidaying around the world and showing up at charity galas. They are the kind of people who are used to The Ritz, not Rosevale Motel.

"I know Chrissy being back is taking the shine off the King and Queen of Coral Bay, but you'd think if their daughter was in this much of a bad place they'd step up and help a little."

I shrug. "Maybe they don't think she's deserving of their help."

"Maybe not. I wonder if the fact that she's been disowned by her own parents proves she is the killer. You don't kick someone out of your life for being a good person, do you?"

196

"I think we can both safely say Chrissy Summers is not and never was a good person," I reply flatly.

We sit in silence for a moment before Amira shudders so intensely the hairs on my arms stand to attention. "I swear, the more time I spend around Chrissy, the more I'm convinced she is responsible. I mean, why bother coming back if you're going to end up living in Rosevale Motel unless it's to kill everyone you think has wronged you?"

I go hot and cold at the thought. The chances that I'm parked outside the home of a serial killer with a vendetta against me are increasingly likely. A terror like nothing I've ever felt before tingles my toes, slowly spreading its way up my body until I'm paralysed by fear. "What do we do now?"

"I guess we wait."

We lock the car doors and fix our gaze on Chrissy's room. Silence rings out, only interrupted every now and then by Amira's catty quips about the people walking past. She laughs at her own jokes, snorting as people with bad haircuts or men who 'clearly don't go to the gym' pass us.

I feel like I'm hearing her properly for the first time in a long time. "Was she always this cruel?" I wonder.

My friends and I gossiped like any other group. 'Did you hear about Madge's husband's affair' and 'do you know that Susan's daughter is bulimic', the usual small town, mindless chatter, but Amira's comments are another level of brutal. She talks about people's appearances and makes assumptions about who they are as people from that. In her mind, overweight is lazy, poor is stupid.

Every time she laughs, I burn with injustice. She doesn't know these people. She doesn't know what is happening in their lives, yet the comments she makes are so cruel and so personal. The more cutting her remark is, the better she feels about herself. In her mind, she is beautiful next to the new mother who can't afford a personal trainer and powerful next to the man she would reject with a putdown so savage it could scar.

Me? I just feel dirty for being a part of it all.

I'm about to snap and say something when Amira's phone rings. "Hello?" she chirps down the line.

I can't stand listening to the sound of her voice anymore. Disgusted, I turn my attention back towards the motel. It's even more hideous than I remember.

"What is Chrissy doing in a place like this? How down on her luck has she got to be here?" I wonder.

Maybe going from having it all to having nothing would turn you into a murderer. I've been at the bottom. I know what it's like. The top is a much, much nicer place to be. If you had lost all that, maybe you would do anything to get it back, even kill.

Amira's irritated sigh rouses me from my thoughts. "That was work – big emergency. I need to go home and sort it out."

I glance back at the motel. "Shall we call it a day then?"

Amira follows my gaze. The door of Chrissy's room is shut, as it has been since we got here. "At least we know where she's staying now. That's something, right? And it doesn't look like she's going out anytime soon. We've been here for almost two hours, and we've seen nothing."

I nod and turn on the ignition.

We drive back to Coral Bay in relative silence. Amira tries her best to talk, but I don't feel like engaging in conversation. The quieter I am, the more she claws at me for a response. Her stories become wilder, her jokes more outrageous, and I retreat further and further into my shell.

I desperately want things to go back to the way they were. Back to before Hallie and Bree's accident where Amira's jokes were close to the bone but ones I could put up with, but something inside me is blocked. I can't help thinking that what I've heard from Amira today was… well, ugly. If anything, I'm relieved when I pull up outside her house.

"Thanks for the ride," she says.

"No problem. Good luck with work."

Amira gathers her handbag and goes to leave but stops once she's opened the car door. She turns to me. "I know I'm not your favourite person, Nat, and I know I never will be, but being popular is all I've ever known. I don't know who I am without it." She bites her lip sheepishly then meets my gaze. "I just want to say, be careful, okay? I really think you need to watch your back. You're in this group too. You're just as unsafe as I am, more so if anything. You've got more to lose than the rest of us. If I were you, I wouldn't relax until I knew Chrissy had been stopped once and for all."

With that, Amira heads into her house, leaving my terrified mind racing into overdrive and my trembling hands gripping the steering wheel for dear life.

33

My heart is in my throat the entire drive home. Once or twice I even debate pulling over because I'm shaking that much. Amira's stark words of warning play on repeat in my mind like an irritating song you can't get out of your head, only this one isn't irritating – it's petrifying.

Somehow, I make it home without causing an accident. I park on the driveway and glance at the front door. It's only a couple of steps away, but right now that distance feels like miles. Anything could happen to me in the few seconds it would take to rush to safety. Chrissy could strike me down on this driveway and no one would know until Lucas came home later.

"That's not going to happen," I try to reason with myself, but no matter what soothing words I whisper, I can't seem to shake the feeling that danger cloaks me.

I check my rear-view mirror. There's no one there, but the hairs on the back of my neck still stand to attention as if to warn me that someone is watching me.

My hands tremble as I reach for my handbag. I want to delude myself that this is all in my head, but the body count of my friends is ever growing. Chrissy lays into me at every opportunity she gets. She knows more about my life than she should for a woman who has just shown up in town. She's creating fake profiles and harassing me online, for fucks sake.

Nothing in my life seems certain anymore, least of all my identity and the part I have to play in all of this.

Inhaling deeply, I clutch my handbag to my chest and push open the car door. Brisk air slaps my cheeks. I poise myself, ready to dash to the house, only a snarl coming from behind freezes me to the spot.

"I fucking knew it!"

I jump and turn to find Chrissy on my driveway, her face contorted with fiery rage. The world around me stops spinning.

"W... what are you doing here?" I stammer.

"I could ask you the same thing, hiding outside my motel for hours on end. What, did you and Amira think I didn't see you? Your obnoxious car was almost as obvious as your shitty disguises," Chrissy sneers, marching over to me with her hands on her hips. She's so close I can smell her perfume, cheap and overpowering. My head swims in the chemical scent.

"I... I..." I fumble over my words, heat scorching my cheeks.

Chrissy rolls her eyes. "Fuck me, Nat. If you weren't so annoying, I'd almost feel sorry you," she spits before folding her arms across her chest. "Did you get what you were looking for, then? Rosevale Motel, I can write the address down for you if you want to tell everyone where I'm staying."

"I'm not going to say anything to anyone."

Chrissy snorts. "Very honourable of you. So, if you weren't trying to get Coral Bay's biggest scoop of gossip, why were you there?"

My voice stays caught in the back of my throat, too afraid to break free. A fraught silence stretches out between us. Chrissy's annoyance is palpable. I shrink under her intense glare, a move that only serves to irritate her more.

"Why the fuck were you there, Nat?" Chrissy demands, taking a furious step towards me, but her face suddenly transforms into an eerily serene smile.

"Nat? Is everything okay?"

I turn to find a concerned Jay in the doorway of my house. My hero. I could fall into her arms and weep.

"Everything's fine!" Chrissy chimes, her voice sickly smooth. "Nat and I were just arranging our next yoga plans."

Jay hesitates, her expression sceptical.

"It's okay, Jay. I'll be inside in a second," I croak.

Jay nods, her eyes full of disbelief. "Okay. Well, I'll be inside if you need me," she replies, closing the door.

When I turn back to Chrissy, her features are no longer arranged into the perfect neighbour mask but are back to the expression of pure hatred I recognise so well. She takes a step towards me and I'm spiked through the chest by an icy spear of dread. I step backwards, but she moves closer still.

I remember this so well – me backing away while Chrissy comes for me until I am cornered with nowhere to run. I'm fifteen again, only this time I'm more scared than I ever was back then. This time, my life really is on the line.

My back hits into my car and suddenly I am trapped.

"I don't know why you were following me or what you want but you will not win this," Chrissy whispers, her face now inches away from mine. "I didn't come back here to have an insignificant speck of dust like you ruin it for me. If you get in my way again, I will destroy you. And don't think I won't – I've done it before."

With that, Chrissy turns and walks away.

It's only when I hear her car turn off my road that I finally dare to breathe again.

34

Jay knows I'm lying when I tell her everything is okay, but she has the good sense to not push me. She just offers a listening ear if I need it. I thank her but I know I will never speak to Jay about what happened on the driveway. Not now what started out as a nagging suspicion has turned into a full body, shake you to the core conviction.

Chrissy Summers killed my friends.

'I will destroy you. And don't think I won't – I've done it before' – what else could that mean?

I need to prove what she has done, and I need to prove it before anyone else gets hurt.

But how? How can I admit to following her without looking crazy? How can I accuse her of murder without concrete proof? No one else heard her on the driveway. It would be my word against hers, and the way Detective Baldie looks at me doesn't fill me with much confidence that I'd be believed.

But I know she did it.

There was never a line Chrissy Summers would not cross. Someone else's boyfriend, drugs, violence, stealing… it was all in a day's work for her. She took what she wanted with confidence and a smile as if it had always belonged to her. Why wouldn't that attitude stretch to murdering someone to get her own way?

With trembling hands, I find myself looking through my yearbook again. Every picture is its own special kind of torture. It is a portal to a life I was always able to view but never participate in. The sports games, the social clubs, the cliques… I was always on the periphery. I'm not in a single photograph – why would I be? Who would want to remember me?

But I was there.

I was *there.*

I remember it so well it brings tears to my eyes. I remember the sweaty gym hall and the way people's trainers squeaked on the floor when they walked across it. I remember the chaos in the corridors between classes, a blur of navy uniforms and excitable babble I was always excluded from. I remember the smell of Juicy Couture perfumes, Lynx, and cheap hairspray, of hope and fear and the dizzying possibility of youth.

I remember Chrissy and her gang and how they made my life hell. The names I can never forget, the scars from wounds too deep to fully disappear when they healed… I remember it all.

I close the yearbook and hug it to my chest.

If I could go back and change everything, I would. I would do anything to be in one of those photos. I would do anything not to be the person I used to be.

I lie on the sofa, desperately trying to hold myself together while everything inside me begs to fall apart. Time blurs until a knock at the front door echoes out into the house. Terror grips me, but I tell myself that if Chrissy is going to kill me, she wouldn't announce her arrival. It's only a small comfort, but one that gives me the push I need to answer the door without tears in my eyes.

When I do, it takes me a second to register the sight of a nervous Becca on my doorstep. "I hope you don't mind me dropping by," she says, "I just thought I'd see how you are after… well, you know. After what happened."

A strange tension fills the air, but I force a smile and push past it. "That's so kind of you! Please, come in," I say, throwing open the door and leading Becca to the living room.

We sit in an awkward silence for a moment before I crumble.

"I'm so sorry I haven't called. I just…" I trail off, not knowing how to finish my sentence.

"It's okay, Nat. I can't imagine what you've been going through after finding... after what you saw."

Melissa's bloodied face flashes before my eyes, an image I quickly blink away. I focus my attention on Becca. Exhaustion has greyed her eyes and breakouts line her chin, worlds apart from her usual glamorous self. Guilt plucks at my chest.

"I went to see Bree yesterday," she informs me.

"How's she doing?"

"She's the same as when we last went, but I could tell she was glad I was there. I squeezed her hand and I swear I felt her squeeze mine back. The nurse didn't believe me, but Bree's mum did. I think she'd really love it if you went to visit her too. We could go together if you'd like."

"I'd love that."

Becca and I share a smile, the stretched ties between us moulding together again as if the events of the last few weeks never happened. It's a beautiful moment, one I didn't realise I needed until now.

Suddenly, Becca spots my yearbook on the table. She reaches for it, stroking the cover with the ghost of a smile on her lips. "Now this takes me back," she says. A dreamy, faraway expression sweeps across her face. She flicks through the first few pages. "What I wouldn't give to do it all again."

"Me too," I reply sadly. "I'd love to go back and do it differently."

"Really? I wouldn't change a thing."

Her words twist in my gut. I fight to shrug them off like I used to whenever my friends relived their glory days, but this time the words won't disappear when I try swallowing them down. I do my best to not look disgruntled, but distaste is written all over my face.

Becca cocks her head. "What's wrong?"

"I... I just..." I study Becca with her quizzical eyebrows and shocked expression, and something inside me snaps. "You wouldn't change *anything*? Nothing at all?"

Becca shakes her head.

"You wouldn't be nicer? You wouldn't not burn James McAllister's school bag even though you knew his family was so poor they'd never be able to afford another? You wouldn't not throw Josephine Riley down the stairs? You wouldn't not call Sonny Peters' mum and out him as gay before he got the chance to tell her himself? You wouldn't be nicer to me?"

"Nat, we weren't that bad -" Becca begins, but I scoff so loudly she jumps.

"What makes you think you get to decide how bad you were? The people who experienced what you did, the people who *lived* it, think you were plenty bad enough."

Becca sits up straighter. "Have you been talking to Amira? Has she put you up to this?"

"Nobody's put me up to anything, Becca. I have my own mind – I'm not like you."

Becca blinks, stung. "That was uncalled for."

"I guess you don't like a taste of your own medicine, do you?" My acidic words burn my mouth as I spit them across the room at my wounded friend, but I can't stop. Now I've opened the flow of abuse, there is no lid that can contain my anger. "You were a bitch, *Bex*, and don't you ever forget it."

Becca lowers her gaze, her cheeks burning an indignant red. "Look, I'm sorry you're struggling at the minute Nat, but I really don't think I should have to defend what I did when I was fourteen."

"No, you've just got to live with it on your conscience for the rest of your life. Oh, and justify it to whoever is coming after you for what you did."

Becca's face floods. "So you have talked to Amira. Well, there's no truth in it. No one cares about school anymore. Chrissy said –"

I snort with laughter. "Chrissy? Becca, Chrissy is the top suspect!"

Becca tenses. "There's no such thing as a suspect. Hallie and Bree had an accident because Hallie was drink driving, and Melissa... Melissa..."

"Melissa what? Melissa fell on a knife? Melissa beat herself to death?"

Becca's shoulders slope inwards like she is physically trying to protect herself from my words. "Melissa…Melissa was hurt, but it was a random attack. A home invasion or something, okay?"

"Becca, two of your friends were murdered and one is brain damaged… when are you going to wake up and realise what is going on? Someone is hunting you down!"

"You don't know that!"

"How else do you explain it?!" I cry. "The only thing tying you all together other than the fact that you were friends is that you were all in the same bullying gang!"

"That's not true!"

"Yes, it is, and you know it is! Or maybe there's another explanation," I hiss. "How about the fact that you were all such good friends with your darling Chrissy, yet you dropped her the second her life wasn't quite so glamorous. No wonder she hates you. Maybe she's right for hunting you down for abandoning her when she needed you the most. Maybe you all deserve what's coming your way."

I level my gaze with Becca. Her bottom lip trembles, willing me to take it all back, but I won't. I refuse to. She can't be this naïve or this in denial about who she once was and the hurt she once caused, not when the memories of it fuel my every move and keep me awake at night.

Becca swallows her tears and rises to her feet. "Do you know something, Nat? The only person I've spoken to who sounds like they want to hurt any of us is you."

With that, Becca storms out of the house just as Lucas gets in from work. I don't feel anything when I watch her go, or when Lucas asks me what's going on.

"Nothing," I shrug.

"Nat, Becca's just left the house in floods of tears and -"

"I said nothing!" I push past my husband, the guy no one could believe I got, the man who will never, ever know what it feels like to be anything other than adored. He will never understand.

No one will. No one knows what it was like to be me back then. A victim. A non-person.

I wonder what would have happened to me if teenage Nat hadn't had her voice beaten out of her. Would I be happy? Would I be safe? Would this nightmare even be happening?

I wish more than anything that I could turn back time and save myself from the danger that is to come, but I'm as helpless now as I was back then.

Then.

Countless cars drive past the girl as if she isn't there. Multiple people have seen her sat on the same bench on Main Street for over two hours now, but not once have any of them come to check she is okay. Everyone always makes out that Coral Bay is so friendly, but it's not. She's clearly been crying, but does anyone care? No. She isn't a Chrissy of this world, so why would they?

The girl draws her knees to her chest, fighting to stay warm. She had meant to go home after school, but as she drew nearer to the house the sound of arguing spilled out onto the street.

He was screaming, the rage and hatred in His voice as suffocating as a chemical. He said the cancer was her mum's fault for being a rotten whore. He said He was counting down the days until she died.

As soon as the girl heard Him say that she knew she couldn't go into the house because if she did, she would kill Him. Then she would kill her mother for accepting His shitty treatment and for making her put up with it too.

So, she turned and ran to Main Street where cutesy boutiques invite customers with fancy credit cards and fresh blow dries to spend their fortune without a care in the world. That is where she has sat undisturbed and alone for the last few hours.

Alone - the story of her life.

Dot from Dot's Designs flips over the 'open' sign on her door so it reads closed. A few seconds later, she's outside locking up. Dropping her keys into the expensive handbag balancing over her arm, Dot turns and spots the girl. Her eyebrows shoot up.

For a second, the girl thinks Dot's worried to see her out so late, but then her brows furrow with irritation and all hopes of having someone care are dashed.

"What are you doing loitering around at this time? Don't you have a home to go to?"

The girl wonders if she should explain herself. She has a home, but He is there. His temper is there. His rage stains the walls. His words and his fists bruise her weakened mother. "I'm scared," she wants to admit. She has nowhere to go, no one to look out for her.

"You know, you're really lowering the tone of the area. Shoo!" Dot snaps, waving her arms. "Go home! Shoo!"

Struck by shock, the girl stumbles to her feet and walks away. She cannot believe she is following the orders of someone who has 'shooed' her like a stray dog. In a life already made up of a series of low moments, the injustice of this one seems to stick with her more than usual.

Something inside the girl breaks and she turns back. "I have a right to be here, you know. I live here too!"

"And what a shame that is," Dot sighs, climbing into her car and driving away without a second glance at the victim of her devastating blow.

The girl watches Dot's car until it disappears from sight. Her eyes stay fixed on the road long after it has gone.

Dot probably has a hot meal waiting for her when she gets home, the girl surmises. There is probably someone there who will ask about her day and offer to run a bubble bath when they hear about the insolent teenager Dot had to put in their place.

The girl daydreams about Dot's life for a while, losing herself in her thoughts so much so that she doesn't notice Chrissy sneaking up on her.

"Boo!" Chrissy laughs as the girl jolts with fear. "What are you doing out here? Don't you live under a bridge or something?"

Chrissy's friends snigger. They've been drinking. She can smell the alcohol on them, strong and pungent. Underage wannabe party girls trying to impress older kids with their miniscule clothing and determination to prove they're all grown up. The way it always is with rich kids who are over life already even though they're only in their teens. People who know nothing about the horrors awaiting some people when they get home. People who are blind to the fact that only the privileged have the luxury of being bored.

"Looking at clothes you can't afford?" Amira says, nodding at Dot's Designs.

"Dot's clothes are fucking tragic, but even they're too good for you," Chrissy grins.

"My mum's cleaning rags are too good for her," Hallie jokes.

The others fall about laughing. The girl lowers her head, letting their words wash over her like waves of the ocean.

"Here, help yourself to some," Chrissy says, picking up a rock and launching it at the window of Dot's Designs.

The glass splinters instantly, the cracks deep and widespread.

For a second, everything stays suspended in a moment of disbelief. No one moves. No one can quite believe what Chrissy has done. She's always taking things to the extreme, but smashing up a business? That's a whole new level, even for her.

"Chrissy, what the fuck?" Bree gasps, half giggly, half terrified. "What have you done?"

"What have I done? You mean what has Fish Sticks done."

There's a moment where the girl hopes that surely they will tell Chrissy she's gone too far this time. Surely they know framing her for a crime she didn't commit is wrong?

But that moment never comes. All she sees is a group of girls with glassy, intoxicated eyes nodding at their all-powerful leader.

"Fish Sticks, you're so bad!" Melissa slurs.

"Maybe your rotten smell has rotted your soul," Bex giggles, a *comment that earns her a high five from Chrissy.*

The girl opens her mouth to protest, but no words come out.

"Come on, we'd better sober up. Someone needs to call the police and report this hideous crime!" Chrissy cries.

At the mention of the police, something inside the girl jolts into life. "But I didn't -" she protests, only to be silenced by Chrissy pushing her hard in the chest.

"Yes, you did, you little bitch. You are a stain on life. You are an embarrassment. The sooner everyone sees that the better, then hopefully you fuck off out of here for good." Chrissy's words are slurred, but her hatred still shines through.

The drunk girls walk away, their tanned, slender arms linked, their taunting laughter ricocheting down Main Street.

The girl watches after them, powerless. It's their word against hers, their lie against her truth. Who would the police believe, Chrissy or Fish Sticks? The girl who can afford to go on shopping sprees in the city every weekend or the girl whose clothes barely fit anymore? The girl with it all or the girl who no one would notice if she disappeared?

She studies the destroyed window of Dot's Designs and, for a moment, she almost believes she did it. Destroying something you can't have would be something an embarrassment to humanity would do, right?

But she knows she didn't do it. Deep down, she knows she is not a bad person, no matter what they say.

Only it's starting to take longer for her to be able to convince herself of that these days. The more they push her, the more she wavers. The more they push her, the more she loses herself and becomes exactly who they paint her out to be.

Now.

35

I wake with a pounding, hangover-like headache even though I didn't drink the night before. My sleep was so restless that in the middle of the night Lucas ordered me to keep still. "I've got to be up for work in three hours," he grumbled.

I waited for him to fall back asleep before siphoning another of his pills to knock me out.

The lack of sleep and my half-dazed-from-medication nature has heightened the irritation swelling between us. We manoeuvre around each other like strangers in a hostel. Lucas pours himself a cup of coffee yet doesn't even get a mug out of the cupboard for me. I respond in an equally 'fuck you' way and only make toast for myself.

We eat in silence. Lucas looks over to me a few times as if he has something to say, but then he thinks better of it and keeps quiet.

"What?" I snap when I catch him glancing at me for the millionth time, my tone so sharp Esme starts to whimper.

"Woah, Nat," Lucas begins, but the doorbell rings and saves us the pain of having this conversation on no sleep.

"I'll get it," I mutter.

Running my fingers through my wild mane, I escape the hostility of the kitchen and throw open the front door. Whoever I was expecting to find on my doorstep, it was not Detective Baldie and Detective Stone.

I blink. "What are you doing here?"

"We're here to buy a painting," Detective Baldie replies.

Detective Stone doesn't even roll her eyes or grimace to chastise him. "Mrs Redding, we're here to invite you down to the station to answer a few questions," she says, her tone cool, her words anything but.

"The station? Can't we answer them here like we usually do?"

"I'm afraid not. With recent findings, we think it's time we spoke to you in a more formal setting," Detective Baldie says. I can't help but notice his eyes gleaming as if payday has come early.

My face burns. "What findings?"

"We can wait for you to get dressed, if you'd like," Detective Stone says, dismissing my question.

"I can't go to the station - I have my daughter here."

Detective Baldie tilts his head. "Well, it's a good job you have a nanny then, isn't it?"

I open my mouth to offer another feeble excuse, but the sound of footsteps approaching distracts me.

"Is everything okay?" Lucas asks, joining us in the doorway with a now calmed Esme in his arms.

"We just need Mrs Redding to come to the station to answer a few questions, that's all," Detective Stone says, smiling at Lucas.

Lucas looks from the police to me. "The station? Why does she have to go there?"

"I think that's a conversation we'd best have with Mrs Redding."

Lucas's frown lines deepen. My head swims. "I... I don't understand," I stammer.

"Alright then, where were you yesterday, Mrs Redding?" Detective Baldie asks.

I think back to yesterday, to Rosevale Motel and to Chrissy on my driveway. My body tingles. "I was home, painting and -"

"Was this before or after you followed Chrissy Summers to her motel and waited outside for over two hours?" Detective Baldie cuts in, bored of my dawdling bullshit already.

Lucas turns to me, his expression a heartbreaking mixture of shock, confusion, and anger. My face crumples. I want to reach for him, but I know that if I try, he will bat me away. This is a step too far for him to understand.

"Or before or after you told Rebecca Harper that someone is hunting her because she used to be a high school bully?" Detective Baldie adds, sticking the knife in a little deeper.

If I thought Lucas's expression was gut wrenching before, the one on his face now makes it look nothing but positive. His grip around Esme tightens.

"It wasn't like that!" I protest, pleading with Lucas to hear me out, but Detective Baldie clears his throat.

"That's something you can explain to us at the station."

I shake my head, trying to make sense of what is happening, of how quickly the tables have turned on me. Everything spins. I move towards Lucas, but he pulls away.

"Mrs Redding," Detective Stone says. "If you could go get dressed now, please."

I look from the stony-faced detectives to my horror-stricken husband and back again. I want to shout at them that I am the victim here, to yell at them for bringing their unfounded insinuations into my home and for looking at me like I am hiding something.

But I don't.

Instead, I trail miserably upstairs, conscious of three pairs of eyes boring into my back and wondering if I really am the person they thought I was.

36

The room I'm left in is sterile and bare, with just two chairs on the opposite side of the table and nothing else. A sad shade of blue coats the walls. The only sound cutting into the eerie silence is the ticking of the clock hung above the door. It's the kind of interrogation room you see on bad police dramas, a comparison that only heightens my fears.

I know I've been left in here alone on purpose. The detectives are probably watching me from a CCTV monitor somewhere and studying how I react to this bewildering situation I have somehow found myself in. Waiting for an innocent gesture they can twist and pin down as guilt.

Well, I refuse to give them anything. I haven't done anything wrong.

I sit with my hands on my lap, hidden from view, and pinch the flesh of my fingers until the skin screams. My blank gaze stares ahead, focusing on the same spot on the table before me. There's a mark on the surface, a scratch from someone been and long gone. I wonder who they were. Why were they here? Were they guilty? Did they feel as terrified as I do?

A bead of sweat trickles down the back of my neck, but the only thing I'm sweating about is my marriage. The way Lucas looked at me when I left the house… I shudder at the memory.

Voices on the corridor outside warn me of the detectives' imminent arrival. I stay still, silent and composed. A few seconds later, they enter the room.

"Sorry about the wait," Detective Stone says as she takes a seat. I'm about to respond reassuringly when I see the trace of a smirk on Detective Baldie's face. I press my lips together in a thin, straight line.

Detective Baldie announces the date and time, then sets his gaze on me. My mouth dries. "Mrs Redding, can you tell us why you're here today?"

Underneath the table, I pinch my thigh. The sharp pain breaks my heightened anxiety and allows me to speak. "You want to know why I followed Chrissy Summers," I reply. My voice sounds strange, like it's being held underwater. I'm furious with myself. I don't want to seem any different to the other times we've met. Detective Baldie doesn't need another reason to suspect me, not when there's already a determined glint in his eye.

"We received a complaint from Chrissy Summers stating that you followed her and waited outside her room for over two hours. She was very distressed," Detective Baldie begins.

I itch to shout that I am the one in distress, that Chrissy should be the one sat in this seat, not me, but I hold the words inside. "Amira called me to say she had spotted Chrissy in Coral Bay and wanted to follow her. She asked me to go with her."

"Why did you say yes to that?" Detective Stone asks.

With nothing to lose, I answer honestly. "Because I don't trust Chrissy Summers's sudden reappearance in Coral Bay, and I didn't want Amira to go after her alone."

"Why is that?"

I level my gaze with the detectives. "Because I don't believe Chrissy is a safe person to be around."

My words hang heavy in the air.

Eventually, Detective Baldie sits back in his seat. "The thing is, we spoke to Miss Johal after our conversation with Miss Summers. She confirmed she had been with you in the car but told us that you were the one who wanted to follow Chrissy Summers, not her."

I blink. "But that's not true."

Detective Baldie shrugs. "Well, I'm afraid at the moment it's your word against Miss Johal's and she was really quite insistent that this was your doing. Following Miss Summers was apparently all your idea."

"But it wasn't. Amira phoned me, Amira asked me." I protest.

My head spins. Why would Amira lie?

I don't have time to think about it, though, because Detective Baldie leans closer, his expression the epitome of patronising. "I'd like to believe you Mrs Redding, I really would, but the part of your story I don't understand is if Amira Johal wanted to follow Chrissy Summers, why would she wait for you? Why wouldn't she just follow her herself?"

"Because she knew Chrissy would recognise her car, so we needed to go in mine," I explain. "Besides, Amira didn't want to go alone. She thinks Chrissy is dangerous."

"And why would she think that?"

Knowing all too well that Detective Baldie already knows the answer to his question, impatience grips me. "Because she wrote a list of people she thinks might want to hurt her and put Chrissy at the top of that list."

"Ah yes, I remember – the list of suspects you helped her to compile. The list of suspects you were adamant Chrissy should be on."

I sit forward indignantly. "Amira wanted to put her on the list too. She brought it up, not me. She thinks Chrissy is as much of a suspect as I do, if not more seeing as she was the one who wanted to follow her in the first place."

"Yet you were the one driving the car…"

My eyebrows furrow. "I only followed her because Amira asked me to."

"What about that day in the supermarket?" Detective Stone asks. Her interjection knocks the air from my lungs. "You were following Chrissy then, weren't you? Amira wasn't with you, but you were still following Chrissy."

"That… that was different. That was a heat of the moment thing."

"And leaving your house in the middle of the day to follow a woman running errands wasn't?"

I'm silenced. What can I say to that? How can I exonerate myself? Why even bother? They've already made their minds up about me. Somehow, despite everything she has done, Chrissy is the victim, and I am the psychopath.

"Well, isn't this a tough one," Detective Baldie sighs. His acting is so blatantly fake it makes my teeth grate against each other. "You say one thing, Miss Johal says another. Who am I supposed to believe?"

"Me!"

"Look, I'll spell it out for you, Mrs Redding - Miss Johal claims that she rang you because she was scared. The list you complied together put Chrissy Summers as a suspect. When Miss Johal ran into her unexpectedly, she was frightened. She claims she rang you to calm down, but that you only confirmed she should be scared and suggested following Miss Summers."

"That's not true!" I argue, my volume rising a decibel.

Instantly, I regret it. Detective Baldie smiles like he has already won. I clench my hands together, imagining his thick neck is between them, and swallow the overpowering urge to lean across the table and throttle him. "Amira and I both wanted to follow Chrissy. We are both scared of her, and with good reason. Chrissy Summers was on my driveway when I returned home. She followed me back!"

"Miss Summers admits to following the car she had seen outside her home to find out who was watching her and why. She was scared."

The absurdity of Detective Baldie's last statement is too much for me ignore and I snort. "Chrissy Summers doesn't know scared. She wanted to threaten me. She was angry -"

"Wouldn't you be angry if you were being followed?" Detective Stone cuts in.

I open my mouth to snap a bitter reply but catch myself just in time. I wrestle for composure. "Look, maybe I should have said no to Amira, but I went because she was scared and she asked me to. She's my friend.

I don't want anything to happen to her. I just wanted to help."

"Just like you wanted to help Rebecca Harper when you told her she was being hunted for being a high school bully? Just like when you told her she, and I quote Miss Harper here, 'deserves what's coming her way'?"

"It wasn't like that," I whisper.

"We have a statement from Miss Harper stating it was just like that. You can read it, if you'd like. It talks all about how Miss Harper left your home in tears after you tried to convince her someone was going to hurt her. Apparently, you were particularly adamant that someone was Chrissy Summers. Is that not the case?"

I want to scream 'no', but what's the point? They're not listening to me. No one's listening to me.

Detective Baldie leans in. "You are friends with Rebecca Harper, is that right?"

"Yes."

"Good friends?"

"Yes, definitely."

"And you were both friends with Melissa Curtis? Good friends?"

Suddenly, I am terrified. I know exactly what's going to come next and exactly how it's going to make me look, but what can I do?

I nod.

"Then why is it since the death of Melissa Curtis, you haven't reached out to Rebecca Harper once?" Detective Baldie slides a piece of paper with screenshots of text messages between Becca and me printed on it. The last four messages are from Becca, asking how I am, telling me she misses me, sending her love.

All four texts I have read.

All four texts I have ignored.

I swallow with difficulty. "I've been struggling with what happened," I reply, but even I know my excuse is weak. "It's been so overwhelming.

I've just wanted to be alone."

"But not alone enough to not answer Amira Johal's call or follow Chrissy Summers. Not alone enough to make sure you meet enough people to put Chrissy Summers's name in the line of inquiry as much as possible," Detective Baldie states.

My head spins. I don't trust myself to speak.

"Why did you come back to Coral Bay?" Detective Stone asks. Her question catches me off guard. "You've told us many times you were bullied here. Plus, we know your mother had cancer for most of your teenage years and sadly passed away." Something inside me twists at the mention of my mother, the pain of losing her still so raw even after all these years. "Life in Coral Bay can't have been easy. So why come back?"

I study my hands, tracing my lifeline with my eyes. There's a fracture in it. When I was younger and at my lowest, I used to tell myself that was the moment something amazing was going to happen to me. That idea used to get me through the worst moments, but now the memory chokes me.

"Coral Bay was my home. It was where my mum and I were happy, at least when I was little, anyway. I didn't want my only story here to be a sad one," I reply, my voice thick from admitting one of my most painful truths to two strangers.

I meet the detectives' gaze. Their hard eyes stare back at me, cold and unmoved. They don't believe me; it's written all over their faces.

But they should. I am the victim here and, yet again, everyone is turning a blind eye to that. History is repeating itself, only this time the consequences aren't a few cuts and bruises – this time it's life and death.

A newfound wave of determination surges through my veins.

"I know not texting Becca looks bad, but I couldn't face it. Loosing Melissa… finding her like that…" I trail off, then pull myself together. "Following Chrissy was wrong, but I promise you that Amira asked me to go. She asked me to help her make the list. I don't know why she's changing her story, but I've sat with her over these last few days. She's just as scared of Chrissy as I am. The person you should be talking to right now isn't me. It's Chrissy Summers."

Detective Stone opens her mouth to speak, but Detective Baldie jumps in first. "Why should we speak to Chrissy Summers?"

I look at him as if he's insane. "Don't you think it's a bit suspicious that bad things only started to happen when she came back to Coral Bay? Everyone who has died has been connected to her, even Blaine Rankin."

Both detectives perk up.

"Blaine Rankin?" Detective Stone asks, her tone measured but she's clearly salivating at the thought of a new thread to pull that all started with me.

I falter but remind myself that all I can do is be honest. "He was someone else we went to school with. He was a bully too. He committed suicide a few months ago. Even at the time of his death, everyone thought it was suspicious. Blaine was just too full of life. Chrissy was in the city at the time it happened. She met up with him two weeks before he died – there are photos on Facebook."

"It's great that you've played social media detective for us," Detective Baldie says dryly, "but you said Blaine died of suicide. If a coroner found that to be the cause of death, then I'm struggling to see how Chrissy Summers can be at fault for that."

I hold his gaze. "Let's just say that I wouldn't put it past Chrissy to make it look like that."

I study the detectives as they digest this new piece of information. Neither of them gives much away, but I've said it now. I have told them the truth that screams in my core - Chrissy is the killer.

My only question is – do they believe me?

37

Detective Baldie instructs an officer to take me home. He waits with me while the officer grabs their keys and holds the door for us on the way out. "Goodbye, Mrs Redding. I'm sure we will be seeing each other again very soon," he says ominously.

I try to not look rattled, but my trembling body gives me away. Head down, I scurry towards the vehicle and slide into the back, praying that the journey home will be quick.

However, the officer driving seems to have other plans. They take the scenic route, parading through Coral Bay with me in the back of the squad car like it's no big deal. Neighbours and so-called friends stare as I pass, turning to gossip as soon as they think they're out of my sight, but I see them. I see the look of shock that turns into delight as their imaginations go into overdrive and they fantasise about my epic fall from grace. Everyone will want to know what's gone on. Everyone will be talking about me and there is nothing I can do to stop them.

Humiliation singes my cheeks. I turn my attention to my phone to avoid making eye contact with anyone else. There are two texts waiting from Arlene Davies, the first reading:

Nat, you are contractually obligated to update me with your progress. I've been trying to get in touch with you for weeks now. You need to respond, or you are in violation of our agreement.

The second is more to the point.

Call me NOW.

I exit the conversation without replying and open 'Finding the Good Life'. Ignoring my bursting inbox, I flick to my latest post, a smiling photo of me at the beach that was scheduled to post two hours ago. I open the comments.

Sure enough, @coralbaygirl747 has commented.

How can Nat be at the beach when I've just seen her heading into Coral Bay Police Station? Seems like she's guilty of more than just being a fraud online…

I bite my lip to hold in a scream, tears prickling my eyes as I see how many interactions this comment has had. My hands tremble as I read the replies.

The police station? Wtf?!

Omg talk about Insta VS Reality…

What was she talking to the police for?!?!

I burn with the injustice of it all. For starters, I want to reply that it's common practice for influencers to schedule their posts, but that's not the part that upsets me – it's the insinuation that I'm not who I say I am. Whatever @coralbaygirl747 says is being turned into fact without anyone checking the merit behind her words.

Chrissy has been so clever with her online campaign of hate. She knew I would be questioned today. After all, she rang the police about me, but of course she didn't go to them because she was scared. She went to them so she could post this comment and bring me down.

I grit my teeth and start writing a post explaining everything going on in my life right now and detailing my hurt at the nasty comments, but I stop myself.

Chrissy cannot know she has got to me. Responding will only encourage her to keep going, that's handling bullies 101.

Besides, I know that as soon as I post anything, I will be inundated with well-meaning messages from my followers. A bunch of strangers telling me I'm great isn't what I need right now – I need my friends.

But what friends? The friends who have been cruelly stolen from me, the ones I'll never get to see again? Or the friends who lied about me to the police?

A fresh swell of rage pumps through my body. Fuelled by anger, I text Amira.

Just heading back from the police station now. Apparently you had a lot to say about me… some friend you are!

I press send then copy and paste the same message to Becca.

Within seconds, Amira replies.

What???? I had to tell them we followed Chrissy! If she's as guilty as you think she is then they need to follow her too. She's a suspect now. Isn't this what you wanted?

I grit my teeth. Trust Amira to miss the point completely.

My problem isn't that they know we followed her – my problem is that they think it was my idea. They're making it sound like I'm obsessed with her!

I watch as the typing bubbles appear, then disappear, then reappear again. Fury chokes me at Amira's inability to message back quickly, but eventually a response comes through.

It doesn't matter whose idea it was to follow her – you're convinced she's behind this and for safety it wasn't wise for one of us to go alone. Maybe you are obsessed with her, but how else can you be if you think she's a killer? Sorry if I've upset you, babe – it's the last thing I'd ever want to do. You know I love you! Don't hate me.

Amira's insincerity grates against me like nails down a chalkboard. Too pissed off to reply, I exit the chat and check my exchange with Becca. She's not even bothered to read my message.

I let out a small, bitter laugh. The officer driving jumps at my sudden outburst, but I don't explain. How can you explain how tragically funny it is that a person can go from having it all to losing it all within the space of a few weeks?

Every fear I have ever had is coming to life and I don't know what to do to stop. Right now, quite frankly, I don't think I have it in me to even try.

We turn onto Maple Drive and I slip my phone back into my pocket. There's no time to hide behind a screen anymore – reality awaits.

I thank the officer for the ride and stand on the pavement outside my house. It's impressively beautiful, I can still admit that, but the sense of tranquillity that usually waves me down the driveway is no longer there. Instead, I notice how imposing the building is, how it looms above me like a teacher chastising a student.

Lucas's car is parked in the driveway. He must have stayed home from work. Normally the sight of his car and knowing he is home makes my heart skip a beat, but not today.

To waste a few seconds before facing his fury, I grab the mail then psych myself up to go inside.

The driveway has never felt so long, but I keep going and soon I find I am inside and slipping my shoes off. "Hello?" I call out into the house.

Silence.

I peep into the living room and Esme's playroom, but they're both empty. For a moment, my heart hammers and I wonder if Chrissy got me out of the house so she could inflict her worst damage, but then a burst of laughter from the kitchen rings out. I follow the sound, pushing the door open to find Lucas and Jay playing a game with Esme. They freeze when they see me as if I'm the ghost of a life they would rather forget. I freeze when I see them because they look so happy without me, I feel like running away and leaving them both to it.

"You're back," Jay says, beaming as if she has done nothing wrong by being so cosy with *my* husband and *my* child.

I open my mouth to respond, but Lucas clears his throat. "Jay, can you take Esme upstairs please?" His tone is icier than I've ever heard it before.

Even Jay looks a little afraid. She nods and scoops Esme into her arms. As she passes me, she offers a small, supportive smile. I don't smile back.

When he is sure Jay and Esme are out of earshot, Lucas finally looks at me. "Why, Nat? Why?"

"Lucas, Chrissy is -" I try to argue, but the look Lucas shoots me stops me in my tracks. I sigh. "I know you don't want to hear this, but I really believe Chrissy is behind everything."

A tense silence hangs in the air for a moment before Lucas crumbles. "It's bad enough that two of our friends have been killed, but this? This I can't handle." He runs his hands through his hair and turns his back on me. The sight constricts my chest.

"Please, just listen to me - it all makes sense if you think about it! She's back in town, people die. She was in the city when Blaine died -"

"Blaine killed himself," Lucas interjects.

"He wouldn't -"

"How do you know he wouldn't? Because you were such good friends? Because staring at him from across a sports field while you sat alone at lunchtime means you knew everything about him?"

Lucas's words hit like a slap. I take a step backwards, but Lucas doesn't come to my aid with open arms and a grovelling apology like he usually does when he takes it too far in an argument.

I blink in the moment.

He has never not come to me before.

Everything falls out of focus. I lean against the kitchen counter for support. I look at my husband, pleading with him to be on my side, but he doesn't move.

"Lucas, Chrissy isn't a good person. She's threatening me online. She keeps commenting on my posts and making out that I'm a liar. She's trying to turn people against me! The account isn't under her name, but I know it's her."

"And how do you know that?"

"Who else could it be?"

Lucas throws his head back. "Oh, come on, Nat! Surely you can hear yourself?! You sound insane! You have a popular Instagram page. You're bound to get hate every now and then. That doesn't mean it's Chrissy Summers. You're pinning things onto her with zero proof."

"The only proof needed is that Chrissy isn't a good person," I fire back.

"And you are, Nat?"

A vein pops out on Lucas's forehead, a vein I have only ever seen once when a drunk man tried to grope me in a bar. I realise how angry my husband is and, with a sinking feeling like nothing I've ever felt before, I realise all his anger is directed at me.

"As if it's not bad enough that you followed Chrissy and waited outside her home for hours, but now you're trying to convince your friends that someone is going to kill them. You want them to admit they were bad people and be hated by everyone, but guess what, Nat? No one cares what happened in high school. Only you. Everyone else has moved on."

"But clearly someone hasn't! Clearly someone is targeting them! Chrissy is that person. Can't you see she has everything to do with this or has she got to you too?"

Lucas lets out a strained noise as if he is trying to stifle a scream. "The only person making themself look like they have anything to do with any of this is you!"

The words are out there now. It's like I can see them, covered in spikes and floating through the air, ready to attack whoever makes the first move.

My husband, my Lucas... does he really suspect I am behind this?

I wipe a tear from my cheek. "I can't believe you think I could be responsible for this."

Lucas sighs. "I don't think you're responsible, Nat, but I think you're making yourself look like a suspect. You need to let the past go."

"It's not that simple," I say, but my words set off another spark of anger in him.

"Then you're going to lose everything. Or maybe you already have, but you're too blinded by obsessing over Chrissy bloody Summers to see it."

Without another word, Lucas storms out of the kitchen. I listen to the sound of his angry footsteps pounding the stairs, then silence rings out. There is nothing and no one but me and my thoughts.

I collapse onto the table, tears streaming down my cheeks.

Not only have I lost three friends, but I've also lost my assistant and now it looks like I'm about to lose my husband too.

How can this be happening? I am not at fault here. Following Chrissy might not have been the smartest move, but *she* followed me back. *She* threatened me.

I wipe away my tears furiously.

How has it come to this? How have my friends been murdered in cold blood and *I'm* the one under the microscope?

"I'm fucking innocent," I whisper angrily, sifting through the mail to stop myself from clawing at my own skin. There's a bill, a letter to Lucas about his pension... and a blank envelope.

The hairs on my arms rise at the ominous sight. With trembling hands, I rip the envelope open and pull out the paper inside.

My world stops spinning when I see what's on it.

Torn from the pages of a Coral Bay High yearbook is the smiling group photo of my friends and the football team, only this image has been tampered with. Large, ugly crosses cover Bree, Hallie and Melissa's faces and a red ring circles another person in the photo.

Lucas.

Lucas is next.

38

"Lucas! Lucas!" I holler, racing upstairs to find him and hold him in my arms so I know he is safe.

"What? What is it?" he shouts back, rushing out of the bedroom and bumping into me at the top of the stairs.

"Oh Lucas," I sob, collapsing into his arms.

He holds himself rigid, the memory of our seemingly endless stream of fights still present in his mind, but he doesn't push me away. Right now, that's all I can ask for.

"What is it? What's wrong?"

Trembling, I hand him the photo. As Lucas takes it from me, all colour fades from his cheeks. "What is this?" he asks. He sounds calm, but I know him well enough to detect the wobble of fear in his voice.

"It was in with the mail," I sniff.

Lucas takes the envelope out of my hand and flips it over.

"There's no name," I say, even though he can see that for himself.

Over his shoulder, I spot Jay hovering in the doorway of Esme's room. "Is everything okay?"

"Lucas has been sent this," I say, my voice cracking as I point to the yearbook page. Jay walks over and examines the photo. Horror fills her eyes. Witnessing her reaction sets my tears off again.

"We need to call the police," Lucas says decisively. He disappears into the bedroom to make the call. His low, muffled voice filters through the air.

"Do you... do you think it was her?" Jay whispers.

"Who?" I ask, but Jay and I both know who she's talking about.

Jay chews her lip. "She was here yesterday, wasn't she? She could have easily posted this."

I force myself to take another look at the terrifying image. Vomit clogs my throat at the sight of an ominous red ring around my husband's smiling face. "She comes back to Coral Bay, people die. She shows up at my house, Lucas gets sent a death threat. Tell me that's not a coincidence, Jay?" I beg.

Jay's face twists, but she doesn't get chance to reply because Lucas exits the bedroom, pale faced but holding himself strong. "The police are on their way."

We sit in the living room and wait for their arrival, the air thick with tension. I hold Lucas's hand, but his fingers slip through mine, limp and lifeless. He's lost in his own thoughts and, no matter how much I try to console him, he feels too far away to reach. A distance between us I've never felt before keeps me at arm's length.

Lucas and I used to be so in sync we could communicate with just a nod of the head or a twitch of the mouth. Looking at us now, I've never felt more out of step with anyone.

An uncomfortable question squirms in my mind like wriggling maggots in rotting meat - have I already lost my husband? A few weeks ago, the idea of asking myself that question would have made me scoff, but now? Now I'm not so sure it's such a crazy thought.

When the doorbell rings to announce the arrival of the police, Lucas leaps to his feet. I hope it's my mind playing a trick on me, but I swear he almost looks relieved to detach himself from my side.

A male officer goes into the kitchen with Lucas to take his statement while a female officer sits in the living room with me to take mine. We are going through basic identification questions when Detective Baldie walks through the door. My insides turn to stone when I see him.

"Twice in one day, Mrs Redding. This is getting too much," he jokes before speaking to the officer. She shows him the yearbook extract, which is now encased in a clear, plastic evidence bag. I shudder at the sight of it, an alien object in my usually comforting home.

"You found this, is that right?" Detective Baldie asks.

"Yes. It was in with the mail."

"Good of you to remember to bring in the mail after being questioned by the police." Detective Baldie's words are heavy with insinuation. I colour under the weight of them.

"I was stalling before I came inside. I knew Lucas wouldn't be too happy about me following Chrissy. I didn't want to face the music straight away."

"Well, I can see why he might not like finding out that his wife was secretly tracking another woman and accusing her of murder without any evidence to support the claim," Detective Baldie says as he takes a seat. His imposing frame takes up so much room on the sofa that the officer has to shuffle down to accommodate him. "What happened when you got back?"

A part of me wants to lie and pretend everything was okay. I don't want Detective Baldie knowing that not only has he got under my skin, but he has impacted my marriage too. Only I can't lie, not when Lucas's life is in danger.

"We fought," I say, sticking my chin out defiantly to show that I'm not ashamed of it. "Lucas was upset I hadn't told him about following Chrissy and he was angry at me for upsetting Becca – she's as much a friend of his as she is mine."

"It seems like every time I show up, you and Lucas fight," Detective Baldie quips.

"Well, you have been the bearer of a lot of bad news recently."

Detective Baldie nods at me as if to say 'touché'. "So, you fought - then what?"

"Lucas went upstairs. I sat at the table and cried, then I pulled myself together, opened the mail and found it."

Detective Baldie holds up the bagged picture and I nod.

"I ran upstairs to check Lucas was okay. I showed him the photo, then he rang you."

"Did anyone else see or touch the photo?"

"Our nanny, Jay."

Detective Baldie turns to the officer. "If you could find Jay and take a statement that would be great." She nods and leaves the room.

Detective Baldie and I sit in an electric silence before he leans back on the sofa and speaks. "So, this photograph – who do you think posted it?" He asks his question lightly, but it's a loaded one.

I don't back down from answering it. "Yesterday, Chrissy Summers followed me home. I told you earlier that she threatened me, but you didn't want to listen. Chrissy stood on my driveway and told me not to get in her way or she would destroy me." Detective Baldie's eyebrow raises at this. I want to shout, 'good, now you're listening to me', but I don't.

"I know you think I have a vendetta against her, but she shows up and my friends are murdered. She finds out where I live and the next day a threat against my husband is posted through my letterbox. These things cannot be coincidences. I'm not making anything up – I'm simply pointing out what's there. That group from high school is being culled one by one and everything points to Chrissy. Her friends ditched her, so she killed them. Lucas didn't marry her so now she wants him dead too. This photo is her warning. He's..." my voice cracks, but I clear my throat. "He's her next victim."

"It all sounds a bit like a made for TV movie to me," Detective Baldie shrugs.

"Well, it sounds like real life to me," I fire back.

Detective Baldie pauses then sits forward, resting his forearms on his knees. He holds my gaze so intensely that my even my breath is afraid to move.

"This could all be true, Mrs Redding, but the fact of the matter is that none of the other victims ever received a note or warning. Your husband is the first and only one. One might argue that instead of being a genuine threat, that note is more likely to be someone trying to throw our attention away from them and focus it elsewhere."

Detective Baldie takes in my stunned reaction then shrugs. "But what do I know about threats and murder and intention? I'm only a detective, after all."

39

With me too shellshocked to speak and Detective Baldie too triumphant to push it, our conversation dries up. After ordering the female officer to take my fingerprints, Detective Baldie leaves me so he can check on Lucas.

"It's lovely weather today, isn't it?" she asks as she stamps the ink-stained pads of my fingers.

I don't reply. I can't, not with my mind spiralling out of control. I want to stay still, to block out the world and hide away until this is all over, but it's too late now. Every move I make, every word I speak somehow implicates me and not Chrissy. My world is caving in. There is nowhere left to hide.

As the process of taking my fingerprints ends, it takes all my willpower to not draw my knees to my chest and burst into tears.

Voices in the hallway stir me. I follow the sound and find Lucas leading the police to the door.

"If you need anything or notice anything suspicious, please just call," Detective Baldie says, showing Lucas more kindness in that one sentence than he has shown me in all our interactions combined.

"Thank you. I really appreciate you taking the time to come out and speak to me," Lucas replies.

I go to his side and put my arm around his waist, but Lucas doesn't lean into me. Instead, he paints a polite smile on his face, one so transparent it makes me burn.

Detective Baldie scrutinises the shift in our dynamic before making a move to leave. Just as he reaches for the door handle, he stops. "Have you redecorated?"

I shake my head.

"Huh," he says, glancing around the room. "It feels different in here." With that as his parting comment, he finally leaves.

I look around the entrance to our home, trying to spot anything unusual. A frosty atmosphere that wasn't there before chills the air, but I doubt that's what Detective Baldie means. "What a weird comment," I say.

"Weird sounds about right after today," Lucas replies wearily. I try to catch his eye, but he looks anywhere but at me. "I'm going for a shower. Leave me for a bit, okay? Just... just leave me."

I open my mouth to respond, but Lucas doesn't wait to hear what I have to say. He heads upstairs, taking two steps at a time. I watch him go, and then I am alone again.

Part of me is glad I was so badly bullied at school. After all, what better preparation could there be for times like this when everyone around me is pulling away?

Maybe, no matter how hard I tried to fight against it, loneliness was always meant to be my destiny. Maybe I should just give in and let things go back to the way they were, the way Chrissy told me they were always supposed to be.

40

Even though Lucas and I barely speak for the rest of the day, so much is said with every hostile movement and blank glance. Every drink he makes only for himself, the conversation he solely directs at Jay, the fact that he sits on a separate sofa to me… it screams volumes.

We lie in bed, side by side but not touching, the thin strip of material between us mirroring a vast, tumultuous ocean. I want to reach out for him, but I don't. I can't bring myself to make the move.

"I'm worried about you," he says into the darkness.

Terror wraps its hand around my throat. I fight to hold back my tears.

I want to tell Lucas I'm worried about him too, especially after finding that yearbook photo. I want to confess that I'm terrified of what is going to happen next, that it feels like no one is listening to me, that I'm petrified Chrissy is going to end me before I get the chance to make any of this right. I want him to know how scared I am, how lonely, how lost, but what's the point? He doesn't understand. He doesn't even try.

So, I say nothing.

Eventually, Lucas rolls over. A medicine bottle rattles, and I hear him take a gulp of water from the glass on his bedside table. Lucas's back is okay today, but he has still taken the medication. There must be another reason for him resorting to a sleeping aid.

"You," I tell myself. "You are the reason."

A few moments later and he is snoring away, dead to the world and finally at peace.

Me?

I lay awake, a captive of fear. My mind races with the events of the last few weeks, replaying moments like a sickening showreel of horror films.

Two of my friends are dead and a detective thinks I am responsible. I have no one around me to turn to for help or support. My husband thinks I am obsessed with my high school bully, a woman who is as dangerous and as unhinged as I am being made out to be.

She knows where I live. She has threatened my family. She knows where my husband parks his car, where my daughter sleeps, where I make a living.

She knows everything.

Like a spider crawling up the back of a bare neck, the sinking realisation of just how unsafe I am creeps upon me.

I lie in bed and stare fearfully at the ceiling until a car slowing to a stop outside makes my blood run cold. My heart thunders as someone closes the door as softly as they can, but not soft enough that it doesn't make a sound in the still of night.

I listen out for footsteps on the driveway.

I can't hear any, but that doesn't mean they aren't coming.

I slip out of bed and pad over to the window, peeking outside. Maple Drive stares back at me, cloaked in darkness and as normal as ever.

But that's what Chrissy would want me to think. Melissa thought she was opening the door to a friendly visitor and look what happened to her.

I step away from the window and head back towards the bed, but then I hear it – the sound of the front door handle rattling.

She's here.

She's coming for Lucas.

I glance at my sleeping husband, his full lips parted as he snores. There's no point trying to wake him, not after a tablet, no matter how much danger he is in.

The question 'would he believe me anyway' furrows in my brain like a burrowing cockroach, but I quash it down. Now isn't the time to worry about my husband's faith in me – now is the time to save his life.

Heart hammering, I pull one of Lucas's golf clubs from their bag inside the walk-in wardrobe and tiptoe out of the bedroom.

My clammy palms grip the club tight. The soles of my feet stick to the cool, wooden floor as I make my way towards the stairs. Blood pounds in my ears, but I force myself to peep at the front door. The handle isn't moving now, but that doesn't make me any calmer. Chrissy wouldn't keep trying the door if she couldn't get in. She would look for another point of entry.

I think of how many windows there are in this house and pray we remembered to close them all before we went to bed.

Trembling with every step, I creep down the stairs.

Even though this is my home, in the darkness it suddenly seems alien to me. Innocent shapes I know to be my sofa or side table look like they're hiding an enemy, their outline sinister and panic inducing.

"Hello?" I call out into the deafening silence. "Chrissy? If you're here, you need to get out. This is breaking and entering!" I try to project an air of confidence, but even to me my voice sounds hollow.

Suddenly, I hear a scraping at the kitchen window.

My heart leaps into my throat, but I don't give myself a second to think twice. I dash into the kitchen to confront Chrissy.

Hitting the lights on, I'm momentarily blinded. I blink rapidly, trying to get accustomed to the sudden onslaught of artificial light.

"Chrissy? I know you're here!"

Silence.

I pace the kitchen, skirting around the dining table and peering out of the window into my blackened garden. Everything is indecipherable in the darkness of the night.

Suddenly, a blur of a shadow rushes across the grass and dashes into the bushes.

I clutch the golf club, ready for whatever comes next. Adrenaline fuels me. My eyes stay fixed on the garden, waiting for a sign of life, but the only movement is the leaves fluttering in the breeze.

Nothing else moves. No one makes a sound.

But still the hairs on the back of my neck stand on end as if I'm being watched.

I squeeze the golf club tight.

"If she comes at you, you're armed. She can't do anything," I whisper to myself, but my words are futile. Chrissy can't do anything? That's the biggest lie of all.

After one last lingering survey of the garden, I concede. Everything is still. No one is here, not anymore.

My relief is so strong that my legs threaten to buckle beneath me. I let out an unsteady exhale and turn to head back upstairs.

It's when I'm walking through the hallway that I spot the face.

41

I scream, the sound that bursts from me so full of horror and undiluted fear it can only be described as blood curdling.

With all my might, I swing the golf club backwards then drive it into the face before me.

The sound of glass shattering makes me stumble backwards and I blink, waiting for the face I had seen to transform into a figure and unveil them self to me.

But there's no one there.

I look around, taking in the smashed-up scene, and realise what's just happened.

Myself.

I'd seen myself.

I don't know whether to laugh or cry. Shards of what was once our hallway mirror litter the floor like murderous wedding confetti, but I don't care about the mess. All that matters is that there's no one here. No one is coming to hurt me or my family.

"You're okay, it's okay," I repeat, doing all I can to still my erratic heartbeat, but my body jars and fights back against the narrative I'm telling myself.

Okay? Nothing about this night is okay.

What if that had been Lucas coming downstairs for a drink in the middle of the night? What if Jay had seen the lights on and come into the house to check that we were all okay?

I would have hit them in the face with a golf club.

I would have killed them.

I look down at the heavy, metallic club in my hand, my weapon of choice. How odd it seems to be carrying it around my home now, how barbaric, yet just a few minutes ago I was ready to cave Chrissy's skull in should she have been here.

I was ready to kill her.

I *wanted* to kill her.

I drop the golf club, letting it clatter to the floor with an almighty bang, and sink to my knees. A piece of mirror embeds itself in my hand. The sudden sharp shock of pain makes me gasp out loud. I watch with fascination as blood trickles from the wound down my wrist.

What is happening to me?

Have I lost my mind?

The face I had seen in the mirror had been terrifying. Possessed eyes, a twisted, determined expression, hatred oozing from every pore… it was like something from a nightmare, and it was me. I hadn't even recognised myself.

I huddle my knees to my chest and rock my body backwards and forwards. My grip on reality is slipping. I can feel my fingertips sliding back inch by inch, barely clinging to the edge anymore, but what can I do? There's nothing left for me to hold onto. Chrissy has taken it all.

42

A cupboard door slamming startles me awake. My first thought is that Chrissy has made it into the house, but then I remember that killers are not known for making noise before they commit murder.

The thought doesn't relax me, though. I'm too bewildered at finding myself in the living room and not in my bedroom to be appeased by it.

Sadness trickles down my soul like rain down a drainpipe as I realise I must have fallen asleep on the sofa. In all our years of being together, Lucas and I have never slept apart, not even after our most raging fights. We even broke tradition and spent the night before our wedding together, yet last night we slept as two separate people.

That line has been crossed now. That action can never be undone. Lucas will have woken to an empty bed. He will have stretched his arm out to find me before opening his eyes in confusion. Instead of his wife, he will have found a cold pillow and an undented sheet.

I flinch as another cupboard door slams shut. Rising to my feet, I stretch, my body stiff from sleeping on a too-small couch, and head into the kitchen to face the music.

Lucas doesn't even look up from making his lunch when I enter the room.

"I fell asleep on the sofa. It was an accident."

Silence.

"My poor back," I joke. "Maybe I'll need to borrow one of your pills tonight."

Lucas adds ham to two slices of bread and continues to ignore me.

"Lucas, say something."

"Say something," he repeats, slicing his sandwich into triangles before setting down the knife and gripping the counter so tightly his knuckles protrude white. "How about 'what the fuck was all that smashed mirror on the floor'?"

My cheeks burn. "I thought I'd cleaned it up."

A strange, twisted sound I've never heard Lucas make before bursts from him. "That's all you can say to that?! We have a baby, Nat. A baby who crawls. How could you think it was okay to leave such a mess?"

"It was late, I –"

"So late night property destruction is okay but late-night cleaning isn't? Why was the mirror smashed, anyway?"

"I… I thought Chrissy had come for you," I explain sheepishly.

Lucas holds my gaze. For a split second, I think he recognises the fear in my eyes and is about to close the cavernous gap between us, but then his face twists. "Chrissy? *Chrissy?!* After everything we talked about yesterday, you're still obsessing over Chrissy fucking Summers?!"

"Someone is trying to kill you, Lucas!"

"And it has to be Chrissy because you don't like her."

"No! It has to be her because of the evidence!"

Lucas looks at me like I'm insane. "Do you hear yourself, Nat? Do you hear how crazy you sound?"

"I'm not crazy, Lucas. I know you don't believe me, but I *know* her. I know what she's capable of. Please, you've got to believe me," I cry, desperately reaching for Lucas's chest but he pushes me away.

"I'm not listening to this anymore," he snaps, picking up his lunch and heading for the door. He pauses before turning back to me. "I wasn't going to tell you this but a few days ago Chrissy sent me a message on Facebook. She asked if we would like to go for a drink – if me *and* you wanted to go for a drink. I didn't tell you because I knew you'd be upset she messaged me, but you're wrong about her. She isn't here to cause trouble. She's here to restart her life."

My mouth hangs open. I look at my husband in disbelief. "You... you're friends with her on Facebook?"

That's the moment it happens – the moment my husband's ability to see me as the love of his life dies.

"That's what you take from what I just said?" he whispers furiously, then he leaves.

For a split second, I debate crumbling, but I don't. I can't taint this house with another dose of tears. I straighten up and hold it together the best I can. "Jay? I'm heading out," I shout. I don't wait for her to respond. Instead, I dash to my car and put my foot down.

On the drive, I blast the rock music I used to listen to as a teenager. My skin tingles, my mind swims in angry lyrics. I don't think about Lucas, though, and right now that's all I can ask for.

As I hurtle through town, I ignore the stares that follow me. Fiona, Hank, Gloria, even Joelle – they all watch me zoom past with cold, cruel judgement in their eyes. Once upon a time, that would have hurt, but right now there's too much agony inside me to care what anyone thinks.

My tyres crunch the gravel of the carpark as I pull to a sharp stop by the beach. My mind tells me to get out of the car, but my body won't comply. It stays fixed to the seat, safe from the prying eyes of the world.

I set my gaze on the shoreline. It's only when the sea and the sand and the sky blur and merge into one indecipherable smudge that I realise my eyes are overflowing with tears.

This time, I don't fight them. I sit and I sob, my cries raw and angry, hitting the steering wheel for good measure.

My heart can't take much more of this. Every day is filled with a new level of despair. My soul hasn't ached this much since I lost my mum. Walking down the cold, clinical corridors of the hospital. Listening to her breathing rattle and rasp. Reaching for her hand that could no longer grip mine... then she was gone.

I remember realising she had died and being so shocked. I knew her death was coming – she couldn't fight anymore, not when she'd already fought so hard and for so long – but then it came, and I couldn't wrap my head around it. I was so used to her being ill, but dead? *Dead?* It was so final, so absolute.

That pain had been the final straw. It pushed me to leave everything behind and run to a new city to start again, but this pain? This pain is a whole new experience.

I rest my throbbing head on the steering wheel and breathe deeply. In and out, in and out.

Lucas will come around.

The police will catch Chrissy.

Things will be okay… won't they?

I lift my head and spot Janis Hopkins and Natasha Everett, two of the biggest gossips in town, watching me. They startle when they realise I've seen them and pretend they're mid conversation rather than mid binge watch, but I know better than that. Those vultures have devoured my pain, ready to excitedly regurgitate it to whoever will listen. Even from inside my car, I can see their eyes lit up with the glimmer of something to talk about at their next book club.

Mortification soaks my soul. I need to get out of here. I need to get away. I rev the engine of my car and reverse out of the carpark. A cloud of dust follows me as I speed in the opposite direction to the beach. The temptation to drive anywhere but here is overwhelming. Foot on the gas, head in the clouds, no map to follow… what a dream.

But of course, some dreams are just for dreaming. Instead of fleeing, I head back home to my daughter who reaches for anyone but me when she cries.

43

"Who's a good girl? Is it you? Is it?" Jay coos. Esme giggles and my heart turns to stone.

I look up from replying to emails and eye the pair of them. It's like a low-budget TV advert has come to life in my living room, all sunny smiles and wholesome fun. Jay's even dressed Esme in a lemon-yellow playsuit, a similar colour to the t-shirt she herself is wearing. Jay's mini me, except Esme's not hers, is she? She's mine, even if all I seem to be doing at the moment is failing her.

Jay catches my eye. Her cheeks flush pink. "Hey, Esme, shall we go and play with mummy?"

Esme warbles in agreement. Jay picks her up, but as my daughter nears me, arms outstretched and smile wide, my throat closes and I scramble to my feet. "No, don't! Don't bring her to me. I don't feel well," I lie. "Maybe it's best to keep Esme away from me for today."

Without waiting for Jay's response, I excuse myself and race to my bedroom. I shut the door behind me, a barrier between me and the world, only it's not a strong enough barricade. People can still get to me. I can still hurt the people I love.

I clutch the duvet to my chest. What is happening to me? I ran from my daughter. The thought of having her in my arms, of being responsible for her safety when I can no longer ensure it has me quivering.

My life has never felt more out of control and I don't know what I can do to change that.

I close my eyes, waiting for a sense of peace to wash over me that never comes. My mind races with a million and one terrifying thoughts, all centring around the horrible ways in which Chrissy could destroy my life and my family. Adrenaline pumps through my veins, ready to fight, ready to run, ready to escape my fate. Ready to do anything but be around the people I seem to do nothing but hurt.

Suddenly, knuckles rap against my bedroom door.

"Who is it?" I call, my voice raspy with fear.

"Nat? Sorry to disturb you when you're not feeling great but there's someone here for you."

I tense. "Is it the police?"

"No, it's Sunaina."

I blink at the mention of my former assistant. Sunaina. I almost forgot she existed.

As if sensing my hesitation, Jay speaks. "She's brought your camera back. She said she needs to speak to you about something."

"I'm coming," I reply, swinging my legs out of bed and reluctantly heading downstairs.

The jarring sight of Sunaina holding Esme greets me as I enter the kitchen. It's such a familiar moment to walk in on, but of course everything about it is now new territory. Sunaina is no longer my confidant, but someone I fired. Seeing her again, I almost can't remember why.

A flush of desire to go back and change everything floods me, but I know better than anyone that words can never be taken back.

As soon as she spots me, Sunaina's smile vanishes. "Nat," she says politely, placing Esme in her playpen.

"Jay said you've brought my camera back?"

"And your laptop. It's all over there." Sunaina nods to a box on the dining table.

"Thank you."

With neither of us knowing what to say next, the air between us thickens until it becomes unbearable.

"I've found a job I'd like to apply for. I wanted to ask about a reference."

"You'll get one. A good one."

Sunaina nods, appeased. She chews her lip, the weirdness of the moment too much to not create a nervous tick. "Right, well... maybe I should go."

My chest lurches, begging me to reach out and make Sunaina stay, but I don't. I can't. I'm hurting everyone around me enough as it is. I can't add another name to that list. So instead, I nod. "Maybe that's best."

Sunaina stoops to collect her handbag, then turns to me with a sad smile. "You know, I was hoping to come here and make it okay with you. Not to get my job back, but because it's the right thing to do. I loved working for you. I wanted to end things on a better note, especially after Amira told everyone at the gym you were struggling -"

"Amira said what?" I cut in, but Sunaina ignores me.

"But what's the point? You haven't even thanked me for everything I did for you. You've changed, Nat. You've become as cold and unhinged as everyone is saying."

At the mention of people talking about me, I bristle.

"I didn't think you deserved any of the things they were saying. I used to defend you, even after you fired me, but now? Now I won't bother. You deserve all the hate you're getting. I'm glad people are seeing you for who you are and that you're finally losing it all."

"Losing it all?" I echo.

"Nat, you've lost almost fifteen thousand followers in two days -"

"What?" I gasp. Sunaina's words knock me off my feet. I frown and shake my head, but Sunaina doesn't tell me she's made a mistake. Instead, she slips her phone from her pocket and loads 'Finding the Good Life', holding her screen so I can see.

She's right - I've lost fifteen thousand followers.

I've lost fifteen thousand followers and I hadn't even noticed.

My stomach falls out of my body and lands in a pulsating pile at my feet.

"What? I don't... I don't understand! What's happened?!"

Sunaina shrugs. "I guess you've been exposed for the fraud you are."

When Sunaina shows me her screen once more, I'm confronted with the @coralbaygirl747 page I have come to know so well, only now the profile isn't blank. Now it is dedicated entirely to me.

The first three posts are of black tiles with the words, *'the truth will out'* written on them... then the venom starts.

The first image is a smiling photo of me at the beach with a teenage girl. The caption reads, *'the day after Nat's supposed 'best friend' dies, she was at the beach acting as if she was on a red carpet... is she for real? She was supposedly 'devastated'... she looks okay to me!'*

My jaw drops. This photo was taken weeks before Hallie died, but @coralbaygirl747 has rewritten the narrative, and judging by the 1725 comments underneath, her version of the story is popular

Is this a joke?! Nat was begging for sympathy over this – wtf?!

What a low life bitch! To think I felt sorry for this faker

AS IF! How could anyone use something as tragic as death for profit?

Injustice burns my soul as I flick back to the profile and skim over the other images. Images that prove I edit my photos. Shots of me walking down Main Street looking like I think I'm better than everyone else. A collection of unflattering, cruel photos, all of them painting a picture of a fraud.

Then I see the latest post – a collection of consecutively dated photos of me out and about in Coral Bay on my own. The caption reads, *'Nat is the first to tell us how wonderful motherhood is... where's the baby, Nat? I'm pretty sure motherhood is only wonderful if you actually bother with the child. A baby is for life, not for likes!'*

A frustrated scream bubbles in my throat, one that never escapes my lips because fear grabs it before it gets the chance. My world trembles as it dawns on me that all my fears about Chrissy watching me are true. She's been following me, photographing me, tracking my every move.

I grab Sunaina by the arm. "You have to help me!"

Sunaina takes her phone back and shakes free. "You fired me, remember? You wouldn't even let me explain. You cast me out like I was nothing." Sunaina's chin wobbles, but she holds strong. "The tide has turned against you, Nat. You can't undo this. You're being cancelled, and you deserve it."

"But it's not true! I'm not what they say I am!"

"What's going on?" I jump at the unexpected sound of Lucas's voice. My bottom lip trembles as I face him, his expression weary at coming home from work to yet another dramatic scene involving me.

"Everyone hates me, Lucas," I whisper.

Lucas frowns, but doesn't ask.

"I just came over to return the camera," Sunaina says. "I'll get out of your hair now." She shoots me one last pitying look and goes for the door.

"Sunaina?" Lucas calls, stopping her. "I just want to say thank you for all your hard work. You were a fantastic asset to Nat and really helped her business grow. It's a shame things didn't work out when you posted the photo of Esme but -"

Now it's Sunaina's turn to frown. "I never posted a photo of Esme."

My heart freezes. The moment runs in slow motion. I watch in horror as the realisation clicks into place for Lucas. He turns to me as if I'm a disgusting excuse for a human. "You," he whispers.

"I... I..." I try protest, but what can I say? My lie has finally caught up with me.

"You said I posted a photo of Esme? Unbelievable, Nat," Sunaina scoffs, storming out of the house. The front door slams behind her, but her hurt isn't what breaks my heart. Lucas's revulsion is.

"I didn't think you'd be as upset as you were. I didn't want you to be mad at me -" I begin but Lucas backs away.

"Just do me a favour, Nat – stay away from me. I don't want to be around you right now. You're toxic."

With that, Lucas exits the kitchen, thundering upstairs and leaving me rooted to the spot in shame.

44

The chokehold of our argument lingers overnight and well into the next day. Neither of us say a word to the other. The only peace I get is when Lucas heads to work, but he's home before I know it and the bitterness continues. I spend the evening glued to my phone, watching in anguish as my follower count decreases.

When observing my life fall apart from the sidelines becomes too much to bear, I focus my attention on the person who got me into this mess. I scroll through Chrissy's social media and read every kind comment sent her way with curled lips.

It's so good to have you back!

Coral Bay hasn't been the same without you, girl!

Ur as beautiful as ever

The sickeningly sweet messages burn my eyes, but I devour every word, gorging on them until vomit lodges in my throat.

"Nat, it's time for Esme's bath," Lucas interrupts. I blink in reality, only now noticing how late it is.

"I'll do it."

Lucas glances at my phone. "What are you looking at?"

"Nothing," I shrug, but Lucas grabs my wrist and takes my phone. The expression on his face when he sees my screen would break my heart if I wasn't already hardened to him. He lets me go as if I burn to touch.

Wordlessly, I take Esme from him. Her heart beats against mine and suddenly I'm startled by the weight of her in my arms. When had I last held her like this? When did I last feel like I could?

Should I even be holding her at all?

I force my worries down. Leaving my phone behind, I carry Esme to the bathroom and bathe her. Sat in the centre of the bathtub, she seems so tiny. Small enough to be lost in the sea of bubbles surrounding her. Small enough to slip under the water at any moment.

Panic grips me and I haul her out of the bath. I hold Esme's wriggling body to mine, water drenching my t-shirt. Shampoo still soaks her hair, but I can't risk putting her back in the water. Not with me around.

Lucas joins me to put Esme to bed. It's a relief to have him by my side, not that I tell him that. His soft, low voice reads a bedtime story. Esme's eyelids flutter, and even I find myself at peace listening to the comforting words of a children's tale when told in my husband's hushed tones.

But when Esme finally drifts off, we head back downstairs and suffocating silence resumes.

Lucas turns on the TV, his gaze fixed to the screen. His stony expression warns me to not approach him, so I don't.

Besides, there are other things I can be doing. Things like watching Chrissy's life consume mine, only my phone isn't on the hallway side table where I left it. I scour the living room and the kitchen, but it's nowhere to be found.

"Really, Lucas?" I scoff to myself. Part of me wants to confront him and demand he gives me my phone back, but I don't. I let him have his moment and the prickly silence between us continues.

Over breakfast the next morning, Jay tries her best to offset the tension with her chipper nature, but her cheeriness grates. "We're going to have such a good day today, aren't we, Esme? We've got big plans... big, exciting plans!"

"Oh yeah? What kind of plans?" Lucas asks, purposely turning his back to me while he puts his lunch in his bag.

"We're going to have a craft day!"

"Sounds good. Aren't you a lucky girl?" Lucas says as he kisses Esme's forehead. "Have a good day you two," he calls over his shoulder as he leaves for work. It doesn't take a genius to work out which two people he was referring to.

I glare at the dregs of my coffee and try to get angry at my husband's cool dismissal, but my eyes swim with tears and betray my hurt.

"Do you fancy joining us?" Jay offers with a kind smile, almost as if she thinks that by being extra nice to me, she can make me forget my marriage is falling apart. I should thank her for her efforts, but I'm too embarrassed to have a witness to my relationship deteriorating to do so.

"I'd best not," I say, rising to my feet. "I need to paint. Don't let anyone disturb me, okay? I have so much work to do. But have fun!"

As I put my mug into the dishwasher, I catch Esme's eye. She reaches for me, but at the sight of her arms outstretched in my direction, a spasm shoots through my chest.

"You're only going to hurt her, Nat. That's all a fuck up like you will ever do," my brain warns.

That's all I need to hear to make me lower my head and scurry out of the kitchen like a guilty secret.

In the safety of my studio, I pull out every tube and pot of paint I own and a fresh canvas. It stands before me, exposed and white, begging to be covered and turned into something beautiful.

I stare at it, waiting for inspiration to strike.

The canvas stares back, its blankness dazzling, my lack of inspiration screaming.

All I see is nothing. Vast, aching, empty nothingness. It dances before my eyes. It mocks me.

Rage fuels my next move. I pick up the pot of paint closest to me and launch it at the canvas, spraying the walls and floor black. Even my most recent red, grief washed works get a dark coating. Paint trickles down the canvases, dripping onto the floor and oozing in a pool at my feet like a wound from a mythical creature.

I smile in satisfaction, my own private fuck you to the world interrupted by a gasp behind me.

I spin around to find Arlene Davies in the doorway of my studio.

"Arlene!" I breathe. "What are you doing here?"

Arlene looks from me to the mess and back again before tucking her sleek bob behind her ears. "I came to check in on my investment. Clearly it's a good thing I did."

Crimson, I study the wreckage of what was once my work. I make a move to clear the scene, but Arlene shakes her head. "Don't bother, Nat. I can't sell them."

"I know the black has -"

Arlene lets out a sharp laugh. "You think the black is the problem here? If anything, it's improved them! They're terrible, Nat. They're not what we agreed on at all. Who would buy them – hormonal teenagers who hate the world? They don't exactly have the budget for high end gallery pieces, do they?"

I squirm under the weight of her devastating critique. "I know they're a new direction for me -"

"A new direction? A new direction would be using more gold tones, but this? This is like the work of an entirely different artist, and one who doesn't know how to paint at that," Arlene snorts, expertly dodging the black splattered across the floor and walking towards my latest canvases. She bends and studies them, shaking her head. "Honestly, Nat, would you hang them up in your home? Would you want your daughter seeing these around the house?"

I eye the paintings, their anger and hatred screaming, then hang my head.

"I've heard you've been having a tough time recently, but this? This is something else."

"I'm just finding it hard to paint like I used to," I admit.

Arlene straightens up and faces me. Her arms fold across her chest, her expression hard. "That's not my problem, Nat. I pay you to paint nice, simple seascapes. That's what you're good at. That's what you earn the big bucks for. You're not expressionist, not abstract, not emotional – you're safe, clean, happy, predictable. That's the life you sell, and that's what people want to buy."

"I know but -"

Arlene raises her hand to silence me. "I don't want to hear it, Nat. You promised me three paintings I could sell, and you are going to deliver on that promise. You are going to paint me pretty pictures of the beach, just like you always do. Now sort your shit out or I'll have to reconsider our contract."

The ground beneath my feet trembles. "Arlene, I've been painting for you for almost three years -"

"So? Everyone has a shelf life, Nat. Don't for a second think you are indispensable to me. You didn't think twice about our history when you were ducking my calls or failing to respond to my emails, did you? This relationship is a two-way street. I owe you nothing."

I open my mouth to argue back, but there's no fight left in me.

Arlene shoots the paintings one last withering look. "Sort it out, Nat, or we are done," she warns before marching past me in a blur of expensive fabrics and spicy perfume. She exits the studio without closing the door behind her.

I stand in silence, paint seeping into the floorboards and the cracks in my life deepening. I close my eyes and wait for the ground to open, swallow me whole and take me away from this mess, but when I open my eyes I'm still here. I'm still living this nightmare with no end in sight.

45

Despite everything inside me begging to crumble, I force myself to act. Ignoring the stained, blackened floorboards, I shove my ruined artwork into the corner and grab my usual tones of blues, greens, golds, and yellows. I add them to a palette ready to go, but there they remain, staring back at me as lifelessly as I stare at them.

"The beach, the beach, the beach," I repeat to myself, my new, desperate mantra, but inspiration never comes.

Defeated, I let the palette slip from my hands and clatter at my feet.

There's no point trying to paint like I used to. It would be a waste of a canvas. As soon as I start painting the ocean, it will become a suffocating, suctioning whirlpool destroying all life and taking me with it. The sky will blacken, the sand will suck me under, the water will hold me down.

My days of painting beautiful seascapes that reflect my beautiful life are long gone.

I sink to my knees and let out a raw, animal-like scream. For the first time in forever, the pressure mounting inside me releases ever so slightly. I let out a laugh then scream again. My lungs sing from the freedom.

Suddenly, there's a knock at the door.

"I said to leave me alone!" I shout, my cheeks burning as I realise whoever it is will have heard my crazed screams.

Jay's meek voice replies from the other side of the door. "I know, I'm sorry, but Amira's here. She wouldn't take no for an answer."

"Tell her I'm working."

"I did, but she insisted on seeing you. Please, Nat. I really think you should talk to someone."

The tremble in Jay's voice plucks at something inside my chest and I sigh. With one last glance at the blank canvas, I stand and open the door. Jay smiles with relief, then her eyes flick over my shoulder. They widen as they see the destruction inside.

"Nat, your art!" she breathes, rushing into the studio. Jay picks up one of the black splattered canvases, trying to figure out a way to salvage the original painting, but it's too late. Even with her impeccable homemaking skills, there is nothing she can do. She looks at me, crestfallen.

"It's okay, Jay. They were no good anyway," I shrug. I hold open the door for her to leave and, after a moment's hesitation, she gives in. We walk across the garden and into the house.

Amira rises to her feet when we enter the kitchen, her smile nervous like it's the first day of school.

"I'll leave you both to it," Jay says, slipping out of the room and closing the door behind her.

A beat of silence rings out before Amira breaks it. "I came around to talk. I was worried you'd fallen out with me, especially when you didn't text me back. I sent six messages – ignoring that many texts isn't cool," Amira says, only half joking.

"I haven't ignored your texts." Amira purses her lips and I sigh. "I'm not twelve, I wouldn't ignore your messages. I just don't know where my phone is."

"You mean the phone that's right here?" Amira asks, reaching into the fruit bowl and holding up my phone. I do a double take. It really is my phone, right there in the centre of the room for all to see.

Heat scorches my cheeks. "It wasn't there earlier, I promise."

"Well, I half believe you."

"You should believe me. I'm not a liar, but you... you lied to the police about me." Tears come for me, swift and brutal. I hold them back the best I can, but my vision blurs from the sudden onslaught.

"I didn't lie, Nat. What difference does it make whose idea it was to follow Chrissy? We both think she's guilty and that's all that matters."

"But the police don't think Chrissy is guilty - they think I am."

Amira softens and extends her arm to me. "Come sit. We need to talk."

I hesitate, but I take her hand. I'm not ready to be alone, not now, and Amira is the closest thing I have to a friend left. I've lost everyone else.

I sit opposite her and she slides a cup of tea towards me. "I made this for you."

I take a sip and swallow my tears. We sit in silence, toying with the handles of our mugs and avoiding eye contact.

"I've been worried about you," Amira comments.

"Not worried enough to stop you bitching about me," I shoot back. Amira's eyebrows raise and I sigh. "Sunaina said you'd been gossiping about me at the gym."

"I hardly call answering people's questions gossiping, Nat. You're the talk of the town right now. What was I meant to do? Just let people say what they wanted? I did what I could to dispel the rumours you've gone completely insane -"

"People think I've gone insane?"

"You were spotted crying in your car and somehow news of you following Chrissy has got out. What else are people going to think?"

"But we *both* followed her."

Amira shoots me an apologetic grimace. "Everyone thinks it was just you."

I groan and run my hands through my hair. "This is a fucking disaster!"

Amira reaches across the table and holds my hand. "I'm worried, babe. Have you been sleeping? You look exhausted, and you're thinner than ever, and not in a good way."

Her kindness breaks me. "I just... I don't feel safe anymore."

"It's Chrissy, isn't it?"

"Amira, she's everywhere. She's chipping away at me, bit by bit. She's made a fake profile and is tearing me apart every chance she gets.

I've lost so many followers already! She threatened me outside my own home, then the next day I found a photo with Lucas's face circled like he's going to be next."

Amira's mouth hangs open. Her horrified reaction sends a shiver down my spine, but it also makes me sit a little taller. *Someone* believes me. *Someone* sees how twisted Chrissy is.

"No one thinks she's behind this. The police doubt everything I say and now even Lucas is pulling away from me. Everyone's telling me I'm crazy but I'm not. I *know* Chrissy is doing this."

"Oh Nat, you're so right – it's got to be her, hasn't it?" Amira breathes. "Have you told the police about the photo?"

I nod. "I told them about Chrissy following me too, but they aren't listening."

"And Lucas?"

I colour. "Lucas… Lucas doesn't think she's behind any of it either."

Amira pulls a sympathetic face and squeezes my hand. "Well, for what it's worth, I think she's behind it all. She's asked to meet me three times this week already and every time she wants me to meet her alone. I'm telling you, that woman is trouble."

A bubble of hope swells in my chest. "Can you tell the police that?"

"I already have. Chrissy's name was on the list I gave them, remember? And I said I followed her with you."

"But if you go to them again maybe they will take it more seriously. Two people who are adamant it's her is more believable than one, right? If you tell them how much she scares you, how evil she is –"

Amira pulls her hand away, a gesture that silences me.

"Look, Nat, if Chrissy really is coming for us and she finds out I've gone to the police to point the finger at her again, what do you think she's going to do? I'll be dead by the end of the week."

"But the police think I'm saying this out of spite," I protest. "I need backup."

"I can't give you that, not more than I already have. I can't go in and make a big deal about Chrissy again. If you can prove she's the killer then I'll be the first person to shout it from the rooftops with you, but until then…"

"But I'm innocent!"

"I know you are, and I've told the police that as much as I can, but I can't go to them again. I'm scared, Nat. Surely you understand that?"

"I know all too well what it's like to be afraid of Chrissy, Amira, but the longer the police suspect me, the more time Chrissy has to do something else. You think you're protecting yourself by keeping quiet but you're not. You're giving her everything she needs to strike again! And in the meantime, I'm being accused of crimes I didn't commit."

Amira shifts in her seat. "I feel for you, I really do, but you live in a house with your husband and a nanny. You're protected, but me? I live alone. I'm a walking target. I don't stand a chance against Chrissy Summers."

"And I do?"

Amira lifts her gaze to meet mine. "You survived her once before – surely you can do it again?"

I sit back in my seat, flattened. The truth is I barely survived Chrissy the first time. Can I really go through all that again and come out okay? Judging by the state of my life right now, the answer is an emphatic no.

46

When Amira leaves, I try to pretend I am okay. I go through the motions of interacting with Jay and Esme but in the back of my mind all I can think is, 'is Chrissy watching us right now?'.

I've never realised before how many windows this house has or how visible we are to anyone on the outside looking in. We are goldfish in a bowl. Targets waiting to be picked off one by one.

As my daughter smiles at me, her innocence shining like a beacon, something inside me snaps. "Can you close the curtains?"

Jay blinks but does as she's asked and we plunge into darkness. I wait for relief to hit me, but it never does.

Even with the windows concealed, Chrissy could still be watching. She has her ways. When I was a teenager, she always seemed to know what I was doing like she was one step ahead of me. Judging by the candid photos of me on the @coralbaygirl747 profile, things are exactly the same now.

Only this time it's life or death.

Esme giggles and a sudden surge of energy overwhelms me. I need to secure my home. I need to protect my family.

I jump to my feet. "I'm heading into town. Don't answer the door. Don't let anybody in and don't go out, do you hear me? Nobody in or out of this house."

Jay's grip on Esme tightens. "Is everything okay?"

I want to scream and ask how she could even think everything is okay when there's a murderer on the loose, but I don't. Instead, I force a smile. "I just want to get a few security bits, that's all. With what happened to Melissa, I think we could do with the protection. Call me if anyone comes to the door but don't answer it. I mean it Jay, don't open the door to anyone."

Jay nods, her smile as tight and as worried as my own. I'm not trying to unnerve her, but I can't help it. I need her to be vigilant. Her life and my family's life may depend on it.

I head into Coral Bay like a woman possessed, ignoring everyone else on the road. I know, 'have you heard? Not only has Nat Redding gone insane but she was so rude to me at the intersection' will now be today's hot gossip, but I don't care. All I care about it keeping my family safe.

I park on Main Street and hop out of the car. Sunlight blinds me. The world seems too big, too loud, too full on, but I grip my handbag and set off moving.

Out of the corner of my eye, I spot Dot waving to me. I lower my gaze and walk on as if I haven't seen her, but a few seconds later she grabs me by the arm.

"Nat, wait. I'm so glad I've bumped into you! I've been wanting to speak to you for a few days. Come into the shop with me?"

I hesitate. Al's Electronics is only two doors away. The surveillance equipment I need is inches from my fingertips, but one look at Dot's big, concerned eyes and I melt. I nod and follow her into her store. Once we are inside, Dot flips the 'open' sign over so it reads 'closed'.

"This must be a serious chat," I comment.

"I'm worried about you, love. I bumped into Amira the other day and my heart couldn't take it when she told me how you've been unravelling recently."

The kindness in Dot's voice pulls at something in my soul and I well up. "Sorry," I sniff, embarrassed by the lack of poise I'm showing in public.

"Don't be sorry for being upset! You've been through such a tough time of it recently, what with losing Hallie then finding Melissa like that.

Oh, sweetheart, come here."

I fall into Dot's arms and she holds me tight. Her small frame takes on every ounce of my pain. I can't remember when someone last hugged me properly. For the first time in a long time, I feel somewhat safe.

When I have no more tears left to cry, I pull away and wipe my eyes.

"How about you take a seat while I make us a cup of tea, then we can talk this through," Dot offers.

"That would be great."

I perch on the counter while Dot heads to the back of the store. The kettle bubbles into life. I pull my phone from my pocket while I wait, a timewasting habit I cannot shake no matter how many New Year's resolutions I make, and check my notifications. Unsurprisingly, there are no messages from Lucas, but there is one from Amira.

I don't know if you've already seen it but that trolling account you told me about has really gone in for you. You've lost even more followers. Hope you're okay babe – call if you need me x

I'm on Instagram in seconds. What I'm confronted with makes me gasp out loud.

Posted for all the world to see is a photo of me exiting the police station looking flustered and... well, guilty.

'I bet naughty Nat won't be posting this on her profile! But why would you when you're being questioned over stalking and MURDER allegations?'

Everything around me spins. My breathing becomes erratic as I read the comments underneath the post.

Murder? Wtf?! As if I used to like this woman...

There was always something I never liked about Nat, but I never could say what. Well, now I know it – SHE IS A MURDERER! So glad this account has shown me the truth. What a vile woman!

I hope she rots in prison for a long time for what she has done to her friends

I can't catch my breath. I can't hold on. I feel myself falling, despair cloaking me and pinning me down. Through the blur of my tears, I flick back to 'Finding the Good Life' and nearly scream at the follower count.

54k.

A few weeks ago I was flying past eighty thousand and now I'm on *54k.*

Chrissy is destroying me.

I go back to @coralbaygirl747 and scan the photos, consuming every bad angle, every sarcastic comment, every poisonous twist of the truth. Chrissy's cyberattack strikes me repeatedly like a knife to the gut.

Just as I am about to break, I spot a post I've not seen before. This one is the scariest of them all.

It's a photo of me taking the bins out looking dishevelled. The caption reads, *'and Nat swears she doesn't edit her photos... LOL'*, but the fact that an ugly photo of me was posted without my consent it not what terrifies me. No, what terrifies me is the fact that someone was outside my house taking those photos.

"Are you okay, Nat? You're as white as a sheet."

I jump as Dot re-enters the room. It feels like I'm stuck in two simultaneous timelines, one before I realised that not only has Chrissy been following me, but she has also been camped outside my home, the other my sickening reality where all my worst fears are confirmed. The two don't mesh. Dot's kind face jars against the idea that we are probably being watched by a murderer right now.

The hairs on the back of my neck stand on end.

"Close the blinds," I command, leaping to my feet.

"What?"

"Close the blinds now!" I yell, running to the shop window. The street outside looks normal, but I can't be too sure. Someone has been taking photos outside my own home and I haven't noticed. Can I be really trusted to make a judgement about my safety when I'm out and about?

"Nat, you're scaring me."

"Someone's following me."

I show Dot my phone, watching her reaction as she flicks through the photos and reads the captions.

When she finishes, her mouth sets in a straight line. "I tell you, those trolls are out of control!" she sighs, handing me my phone and going to the window to open the blinds.

I blink. "What are you doing?"

"Nat, come on," Dot says, turning to me with a reassuring smile. "I know this isn't nice, but what do you expect? You're a bit of a celebrity around here. A lot of people are jealous. I'm not saying it's right or that it's nice, but a few unflattering photos aren't to be unexpected when you do what you do for a living."

"Dot, someone took a photo of me outside my own home."

"I know, it's terrible, but you live on a normal street, not a gated community. What can you do?"

"Dot, Chrissy is -"

Alarm flashes across Dot's face. "Chrissy?"

"Chrissy is behind this," I explain.

Dot studies me closely and my hope rises. Surely Dot remembers what Chrissy is like? She nearly ruined her business. Dot knows better than anyone what evil Chrissy is capable of.

But my hopes are shredded when Dot's worry lines deepen. "Oh, Nat. I've heard the rumour you've been having a little trouble readjusting to Chrissy being back, but this is worse than I thought. Chrissy didn't set up that profile, love. She wouldn't do that."

I take a step back as if I've been shot. "She wouldn't do that? Are you... are you fucking kidding me?"

Dot blinks, my foul language cutting through the friendly atmosphere like an axe chopping wood.

"Chrissy Summers is a toxic bully," I spit.

267

"She's changed, Nat. She's grown up! Sure, she had her moments -"

That's when I lose it.

"Her moments?! Her fucking moments?! You, like the rest of this stupid town, seem to have a very short memory. If Chrissy had her way, you would have lost everything. She convinced everyone to boycott your store! If it hadn't been for me taking pity on you, you would have closed years ago!"

I know as soon as I've finished speaking that I've gone too far. Dot is Coral Bay's mother. You don't upset her. A line has been crossed, one that I'll never be able to claw my way back from.

Dot's face closes like a shutter. "You need to leave," she says calmly.

"Dot, I -"

"Leave, now," Dot commands, her eyes flashing with fire.

I stand for a moment, my breathing heavy, then snatch my handbag from the counter. "Just you wait, Dot. When she murders you, then you'll be sorry," I snap, unable to leave without having the last word. I march out of the door, my legs like jelly.

"The only person here acting crazy enough to be a killer is you, Nat," Dot calls after me, just loud enough for the people on Main Street to hear. They turn to watch the scene unfold, their curiosity pricked.

I look around, the judgement in everyone's eyes blazing. I open my mouth to argue back, but what's the point? No one believes me anyway.

"What are you looking at?" I snarl at the crowd before quickly heading to my car.

Halfway into my journey home, I realise I forgot to pick up the surveillance equipment, but it doesn't matter. After my public showdown with Dot, every eye in Coral Bay will be on me, waiting for me to slip up again. Who needs CCTV when you're the target of everyone's stares anyway?

47

I shut myself in the living room as soon as I get in. Jay knocks on the door and asks if I'm okay, but I tell her to leave me alone. I don't trust myself around people, not when I'm destroying relationships left, right and centre.

Once cocooned inside, I pull out a pen and paper and plot a timeline of events, starting with Hallie and Bree's crash and ending with the latest round of online hatred posted about me. I make a note of every time Chrissy has cropped up unexpectedly, every time her whereabouts have been unknown and every knife like phrase she has said to me. The more I write, the guiltier she looks.

I'm so tired of being the only one who can see the truth. I'm exhausted from looking over my shoulder every few seconds, of living in fear. Before I realise what's happening, my eyelids droop and the next thing I know I'm fast asleep on the sofa.

My dreams follow their usual haunting pattern of the last few weeks – Chrissy making her way towards me one menacing step at a time. Melissa reaching out, blood dripping from her fingers as she begs me for help. Screaming and running with nowhere to go and no one to help, and all the while Chrissy gets closer and closer.

I startle awake at the sound of the front door closing. I sit up, gripping the cushion next to me in terror. "Chrissy?"

The living room door opens, and I'm confronted not with the face of my enemy, but of my husband. From his expression, though, you'd think we were enemies.

"Did you just call out for Chrissy?"

I don't need to speak to answer Lucas's question – the look on my face says it all.

"Why are all the curtains closed?" he asks. Again, I don't answer. Lucas sighs irritably and opens them. Blinding sunlight floods the room. I wince, shrinking from its glare. When my vision resets, I find Lucas scanning over my jottings about Chrissy. "Really, Nat?"

"Lucas, she -"

Lucas waves his hand in the air to silence me, then frowns. "Where's Esme?"

I blink, uncertain for a moment. "With Jay," I reply, but it's too late – Lucas caught my hesitation. His judgemental glare twists my gut.

"Jay?" Lucas calls out.

"Up here!" comes a cheery response that jars against the spiked atmosphere.

Lucas thunders upstairs and I follow, although I'm not sure I should. By the time I make it up there, I find Lucas crouched beside Jay on the bathroom floor, grinning at Esme as she splashes in the bath.

"There's my little monkey!" he coos, then he faces Jay. "Thanks for bathing her."

"Oh, don't worry about it. We were finger painting, but it turned into body painting with this one! I thought we'd best have bath time early and save you both from the mess."

My eyes sting as I watch my husband and the nanny laughing together from periphery. It's a scene of picture-perfect family bliss... a picture I'm not included in.

But that is my husband, my daughter, my family.

A balloon of indignation inflates inside me. "I can take over from here," I interject, pushing my way into the bathroom.

"Oh, it's okay -" Jay begins, but I cut her off.

"I'm her mother, Jay, and I said I can take over from here."

Jay rises to her feet, blushing. "Of course, I'm sorry, I just -"

This time, Lucas interjects. "There's nothing to be sorry for, Jay. You were just doing your job." Lucas doesn't say more, but I know the rest of the sentence that's on his mind – 'you were just doing the job that Esme's own mother is incapable of doing'.

I glare at my husband and he glares back. The room beats with tension.

"I'll start dinner," Jay says meekly before slipping out of the room.

When she's gone, I turn back to Lucas. The expression on his face riles me up even further. "What?"

"What do you mean, 'what'? That's no way to speak to someone!"

I press my lips together. "I have to make a stand at some point, Lucas. Jay is taking over a little too much, don't you think?"

"She's just doing her job."

"Taking Esme when I'm at home isn't her job."

"When you're at home fast asleep in the middle of the day I think it might be."

Even though Lucas is right, I recoil from him.

"Don't look at me like that, Nat. Jay has been amazing these last few weeks when you've..." Lucas trails off, suddenly embarrassed by what he's trying to say.

I prickle. "When I've what?"

"Nat -"

"When I've what?"

"When you've been obsessing over Chrissy Summers!" Lucas shouts. His words echo around the bathroom like a bully's taunt.

"Lucas, she –"

Lucas holds his hand up wearily. "I'm not doing this with you, Nat. I am not having this conversation again. You need to stop. I want my wife back. Esme wants her mother back."

"Are you trying to say that I'm a bad mother?" I ask, the threat of tears squeezing my throat.

"You know I'm not saying that, but I am asking you to stop with the craziness and the following -"

"I'm trying to protect my family!"

From the bath, Esme starts to cry. I pull my attention away from my irate husband to my upset daughter. Her wobbling lower lip breaks my heart. I march over to Esme and pull her out of the bath.

"What are you doing?" Lucas says, trying to stop me, but I have Esme in my arms. She's wailing properly now, a full, hearty cry that rattles the air from my lungs. "Nat, you're scaring her!"

"Scaring her? I'm her mother!" I yell, carrying Esme out of the bathroom. In the heat of the moment, I forget to pick up a towel on the way out. Esme's wet body soaks my clothes, but I refuse to go back for one. I won't give Lucas the satisfaction of knowing I forgot yet another vital component of caring for my daughter.

Esme's cries are ear-splitting now. I sit on my bed and bounce her in my arms, trying to shush her but doing little to soothe her pain.

"Nat, at least wrap her up, for fucks sake!" Lucas snaps, entering the bedroom with a towel. I snatch it from him and bundle my sobbing daughter inside. I try to hold her close, but she puts her arms on my chest and pushes away, screaming at the top of her lungs.

"It's okay. Mummy's here," I whisper, but it's no use. Esme's anguished cries continue, fat tears rolling down her cheeks. Her hands press against me, her tiny body doing all it can to resist my embrace.

"Nat, you're going to hurt her. Give her here," Lucas pushes.

"No!" I shout, trying to hold my daughter's flailing body in my arms. "Give her to me NOW!"

I've never heard Lucas so angry before. My mouth hangs open, my arms go limp. Immediately, he scoops my daughter up and carries her away from me. His footsteps pound down the stairs. Esme's cries ring out in the house, but they are softer now, calmer.

She's okay now she's not around me.

She didn't need me - she needed anyone *but* me.

A loneliness I've never felt before, even when I was friendless, the butt of everyone's jokes and without a mother, suffocates me. First Hallie and Bree, then Melissa, then Sunaina, then Dot, and now Lucas and Esme... who else am I going to lose before life stops fucking with me?

At this point, is there even anyone left?

48

We eat dinner in stony silence. My red-rimmed eyes burn, but Lucas doesn't ask if I'm okay or comfort me. In fact, he barely acknowledges my existence. Each bite I eat struggles down my throat, landing heavily in my stomach like a stone dropping down a well.

I practically faint with relief when the doorbell rings halfway through dinner.

"I'll get it," Lucas mutters. I watch his strong, broad frame slink away from me. When he is gone, I feel less alone than I did when he was sat opposite me. I sink into my chair and finally breathe.

I only get a moment of respite, though, because suddenly shouting echoes out through the house.

"Is she here? Is she?!"

I'd recognise that voice anywhere. Heart racing, I rush to the hallway where I find Chrissy on my doorstep radiating with anger. Her eyes flash with pure hatred when she sees me, a sight so terrifying I almost collapse.

"What the fuck is wrong with you?!" she screams.

"Hey," Lucas says, holding his arms up to block Chrissy from lunging at me. "What's going on?"

Chrissy jabs her finger in my direction. "*She* keyed my car!"

My mouth hangs open. "I did not!"

"Oh, come off it, Nat! You're the only person who knows I'm staying at Rosevale Motel!"

"That's not true - Amira does too!"

Chrissy's jaw clenches. "Fine, you're the only person who knows I'm staying at Rosevale Motel and hates me. Hates me enough to key my car, anyway!"

"I didn't key your car!"

"Stop lying!"

"Chrissy, I have a baby upstairs," Lucas interjects.

Chrissy's expression softens, and she looks at Lucas through big, sad eyes. "I'm sorry, Lucas. I shouldn't have come barging in here like this. I'm just angry, that's all. That car is one of the only things I've got."

"Hey, I'd be pretty pissed if my car was keyed too," Lucas nods.

Chrissy smiles a simpering smile. My fingers itch to claw her eyes out. I plant myself firmly beside Lucas. "I didn't key your car."

Chrissy rolls her eyes. "The only person it could be is you. First you keep telling the police I'm a killer, then you follow me -"

"Amira was there too!"

Chrissy scoffs. "Please, the only reason Amira went along with you is because you scared her with your crazy theories."

"That's not true! They're her theories!"

"Amira's going for drinks with me on Saturday. Do you really think she'd be doing that if she thought I was a killer?"

I blink. Amira was with me just a few hours ago saying she was afraid of Chrissy. Why would she be meeting her if that were true?

"You... you're lying."

"Nat, the only liar here is you. I ignored you the first few times you tried to push me out, but accusing me of killing people and now keying my car? You've gone too far."

"But you followed me back! And you came to my house at night when everyone was sleeping."

"What?" Chrissy and Lucas both say.

"The other night! You came back in the middle of the night and rattled the door and..." I trail off as I sense Lucas turn to stone. I meet his gaze, his eyes betraying his horror. "That's why I smashed the mirror. I thought... I thought someone was there..."

Lucas struggles to find the words to say to me, but he doesn't need to say anything. He shifts his bodyweight so that he's no longer stood beside me. If anything, he looks as if he's leaning towards Chrissy.

My heart cracks so painfully I swear they must have heard it break.

"Nat, I did not come to your house at night," Chrissy says.

"You did," I protest, but there's no point. She would never admit it in front of Lucas. I glare at Chrissy, her demeanour mirroring one of a worried therapist but her eyes glinting with the shine of an evil genius.

Chrissy turns to Lucas. "Look, I'm going to the police tomorrow. I need to report this. This harassment can't continue."

Lucas sighs. "I get it, Chrissy, I really do, but please don't. Nat's really struggling with everything that's happened recently. Please don't add to it. Is there anything we can do to change your mind?"

Chrissy acts as if she's having a moral dilemma. "If you drop these accusations and pay for the damage, I can pretend this never happened. But you need to *drop* this, Nat. I'm not trying to hurt you, your husband, your daughter, or your friends. I'm not here to hurt anyone. I'm trying to have a life in Coral Bay, that's all."

I don't break Chrissy's gaze. She smiles at me, the same smile a parent gives their child when tricking them into eating vegetables.

Hope radiates from Lucas. His eyes plead with me to take this offer and move on.

But I can't. I can't let her get away with this. I can't let her win, not again.

"Chrissy, I did *not* key your car," I repeat, and then I walk away.

"Nat! Nat! Come back! Nat!" Lucas calls after me, but I don't turn around. I ascend the staircase and go to my bedroom, leaving my husband and my enemy in the doorway of my house alongside any hope of saving my marriage.

49

Lucas doesn't come to bed with me. He shuffles around the guest bedroom for a few minutes then the gentle sound of his snores ring out through the house.

The bed feels empty without him in it. So does my heart.

I throw my head back onto my pillow. Our second night apart. Separate rooms, separate lives. How did this happen?

Perhaps the more appropriate question would be - who made this happen? For that there is only one answer.

The way Chrissy looked at Lucas flashes before my eyes. A simpering, pouty damsel in distress, and Lucas fell for it. He didn't even stop to ask when I was supposed to have disappeared to Rosevale to key Chrissy's car. Rage flutters inside my chest. What kind of power does she have over him that he didn't even think to check her side of the story?

I stew on my festering thoughts until I hear it again – the sound of the front door handle rattling.

I bolt upright.

"You're not getting away from me this time," I think, grabbing a golf club and thundering downstairs. Ignoring the pounding in my chest, I wrench open the front door like I'm about to go into battle.

There's no one there, but the upright hairs on the back of my neck tell me to not trust the scene.

A cool breeze tickles my skin. I take a tentative step forward, crossing the boundary of my house to my driveway, and study the darkened world before me. I can't see anyone, but why would Chrissy make herself visible? That would ruin the fun. She will want to taunt me before she kills me, toying with me like she's the cat and I'm the mouse.

The imposing frames of our cars are the perfect place to hide. Gripping the golf club tighter, I take one step forward, then another.

"I know you're here, Chrissy," I call out into the darkness.

She doesn't reply, but I don't expect her to. She wants to rattle me. She wants me scared.

Well, I'm not scared anymore. I've spent too many years of my life scared of that woman. Too many years cowering in corners, averting my gaze and trembling in her presence.

But not anymore. Today I fight back.

I circle my car, then Lucas's. No one jumps out at me; no hand grabs my ankle... but that doesn't mean she's not here.

Every sense I have is heightened. I *know* she's here. I can feel her presence. Her eyes bore into my skull, her fingers itch to grab me. I can taste her murderous anticipation on the tip of my tongue. She's close, so close...

Suddenly, a slam rings out behind me. I spin around and the blood drains from my body.

The front door – it's closed.

I don't have my key.

I can't get back inside.

It's a windy night, but not windy enough to close a door by itself. No, someone purposely shut the door.

It's Chrissy. She's here... and now she's in the house.

50

Throwing the golf club to the ground, I race to the door and pound it with my fists.

"Lucas! Lucas!"

My frantic, trembling hands jab the doorbell repeatedly, trying to make as much noise as possible to wake my husband.

"Lucas!" I holler, but still the lights remain off. Darkness. The perfect camouflage for Chrissy to do her worst.

She's in there. She's in there with my sleeping husband and my vulnerable baby.

She's going to kill them both.

Snot dribbles down my chin as I scream for Lucas and attack the front door with all my might.

Suddenly, I spot the golf club glinting in the moonlight. The one thing that can stop Chrissy and save my family.

Without a second thought, I pick it up and drive it into the living room window. The cracking of glass is ear-splitting. I swing the golf club back and attack the window again. The glass splinters and shatters, sharp shards falling to the floor like a stream of dangerous icicles.

I chisel at the pointed remnants jutting out from the windowpane with the golf club but making a clear entryway is too time consuming. Time I don't have.

Biting my lower lip, I press my hand onto the window ledge, ready to haul myself inside. Glass tears into my palm and shreds me open, but I barely feel the pain. I know however sore it will be, it's nothing compared to what Chrissy will do to my family if I don't stop her.

I'm about to heave myself into the house when my face illuminates with the glow from the hallway light. My legs almost buckle from the rush of relief.

Thundering footsteps race towards the front door. I peel myself from the window, blood trickling down my fingers and dripping onto the driveway, but I couldn't care less. Lucas is coming. Lucas is okay.

He throws open the front door and I fall into his arms. "Oh Lucas," I sob. I want him to hold me, but he doesn't. He pulls away and keeps me at arm's length, my blood smeared across his bare chest.

"Nat, what the fuck is going on?" he asks, but he looks past me to the golf club and the broken glass and answers his own question. He lets me go like I'm cursed. "What… what have you done?"

"Lucas, she was here…" I trail off. I can't finish my sentence, not with my husband looking at me like he is afraid of me. I make a move towards him, but Lucas holds his arm up.

"You've lost it, Nat. You've well and truly lost it."

I open my mouth to protest, but no words come out. I glance over my shoulder, examining the scene through Lucas's eyes.

It doesn't look good.

"I knew you were struggling, but this? This is too far. Look at the house, Nat. Look at your hand."

"I can explain. Please, let me explain," I beg, but we both know I'm lying. How can anyone explain this?

"Amira told me you weren't in a good way, but I never thought this…" Lucas gulps. His eyes trace my body, lingering on my maimed hand. "We need to clean that."

Without another word, he walks through the house towards the kitchen. I follow him because I don't know what else to do.

Lucas doesn't look at me while he unpacks the first aid kit, nor when he cleans my hand. I wince as antiseptic burns my wounds, but Lucas says nothing. The cold, clinical way in which he deals with me hurts more than any cut ever could.

As soon as my hand is bandaged, he drops it. "That should be okay for tonight, but if it doesn't stop bleeding we might need to go to the hospital tomorrow. Some of the cuts are pretty deep." He clears away my bloody tissues, his body vibrating with tension.

"Lucas," I whisper, taking a step towards him, but he shakes his head.

"I can't deal with this right now, Nat. I have work in five hours. We'll talk when I get home, okay? We'll get you some help. I'll ask Jay to look after Esme so you don't have to worry about that, but for now please just go to bed. Go rest, and without having one of my pills, okay?"

I jolt at the mention of the medication. I thought I'd hidden taking the pills so well. As my face flames, Lucas's stays impassive.

"Go rest, and don't do anything else…"

"Crazy," I finish his sentence for him.

I want Lucas to protest that he doesn't think I'm crazy, but he doesn't say a word. Of course he doesn't because why wouldn't he think that? Confronted by this scene, what else would he think?

But I know the truth. Someone was here. Someone wanted to coax me outside and for Lucas to see me like this. Someone wants me to lose everything, and it looks like they're getting their wish.

51

I make sure I wake up before Lucas. I can't face seeing him, not after last night. His disappointment haunted my dreams. I'm not ready to face it in real life too.

My hand throbs, my bandage patchy with crusted blood, but I don't change it. Let me bleed. Let the world see how much I hurt.

I throw on my running gear and leave a note by the coffee machine to explain where I am, not that I suspect anyone will care, then slip out of the house. Sticky, muggy air greets me, as does a splatter of my blood on the driveway. My organs jar when they see it. I set off running, speeding away from what I did and the pain I have caused.

With my brain fried from last night, my feet automatically take the route to Hillman's Trek.

The rising sun greets me as I pound my way down the silent streets of Coral Bay. At this time, everything is peaceful and still. As I pass rows of suburban dream homes and shops that once waved me in like an old friend, I almost forget that once again I'm an outsider here.

Almost.

At the foot of Hillman's Trek, I pause. The incline snakes ahead of me, imposing and giant. "Do I have it in me to get to the top?" I wonder.

My feet answer the question for me. They set off at full speed, sending my body hurtling towards serenity at the end of the track. My lungs ache, my calves scream, but my feet won't stop. They can't stop. They know I need the win of reaching the summit.

The further I run, the more rejuvenated I feel. It's like the closer to the top I get, the more I become myself. I need that feeling now more than ever. Desperately, I chase it, my feet hitting the ground hard and fast.

I'm halfway to the top when I notice something on the path ahead of me. My heart flickers, but whatever it is isn't moving, so I keep going.

It's only when I'm about ten feet away from the shape that I slow down.

There's a shoe.

A neon pink running shoe belonging to someone who is half on the path, half buried in the wilderness.

Someone who isn't moving.

With my heart in my throat, I take a cautious step towards the person. "Hello? Hello? Can you hear me?"

There's no reply.

Trembling, I take small steps towards the figure. More of it emerges the closer I get.

Ill-fitting, well-worn leggings.

A t-shirt, dusty from the dirty ground and splattered in blood.

Badly fake tanned skin.

Blonde hair.

Matted, bloodied blonde hair.

And then I see the face. Or, more appropriately, what's left of it.

Chrissy Summers, her mouth stuck forever in a twisted, agonised scream, dried blood crusting the side of her concaved skull.

Chrissy Summers... dead.

52

I stumble backwards. I can't catch my breath, can't stop the world from spinning off balance like a broken fairground ride. I glance back at the maimed corpse of my tormentor and gag, acidic bile rising in my throat and threatening to spill out onto the floor.

Chrissy Summers is dead.

Head caved in, blood everywhere... dead.

My knees buckle beneath me and I crouch on all fours, panting for air.

Chrissy Summers is dead.

She isn't responsible for killing my friends. Someone else is... someone who's still out there.

The thought has me doubled over. I cry into my hands, loud, gut-wrenching sobs that hurt to let out.

What happened here?

What the fuck do I do?

I wipe my nose on the back of my hand and glance at Chrissy's battered body once more. A strangled noise escapes my lips. The blood, the overwhelming fear... it's all I can see.

Whatever I thought of Chrissy, the fact that she died up here scared and in pain makes me want to start crying all over again.

I don't want to leave her alone like this, but I don't have a choice. My phone is back at the house. I know Hillman's Trek well and it will be lucky if someone else runs the route this week. No one will find her if I don't tell them, but to do so I must leave her body behind.

I stand on unsteady legs. Before I leave, I take another look at Chrissy's smashed face, frozen in a moment of pure terror. Tears fall from my eyes once more.

"I am so, so sorry," I sob. "You didn't deserve this."

It pains me to realise the truth in what I'm saying. I wanted to make her pay for what she did to me, but not like this. I wanted an apology. I wanted to be better than her, to have a life she was jealous of, but hurt her? Erase her from the world? No, never.

Chrissy did bad things, but did she deserve to die like this? Does anyone?

I lean down and squeeze Chrissy's hand. Her skin is cold to touch, her hand hard in mine.

Chrissy Summers is dead. Those words, however implausible they seem, are true. She really is gone.

"I'm sorry," I whisper to her lifeless corpse. My bottom lip trembles, but I force myself to turn my back on her body and walk away.

By the time I reach the bottom of Hillman's Trek, my breathing has calmed, but my mind races faster than ever.

The police already think I'm responsible for everything. What will they think when I'm the one who finds Chrissy's body on a notoriously quiet running track?

Guilty.

I pause at the end of Maple Drive, but I don't go down it. I need time to think. So, instead of going home, I head to the beach.

My feet sink into the soft sand. The waves cheer me on, drawing me closer until I sit heavily where the water and sand meet. Waves lick my toes, but I barely register them.

If I say what I've found, I look guilty. If I don't and the police find out I already knew Chrissy was dead, I look guilty too.

I am trapped in an impossible situation. Trapped and destined to look guilty… exactly how someone wants me to look.

I think back to the list I made with Amira. I run through the names, but it makes no sense. Why would anyone on there want to set me up? I was as much of a victim as they were. Why would they turn on me?

"I've got it wrong," I realise. It can't be anyone on the list. It must be someone closer, someone who understood my past with Chrissy and my fear at having her back.

It must be a friend.

I go hot and cold at the realisation.

Suddenly, a dog barking makes me jump. I spin around to find Joelle being dragged across the sand by her Golden Retriever, Bo. She slows when she sees me.

"Morning Joelle," I call, pushing myself to smile.

"Morning Nat," she replies, her grip on the lead tightening.

As I rise to stand, Joelle takes a small step away from me, a move I choose to ignore. "How was the Arts Council meeting?"

"Good. It was good."

"And the grandkids? How are they?"

"They're good."

I wait for Joelle to return the question, but she never does.

"What's going on, Joelle? It's just me," I push, taking another step forward but I stop in my tracks as a spike of terror flashes in her eyes.

No one's ever looked at me like that before.

Burning from head to toe, I run back up the beach and into town.

The world has woken up in the time I've been lost in my thoughts. People mill around, starting their day, blissfully unaware that yet another Coral Bay resident is no more.

I walk down Main Street with tears in my eyes. I pray no one sees me crying in public again, but with the way Joelle looked at me looping in my mind it just might happen. All it will take to set me off is someone asking if I'm okay. In Coral Bay, questions like that are routine.

Only no one speaks to me. No friendly greeting, no enthusiastic wave, no conversation, nothing. It's like I'm not even in Coral Bay anymore.

I look around and notice that while no one approaches me, everyone is watching me. They've all seen I'm upset, but they don't care.

"Did they ever?" I wonder, a thought that ties my stomach in a knot.

With my head down, I keep walking, trying my best to ignore the stares even though they are lasers scorching chunks off my soul.

"I've heard she's well and truly lost it," someone whispers.

"Have you seen the front of her house? Blood everywhere, window gone. Annie Greenwell says she woke up in the middle of the night to find Nat smashing it with a golf club!"

"Poor Lucas. How the mighty have fallen, eh?"

Their comments burn like acid, the malicious words booming around my skull as if shouted through a megaphone.

Halfway along Main Street, I glance over my shoulder to find everyone still watching me. I expect them to blush and turn away when they realise I've heard what they've been saying, but they don't. They're not ashamed of gossiping. Why would they be? You only care about being caught if you care about the person you're talking about.

I scan the crowd, noting the judgemental faces of people I would usually consider a friend, and open my mouth. "You're not perfect, you know," I shout to my audience. "I could list a million and one things each of you have done that make you a bad person."

Hot tears spill down my cheeks. I wait for someone to break from the crowd to come to my aid, but no one makes a move. They just stare, half embarrassed on my behalf, half engrossed by my spectacular outburst.

I take one last look at them all. "Fuck you," I spit, even though I don't mean it, then I break into a run. I don't stop until I reach home.

I arrive in time to find Lucas pulling out of the driveway to go to work. He stops the car when he sees me and instinctively I wave, a gesture he doesn't return. His lips remain drawn in a tight line as he speeds away without a second glance in my direction.

An all-consuming ache splits my chest open. I've lost him, and that's before he finds out about my outburst on Main Street.

I trail into the house and head to the kitchen where I find Jay feeding Esme.

"Morning," she chimes, but one look at me and her features fall into a concerned frown. "Are you okay? Here, sit down and let me bring you a cup of tea."

"That would be great," I nod, sinking into a chair and facing Esme. She's covered in her breakfast, as always, and she's smiling, as always. Only this time I notice that she's smiling at me, her eyes full of a love that just a few days ago I didn't think was there.

Something inside my chest pulls tight.

Chrissy once looked at her mum like this. She was once someone's baby. Despite what she did to me, what she did to so many people, she was once this small, this innocent, this vulnerable. Her terrible choices will always define her to me, but to someone else she was simply just their daughter.

And now she is dead on Hillman's Trek.

Jay sets down a cup of tea and I take a large gulp, then another.

Even though I'll look guilty for it, I know what I need to do. Detective Baldie might not like me, but he can't pin crimes on an innocent woman. Instead of worrying about being liked, I need to worry about doing what is right and that is giving Chrissy the dignity in death she deserves. Who knows, maybe by doing that the whispers will stop. Maybe Lucas will see me as his wife again. Maybe by finally putting my past to rest I will be able to piece my life back together bit by bit.

I drain my tea and rise to my feet. "Have you seen my phone?"

"No, why?"

"I need to ring the police. It's Chrissy Summers… she's dead."

Jay looks at me for a moment before her face splits into a wide, beaming smile. "I know, and about time too, right?"

Then.

Mrs Hendricks sighs when she sees the girl outside her office, bloody nosed and trying her best not to cry. "Back again?" she asks, pushing the door open and inviting the girl inside.

As they enter the room, Mrs Hendricks makes sure she opens the window. She will be thankful for that after a few minutes in a confined space with this one.

"What happened this time?"

"What do you think?" the girl replies sullenly, gesturing to her face.

Mrs Hendricks sucks teeth. If there's one thing she cannot stand about teenagers, it's their attitude. "Here," she says, handing the girl a tissue.

The girl wipes the blood from her nose, wincing as she does.

"It's not broken. I can tell by looking," Mrs Hendricks informs her.

The girl doesn't react. Her features remain in the same impassive, expressionless mask the teacher has come to know so well. A hard face, the face of someone with no life behind the eyes. Mrs Hendricks finds herself wishing the girl had some fight to her, a little more spark. Maybe then being in the same room as her wouldn't feel quite so torturous, even with the smell.

"Why don't you tell me what happened?"

"What always happens – they got me," the girl shrugs, sinking into her seat.

Mrs Hendricks doesn't even bother to act surprised. She gave up that pretence months ago. Every time she opens her office to this girl, she knows what the story will be, but what can she do to fix it? They won't stop, not now they've smelled a weakness.

"Well, they've smelled something alright," she thinks, scrunching up her nose.

Mrs Hendricks studies the girl's face, noting how her left eye is swelling and how the energy she radiates with seems to suck the life from the room. "She's a funny little thing," Mrs Hendricks surmises. She's not grown into her features yet, still too small here and too big there. And the smell – dear God, the smell.

"Was it about your… your…?" Mrs Hendricks wonders how you say 'repulsive odour' without offending someone, but the flush on the girl's cheeks tells her that the girl is already aware of her stench. "Have you ever thought of trying to blend in a little more?"

The girl looks up, the first time she has looked Mrs Hendricks in the eye in months. Her gaze is piercing, alarming even.

"Blend in?"

"You know, trying to be more like the others so they don't notice you as much. It doesn't take a lot – they all wear their hair the same way these days! And how about a little deodorant? They do some wonderful scents. I have one with three kinds of flowers in it!"

The girl thinks to her cupboards at home, bare of food, never mind deodorant. "Do you think it will help?"

"My dear," Mrs Hendricks smiles, unable to hide her joy at this breakthrough moment. "Fitting in always helps."

The girl sits back in her chair, her mind ticking.

Fitting in – Mrs Hendricks makes it sound like it's so simple. Films and TV shows make it seem so simple too. All you need is a coat of makeup, hair straighteners and a push up bra and everyone forgets you were ever a social pariah, right?

Wrong. It doesn't work like that. She knows it doesn't, not for her anyway.

She will never be anyone other than the waste of oxygen they say she is. Mrs Hendricks can smile all she likes, but the girl knows the truth –

she just wants her gone like the rest of them do.

Fit in, huh?

She swears to herself there and then that one day she will fit in so well they won't even recognise her. One day she will fit in so well they'll never see her coming, and then they will be sorry.

Now.

53

The world is on pause, life suspended in a moment of pure disbelief. Jay's grinning face looms before me, her words looping in my mind.

Jay?

Jay did this?

"The look on your face!" Jay giggles. "Oh, Nat, it's a picture!" She reaches out and squeezes my hand, but I pull away sharply.

"Don't touch me," I whisper.

Jay pulls a mock sad face. "Come on, Nat, don't be like that! You can't turn on me. I've been the best friend you've ever had these last few months! Taking your baby at the drop of a hat, supporting you when everyone else turned their back on you. I was the only one really on your side!"

"Of course you were if you were the one doing it all!" I snap. My head spins, the truth shape shifting before me like phantom. "I don't understand, Jay. I just don't understand."

"Really?" Jay asks, tilting her head. "You don't understand why those monsters had to die? You don't understand that they had to pay for what they did?"

I open my mouth to argue but close it in defeat.

Jay nods. "There you go. You know exactly who they were, exactly why I had to do what I did."

The collar of my t-shirt sits tight on my neck. I tug at it. I'm inexplicably warm, the intense flames of Jay's revelation licking my face, but there's no way to comfort myself. Not after this bombshell.

My voice trembles as I speak. "Did you kill all of them? Hallie? Melissa? Chrissy?"

Jay holds my gaze, her sparkling eyes answering my question.

I hang my head, Hallie's carefree, smiling face swimming before me. "I can't believe it," I breathe.

"Can't believe it? Nat, you should be thanking me!" Jay cheers, clapping me hard on the back.

My head snaps up and my vision blurs. I shake my head, but the movement comes out slow and clumsy as if my neck can't support the weight.

"Why, Jay? You didn't even know them."

Jay's face splits into a wide, amused grin as she perches on the kitchen counter. "You really don't recognise me, do you?"

Dread rolls down my body at her words. I try to study her features, but they slip and slide in and out of focus. I blink to correct my vision, but nothing seems to be working the way it should be.

"I went to Coral Bay High, Nat, just like you."

I frown. "No, you're from... you're from..."

It's then that I realise I cannot complete my sentence. "Where did Jay grow up?" I ask myself. I don't have a clue.

My heart ices over as it dawns on me that I know very little about my nanny, the woman I moved into my home and trusted to look after my daughter.

Jay laughs. "You've literally no idea, do you? Did you even read my CV or were you just too excited to hand the baby to someone else to bother with the details?"

I look over to Esme. She beams at me, a smile so dazzling my heart spasms at the sight of it.

I read Jay's CV, of course I did. Our search for a nanny had taken months. We interviewed a lot of people before her, but Jay stood out. I remember taking her references – glowing ones - and being grateful that she had so much experience with children, but I can't remember much else about her life before I invited her so enthusiastically into my own.

"Let's be real, Nat. You were so desperate to fill the post you barely interviewed me. All you wanted was for someone, for anyone, to hold the baby while you took photos of your amazing life for strangers on the internet... so there I was. I started the day after we interviewed. I mean, really, I could have been anyone."

"But you... you never wanted to talk about your past. You had a bad breakup. I didn't want to pry!"

"I'll give you that - the bad breakup part is true." Jay's face clouds over, a sight that sends a shiver down my spine. "I got out of Coral Bay at sixteen with the scummiest guy on the planet. Luckily, his nasty streak taught me a thing or two about where it hurts most to hit someone." Jay winks at me and I recoil.

"But everything happens for a reason, right? I got to walk away with his surname. A box of hair dye, a little weight gain, some makeup and a new last name was all it took to fool you into thinking we'd never met before."

"You're not called Jay Scott?"

"I am, but you might know me better as Jay Riley. Sorry, should I say Josephine Riley."

The blood drains from my body.

Suddenly, I know exactly who Jay is. More importantly, I know exactly why she is here for me.

<u>Then.</u>

It's a scorching day, but Josephine can't feel the heat. She's too numb to feel anything.

Her mum is dead.

*Her mum is **dead**.*

Josephine has repeated those words over and over again for the last hour, but they still don't seem real. None of this does.

Her life changes from here, she knows that. Her mum won't be sleeping off her pain when she gets home from school. She won't be telling her to reach for the stars and do better than she ever did. She won't be coming back from the hospital, not this time.

Where does that leave Josephine?

At best, she will be stuck with Him until she can escape here and never look back. At worst, He will kick her out and she will have nowhere to go.

Her mum is dead.

*Her mum is **dead**.*

A bursting dam of emotion brews inside Josephine. She wants to release the strangled cries building inside her but she's scared if she does then she won't ever be able to stop her tears. She's never experienced pain like this. Every day of her life so far has been torturous, but this? This is something else. This is a whole new level of agony.

Her mum is dead.

*Her mum is **dead**.*

Suddenly, Josephine burns from head to toe, her instincts screaming that someone is watching her. She stiffens, waiting for Chrissy and co to pounce, but relaxes when she realises it's not them making their way over to her.

It is someone from school, though. The art girl. Nicole? Nancy? She's not in any of Josephine's classes, but she's seen her around the hospital a few times. She's never asked what she's doing here, though. In fact, they've never spoken. Chrissy's ruling of who is a social leper extends well beyond the walls of Coral Bay High.

But then the art girl offers Josephine a shy smile and breaks the rule. She sits beside her, sweat glistening on her forehead.

"I heard a nurse talking about your mum. I'm sorry."

Those words of kindness wrap a blanket around Josephine's broken heart. "Thank you," she croaks.

She wants to say more, to tell this girl about her mother before He and the cancer ruined her, but the words are too painful to say out loud.

"I'm Nat, by the way."

Nat. Fat Nat. Nerdy Nat. The art geek, another person on the lower rungs of the popularity scale. Not as low as Josephine, but low enough that her life has been scarred irrevocably by Chrissy Summers and her friends.

"Josephine," she replies.

Nat nods. Josephine wonders if this is the first time Nat has heard her real name. Usually she's only referred to as Chrissy's defamatory slur.

"My mum's in here too. Breast cancer. This is the second time she's had it. It's spread to her lungs." Nat stumbles over her words, her pain catching in the back of her throat. She faces Josephine. "Not many people understand what this is like, but I do. I know you're feeling alone right now - I guess you're always feeling alone, actually - but you're not. If you need to talk, you know where I am."

Nat squeezes Josephine's hand, then she leaves.

Josephine stays on the bench for the next few hours. Even though Nat has long gone, Josephine can still feel the ghost of her touch. Her skin tingles with hope.

For years people have recoiled from her, but Nat? Nat bridged the distance. Nat gets it, all of it. She's on Chrissy's hit list too. Her mum is sick with an illness that destroys more than just the person with it. She knows what it's like to carry hurt around like a backpack filled with rocks that you can never take off. She knows what it's like to be so alone, so unloved, so invisible you often gasp at the sight of yourself in the mirror when you realise you actually do exist.

If life so far has taught Josephine anything, it's that she shouldn't get her hopes up, but she can't help herself. The thought shines in her like a beacon... Nat could be a friend.

That night, even though her mum is no longer in the room next door and her life is filled with uncertainty and pain, Josephine sleeps. She sleeps well. She dreams of a time where life isn't like this, where it's her and Nat against the world and where loneliness is a thing of the past.

The next day, their taunts on the bus don't hurt as much as they usually do. She doesn't mind when people shove past her then scream because they made contact with her gross, slick with sweat body. She glosses over the part where they throw scrunched up paper at the back of her head all the way through science when the teacher's back is turned, and sometimes when the teacher's back isn't.

Josephine ignores it all because when she closes her eyes, she can still feel the warmth of Nat's hand on hers, the fizzing, all-consuming comfort of friendship.

Josephine spots Nat at lunch. She's sketching, something she does every day. People think Nat is art obsessed, but Josephine knows what she's really doing – keeping her head down in the hope that Chrissy won't find her. It's a tactic that more often than not doesn't work, but for the rare times it does, it's worth a try.

Butterflies flutter in Josephine's stomach as she makes her way over to Nat. "Hey."

Nat looks up, alarmed to hear someone talking to her. That alarm transforms into pure horror when she realises who it is that's speaking. "Oh, hey," she replies, her face burning.

Nat snaps her sketchbook shut and for one brief, brilliant, delusional second, Josephine imagines it's because she's about to pat the grass beside her and ask Josephine to sit down.

But the next thing she knows, Nat is on her feet. "I need to go to class," she mumbles.

"But lunch has only just started."

"I know but I... I want a good seat."

Nat tries to get past, but Josephine blocks her.

"But you said we could talk. You said I wasn't alone." There's so much hope in her voice it sounds desperate, Josephine knows that, but she can't help it. She is desperate. Nat threw her a lifeline just as she was about to give up... doesn't she realise how much that meant? Why would she take it away now when Josephine needs it the most?

"I know but -"

Then they hear it - the voice that could trigger a thousand night terrors.

"What the fuck is this?! Are you two an item now?"

The all too familiar feeling of ice-cold dread rolls its way from Josephine's head to her toes. She turns and faces the line-up of her tormentors.

"Chrissy," Nat tries to explain, but Chrissy shoots her a look so poisonous even the newest flower would shrivel if caught in its glare.

"Are you two a couple?" Chrissy spits gleefully.

Josephine looks at Nat, her heart racing. "Please," she pleads with her eyes, "please stick with me."

Surely she didn't imagine the kindness? Surely having someone who knows what it's like to deal with a parent who has cancer is more important than avoiding Chrissy Summers? Surely Nat won't cast her out just as she had invited her in?

But, of course, life for Josephine only ever goes one way.

"No, no!" Nat protests, shaking her head in disgust to emphasise her point.

Her denial hits Josephine like a truck ploughing over a mouse.

"Then why the fuck are you talking?" Chrissy laughs, moving closer.

Nat looks at Josephine, her fear and desperation enough to send a shiver down Josephine's spine. Josephine wants to reach out, to say it's okay, to reassure her that whatever Chrissy does they can take now that they aren't alone, but then Josephine sees something flash in Nat's eyes.

She knows what's going to happen before it does. "No," she thinks. "No, please, no."

"Her mum just died," Nat says.

Those words, no matter how softly they were spoken, split the atmosphere wide open. There's a beat of silence so alive it has its own pulse.

"What?" Chrissy asks.

"I... she... her mum just died."

Nat wants to take the words back as soon as she's said them, but she can't. They're out there now. They're in the air. She's breathing them in, their hateful sentiments filling her lungs and choking her.

Nat never thought she would become this person. She never thought she had a malicious bone in her body. She would never have believed it of herself.

But Josephine can believe it. She believes the worst of everyone. It's all she's ever been shown.

"Fuck," Chrissy cackles. "I mean, wouldn't you want to die if that was your daughter?"

As Chrissy and her circle snigger, Nat takes a step back from the scene. She can't distance herself enough from what she's done, though. Those words can never be taken back. The trauma of this moment will never be forgotten.

She wants to take Josephine by the hand and say I'm sorry, I'm so, so sorry, but she doesn't. Her apology will never make up for what she's done, and it won't change what's about to happen. It's too late. Josephine will have to take the hit, like she always does.

"She's used to it by now," Nat tries to tell herself, but she knows this is different. This has gone further than anything that's ever happened before. What she has done is unspeakably despicable, and the shame will burn inside her forever.

As for Josephine, she learns important lessons that day. She learns that fear overrides sense and that grief and loss don't excuse you from more pain. Most importantly, she learns that even though she thought life was the cruellest it could possibly be before, it can always get worse.

Josephine turns and faces her tormentors head on. She's ready for it. Whatever they throw at her, whatever they do, she will take it. There's nothing left for her to care about now, anyway. Everything positive in her died the moment Nat showed her how truly cruel people could be.

Now.

54

"Jay, I'm so -"

"I don't want your apology. It's years too late."

"Jay, I was young and -"

"Oh, please!" Jay scoffs. "All I've heard you bang on about for the last few weeks is how your friends knew exactly what they were doing and that being young is no excuse, so don't try that one with me now."

I hang my head in shame. "My mum died a few months after what happened. I always... I always thought I deserved it because of what I'd done," I admit. "I can't describe the pain of losing her. If I'd have known what they'd do..." I close my eyes, trying to block out the memory of the cruellest thing I've ever done, but it consumes me.

Jay rolls her eyes. "What did you think they would do – feel sorry for me? Realise how toxic they'd been and apologise? Did you think we'd start having sleepovers and braiding each other's hair?"

"No, but I didn't think they'd be that bad! I didn't think they'd tease you over your mum dying." My lower lip trembles as memories of their vile taunts flash before my eyes. Josephine had looked like the most broken girl in the world, and I was responsible for that.

I have repressed the memory of what I did that day for so many years, but here it is in my kitchen, alive and kicking and rightfully furious.

"You knew what they'd do, Nat. That's why you said it – so they'd get me and not you."

I open my mouth to argue, but she's right, of course she's right. Anything to give myself five minutes of peace, right? Even if that meant destroying someone else at the lowest point in their life.

"I'm so sorry," I whisper.

"I said I don't want your apology!" Jay yells, slamming her fist on the counter.

The noise startles Esme and she begins to cry. I try to reach for her, but my arms won't move when I tell them to.

"Shh, baby girl, shh," Jay whispers, picking Esme up and rocking her.

My heart leaps into my throat at the sight of my daughter in her arms. "Put her down," I plead.

"Or what? What are you going to do?" Jay looks at Esme and kisses her forehead. "She likes me more than she likes you, anyway."

Her words whip me. I look at my daughter nuzzling into Jay's neck like it's home and my eyes fill with tears. Jay's probably right. She has been there for Esme these last few weeks while I've been chasing Chrissy Summers, after all. Why wouldn't Esme prefer her to me? At least Jay is present in her life.

But Jay isn't Esme's mother – I am.

"Give me my daughter," I command.

Jay just laughs.

"Give her to me!" I shout, rising to my feet.

Or at least, I try to rise to my feet. I barely take one step before my legs give way and I collapse to the floor. The air is knocked out of my lungs from the shock. I grapple with my limbs, trying to push myself to stand, but nothing is working the way it should.

Jay doesn't help me up. She stands over me and watches as I flail about on the floor.

I try once more to push myself to stand, but I can't. My limbs refuse to take orders. I look up at Jay, her smiling face looming above me. Dread trickles down my soul like rain on a windowpane.

"What... what have you done to me?"

Jay picks something up from the kitchen counter... Lucas's pain medication. She shakes the bottle, but the usual rattle of pills can't be heard.

It's completely empty.

An anguished wail escapes my lips. "Jay, it will kill me!"

"That's the point..." Jay responds, amused it has taken me this long to realise what she is going to do. She sets a now calm Esme back down in her highchair and crouches before me. My heart stops inside my chest. "There are two options here Nat – you do exactly as I say, or you don't. But just to warn you, if you do what I say then you will die."

Even with my senses slowly numbing, my body still turns to ice. "And if I don't?"

Jay nods at Esme and pouts. "Then unfortunately Esme dies too."

I make a move to claw her evil face, but my arms loll by my sides, feeble and useless. Everything blurs and swims. I try to scream, but the only sound that leaves my drooling lips is a strange, strangled wail.

"Shh, Nat. We've only got one chance to get this right. Don't go using all your energy up now and spoil it."

I fix my gaze on Jay, my face wet with tears and damp with sweat.

"That's better. Now, I need you to get up and sit back on your chair. I can help a little, but not too much. If I drag you, you might bruise and then... well, then your favourite detectives might not get all their loose ends tied up as neatly as planned. So," Jay says, kicking the bottoms of my feet. "Up you get."

I try to sit, to move my limbs into compliance, but they feel so heavy. It's like my body has turned into a statue without my consent.

"Up you *get*," Jay repeats, kicking me harder.

I can't do it. I can't follow her orders. I try my best to, but I stay fixed to the floor, a pathetic, immovable mass.

"Oh, for fucks sake," Jay snaps, heading over to the kitchen and picking up a large knife. She strides over to Esme and holds it in front of her, pointing the blade at her tiny chest.

An animalistic scream bursts from me. "I'll do it!"

Jay lowers the knife. She watches me roll onto my stomach, putting as much of my weight onto my forearms as possible. Slowly, I drag my body towards the chair, gripping the chair leg with one arm as best I can. The effort of the manoeuvre is exhausting.

"I… can't…" I pant.

Jay sets the knife on the table and slips her arms under my underarms. I push with my feet and she hauls me up at the same time, then my cumbersome body lands heavily in the chair.

"There. That wasn't so hard, was it?" Jay says brightly, pushing my seat up to the table.

My blurry vision fixes on Esme. I try to smile at her, to let her know it's going to be okay, but my features won't obey orders. My tongue feels clumsily large and choking. I need to stick it out of my mouth, but my lips won't open when I tell them to. Tears fall down my cheeks, but I can't lift my arms to wipe them away.

"How the mighty have fallen," Jay mutters as she sits opposite me.

The back door calls to me from over her shoulder. It's so close. If I could run to it, if I could make outside, if I could scream…

Jay follows my line of sight. "Oh Nat, are you really thinking about trying to get away?" I flick my gaze back to her and she gives me a pitying smile. "I admire the fight, I really do, but you don't stand a chance. You've got so many pills inside you that you wouldn't even reach the door without passing out."

I want to argue back, but it's taking all my concentration to stay awake.

Jay rises to her feet. She ruffles Esme's hair as she walks past her then picks up the empty pill pot and my laptop, bringing them both to the table.

"Your suicide note is set to go live in half an hour. Not the most original ending for a serial killer, I know, but it rounds everything up so neatly it just had to be done."

Jay turns the laptop to me. On the screen is a smiling photo of me, Lucas, and Esme. It was taken at the beach. It was taken when we were happy.

It was taken before the arrival of Jay.

My eyes swim. I try to read what she has written, but the pills have destroyed my vision. "What... what..."

"What does it say? I won't bore you with the details – we don't have the time for that - but it's your confession, Nat. It tells the world what a fake bitch you are, even though most people know that already by now. It's the story of how you came back here with a vendetta, determined to be queen of Coral Bay. How you lied and manipulated your way to the top and deluded poor, innocent Lucas into falling for you. How you secretly hated your friends and wanted them gone so tore them apart from the inside. How you couldn't stand it when Chrissy returned and people liked her more than you."

I try shake my head, but the movement comes out wrong.

"Oh, you should see your face! Did you really think I was going to kill everyone and go to prison for it myself? No chance! You're not ruining my life for the second time. No, this all lands on you, Nat. The world will hate you forever for what they think you've done."

It takes all my might, but I manage to speak one word. "Why?"

Jay picks up the knife and rests the point on the table. She spins it, the blade glinting in the sun.

"I tried to get over it all, Nat, I really did. I left Coral Bay as soon as I could. I married a psychopath who beat me, but I left. I wasn't Josephine Riley anymore – I was Jay Scott! I got a job, I made friends, I dyed my hair, I worked out - I was not the girl I was before. I mean, when I came back here you didn't even recognise me. No one did. That was all I ever wanted. I tried to put so much distance between me and the girl I was, but…"

I finish her sentence for her. "You couldn't."

Jay smiles at me. "Once a victim, always a victim, right?" She laughs bitterly. "My husband kept outing me as a loser. He ridiculed me in front of everyone. He beat me and humiliated me like it was a sport. The friends I'd made left me behind because of him. So, I killed him."

Jay's cold, cruel eyes stare into my soul. My stomach spasms, but I'm not sure if it's from the intensity of her gaze or from the medication attacking my organs and shutting them down one by one.

"I made it look like he left me. He wasn't a nice guy and didn't have many friends, so no one really missed him. That's when I realised I didn't have to be Josephine Riley ever again. I could start over. I could reinvent myself. And, more importantly, I could stop anyone who tried to make me become the girl I used to be."

"I started going out. I got a *lot* of attention. After years of being invisible, it felt good. Then one night I bumped into Blaine Rankin. He started talking to me… *he* started talking to *me!* I couldn't believe it. We went on a couple of dates and things were going well then…" Jay's face twists, but she pulls herself together. "Then we slept together. The next morning, all Blaine could say was what a perfect match we were. He said he couldn't believe he'd never met someone as amazing as me before, so I told him he already knew me."

From the look on Jay's face, I can tell the news didn't go down well.

"He was horrified. Disgusted. He called me… he called me Fish Sticks," Jay spits the name like it's poison. "I left, then the next day I waited for him outside his apartment. I begged him to speak to me, but he said he didn't want his flatmate seeing us together. He was *embarrassed* of me," Jay hisses. "So, I told him I'd taken a photo of him naked and was going to send it around if he didn't speak to me. He wouldn't let me in his apartment, but his building had a communal rooftop, so we went there for our chat." Jay's eyes glitter. "He lunged for my phone.

He thought he could throw it off the roof and he'd win again. He didn't realise the only thing falling from up there was him."

A shudder travels through my core.

"I should have felt bad, but I didn't. If anything, I felt amazing. He deserved it, after all. So, I got thinking... who else deserved it?"

Jay shifts her gaze onto me. If I weren't already immobilised from the drugs, the hatred in her eyes would have pinned me to the spot anyway.

"I found you so quickly, bragging about your fantastic life, your amazing husband, your perfect baby... it was sickening. You didn't deserve any of it. I was only going to toy with you, maybe break up your marriage... but then I saw the photos of you and *them*." Jay's nose wrinkles. "It was bad enough that you forgave them, but worse than that you *became* one of them."

Jay's words crucify me. I think of my filtered, carefully crafted, smiling group photos blasted all over the internet with #squadgoals plastered proudly underneath them. I think of the matching dressing gowns we wore for my wedding, the expensive girls' trips we lowkey bragged about.

But worse than that, I think of the people who used to be kind to me at school. The people who would offer me pitying smiles whenever Chrissy and her friends did something horrific or who would tell a teacher to check on me after I'd been hurt. I pass those people on Main Street all the time, but I've never once thanked them. I've never once invited them out or made them a part of my life. Why would I? I didn't want to befriend *them* – I wanted to be a cool girl!

In all the time spent remembering how horrific school had been, I forgot the moments of kindness I experienced. I chose the wrong people to be my friends. I became someone I never should have been.

And I will pay the ultimate price for it.

I struggle to hold myself together. Snot dribbles down my chin as I cry for the mistakes I have made and the punishment I am receiving for them.

Jay watches me crumble in delirious fascination. "Has anyone ever told you you're a really ugly crier?"

My head drops, the ability to keep upright something I'm quickly losing. Drool and tears pool on my collar.

"Don't cry, Nat – this story has a happy ending!" Jay says, pushing my head up so I can look her in the eye. A demonic smile plasters her face. "Maybe not so happy for you, but I think you're going to like it. Originally, I was going to kill Lucas. This was going to be a murder-suicide situation, but he changed my mind. Do you remember what he said to you in the kitchen that day? He said, 'no one got as raw a deal as Josephine Riley'. He remembered me. *He* remembered *me*, my real name and everything! And he didn't dismiss what I went through like he did with you. So, I decided that he can stick around. I'll be his shoulder to cry on when you're gone," Jay winks.

I want to lunge at her, but I can't. My hand twitches, but that's it.

My pathetic attempt at fighting for my husband serves only to amuse Jay further. "You're so funny, Nat. You should see how hilarious your body looks spasming and twitching like that," she grins, setting the knife on the table and sitting back in her seat. She glances at the clock on the wall. "Any minute now you should be blacking out."

Her words kick something inside of me into life. I think of Lucas coming home from work and finding my body slumped over the table, the man I love who will spend the rest of his life believing the worst of me if I don't stop this. I think of my daughter sat inches away from me, blissfully unaware that she is witnessing my slow, painful death.

This cannot be it. This cannot be how my story ends.

Using the last scraps of strength I have, my arm shoots across the table and I grab the knife.

Or I try to grab the knife, at least, but my fingers are clumsy and disobedient. They graze the blade, not gripping the handle and driving the metal into Jay's cold, murderous heart like I intended.

Jay roars with laughter. "I knew you'd go for the knife! I couldn't resist leaving it out and watching you try to fight back! Oh, that was too precious!"

Wiping tears of joy from her eyes, she bats my hand away and slides the knife out of reach. My defeated body falls forward onto the table, my useless fingers outstretched as if they still half believe they have a chance of getting the knife and using it against Jay.

"Look, Nat, trust me when I say that death is the best option here. It's either death or life in prison for multiple murders."

My head rests on the cool wood of the dining table, too exhausted to remain upright.

"I'm going to get away with this, Nat. Not only are you going to post a confession to the world in a matter of minutes, but all evidence points to you. Your car is the car that scared Hallie and Bree into driving off the road. I used your laptop to sign up to dating websites so I could talk to them – it's all on your web history, as is the fake profile you made to troll yourself. The hideous candlestick that's missing from your hallway? That's the weapon Melissa was killed with. It's in the bag of items to be donated to her work's auction. You were taking it around to hers when anger took over and you caved her skull in, or so the story will go. Your yearbook has a page missing – a page that was found in your letterbox by you. Becca was -"

My eyebrows furrow at the mention of Becca's name.

Jay smirks. "I forgot she's not been found yet. It's been a few days – I can't imagine what she looks like now," Jay grimaces. "But Becca's dead too. Tragic, isn't it? I didn't get around to killing Amira, but I guess one can get away for now. I'm sure I'll find a way to make her disappear soon. I always do."

A sob escapes from my lips. My insides are both completely numb yet screaming in pain. I can feel death coming for me, rolling over my body bit by bit.

Jay pats my shoulder. "Don't be sad, Nat – Becca was a bitch. Did you know she was sleeping with two married men and getting another to pay her rent so she didn't tell his wife about their affair? I – we – did the world a favour. We did the world a favour with them all."

My neck jerks, a pathetic attempt at a shake of the head.

"Oh, don't be so humble, Nat! This was a team effort! You're as responsible for this as I am. You brought me into your life. You showed me a way to get to them all. You made this so easy for me."

"No," I moan.

Jay pats my hand. I want to snatch it away, but I don't have the energy to make such a bold move.

"Face it, Nat - there isn't a jury in the world who would find you not guilty. I planted enough physical evidence to implicate you, and you? You did the rest. Really, even in my wildest dreams, I'd have never thought you'd have gone as crazy as you did. I could never have predicted your Chrissy issues ran that deep! Really, I owe her as much as I owe you in all of this. You hit her with a rock, by the way. What a stroke of luck that you both pick the most obscure route in the world to run," Jay laughs.

My cries get louder, anguished, pained sobs that come from the pit of my soul.

Suddenly, Jay is at my side, stroking my hair. It hits me that her face might be the last thing I ever see, a thought that shatters my heart into a million pieces.

I don't want to die. I don't want to die, not like this.

I flail my arms to push her away, but they barely move. A low moan rings out, the only sound I seem capable of making now.

"Nat, you're making this so much harder than it needs to be," Jay sighs, pressing the empty box of pills into my hand and curling my fingers around it. "Do I need to bring Esme closer for you to remember what's at stake here? Do I need to hand her the knife? Killing bullies is one thing, but do you really want the world to think you murdered your own daughter?"

My vision flicks to Esme. Her edges are hazy, but I see her. I see her, my beautiful, wonderful daughter. "I love you," I want to scream. "I love you so much."

But my words stay bottled inside my immobilised lips.

"That's it," Jay whispers. "Do the right thing, Nat. Do what you should have done all those years ago when you made the choice to tell Chrissy my mum had died."

I choke on my tears. Everything is slowing now. My breathing, my vision, my life. It's all just slipping away.

"We all have a choice to make, a fork in the road that will change our future forever. You chose the wrong one before, but now you can make it right. I'm giving you the chance to redeem yourself here."

"Esme," I try to say, but her name comes out indecipherable and wrong.

"Shh, don't scare her. Just let go. Aren't you tired of pretending to be someone you're not? Aren't you tired of this half-life you've been living? Just stop. Give up, give in."

I want to push back against Jay's words, but with what? The very essence of my life is being sucked from my body with every aching breath I struggle to take.

Besides, I *am* tired. I am not the wife Lucas thinks I am, the person I present online, the friend I pretend to be.

I look back at Esme. She's whimpering now, her large, blue eyes confused and scared. "Mummy's here," I want to say. "Mummy's here and it will all be okay."

Something inside me kicks.

I may have pretended to be many things, but I never pretended to be her mother. That love was always there. That love was always true.

As her cries get louder and my muscles grow weaker, I realise that I'm still fighting. I'm not fighting for me, though – I'm fighting for her. My daughter is my greatest achievement, my most genuine love, the purest thing in my life.

My daughter will not die for a mistake I made as a teenager.

She will never know of the choice I made for her, but she will live for it, and that is all I can ask for.

Everything around me dims. The colours blur, the world smudges. The last thing I see before everything fades into nothingness is Esme, the thing that was always, always worth the fight.

Epilogue

Sixteen Months Later

She sets the freshly brewed coffees on the table, the final touch to the breakfast she has spent the last half an hour lovingly making. She swells with pride. It's perfect, like something from the pages of a magazine.

"Lucas, it's ready!"

"Coming!"

On the kitchen counter, her phone buzzes. She bites back her irritation at having her morning interrupted and glances at the message.

Babe, you are a HERO for helping me out! Seriously the BEST! See you tonight... I'll bring the wiiiiiiiine!x

She doesn't reply, not now. Not when she has choreographed the perfect breakfast for her and Lucas to share. Romance needs to be worked on, cultivated, and kept alive, that's what everyone says, and she is not going to let this one die by replying to Amira.

She rearranges the flowers so they look symmetrical then takes her usual seat, the one directly opposite him. The place she was always destined to sit, she just didn't know it.

She smooths down her appearance and tucks her hair behind her ears. Smiling, easy going, laid back - the girl of his dreams.

She butters her toast – one slice, even though she wants two – and sets it on her plate. Seconds later, Lucas walks into the room with Esme.

"Sorry, this one did *not* want her hair brushing this morning," he says, leaning in and giving her a slow, lingering kiss. Her soul sets on fire.

Lucas Redding, the best she's ever had. She could kiss those lips forever. She *will* kiss those lips forever – she has it all planned out. Starting his day with the perfect breakfast is just part of putting that plan into action, as is always looking beautiful and being the best, most caring mum she can possibly be. How could he resist that? How could anyone?

"Not a problem," she beams. "Here you go, sweet," she says, sliding Esme a plate of food. The child tucks in greedily. She glances at the infant's head, her wild mane of curls as untameable and as infuriating as ever. The only marker of the woman that came before her.

She sniffs. She will straighten those curls into submission as soon as it is socially acceptable to do so.

Lucas takes his seat. "This looks amazing! You really are the best," he enthuses, piling his plate high with sausages and eggs and bacon, everything she has made just for him.

She comes alive at his words. Smiling coyly, she stabs a mushroom with her fork and pops it into her mouth. "I hope you don't mind, but Amira is coming over tonight. She wants my help picking out an outfit for the book launch."

Lucas's shoulders tense. "What's the book called again?"

"'Coral Bay Girl – A Survivor's Story'," she replies, biting back a smirk at the ludicrous title and Amira's delirious notion she was spared for a reason.

Lucas rolls his eyes. "Amira always did have a flair for theatrics."

She laughs and they share a smile. So much has changed between them in the last few months. So much has blossomed. Sometimes she can't believe she is sat across the table from *the* Lucas Redding in skimpy nightwear, but here she is. Here she is and it is perfect.

But there is something else they need to talk about today, an ugly reminder of the past that will be far more painful than casually acknowledging Amira's book. These conversations never go down well, but what can she do? If she doesn't tell Lucas now, he'll only be blindsided by the gossip when he gets to work. That's the way it is in this hellhole of a town.

"If only we could leave," she thinks wistfully. But she never can. She never will. This place always seems to pull her back. It's her anchor.

Inwardly, she sighs, building herself up to deliver the blow. "Have you seen the paper?"

"No?"

Wordlessly, she holds the day's newspaper in the air. The headline, 'Serial Killer's Art Breaks Gallery Record', screams in bold, the family photo from Nat's suicide note slapped beside it. Esme's face is pixelated out, but it might as well not be. So many people saw her when the confession was shared online. Esme almost became as recognisable as her murderous mother.

The colour drains from Lucas's face, but he says nothing.

"Arlene Davies said they're a cultural phenomenon. She said they might just be the most important works of our time. She said -"

"I don't care what she said. All that matters to me is that Esme gets her chunk of the commission and we never, ever have to think of that woman again."

She nods, skewering another mushroom. She understands Lucas's rage, of course she does. He is the ex-husband of a serial killer, after all, but does he really have to use that tone with her?

"There are positives to this, Lucas. The money will change Esme's life, and some of the things Arlene said about the paintings are really nice. Maybe it will mean a lot to Esme to see her mother's work was so important. You never know, Nat's story might help more people understand the impact of bullying and -"

"Bullying? That's what you think it was all about?" Lucas cuts in.

She blinks. "What else could it have been about?"

"Being called a few names when you're a teenager doesn't make you do things like that. You have to be a special kind of psychopath to do what she did." Lucas shakes his head angrily. "Arlene Davies can call those paintings what she likes, but she's fooling no one. She's profiting off a mass murderer. Nat had a part of her brain missing, a part of her heart. Her actions can't be excused or justified because she was bullied. At some point, you've just got to get over it."

She grips her knife like she is gripping onto the edge of a cliff. "Get over it?"

"Get over it, grow up, move on – whatever you want to call it. Just not murder everyone you think ever even slightly wronged you."

The ground beneath her feet tremors.

"What's going on here?" she wonders in broken disbelief. Lucas sounds so sure of himself, so arrogant in his convictions. Where is the Lucas she knows? Where is the Lucas who reminded Nat of all the times others got it worse? Where is the man who remembered her when no one else did?

"You don't think bullying is bad?" she asks, her voice barely a whisper.

"Of course I do, but it's something you get over. Something normal people get over, anyway." Lucas shovels egg into his mouth. Yolk dribbles down his chin. He licks it away with a quick flick of his tongue. For the first time ever, she is repulsed by him.

"Maybe Nat couldn't get over it. Maybe the pain was just too much."

"Yeah, well," Lucas says, rising to his feet. "She didn't think much of the pain she left behind, did she?"

Lucas takes his plate to the sink and throws it in there. The jarring clatter of porcelain and cutlery marks the end of breakfast, the morning now a complete write off. Esme blinks at her daddy's uncharacteristic show of rage, a piece of half-eaten toast mushing in her hand.

She doesn't move. Her gaze doesn't follow Lucas or his angry outburst. Instead, she stares at the wall ahead until the harsh, sterile white burns her eyes.

Everything is ruined, and not just because of the news about the paintings. Lucas ruined it all with his poisonous words. Why did he do that? Didn't he want their life together to be perfect? Didn't he want to understand?

"Jay!"

She jumps, sucked back into reality by Esme's shocked outburst and the sight of Lucas rushing to her aid.

"You're bleeding!" he cries, taking her hand in his. Jay looks down to find her finger oozing crimson, blood dribbling down her wrist.

Lucas pries the knife, the source of the damage, from her hand and sets it on the table. Blood drips from the blade. The puddle acts as a red reminder of the life inside her that Jay could swear disappeared when she was younger.

"This is a bad cut, Jay. How did you manage to do it?" Lucas asks, bundling a towel around the deep wound.

Jay blinks. How did she do it?

"I don't know. I didn't feel it. I didn't feel anything at all," she answers, a statement so true it takes her breath away.

Acknowledgements

There are many people who have helped me get to this point, a moment in my life that for so long felt like it would only ever be just a dream. A few lines at the back of book will never match the care, support and love these people have given me, but I'm going to write them anyway.

First of all, I'd like to thank the team at Kingsley Publishers for taking the chance on me and this story. You'll never know how much what you have done means to me.

Thank you to my dear friends and test readers – Katie Evans, Charlie Rolfe, Laura Shallcross, Sanchana Venkatesh and Emily Chandler. Your feedback was more valuable than you will ever know, as is your friendship. A special shout out to Katie Evans and Charlie Rolfe for cheering me and this book on every step of the way.

Thank you to James Knox, who quite literally changed my life. I think of you and miss you every day.

Thank you to Amber Lewis, whose postcards and messages from home have helped me through some of my most anxious, doubting moments.

Thank you to Rachel Harrison, Rachel Dyer, Sarah Clarke and Laura Sheerin – friends like you are hard to find. Also a huge thanks to Sunaina Patel for not only being a great friend but also letting me use your name for arguably my favourite character!

Thank you to Grace Greenwell and Amy Watmough for being the best friends a girl could wish for. Even when I'm on the other side of the world, you're still the people I go to first. I miss you more than you'll ever know.

Thank you to Jackie Hudson and Christine Burns for being the most inspiring, caring and nurturing teachers. You showed me from a young age that I had a voice and encouraged me to use it. Without you, I genuinely don't believe I would be writing today.

Thank you to Jenny, Mike, Tom, Meg and Jude for making Australia feel like home. Your encouragement and support helped me stick with this project at times when I felt like giving up – thank you!

Thank you to James and Victoria for putting up with a sister who had a vivid imagination and a flair for dramatics. I don't say it enough, but I love you both so much.

Thank you to my mum and dad for always supporting and encouraging my dreams, even the ones that took me to the other side of the world. If I could pick anyone to be my parents, I'd always pick you.

And finally, Jack. The words 'thank you' simply aren't big enough to express my gratitude to you. For every word of encouragement, every time you believed in me when I didn't believe in myself, every extract you read after a long day at work… the list is endless, as is my love for you. I'm so happy that you're the person by my side for this journey.

Author Bio

Jess Kitching is an avid reader, writer and binge-watcher. Originally from Bradford, England, she currently lives in Sydney with her fiancé Jack. Her two goals in life were to move to Australia and have a book published. To be able to say she has done both is something she still can't wrap her head around.

CPSIA information can be obtained
at www.ICGtesting.com
Printed in the USA
LVHW082003151021
700579LV00013B/421

9 780620 941273